ARGREN BLUE

A Spirit Song Story

ROSS HIGHTOWER & DEB HEIM

Black Rose Writing | Texas

The author grants the final approval for this literary material.

First printing

This is a work of fiction. Names, characters, businesses, places, events, and incidents are
either the products of the author's imagination or used in a fictitious manner. Any
resemblance to actual persons, living or dead, or actual events is purely coincidental.

ISBN: 978-1-68513-198-2
PUBLISHED BY BLACK ROSE WRITING
www.blackrosewriting.com

Printed in the United States of America
Suggested Retail Price (SRP) $24.95

Argren Blue is printed in Andalus

*As a planet-friendly publisher, Black Rose Writing does its best to eliminate unnecessary waste to
reduce paper usage and energy costs, while never compromising the reading experience. As a result,
the final word count vs. page count may not meet common expectations.

We hope you have as much fun reading this story as Deb and I had writing it. We would like to thank the staff at our local brewery who plied us with beer while watching our passionate discussions about plot and characters. Also, we want to thank our early readers, especially Cathy and Annette, as well as my coach and friend, Kathie Giorgio.

MAPS

You can find maps and more at rosshightower.com/argren

ARGREN
BLUE

Chapter 1

More Rabble than Rebel

Alar wasn't as nervous as he should have been. At least, he wasn't as nervous as his fellow rebels. They peered at him through the underbrush with wide eyes. Seeking reassurance. He gave Lief, the youngest member of their party, a smile and nodded toward the road. The ambush would be the boy's first taste of the kind of violence Alar was used to. He promised himself he would keep the boy alive. If possible. Lief, his face even paler than normal, nodded stiffly and looked away.

It was a beautiful day. The sun, finding its way through the green canopy, was a warm contrast to the cool breeze wafting down from snowcapped mountains to the east. A typical summer day in the foothills of western Argen. A nervous giggle joined the chatter of a gregarious flock of sparrows. He followed the sound to the branches of an old oak across the road and caught a flash of Tove's red hair. Their only archer's face appeared, breaking into a nervous smile, when she noticed him watching her. Suddenly, the birds hushed, and in the silence, a horse whinnied. Tove looked toward the sound, glanced at Alar, and retreated from view.

The horse whinnied again, joined by the jangle of a wagon's traces and the driver's shouted encouragement to his team. Alar leaned out and peered at the heavy wagon as it mounted the steep slope of the hill on which they waited. A hint of movement through the narrow, barred windows of the wagon was the only evidence of his unfortunate countrymen inside. Slaves on their way to a grim fate. He settled back and caught Sten's eye, lifted two fingers, made a fist, then lifted two fingers again. Two riders, followed by the wagon, then two riders bringing up the rear. The older man, the leader of their small band, nodded. Five Imperial soldiers, including the driver. One would think the Imps would bring a larger escort deep into Argren, but they had learned to rely on the *Alle'oss'* peaceful nature. They would learn a different lesson this day.

He held his breath, studying the first two mounted guards through the tangled branches of an elderberry as they passed. Bored, exhausted … unsuspecting. His comrades' tension, as of drawn bowstrings, was so palpable he couldn't believe the soldiers didn't feel it. Taking a deep breath, he sighed it out and forced his sweaty fist to loosen on the hilt of his sword.

The wagon topped the hill. The moment had arrived. But, still, the signal didn't come. He was wondering whether he should simply lead the attack himself when Tove's arrow flew. They knew it was coming, were waiting for it, but when the arrow struck one of the trailing soldiers on the arm, there was a breathless, startled moment before they burst out of the forest on both sides of the road, whooping and brandishing their swords.

They expected the guards to flee. After all, the rebels outnumbered them two to one, and *Alle'oss* slaves were cheap. Instead, the Imps responded aggressively, gleefully laying about with their swords from atop their massive destriers. Even the sergeant Tove wounded joined in, the arrow shaft protruding from his arm, waving like a banner. The rebels' triumphant shouts died quickly, replaced by the bright clang of steel on steel.

The plan required Alar and Lief to free their countrymen while his companions kept the guards busy. He leapt from the underbrush beside the wagon, a nervous Lief close by his side. With a quick glance toward the front, he ensured Frode and Erik were keeping that guard busy. He turned toward the back of the wagon, expecting to find Sten and Estrid busy with their task. Instead, the Imp on his enormous black horse filled his vision. On instinct, Alar shoved Lief into the elderberry bush before spinning away. The act took half a heartbeat, but it was too long. The horse swiped him as it passed, throwing him violently against the side of the wagon.

***

Alar's eyes fluttered open to panicked shouts, guttural laughter, the crunch of horses' hooves on crushed stone. He lay on his back, squinting, trying to understand what he was looking at. Wide, weatherbeaten oak planks spattered with mud from a recent rain. The underside of the wagon. In the time it took him to orient himself, the sounds of battle died away. Only moments into the fiasco, it was over.

He rolled to his hands and knees in time to see Frode disappear into the trees. The last of the mounted soldiers followed, calling "Taa-hoo-aloo," like a lord on a fox hunt. Alar crawled out from under the wagon and pulled himself upright on the spokes of the wheel. Putting his back against the wheel, he brushed dirt from his hands and glanced around. He was alone. A small smile touched the corner of his mouth. Despite everything, there was still a chance for success.

Pushing himself upright, he teetered for a moment on unsteady legs, then he scooped up his sword and stumbled toward the back of the wagon.

"Alar, look out," Tove shouted from high in the oak tree.

He rounded the corner and came face-to-face with the wagon's driver. The burly Imp was peering into the interior of the wagon, the big iron lock that secured the door in one beefy hand. At Alar's appearance, his head snapped around. The surprised expression on his lopsided face would have been comical under other circumstances. As it was, all Alar could see were the copious scars crisscrossing the Imp's face, a roadmap of a violent life. Alar's legs quivered with the need to run, but still woozy from his momentary departure from the world, he could only watch, fascinated, as the Imp let the lock drop on its thick chain, then pivot toward him, bringing his sword up.

"And here I was thinking I was going to miss all the fun."

Thok. Tove's arrow rebounded off the hard oak planks of the wagon door into the Imp's face. He swatted at it as if it were a mosquito, and in the moment of distraction, Alar's sword flicked out and nicked the man's forearm. Both men froze. Watching the driver gaping at the bloodstain growing on his sleeve, Alar had to suppress an irrational urge to apologize. The driver's head snapped up at Alar's strangled giggle.

"Why, you little—"

Alar ran. He intended to follow his comrades into the forest, but the Imp followed surprisingly fast for a such a hulking man, forcing Alar to turn and defend himself. He backpedaled in the narrow space between the wagon and the forest, frantically blocking a flurry of indignant blows. The end came so quickly, he wasn't sure how it happened. One moment, Alar was congratulating himself on his fine swordsmanship, the next moment his weapon was spinning away into the underbrush. Defenseless, facing a trained killer, Alar's death seemed imminent. Fortunately, his opponent allowed himself a moment to gloat, sneering and twirling his sword. Alar plunged into the forest.

At first, his slight frame allowed him to weave through the trees and open the gap his sudden departure gained him. But his last substantial meal, a loaf of bread he stole from a baker's cart, was a distant memory, and adrenaline could only sustain him so far. It wasn't long before he was flagging. His only hope, that the soldier would lose interest, was dashed by bellowed threats that carried a promise. And they were getting closer. Alar could not outrun him.

Heart galloping, breath coming in ragged gasps, he careened drunkenly through the dense undergrowth on wobbly legs. Ducking his head to plunge through a line of densely packed firs, he stepped into air.

In the moment before he pitched forward, he glimpsed a man standing in a narrow road at the bottom of a muddy embankment, his face just beginning to register his surprise. Then Alar was rolling head over heels down the slope, coming to a sudden, violent stop on the hard-packed surface of the road. With a groan, he opened his eyes and looked up at the stranger staring down at him.

"You can't run forever, you scrawny *l'oss!*"

Alar and the red-headed stranger looked up at the driver's threat. "Run!" Alar shouted, and without waiting to find out if the stranger complied, he jumped up, sprinted across the road and scrambled up the bank. Hauling himself the last few feet using an exposed root, he managed to get his upper body over the lip, then scrabbling with his feet against the muddy bank, he dragged himself into the bushes. Lurching to his feet, he pitched forward onto a small sapling. The thin maple gave with his weight until he rolled off, releasing the tree to spring upright.

He lay, spread eagle, staring at small patches of blue sky, counting what were undoubtedly the last thudding beats of his heart. This was it. He had nothing left. The Imperial soldier might decide he had more value as a slave than a corpse, but Alar doubted it. The minor cut he inflicted on the Imp's arm signed his death warrant. He let his eyes close, waiting for approaching footsteps.

"You!" It was the same voice that had questioned his parentage, but it wasn't nearby.

"What?" Another voice. It must be the stranger Alar saw on the road.

"You're with those rebels."

"Reb—" The voice rose several octaves. "What?"

"What are you doing on this road all alone?"

Alar rolled onto his stomach and crawled toward the road.

"I was in Richeleau. On business. I'm going home."

"Took the wrong road, son."

"You're looking for that other guy, the … rebel. He went that way."

Alar peered at the men from beneath a mountain laurel. The soldier, bent over, one hand on his knee, waved the tip of his sword toward the red-headed stranger, who appeared to be near Alar's age, sixteen or seventeen at the oldest. The Imp straightened, kneading his lower back with his free hand. Alar couldn't help grinning when he noticed the blood moistening the man's sleeve. The kid backed slowly away, one hand held up as if warding the Imp away and the other pointing to where Alar escaped into the forest. He was *Alle'oss*, one of Alar's countrymen. The beads entwined in the thin braids by his left ear suggested he was from central Argren. He was a long way from home.

The soldier glanced in the direction the boy pointed, his eyes going to the scrapes Alar's feet made in the mud, but made a dismissive gesture. "I'm tired of running. 'Sides, it's all the same to me, one *l'oss* or another. By the looks of you, you'll last longer in the mines than that skinny whelp, anyway."

"Mines?" The boy adopted a tone that suggested he had finally gotten to the bottom of the misunderstanding and could now explain. "No, see, I went to Richeleau for my father. He let me go pay our taxes and meet potential buyers. *Imperial* buyers."

Alar shook his head. The boy said that last bit as if he thought it would make a difference.

Rummaging through the satchel hanging from his shoulder, he pulled out a slip of paper. "Look, I got the receipt. For the taxes."

Alar let his head drop into his arms. He had seen too many scenes like this. It wouldn't matter if he had a note from the emperor. He was *Alle'oss* and the soldier had decided he was a slave. Nothing was going to change his mind. He looked up in time to see the man rip the receipt from the boy's hand and toss it aside. Instead of displaying the fear he should have, the stranger stood straighter, an outraged scowl on his face.

Alar ignored his retort and backed away. This kid was just unlucky, like so many others. Wrong place, wrong time. Looking back, he listened to the boy complaining bitterly. He watched through tangled branches as the soldier prodded the boy forward at the point of his sword. If he truly was destined for the mines, he would likely never reach his twentieth summer. Alar watched them, gritting his teeth. He should just go. Count himself lucky for a miraculous escape. But even before the thought fully formed, he knew he couldn't leave. The boy was, after all, only in the wrong place because Alar led the soldier to him.

He eased forward and peered down the road. From the top of the embankment, he could see the bald patch on top of the soldier's head. Alar lost his sword, but as he studied the situation, a plan began to take shape. It was foolish, but he had been riding the ragged edge of foolish since he joined the resistance six years before. He worked his way backward, until he could get to his feet, then moved as quietly as he could, paralleling the road until he found a small gap between the trees ahead of the two men.

He held his breath and listened, judging their position by the boy's plaintive objections. *Now!* Alar bounced on the balls of his feet twice, took a breath, whooshed it out, then sprinted toward the opening.

The pair on the road looked up at Alar's sudden appearance. He had only a moment to realize he mistimed his attack. Arms pinwheeling, he pivoted and spread his legs to avoid kicking the boy in the head. Instead, he collided with him and rode him to the ground, landing light as a feather on the boy's chest. He looked down between his legs at the stranger's pained expression, then rolled away only to find himself looking up at the soldier's leering face.

"Nice try, little *l'oss*," he growled. He bent over, laughing and blasting Alar with surprisingly minty breath. "They'll like that spirit where you're going. You might last a couple of months."

Alar kicked upward, driving his foot into the man's groin. The soldier squealed, bent over, bringing his hands to his injured nethers. Alar pressed himself back against the hill, lifting his chin as the tip of the man's sword swung across, leaving a small stripe along his jawline.

"You're dead now," the soldier spat past clenched teeth.

Alar scrambled to the side, away from the sword. The boy, still trying to catch his breath, gasped as Alar's weight landed on his stomach. Crab walking backward across the boy's body, Alar felt something hard.

The soldier, growling through bared teeth, a hand still covering his injured parts, swiped weakly at Alar with his sword. Alar wrapped his hand around the hard object, pulled it free of an obstruction and swung it at the man's knee. The high shriek that emerged from the burly man was so unexpected Alar let out a bark of laughter. He scrambled away from a wild swing of the Imp's sword and stood gaping at the hilt of a knife protruding from the soldier's knee. The Imp wrapped his hand around the hilt, bellowing incoherently. Casting about for a weapon, Alar found the boy's satchel lying at his feet. He scooped it up by the strap and swung it with all his might. The hollow thunk of the satchel impacting the soldier's head reminded Alar of the time he threw a honeydew melon from the barn roof. The soldier dropped like a sack of potatoes and lay still beside the stranger.

In the sudden silence, Alar grinned down at the boy, hefted the heavy satchel and said, "What you got in here?"

The boy's head swiveled from the body toward Alar. "What did you do?"

"What? Save your life?" Alar asked, smirking and offering the satchel.

The kid clawed himself upright on the embankment, snatched the satchel and backed away from the body. "He could have told everyone I didn't have anything to do with ... whatever you did."

Alar looked down at the blood pooling in the dirt. "I don't think he's going to tell anybody anything now."

"He's—" The boy froze, his face going slack for a moment before something like fear climbed into his expression. He pointed at Alar, backing slowly away. "You're going to hang for this."

"They'll have to catch me first. Besides, I'd hang for a lot more than this."

They stared at one another for a moment, then the boy's face cleared. He straightened and looked around. "I'm getting out of here." He started walking, stopped, turned around and walked back the other way. When he reached Alar, he moved as far to the other side of the road as he could, glaring as he passed.

"Good idea." Alar looked down at the soldier's sword. "Hold on," he called, bent over and unbuckled the soldier's belt.

"You're robbing the dead?"

Alar looked up. The kid had stopped and was watching, incredulous. "Well, he doesn't need it anymore." Alar pulled the belt free, rolling the corpse over. He searched the man's pockets and was delighted to find a small coin purse with a handful of iron pennies in it. He jingled the contents next to his ear, then stuffed it into a pocket and picked up the sword. It was no great shakes. The edge was notched and rolled in spots, but it was a far cry better than the one he lost. With a shrug, he sheathed it and walked toward the boy.

"Where do you think you're going? Get away."

"You, uh, don't have any food in that satchel, do you?"

"Go away."

Alar stopped and watched him until he disappeared below the crown of the hill on which he stood. "Now what?" he murmured. Turning around, he gazed at the Imp's body. Who would miss him? A spouse, children, friends? Unlike some of his comrades, Alar knew killing Imps wouldn't drive the Empire from Argren. The soldier undoubtedly deserved death. His role as the driver of the slave wagon was guilt enough for Alar. If he was anything like the other Imps occupying Alar's homeland, he had much more to answer for than one slave caravan. But this man's death meant next to nothing to their Imperial oppressors. No, killing a few Imps would not free their homeland, but he would feel no guilt. Alar closed his eyes, enjoying the cool breeze on his face. It was a beautiful day, and he was happy to be alive.

"Wish you were carrying some food," he said before noticing the knife still embedded in the soldier's knee. "Hey!" he shouted after the boy. "You want your knife?" He slapped a hand over his mouth and winced. "Stupid," he mumbled and listened. A grumbling squirrel, a pair of flirting goldfinches, the wind in the trees. No sounds of pursuit. Still, the other Imps would undoubtedly be along soon. He bent over, grasped the hilt of the knife and heaved, stumbling backward when it popped free.

After wiping the blade on the soldier's uniform, he strolled in the direction the boy took and examined the knife. It had a curved blade that was much shorter than the hilt. "Paring vegetables, maybe?" Noticing a wadded-up piece of paper next to his boot, he bent to retrieve it. It was the tax receipt the boy offered to prove his innocence. "Ukrit Woodsmith from Lirantok."

Alar's heart sank. The slave wagon was coming from Lirantok. The village was in a valley between two spurs of the *Na'lios* mountains in central Argren, an area that had been relatively free of Imperial depredations. Fertile ground for the slavers. It was Lief who told them about the wagon. The boy was from one of the other villages in the valley and was visiting family when the Imps arrived in Lirantok. Alar let the receipt hang from his hand and gazed down the road, catching sight of Ukrit cresting the next hill. Should he catch him and tell him what he was returning to? No, what good would it do? The walk to Lirantok would take days and there was nothing the boy could do but worry until he got home. He stuffed the receipt into a pocket. Nothing to do but return to their base and discover the fate of his fellow rebels. He shook his head and chuckled. Rebels? More like rabble. His grin faded at the memory of Lief's pale, worried face, looking to him for reassurance before the ambush. He hoped everyone survived.

Chapter 2

A Fateful Decision

By the time Alar made his careful way back to the sight of the ambush, it was deserted. He took it as a good sign there was no blood or bodies. Maybe everyone managed to lose their pursuers in the dense forest. Faint ruts and hoofprints in the road showed the Imps continued on to their destination in Richeleau, one of the few large cities in Argren and home to the Imperial governor. As he was about to depart, he noticed Tove's arrow, snapped in two and left in the road. He picked the pieces up and slid them into a pocket. Tove, who laboriously flaked the arrowhead from flint, could reuse it. The fletching he would weave into his braid, a talisman of a lucky escape.

He swung through a nearby village in a fruitless search for food and arrived home in the early evening. Their base was a narrow cleft, high on a granite ridge. To reach it, they either had to climb the back side of the ridge or traverse a narrow ledge along the face of the ridge. Though it was inconvenient to get to, it was the perfect place to hide. It was sheltered from the worst of the winter winds, hidden from prying eyes, and from the top, they could see anyone approaching.

Dread settled on him as he climbed to the top of the ridge. Someone should have challenged him before he got this far. When he reached the top, he crouched and listened. There was no sign of a sentry and none of the chatter that arose around the fire in the evenings. He crept quietly along the spine of the ridge, until he spotted the sentry sitting with his back to a boulder, legs splayed out. It was Lief. For one chilling moment, he thought the boy might be dead, but then he heard a light snore.

Vo kustuk. He walked up to stand beside him, not bothering to be silent. When the boy didn't wake up, Alar knelt and whispered in his ear, "The Imperials would kill a man for falling asleep on sentry duty."

Lief snorted. His eyes opened and swiveled around. "Hello, Alar."

Alar stared at him.

"I … uh … I was just resting my eyes." Lief licked his lips and swallowed. When Alar remained silent, he sighed. "I'm sorry, Alar. I'm just so tired."

Alar took the boy's hand and helped him to his feet. "We're all tired, Lief." He clapped the boy on the shoulder, and said, "Glad to see you alive." When Lief thanked him for shoving him out of harm's way, Alar brushed it off and asked, "The others back?"

"Most of them, anyway."

They stared at one another for a long moment, then Alar gave him a gentle reminder to stay alert and turned away.

He paused at the edge of the ridge and gazed west to the smoke rising from the hearths in Richeleau. Another world where people had plenty to eat and slept soundly in safe beds. When he finally looked down into their small camp, he counted fewer people around the fire than before they left that morning. Otherwise, everything looked normal, though a bit grimmer, if that was possible. No one looked up, so he retreated to the spot that offered a way to climb down out of view of the group around the fire. At the bottom, he drew in a deep breath, fixed an easy smile onto his face, then stepped into view. The men and women gathered around the small fire tensed when he appeared, but once they saw who it was, they settled back in their seats. "No, no, don't get up," he murmured.

When Tove saw him, she leapt up, wrapped her arms around him, then stepped back and pushed him hard in the chest.

"What's that for?" Alar asked.

"For running off and making me worry." When she spoke, the scar that cut across her lips pulled her mouth into a grimace. She had the scar when Alar found her. He knew she acquired it at the hands of the Inquisition, but she had never been willing to talk about it. She glared at him before remembering, then dropped her head, hiding her face behind her hair.

Alar smirked and waited until Tove peeked up at him, then pulled her into a hug. "Glad you got away," he said.

Tove disentangled herself and returned to her spot by the fire. "Was going to come after you, but by the time I got out of that tree, the other Imps were back." She looked up, hiding her mouth behind a hand. "What about the one chased you?"

Alar grinned, drew his new sword, and held it up. Tove's hand dropped, rewarding him with a rare glimpse of her smile.

"How'd you manage that?" Sten asked, twisting around to get his good eye on Alar.

"Natural good looks and charm," Alar said. He found a spot on the log next to Tove. To Sten's scowl, he said, "Got lucky. Clumsy oaf fell and cracked his head." He searched the faces around the fire. "Estrid and Frode," he said.

"Ana saw Estrid get it. No one's sure about Frode," Sten said. He looked around at the other faces. "Not optimistic, but then we didn't have much hope for you, either."

The blase way the older man recited their comrades' brief obituary said a lot about what the group had been through in recent years. Vivacious Estrid, perennially optimistic, an open book, always quick with a joke. Frode, her direct opposite, quiet, dour even, reluctant to talk about how he ended up with them. Alar would miss them, but he missed all the people they lost.

Estrid was supposed to be fighting alongside Sten, distracting the soldier whose horse nearly trampled Lief. Alar didn't remember seeing either Sten or Estrid during the brief altercation. And now Estrid was dead. He watched Sten staring into the fire, but instead of asking the question he wanted to ask, he asked, "The slaves?"

The older man shook his head. "And it's worse."

"Word is, the garrison in Richeleau is sending a company of Imps to Lirantok," Tove said.

"Word is?" Alar asked. "A rumor or what you know to be true?"

"Lief circled back and followed the caravan to Richeleau. Must have kicked the hornet's nest, because the company set out almost right away." Sten shrugged as he bent forward to turn a spit suspended over the fire. "Might be a coincidence," Sten said, sitting back and resting his forearms on his knees, "but Torva, that gendarme Lief knows, says they're headed up that way."

If they were going to Lirantok, the Imps would undoubtedly encounter Ukrit. The boy was too naïve to avoid them. "Why Lirantok?" Alar asked.

"Maybe they think the people who attacked the slave caravan were from Lirantok," Tove said. "They're wrong, but it makes some sense."

Alar watched her running a whetstone over her knife, trying to ignore a nagging sense of guilt. *Not my problem.* His stomach grumbled its agreement. Shoving the boy's inconvenient predicament aside, he nodded at the roasting rodent. "Squirrel?"

Tove grinned. "First shot."

Alar patted her on the back and forced a smile. "You keep getting better with that bow, we'll be eating like the emperor before long."

"I missed," she mumbled.

It took him a moment to work out what she meant, then he remembered the arrow that narrowly missed the driver's head. He retrieved the arrowhead, handed it over, and said, "It was close enough to give me a head start." Her eyes lit up as she took the broken arrow shaft. "Saved my life."

She scowled and dipped her head. Alar took in the small group lounging around the clearing. The *Alle'oss* were not fighters. When he joined their small band, none of them had a sword, much less trained with one. That wasn't unusual in Argren, but it was bad luck none of them had the slightest bit of woodcraft. There were plenty of skilled archers among the *Alle'oss*. After all, hunter was an honored profession in Argren. But the *Alle'oss* feared being associated with rebels, and their attempts at recruiting had, so far, been unsuccessful.

Tove took it on herself to carve a bow from a sturdy piece of ash. The sinew and the arrows proved more problematic. Four months ago, they stole a quiver with two arrows from a hunter who made the mistake of sleeping late. Alar smiled, remembering how they gathered around, passing the arrow around, trying to discern its secrets. Their first attempts to replicate it were pathetic, but Tove was persistent.

Tove set the whetstone aside and picked up the long piece of yew she was using to carve a new bow. Lost in concentration, she forgot her usual reticence, pushing her hair behind her ears to keep it out of the way as she bent to her task. Alar watched her face, brow furrowed, lips pressed tight, the scar puckering the corner of her mouth. The knife was too large for both her small hands and the finer details on the bow. Reaching into his pocket, he retrieved Ukrit's knife, nudged Tove and held it out to her, hilt first.

Her eyes lit up. "Where'd you get this?"

"Found it."

"Lucky you."

"No, lucky you. You can have it."

She took the knife, weighed it experimentally, then set the hunting knife aside and set to work with a satisfied grin curving her mangled lips.

Alar looked at Sten. "When did the Imps leave Richeleau?"

Sten scrunched up his face. "Early this afternoon."

"How long to get to Lirantok?"

"Walking or riding?"

"Either, both."

Sten looked to a man sitting across the fire. "What you say, Erik? You're from up that way."

Erik was Sten's closest companion and might have been considered second in command if they were actually organized. He looked up from his attempt to repair his tattered boots, brushing his long, dirty hair from his face. Looking from Sten to Alar, he said, "Walking … maybe four, five weeks if you hump it."

"What about if you're on horseback?"

"Imperials?"

Alar nodded. One of the few advantages the rebels had was the Imps rarely ventured far from the roads in Argren. That was true of all the Imps except for the Rangers, but that elite force would not be wasted on a village like Lirantok.

"They'll follow the Imperial Highway south, then turn east and north." He waggled his head, pursing his lips and thinking. "Two, three weeks. Maybe a little more."

"What are you thinking?" Sten asked.

"Was thinking of going to warn them."

Sten and Erik exchanged a look, then Sten said, "No, we need you here."

Alar looked from Sten to Erik, who was nodding. "Need me for what?" he asked.

"It's just not a good idea for any of us to be running off on their own," Erik said. "Besides, we don't know for sure that's where they're going."

"Right, might be something comes up and we need everyone here," Sten said with a firm nod, as if the argument was closed.

Alar gazed at him. It was Sten who found Alar hiding under the porch of a general store when he had ten summers. He was alone, emaciated, and wouldn't have survived the coming winter on his own. The older man saved Alar's life and gave him something even more important: a reason to live. It was true, they were few, but Sten assured him the *Alle'oss* would tire of the Empire's oppression and flock to their cause. Sten's fiery speeches ignited Alar's imagination and gave him purpose. He was excited when they finally let him take part in an operation, and equally shocked to discover they were stealing corn from a local farmer, one of their own. Sten assured him it was necessary, a temporary expedient. But it was only the first in a long series of dispiriting compromises.

The heady days of hope and expectation were long past. Alar looked at the group of people slouching around the fire and saw fatigue and, worse, resignation. The attack on the slave caravan was a rare spasm of initiative, and it brought with it a harsh lesson. His gaze settled on Sten, who stared into space, his face slack. He had never openly defied their leader before. But it wasn't just Ukrit who would pay for their transgression. If the Imps were going to retaliate, the innocent residents of Lirantok would suffer.

Tove, bent over her work, twisted her head and caught his eye. Alar leaned toward her. "Lief said he got back from Lirantok in two weeks," she whispered. She knew what he was thinking. He had to try. Even if it meant defying Sten and Erik.

Chapter 3

Spirit's Luck

Tove was right. Lief knew of a pass through the mountains that would allow Alar to get to Lirantok in two weeks. It was rugged, the trip would be exhausting, but it could be done. Tove and Lief offered to accompany him, but he declined. As broken as it was, their small band was their only home. He didn't want his friends to lose that. He waited to leave until well past sundown, when everyone was asleep. Tove made sure she was on watch when he left.

"You're going to be careful, right?" she said when Alar arrived on top of the ridge.

"Always," Alar said with a grin. "You know me, Tove."

It was at least an hour before the moon rose. With shadows cloaking her face, Tove looked directly at him. "Alar, you're the most reckless person I know."

It was true. Gambler's luck was what Sten called it. When he survived jumping off the roof of his family's farm when he had seven summers, his mother called it spirit's luck. Whatever that meant. "I'm just going to warn them the Imperials are coming. I won't get involved, I promise," he said and meant it. What was he going to do against a company of Imp cavalry, anyway?

"What do you want me to tell Sten and Erik?"

"Tell them … tell them I left early for Richeleau. Looking for food. I've done that before." He shrugged. "They might even believe it. But even if they don't, they'll believe you didn't know any different."

They said their goodbyes and Alar made his careful way down the face of the ridge. From the bottom, he looked up and could just make out Tove looking down, her face a pale moon against the dark sky.

***

As he walked, he tried to remember everything he knew about Lirantok. He heard of it before but couldn't remember how until Lief reminded him. One of a handful of villages in the Ishian River valley, Lirantok gained fame as an artists' community. He knew of Lirantok because of his sister. As a child, he would sift through the ashes in their hearth, searching for just the right bits of charcoal she could use to sketch on the rough planks of their family's barn. When rain wiped her canvas clean, she would begin again, with Alar sitting on a stump in their yard, exclaiming when he guessed the emerging image. Recognizing her budding talent, their parents acquired, at a dear price, a rare set of watercolors from Lirantok. It was the vibrant colors that attracted the artists to the valley. The surrounding hills were rich in the plants and minerals required to produce the vivid hues the *Alle'oss* loved. The inhabitants of the valley grew rich on pigments coveted throughout the Empire and beyond.

Alar traveled fast, stopping only occasionally to catch a few hours of sleep. If it took the Imps three weeks to reach the valley, he might beat them there. Though he brought no food with him, he took advantage of summer's bounty, finding berries and mushrooms as he walked. Two of the dead soldier's iron pennies bought ten early apples from an old farmer. Feeling virtuous for being able to pay for something for a change, he climbed the pass, chewing the sweet fruit and thanking the Mother for her generosity.

The cavalry would head south from Richeleau toward the main highway, then turn east until they met the spur of the highway that headed north into the valley. The pass Alar used was too rugged for horses, but not too difficult for a man born to the mountains. Still, by the time he reached a precipice from which he could see the valley to the north, he was nearing the end of his strength. The Ishian River, sedate for a mountain river, except where it plunged through the entrance of the valley, glinted in the afternoon sun below him. The sapphire blue lake that was the source of the river was just visible over the intervening hills. Lief told him the water was so clear, you could see the bottom two hundred paces below the surface. Though he couldn't see Lirantok, he knew it was on the southwestern shore of the lake. It was the largest and most prosperous village in the valley.

He descended until he met the highway where it turned north, paralleling the river as it left the valley. With a groan, he knelt in the center of the road and studied the packed dirt. Wagon ruts. A few hoof prints, but they were the wide hooves of *Alle'oss* mountain horses. He looked west along the road and listened. Nothing but the reassuring sounds of the forest. If he was lucky, the Imps headed somewhere other than Lirantok. In any case, no Imps passed this spot since it rained last, and they were not near.

Just as he set off, the sun dipped below a mountain peak, throwing the road into shadow. Over the course of the last day, the wind shifted to the northwest, plunging down the peaks that cradled the valley and picking up speed as it rushed through the narrow entrance. He closed his eyes, enjoying the refreshing chill on his sweaty face. Exhausted before he set out, after two weeks with little sleep and only enough food to stay alive, it was all he could do to put one foot in front of another. He gazed longingly at the soft ground beneath the underbrush that bordered the road, but if he stopped now, he might give up the lead he worked so hard to gain. Besides, if the soldiers were coming, he would need as much time as possible to convince the residents of Lirantok death was descending on their idyllic village.

He had only six summers the day his sister received the watercolors from Lirantok, but her joyful response etched the day in his memory. He reached into a pocket he sewed inside his shirt and withdrew a bundle of waxed cloth. With the delicate precision of one handling a priceless artifact, he unwrapped the cloth, exposing a folded paper within. That it survived the early days, when he was alone, was testament to how precious it was to him. The paper was smudged and worn, the creases bit almost all the way through the sheet, but it was still intact, the colors still recognizable.

He unfolded it as he walked, cradling it and looking down at himself, or at least, the six-year-old version of himself. How often had he gazed at this portrait in the years since? Countless times. It was the first painting his sister attempted with her new treasures, and she chose to paint her little brother. Alar was a busy child, and it said a lot about how much he loved and admired his sister that he sat long enough for her to complete the painting. An untrained hand created the portrait, but the talent was obvious. It was unmistakably Alar. She captured the subtle signs of his impatience so perfectly, it never failed to make him smile. She even used a bit of the precious blue hues, Argren blue, to depict his eyes. He folded it carefully and returned it to its hidden spot. The painting was the only surviving relic of his family.

He scrubbed his face with both hands, shook himself, and picked up his pace. If Lief's directions were right, he would be in Lirantok sometime tomorrow morning.

***

The sun was making its presence known behind the mountains to the east as Alar approached the entrance to the valley. The road climbed a long straight slope, leaving the river to plunge through a narrow gorge below. He topped the hill as the sun emerged between two mountain peaks. Standing in the middle of the road, his last apple dangling from his hand, he watched the jagged shadow line crawl across the valley floor, leaving behind a painting in golden hues. The glittering blue lake emerged slowly, surrounded by evergreens and hardwoods, a collage of summer greens. A boat crossed into the light, rocking in a light chop, its white sail luminous. Lirantok was just visible among the trees. It was the largest village in the valley, but he could see the smoke from at least two others to the north and east.

He was steeling himself for one last effort when he heard them. Cold sweat prickled his back as he spun around. The cavalry was approaching the base of the hill, emerging from the fog that often lay in the low places in the mountains. They were still far away and in no hurry, coming on at a slow walk. Alar turned and ran.

He only took a few steps before he knew it was useless. He spent his reserves getting to this point and had nothing left. He felt as if he were plowing through waist deep snow. Leaden legs refused to respond to his urgent pleas. His feet ached, and every jarring step sent sharp spikes into his hips. For one fleeting moment, he considered ducking into the forest and abandoning the citizens of Lirantok to their fate. Maybe the Imps were only here to arrest the village elders. Besides, even if they had darker intentions, what was he doing jumping into the middle of it?

But still, he ran on, grateful, at least, he was running downhill. He crossed a narrow meadow at the entrance of the valley and entered the forest that surrounded the village. Risking a glance over his shoulder, he found the horses stopped at the top of the hill. The officer, sunlight glinting off gold ornaments on his blue uniform, pointed toward the village. That must be Captain Brennerman, the commander of the cavalry detachment in Richeleau, and no friend of the *Alle'oss.* Alar had seen it before. They would gather themselves, finalizing their plans before descending on the village at a gallop to maximize shock and minimize resistance.

"Oh no, oh no," Alar huffed out. Turning his back to the threat, he bent his head and pumped his arms, but only managed a few more steps before he stumbled and sprawled across the dusty surface of the road. For a moment, the memory of that day long ago came back to him. The day the Empire stole his life. His body convulsed, desperate for air, but his limbs were frozen. The feeling of helplessness that stalked him since that day pounced, freezing him in place. He lowered his forehead to the ground.

But he was no longer eight years old, no longer the helpless son of a farmer. "Not this time!" he growled, threw himself upright and took a few stumbling steps. "*Sheoda.*" He was so close!

And then, amid the turmoil in his mind, something tore. He gasped, stuttered to a stop on stiff legs and bent over, hands clamped to the sides of his head. He could *feel* his mind tearing deep behind his eyes, a wet, rotten burlap rending. "Arrgh!" He pressed his hands to his temples, as if he could hold the ragged edges together.

And then it stopped.

Through slitted eyes, he stared at his boots planted on the road's brown surface. He was conscious. He dug his fingernails into his scalp above his temples. He could still feel. In fact, outwardly nothing had changed. What happened to him? He straightened, letting his hands drop to his sides. When he had six summers his mother's brother suffered a brain injury that left him partially paralyzed and feeble. Afraid what he would find, he turned his attention inward, but instead of the debilitating fog he imagined cloaked his uncle's mind, he found a quiet serenity centered on the spot where he felt the tearing sensation. Closing his eyes, he focused on it.

A note, high and pure as a bell's peal, emanated from the spot, accompanied by overpowering waves of euphoria that suffused his mind. He jerked upright, fists clenched, shivers rolling up and down his limbs.

As the note faded, the waves ebbed, lapping at the corners of his mind and leaving behind a mellow bliss. He opened his eyes but focused on what was happening inside his mind. The cool spot was still there, but he shied away from it. He lifted his arms out to his sides and rose up onto his toes. The accumulated aches and fatigue had evaporated. In fact, he felt better than he had in weeks. Like he slept for hours.

Imperials! He glanced over his shoulder. The cavalry was on the move, still walking for the moment, but they would come fast. Shoving aside the riddle of what happened to him, he flew toward the village.

The citizens of Lirantok were already out and about when Alar appeared. "Imperials! Run!" He slid to a stop in the town square, shouting at the top of his lungs and waving his arms, but his warnings only drew curious stares. "Run you fools!"

"Boy!" An elderly man grabbed his arm and pulled him around. "What are you talking about?"

"Imps!" Alar pointed back the way he came. "Imp cavalry." When the man looked confused, Alar shouted, "Slavers!" Invoking their recent experience finally got people moving. Alar snagged the retreating man by his tunic. "The Woodsmiths? Ukrit?"

The man pointed west and said, "Outside town, up the hill." He pulled his tunic free and ran toward the lake.

The bright clop of horses' hooves on cobbles chased Alar from the square. Screams and the soldier's whoops followed him through the narrow lane that led out of town. Beyond the western boundary of the village, the road wound up a hill. The Woodsmith's tidy house perched on the crown of the hill. He paused at the top to look down at the chaos erupting in the town. The Imps were not merely here to arrest the elders. The western wind at his back muted the screams, but people were fleeing in every direction, and smoke was already rising. Turning away, he scanned the Woodsmith's homestead. Besides the main house, there were two other buildings, but none of the family was in sight.

He ran to the house and burst through the door. The common room was empty except for a girl, who screamed and leapt up at Alar's entrance.

"Where are your parents?" Alar asked.

Instead of answering, she fled into an adjacent room and slammed the door. Alar took a step to follow, then heard hoofbeats behind him. He dodged to the side and peeked around the doorjamb in time to see two Imps reining up in the yard. One of them pointed to the other buildings, then dismounted and came toward the house. Alar put his back to the wall, panting, blinking away the sweat dripping into his eyes. He drew his sword as the soldier's boots sounded on the porch, then, without thinking, he pivoted and drove the blade through the doorway.

He met resistance, as if he were thrusting through a bale of hay. There was a low grunt, then the sword was jerked from his hand. He edged over and peeked through the door. A soldier lay on his back in the yard, his boots still on the porch, his hands clutching Alar's sword protruding from his abdomen below his ribcage. Alar jumped back, spun around, searching frantically for a place to hide. He leapt onto the table that stretched across the middle of the room and cast about. He was heading to the open door on the right side of the room when he remembered the girl. Crossing back to the closed door, he knocked lightly and put his ear to the door.

"Hello," he said and winced. "We, uh, have to get out of here. Can you let me in?" There was a squeal followed by a thump from inside the room, but the door didn't open. He rattled the latch. Locked, and the door was sturdy.

"Klaus!" The other Imp's voice, faint, came from outside.

His sword! Alar ran to the door and peeked outside again. The body was still there, the sword protruding from its abdomen. Seeing no one else, he stepped warily on the porch, peering around for the other Imp.

"Klaus, there's no one here." This time, the voice was nearby, just around the corner.

With one last glance at his sword, Alar slipped around the opposite corner.

"Klaus!" Surprise and anger.

"Oh, *sheoda*," Alar muttered under his breath. The forest pushed up close on this side of the house. He took a step toward the shadowy refuge when he noticed the window. The girl. They would find her, and they would kill her, or worse, for what he did to Klaus. He hesitated for only a heartbeat before running to the window and tapping on it. He didn't expect her to respond, but to his surprise, a pair of wide blue eyes, in a round face framed by blond curls, appeared. Alar beckoned, then pointed to the front of the house, trying to convey the danger she was in. He saw her lips moving, and winced, putting a finger to his lips, miming opening the window. She stared at him, started to shake her head, then something heavy struck the door to her room. Alar could hear it through the window.

She jumped at the sound and disappeared, as the soldier let loose with a stream of furious threats, leaving no doubt as to his intentions. Alar bent over, looking for something he could use to break the window, when the sound of the soldier's voice rose in volume. He jerked upright and bright lights exploded in his head. *Oh Mother! Whatever tore before gave way.*

"You okay?"

Hands rubbing the top of his head, he forced his eyes open and squinted up at the girl. She had one leg out the window, which swung out on hinges. Another crash on the door, accompanied by an ominous splintering sound, got her moving.

"Come on, hurry," Alar said, reaching up to take her hand. "If he sees which way we go, we'll never lose him."

The girl ignored his offered hand and hopped deftly to the ground. Alar turned toward the forest, but the girl took his hand and pulled him toward the back of the house. The unmistakable sound of the door giving way followed them around the corner. She led him across the backyard, avoiding the soft earth in the beds of their summer garden. Unlike the gradual climb in the front, the hill fell away steeply here for ten paces, exposing a rough granite face. She sat on the edge, scooted forward and slid to the bottom, then, without a backward glance, she disappeared into the trees. Alar sat, scooted over the edge, trying to mimic her movements. Instead of sliding gracefully down the stone, he rolled, leaving skin on the rock's rough surface and coming to a painful stop at the bottom.

He opened his eyes to find her looking down at him. "Something familiar about this," he murmured.

"You coming?" she asked, then turned and disappeared again.

"Must be Ukrit's sister," he muttered. He pulled himself up on the rock face and limped after her.

She led them far enough into the densest part of the forest they could no longer hear screams nor smell smoke, then dropped to sit on a log. Alar knew what would happen next. He had seen it often. She was one of the lucky few who coolly navigated violence's terrible turmoil. But, the immediate danger passed, she would begin to process what happened to her. He watched her panting, wild eyes casting about the dim clearing, wondering which way she would go. When she spoke, there was a dangerous, hysterical edge to her voice. "Who were those people? Why—" A sob convulsed her body.

Alar stared, feeling suddenly awkward. He took a step toward her and stopped. It wasn't as if he had no experience with this type of trauma. It was, in fact, depressingly familiar. If it were one of his fellow rebels, he would sit with them, put his arm around their shoulders. Let them rage or weep until the crisis passed. But he didn't know this girl. What was the protocol? She might respond violently if he touched her. He stood awkwardly for a moment, hands making inarticulate gestures, then he sat on the log, close enough that she could lean on him if she wished, but far enough to be proper.

Finally, she quieted and sat up. She looked at him and searched his face, wiping her nose on her sleeve. "Who are you?" she asked.

Relieved, Alar started to answer, then shut his mouth. That was a complicated question. He was the person who brought this calamity into her life, or at least he was partially responsible. It may be Imperial soldiers who were busy killing her neighbors and burning her village, but that was the result, not the cause. They wouldn't have come if he and his fellow rebels hadn't attacked the slave wagon. But instead of giving a complicated answer, he said, "A friend of Ukrit."

She stared at him, a small furrow appearing between her brows. The puzzle seemed to focus her mind, and she asked, "Ukrit? How do you know Ukrit?"

"I, uh, met him in Richeleau. Or on the road to Richeleau, actually."

Her face smoothed, and she nodded. She wiped tears from her cheeks, and after a moment, she asked, "Where *is* my brother? Did he come back with you?"

"He's not back yet?"

"No, we haven't seen him for weeks."

Alar chewed his lips and looked up at the patches of blue sky visible through the thick canopy. That was not good news. If he wasn't back and Alar didn't see him, he probably took the same road the cavalry took. The boy didn't seem to know how to deal with hostile Imperials. Still, they didn't normally kill or capture random *Alle'oss* they encountered. There was a good chance they ignored him. Which meant he would return to this devastation. Alar looked back at his sister and asked, "Where are your parents?"

Her face froze. She was up in a flash and had taken a step toward the village before Alar grasped her wrist and jerked her to a stop.

"Let me go!"

"If you go back, they'll kill you." He took a breath and let it out. "Or worse."

"My ma and pa went into town this morning," she said, trying to yank her arm free. Alar may have had little skill with a sword, but he had the rock-hard calluses and iron grip of one accustomed to its use. When it became obvious she couldn't escape, she stopped struggling and gave him a pleading look.

"I warned them in town," Alar said. "They had little time, but there's always a chance they got away." He forced a small smile, willing himself to hide the lie. A flicker of something that might be hope crossed her face, then she sagged and looked pointedly at his hand wrapped around her wrist. He looked into her eyes, gauging her intentions. She gazed steadily at him, showing no sign of the wild panic he saw before. He let go, tense, ready to chase her if she bolted. Instead, she returned to her seat on the log. After a moment, she looked up at him and said, "How long?"

"Hard to say," he said. "A couple of hours. Then we'll go check." He sat, elbows on his knees, and stared into the shadows between the trees.

"I'm Scilla," she said, dully.

"Alar."

Chapter 4

Frayed Threads

Hours later, Alar and Scilla peeked over the edge of the hill behind what was the Woodsmith's cozy home. The house was ablaze, but there was no sign of the soldiers. Alar pulled himself over the rim, offered Scilla a hand to pull her up, then they made their way around the inferno, arms up to shield their faces from the heat. They found the bodies in the front yard. Somehow, her parents escaped the chaos in the village and made it home, undoubtedly becoming a convenient target for the angry soldier Alar left alive. The bodies were so close to the flames, the clothing smoldered sullenly. Forgetting his awkwardness, Alar pulled Scilla into his arms and let her weep against his chest.

By the time the fire died to a few fitful flames, her eyes were dry. She knelt next to the bodies of her parents, hands cupped in her lap, but she didn't cry. Feeling as if he were intruding on a private moment, Alar left to search for his sword.

When he returned, empty-handed, she stood beside the bodies. She handed him a spade and pointed to a majestic elm near the western edge of the hill. "We'll bury them over there." Her hand dropped to her side. "I'm going to go see if I can help in town." She looked at him. "Can you dig the graves?"

"Sure," he said. She gave him a nod, turned, and walked away. He watched her until she disappeared below the crown of the hill. Every person reacts to violent trauma in their own way. Some retreat into themselves, fleeing from further harm. Others rage, searching for someone to blame, lashing out with no thought of who might get hurt. Scilla was the third kind, the kind who got on with it, gathering the frayed threads of their life and knitting them together into something recognizable. With a sigh, he rested the handle of the spade on his shoulder and trudged over to the elm.

***

Scilla returned from town with two bedsheets. They wrapped the bodies and lowered them into the ground. Alar filled in the graves while Scilla stood aside, her face to the sun, blond curls pulled from her face by the breeze. When he was done, he drove the spade into the ground and stood beside her. Scilla turned around. With the wind at their backs, pushing the smoke to the east, it could be any beautiful Argren day. He tied his hair back while he dug in the rocky soil, and the chill breeze raised goosebumps on his exposed neck. Lowering his eyes from the wispy clouds in the blue sky, he gazed at the twin piles of black earth.

He glanced at Scilla, wondering if he should say anything. *Alle'oss* burial rituals were simple, but beyond vague memories of a boisterous celebration of his grandfather's life, he was unfamiliar with them. The rebels had little time to mourn the dead. Their rituals involved swapping stories about the fallen around the fire in the evening. While he was racking his brain for some appropriate words, Scilla began to sing. He was startled when he realized the words were *Alle'oss*, their own language, which the Empire had nearly eradicated. She would be arrested if the wrong people heard her, but he supposed that was the least of her concerns at the moment.

To Alar and his comrades, reviving their language was one of their few victories. Initially, they did it out of a sense of rebelliousness and the need to take back a part of their culture the Empire took from them. But later, it became a secret way to communicate. The trick was to find native speakers to teach them. They were generally very old and frail. Traveling with the rebels was not an option for them, so Alar and his companions sought them out. It was difficult, and at first, their progress was slow. They spent many nights crowded together at the feet of an elderly *Alle'oss,* whispering to avoid alerting the younger members of the family, who often feared Imperial retribution. Still, they learned what they could, and though Alar wouldn't say he was fluent, he and the other rebels developed a patois they understood. The term they adopted for themselves, *oss'stera,* was an archaic construction that translated as 'our struggle', a much safer term than rebel or resistance.

He couldn't understand all the words to Scilla's song, but he guessed she didn't understand any of it. It was a bawdy tavern ballad he was sure would bring a flush to his cheeks were his vocabulary wider. He doubted anyone sang it like Scilla did. She sang it slow, her low, throaty voice lending it a melancholy brittleness. Despite the ribald lyrics, Alar felt his eyes prickling. After the last note faded away, they stood silently for a moment more, then looked at one another.

"Now what?" she asked.

Alar knew all too well what came next, but he had no answer for her.

"Scilla!"

They looked up at a breathless Ukrit topping the hill. He dropped his satchel, glanced at the remains of their home, then looked at the graves.

"Ukrit!" Scilla ran and threw herself at him.

Alar couldn't help a small grin, watching the siblings hugging one another. At least they wouldn't be alone. When they parted and talked quietly, Alar retrieved the spade and gazed down at the graves, not wanting to intrude. He was so busy with his own thoughts, it startled him when the two stepped up beside him. He was turning away, wanting to give them some privacy, when Ukrit glanced at him. Alar braced himself for his reaction, but the boy showed no sign of recognition. Sighing his relief, Alar walked away.

"You!"

Alar remembered that indignant tone. He had neither the energy nor the patience for Ukrit's accusations, but he hitched a smile onto his face, turned around and was forced to take a step back when he found Ukrit standing a hand's breadth away. "Me."

"I might have known." Ukrit's pale face had taken on the hue of the apples Alar purchased from the old farmer.

Apparently, Ukrit was the type who lashed out and was looking for someone to blame. To be fair, after their encounter with the Imp near Richeleau, Ukrit had a right to be suspicious. What were the odds Alar happened to show up at the twin disasters? And he wasn't wrong in the main. Alar *was* to blame. But when the pampered boy thrust his finger an inch from his nose, Alar's mind went still. And in the quiet, he heard, sensed, the spot behind his eyes emitting a low hum that relaxed him and calmed his racing heart.

Fingers tightening around the handle of the spade, he pushed Ukrit's hand aside and asked, "You might have known what?"

Ukrit hesitated at Alar's tone. Uncertainty chased the anger from his expression for a moment, but the taller man gathered himself and leaned toward Alar. "We never had a problem with the Empire before you appeared. You led that soldier to me on the road and nearly got me arrested. You show up here and ... this!" He threw his hand out toward the graves of his parents.

Suddenly, the hum in Alar's mind rose in pitch. The sunlight dimmed, as if a cloud obscured the sun's face. Alar glanced up, but then noticed Ukrit's hand rising slowly from where his fist hung clenched at his side. Without thinking, he stepped to the side, hooked Ukrit's ankle with the spade's blade and jerked. And as quickly as it dimmed, the world brightened and snapped back to its normal pace.

Ukrit lay on his back, staring up at him. Alar lifted the spade and stared at it, distantly aware of Scilla rushing to her brother's side.

Ukrit pushed his sister away and got to his feet, but before he could rush Alar, Scilla stepped between them and put her hand on her brother's chest. "Ukrit, stop. He, Alar, saved my life." She glanced over her shoulder at Alar and said, "And Old Jep said his warning allowed a lot of people to escape."

When she was sure Ukrit would not resume his attack, she turned to Alar and said, "I thought you said you and Ukrit were friends."

Alar shrugged and let the blade of the spade drop. "Yes, well, I might have exaggerated a bit."

When Ukrit started to speak, she put her hand up to silence him and asked Alar, "Why *are* you here?"

"Because he's a rebel. He was probably trying to run away from the Imperials and led them right to us," Ukrit said. When Scilla scowled at her brother, a petulant tone entered his voice. "He's done it before."

"Let him answer," Scilla said. They looked expectantly at Alar.

"I, uh, I belong to a group called *oss'stera*. It's a—"

"He's a rebel!"

"Shut up, Ukrit." When Ukrit clamped his mouth shut, Scilla turned back to Alar. "Oss.."

"*Oss'stera*, it's an *Alle'oss* word that means our struggle." When they stared at him blankly, Alar added, with a sigh, "We're rebels."

"I *told* you!"

"But why are you *here*? Did you lead them here? How do you two know each other?"

"No, I—" He didn't *lead* them there, not directly, anyway. "I ... we ... one of our informants told us the cavalry leaving Richeleau was coming to Lirantok to punish the town for an attack on a slave wagon that came from here."

Scilla stared at him, her lips parted. Her brother nodded and said, "So, you may not have led them here, but they came because of you, you and your criminal friends."

"You rescued the slaves," Scilla said, ignoring her brother. "The people the ... Imps took."

Alar dropped his eyes, feeling his face heat. "I'm afraid we weren't able to rescue anyone." When he looked up again, Scilla's eyes narrowed slightly, but instead of the anger he expected, a kaleidoscope of emotions crossed her face as she worked through his revelation.

"Right," Ukrit said, pushing his sister aside. "It's like I said." He took two long strides and was in Alar's face again. "The Empire barely notices you and your ragtag friends. All you do is provoke them. If it wasn't for you, they would leave us in peace." He pointed at his parents' graves. "All you do is get people killed." His voice broke on the last word. He lifted his hands again and hesitated, but when Alar didn't react, he shoved Alar in the chest.

Alar saw it coming and took a step back to stay on his feet, but didn't respond. He even let Ukrit yank the spade from his hand. But when the boy pulled the spade back, preparing to swing it at Alar's head, he had enough. Stepping inside the shovel's arc, he blocked Ukrit's arm with his forearm, sending the spade spinning across the yard. Before the surprised boy could respond, Alar punched him, dropping him to the ground again.

Alar bent over the boy, ignoring Scilla pulling on his arm and brushing aside the guilt he felt at the shock on Ukrit's face. This coddled kid would not lecture him. "It's true the Imps came today because of us. Because we tried to rescue your neighbors, people you know, taken for no other reason than they are *Alle'oss.* I would think that would matter to you, but I guess not. Call us criminals. But if we're criminals, what would you call the people that decide to massacre an entire village instead of tracking down me and my ragtag friends? I'm sorry about your parents, but you aren't the only one who has lost loved ones. Some of us have lost a lot more." Alar took a step back, breathing hard, letting Scilla interpose herself between them.

Ukrit got to his feet, wiping blood from his upper lip with the back of his hand. Scilla helped him up and stood next to him. She met Alar's eyes and looked like she was going to speak, but Alar turned and walked away.

She caught up to him as he started descending the hill, taking his arm and pulling him to a stop.

"This ... *oss'stera.*" She looked at him and he nodded. "You're fighting against the Imperials?"

Alar nodded. When she said it, it sounded much more impressive than the reality, but he decided a full accounting of their ineptitude was unnecessary.

She looked back at her brother, who had retrieved the spade and was staring at the ruins of their home. "I have to stay, to help put things right, but—"

When he realized what she was going to say, he cut her off. "You don't want to come with me. It's dangerous. I've lost so many friends, I can't remember them all. We live hand to mouth most of the time." He looked over her shoulder at Ukrit and finished, "And most people agree with your brother." Before she could respond, he turned and left.

***

He was surprised to find most of the village intact. There were a few bodies beneath sheets lined up near the harbor, but there were far more people moving about. Alar stood in the center of the square, turning slowly. Only a quarter of the village had been burned. It could have been, and usually was, much worse. Maybe the soldiers were art lovers. With a sinking sensation, he realized the only reason the Imps burned the Woodsmith's home and killed their parents was because he killed the Imp on their doorstep. Gazing around at the villagers cleaning up, treating each other's wounds and consoling one another, he guessed they would rebuild soon enough. The scars would remain, but they would put it behind themselves, promising each other they would remain small to avoid provoking the Empire. They were luckier than they realized.

"*Lehasa.*"

Alar started at the *Alle'oss* greeting. He turned and found the old man whom he spoke to when he arrived, Old Jep. His hair was pure white, contrasting with an improbably red beard. "*Hasa*," he answered.

The man's brows rose. "*Kisu Alle'oss da?*"

Alar shrugged, lifted a hand and waggled it back and forth. "*Da. Bita.*"

The man smiled and rattled off a string of *Alle'oss*, most of which flew over Alar's head. When he noticed Alar's confusion, the man gave him a small smile and said, "We want to thank you."

Alar looked at the row of bodies.

"It could have been much worse," the old man said, following his gaze.

"Maybe. Probably. Usually is," Alar said. He looked around at the remaining buildings. "Maybe they were in a hurry." He peered up at the old man. "Did they say anything?" When the man gave him a confused grimace, he added, "Anything that might say why they left so quickly?"

"*Tsa.* Just up and left of a sudden."

"What will happen to the Woodsmiths? Ukrit and Scilla?" Alar asked.

"*Da*, Scilla told us what happened," Jep said. "It's a shame." He glanced over at the line of bodies. "They'll have company, at least." He turned and looked toward the Woodsmith's home. "Their older brother is off to Kartok. He'll look after them."

They were silent for a time, and then Jep turned to face him. He eyed the state of Alar's clothes and the beads in his braid, which showed he was from the region around Richeleau. "I don't think we need to ask why you happened to be up this way." When Alar started to answer him, he waved it off. "No explanations necessary. Not sure I want to know, to be honest. Is there anything we can do for you?"

Alar shook his head, but then noticed the burned-out ruins of a small bakery at the edge of the square. He walked over and picked up two slightly charred loaves of bread, and held them up, with a small grin. He could have asked for much more. The Mother knew *oss'stera* could use it, but looking around at the devastation, he didn't have the heart to. He didn't deserve more.

"That's it?" the old man asked.

"*Da.*" He waved one of the loaves as he turned to head out of town. "*Andsutra,*" he called over his shoulder.

"*Andsutra, anama eso.*"

Alar shoved a loaf into his pack, settled it once more on his back and tore a piece from the other as he walked. When was the last time he slept? He tried to organize the events of the last two days, but gave up. He was too exhausted to think straight. Each step was an effort. He could have asked the old man for a place to sleep for the night, but, though Old Jep didn't ask questions, others would. Besides, he'd had no time to consider what happened inside his brain this morning and wanted to be alone.

He neared the spot where it happened and slowed to a stop. Closing his eyes, he listened to the birds singing their evening songs. Alar had only six summers when his mother's brother suffered his injury. His uncle Othan was a happy man, always joking and telling stories. Alar didn't understand what happened to him, and his mother's attempts to explain only terrified him. She led her brother out to sit on the porch on nice days, where he sat for hours staring at nothing. Alar would peer at him from the cool darkness of the barn, wondering what was going on inside the old man's mind.

When he imagined what his uncle experienced, it was like what he experienced that morning: a wet ripping sensation in his mind. But whatever happened to his uncle, it was not what happened to Alar. Could someone hurt their brain in a way that made them better? He never heard of such a thing. The spot was still there, as distinct from the rest of his thoughts as his hand or his foot. But after this morning, other than the note he heard when Ukrit attacked him, it remained stubbornly dormant. He had been prodding it all day, but wasn't able to replicate the boost of energy it produced that morning. Whatever it was, he decided it was better to keep it to himself until he understood it better.

He started moving again, trudging up the hill toward the entrance to the valley. At the top, he looked down into the valley, shadowed by the mountains to the west. Was it only that morning he stood here, watching the sun rise in the east? The hill on which the Woodsmiths lived was just visible above the trees. Ukrit and Scilla might have been beneath the elm tree, but he couldn't be sure. He took a bite of bread and prodded hopefully at the spot in his mind, but no rush of energy emerged to wash away his fatigue. With a sigh, he crawled beneath a spruce at the side of the road, laid his head on his pack and was asleep almost immediately.

Chapter 5

Ērtsa oss'stera!

Adelbart's eyes roamed his office, sliding past familiar objects without seeing them. He wasn't so delusional, he didn't understand how he ended up in his current predicament. Focusing on the painting mounted on the wall across from his desk, he sighed. He had sophisticated tastes. Expensive tastes. And as his mother so often reminded him, he hadn't inherited his father's business acumen. Her pinched scowl still haunted his dreams even now, though he hadn't seen her in the two years since he arrived in Richeleau. The old bat couldn't even muster a kind word on the day her brother, Emperor Ludweig II, appointed Adelbart as Imperial Governor of the District of Argren. To be fair, his appointment was more a testament to his mother's influence over her younger brother than anything her son accomplished on his own.

Even so, the day he moved into the governor's mansion in Richeleau was the second happiest day of his life. Just being free of his mother's incessant insinuations and carping would have been enough, but it wasn't long before he came to love Argren and everything *Alle'oss*. He slouched back in his chair, propped his chin in his palm and gazed out his office window. Richeleau represented everything he loved about Argren. The city had a vibrancy, a life, an optimism, absent from Imperial cities. The *Alle'oss* preferred to work with the land when they built their cities, tucking their buildings in among the trees and winding their streets around the hills and streams. To most Imperials, the result appeared chaotic, but Adelbart found it charming.

He lifted his gaze to the snowy peaks visible beyond the foothills in which the city nestled. His office was on the top floor of the governor's mansion, which loomed over Richeleau from atop the highest hill in the city. Viewed from his office, the red-tiled rooftops dotted the leafy canopy like a colorful archipelago in a green sea. The Empire intended to raze most of the trees and construct a proper Imperial city, of course, but he would enjoy it while he could.

He let his gaze drift to the painting again and contemplated the unhappy circumstances he found himself in. Freed from the constraining hand of his mother, Adelbart proved less than capable of handling his own affairs. Lavish parties, expensive cuisine, wine, women, art ... The list of his indulgences was endless. Not that his income was inconsiderable. It was just that his tastes were extravagant. Still, it wasn't until his creditors threatened to go to the emperor that he was forced to rectify the situation. The emperor would tell his mother. He intimidated most of them, briefly arrested the less compliant, even resorted to torture for one recalcitrant wine merchant.

It wasn't until the social season approached that the downside of such tactics became evident. No one would extend him credit. He could, of course, take whatever he needed, but that was a self-defeating strategy in the long run. Coercion and intimidation were not the building blocks from which scintillating social events were built. Chefs, musicians, artists and the like, in Adelbart's experience, performed best when free from fear. Besides, he genuinely loved Argren, and didn't want to be the monster they assumed he was. So, he went into business with people who could provide the income he required. Unfortunately, his lack of business sense let him down once again. Now, he owed money to people not even an Imperial governor could intimidate.

A knock on his office door brought him back from his thoughts. He could tell from the familiar cadence it was Gerold, his assistant.

"Come," he called sullenly.

Gerold entered, approached the side of Adelbart's desk, leaned forward and murmured. "There is a contingent of *Alle'oss* from Lirantok here to speak with you."

"Lirantok?" The governor looked up at his assistant, his brows rising. "Good news?"

"I think so, sir. They said they want to discuss your proposal."

"So, the good citizens of Lirantok have finally seen reason," Adelbart said, sitting up. "You remember what we discussed?"

Gerold nodded. "Yes, sir."

"Good, show them in." As Gerold left, the governor gave his desk a quick scan for anything out of place.

Four *Alle'oss* entered, peering around at his office. Adelbart had never set eyes on any of them, as his assistant had handled the *negotiations* so far. Gerold entered after them and stood beside Adelbart's desk. The man in front wore his long white hair pulled back in a tail. He stopped in front of Adelbart's desk, wiped his hand down his red beard, glanced at the painting on the wall behind Adelbart and sighed. With a visible effort, he met Adelbart's eyes.

Adelbart's thin lips stretched into a smile. He waited for the man to speak. It was a negotiating tactic he saw his father use on many occasions. "Let them wonder what you're thinking. Makes them nervous," his father told him, and Adelbart could believe it. His father's silence always made him uncomfortable. But before the moment could drag out, one of the other *Alle'oss* spoke from the back of the room.

"Where did you get that?" The indignant tone, so much like his mother's, set Adelbart's teeth on edge.

The old man turned and stepped aside, revealing a younger man, a boy really, with red hair. The boy glared at the painting on the wall behind Adelbart.

"I asked where you got that," the boy said, aiming his glare at Adelbart.

"Ukrit!" the old man said. "You remember the condition you agreed to before we let you come?"

Ukrit's eyes flicked to the old man and then fell to the floor. After a moment, he turned on his heel and left the room.

The remaining *Alle'oss* watched him go, then the old man turned back to Adelbart. He expected an apology, but the old man glanced at the painting and said, "The boy may be rash, rude even, but he has a point. If I'm not mistaken, the artist of that particular painting paid with his life for its creation."

Adelbart smiled. "You have a good eye, Hera ..." He hitched an eyebrow at the old man.

After a long moment, the old man said, "Olafson, Jepson Olafson."

"Yes, of course. As I said, you have a good eye, though I would expect no less from a Lirantokan ... Lirantokian ... Lirantokite? My, that's a mouthful." He grinned widely, but Jepson merely stared at him. "Yes, well, now, Gerold mentioned you are ready to accept my proposal?"

"We have considered your *offer* and are prepared to pay you twenty percent of our net."

And as simple as that, Jepson swept away the murk clouding Adelbart's future. The governor took a moment to breathe, feeling the taut muscles at the base of his neck easing. But though he would have been satisfied with twenty percent of their net before, a substantial sum, they would have to pay for the inconvenience they put him through. "Oh, no, no," Adelbart said, shaking his head. "I'm afraid that offer expired when you forced me to send Captain Brennerman's cavalry to convey the seriousness of my offer. Now, the best I can do is sixty percent of the gross." Before the man's face could completely register his outrage, Adelbart raised a finger and said, "In return, I will assign a contingent of the emperor's best to accompany you. It's only fair, now that we are in business together, that I ensure the village is well protected."

The old man stood quietly for a long moment. "Why don't you just steal the pigments?"

Adelbart let his smile freeze. Despite his mother's constant insinuations, Adelbart was not a stupid man. Indolent, certainly, some might say debauched, but not stupid. He chuckled and shook his head. "I am not a thief. I am a businessman." When the old man didn't respond, Adelbart continued, "You see, this way we can both look forward to a long, mutually profitable relationship." The old man's face fell, and he dropped his gaze. An inexplicable twinge of sympathy prompted the governor to add, "If I might offer some advice, you can make up your share by increasing your production."

"We can't simply—" The man stopped, mouth still open. His eyes rose briefly to the painting again, then he said, "Sixty percent of the gross will be acceptable, *if* you will return our neighbors the slavers took."

Adelbart looked up at Gerold.

"As a show of good faith, we will do our best to locate your neighbors, though they may have already been transported elsewhere," Gerold said.

The governor smiled again. It was a generous offer. "So, it's settled. Now, when can we expect the first payment?"

"We ship on the first day of Talavamon."

Adelbart frown.

Gerold leaned over and said in a soft voice, "That is the middle of the month of Lianapok, governor."

Adelbart barely heard his assistant dictating the details of the deal. *How could he have been so stupid?* Of course, it would take that long. Although the secret of the pigments' manufacture was well guarded, he knew it involved plants that grew only in the valley. They would have to wait until the proper time to harvest them. The conversation died, and it was a moment before he realized the old *Alle'oss* man was addressing him.

"We will provide a list of names of our neighbors to your assistant," Jepson said. Adelbart nodded vaguely. "Governor," he said, turned and herded his two companions out of the office.

Gerold followed before Adelbart could say anything. The governor stared at the closed door, his mind racing. He was so close! Lianapok was four months away. Too long. He stood, came around his desk and stood in front of the painting on the opposite wall. It was called *A Summer Day*. It depicted a young *Alle'oss* couple walking down a small mountain road. He carried a bucket and was gesturing with the other hand, as if he were telling a story. Her arms were full of what appeared to be laundry. They were looking at one another, laughing, their joy at being in each other's presence palpable. Adelbart grinned, despite his worries. It was the first painting in what the *Alle'oss* called the new school style. "*Ākana si.*" He whispered the *Alle'oss* phrase, then glanced guiltily over his shoulder. Of the many aspects that distinguished the new school, it was the colors which the governor appreciated the most. "Because they will appreciate in my accounts," he murmured and chuckled at his joke. The red of the bucket and the man's hair, the greens of the fields and forest, the golden yellow of the woman's hair. There were none like them and the new school had ignited a frenzied demand for them throughout the art world. He focused on the woman's dress. Argren blue. More valuable than gold, its secrets known to very few, and no one outside the Ishian River valley.

Yes, he could burn the village to the ground, steal their existing stock of pigments, maybe try to extract the secrets through torture. But Gerold had been too clever for that. It was his assistant who suggested they pressure the citizens of Lirantok into sharing their profits. As the Imperial governor, Adelbart could have imposed a tax on the pigments, but then the revenue would come to the attention of the Imperial Exchequer. No this way was much better. The *Alle'oss* would do all the work and Adelbart would take most of the revenue.

He would have to find some way to satisfy his creditors. Perhaps they would accept the news of his deal with Lirantok as collateral to buy him more time. Yes, that should work, and once he paid them, he would have the revenue to fund his lavish lifestyle for years to come. He walked over to the window and looked out over the city, clasping his hands behind his back. He would have to do something nice for Gerold. Maybe a bottle of wine. Yes, that would do nicely.

***

As Alar expected, Sten and Erik were furious with him for going to Lirantok. He sat quietly through Sten's lecture, not bothering to excuse himself. He expected it and was prepared to pay whatever penance Sten demanded of him. But the older man's lecture was perfunctory, with no trace of the fire he would have mustered at one time. In a surprisingly short time, he began to wind down, pausing between seemingly disconnected thoughts. When Sten looked away, Alar exchanged a grimace with Tove, then let his gaze travel across the other members of *oss'stera*. What he saw was alarming. There were fewer faces than before he left. Only twelve people remained. Though they were pretending to ignore the situation, their furtive glances reflected his own embarrassment.

In the end, Sten assigned him extra guard duty and extracted a promise not to disobey him again. When Alar agreed, the man who rescued him as a child turned away, dropped into his customary place beside the fire and stared into space.

Later, while Alar was serving his first stint as sentry with Tove and Lief keeping him company, Tove explained. "They left in the middle of the night, Sigmond, Greta and the others. Erik said that's what happens if you let people do whatever they want." She gave him an apologetic smile.

Alar gazed at the distant rooftops of Richeleau. People came and went. It was to be expected, but their numbers had been diminishing steadily for some time.

"So, you gonna tell us about your trip?" Tove cut into his thoughts.

"Yeah," Lief added. "Did you get there in time? What did the Imps do?"

"Surprisingly little, to be honest," Alar said, and before Lief could ask, he added, "They left your hometown alone."

"So?" Tove prompted.

Never one to cede the stage, Alar made sure they weren't disappointed. When he came to the part where something tore inside his head, he hesitated, taking in Tove's shining face. Then he skipped past the moment without mentioning it. He told himself he would confide in her when they were alone. But when the time arrived, he kept his silence. On his way back from Lirantok, he poked and prodded the spot, but it remained inert. He could still feel it, cool, quiet and separate from the rest of his mind. But he began to think he imagined the burst of energy or the moment when time seemed to slow. Eventually, he gave up, merely prodding at it idly like a tongue that returned repeatedly to the space left by a missing tooth. They would think him crazy if he tried to explain it. He promised himself he would tell her if anything unusual happened again.

***

Six weeks after he returned, he was once again on sentry duty, looking down at Lief approaching the base of the ridge at a run. His first thought was the boy was being chased, but he kept looking up as he ran, not over his shoulder. It was more like he had news he was desperate to share. Whatever it was, it didn't look good. Alar heard someone behind him and turned to find Tove, her new bow in hand.

He gave Lief another glance, then walked over to join her. "You finished it," he said, taking the offered bow.

"It's done, but it's not right. I made it the same way as the other one. I don't know what I did wrong."

It was just the two of them on the top of the ridge. Tove, forgetting her scar, glared at the offending bow, her lips twisted. Alar held the bow at arm's length and pulled the sinew to his ear. The arc of the top arm was more pronounced than the bottom arm. Easing off the tension, he held the bow horizontally and ran the two arms between his thumb and fingers. They felt the same, but it was hard to tell.

Tove took the bow back, dipping her head as her usual reticence returned. "We need someone who knows the right way to make one."

Alar could hear the frustration in her voice. "Tove, bowyers spend years as apprentices learning their craft." He rested his hand on her shoulder. "You've only made two bows, and one of them is pretty good."

Tove peeked up at him. "It's just, it's a lot of work, and when it doesn't turn out, I don't know why."

"You're right," he conceded. "We need to find someone to teach you." He looked out over the forest canopy, at the height of its summer glory, tossed about by a gusty breeze. They once nurtured glorious fantasies of standing toe-to-toe with the Imps, cold steel in hand. When they weren't trying to feed themselves, they bent all their will to finding swords, axes, anything they could wield in hand-to-hand combat. Their first encounters with trained soldiers disabused them of their fantasies. The *Alle'oss* had no expertise nor tradition with swords and spears. Even if they found someone to teach them, it would take years to match up with their oppressors. The one weapon that might provide an advantage in their mountains was the bow. The problem was, no one in their small band knew the slightest thing about archery. It was a conundrum Alar had been worrying at for some time.

"What about that bowyer in Richeleau? What was his name?"

"Bjorn." Alar shook his head. "He threatened to call the gendarmes the last time I talked to him." He smiled at her. "We'll just have to look elsewhere." He turned as Lief clambered onto the top of the ridge. The boy hurried over to them, his red hair, lank with sweat, sticking to his cheeks. He held up a hand, bent over, and rested his hands on his knees, chest expanding and contracting like a bellows.

Alar exchanged a look with Tove, feeling a chill run up his spine. "Lief, you've been gone a long time. You run into trouble?" he asked, trying to keep the tension out of his voice.

The boy straightened abruptly, splattering them both with sweat. "Alar, we have a problem," he said.

"What?" Alar asked, wiping his cheeks with both hands.

"Someone has been asking around Richeleau for you. Throwing your name around."

Alar looked from Lief to Tove's vaguely accusatory expression. His incessant lectures on the subject of security were a continuing source of annoyance to his companions. "How do you know they're asking for me? It could be some other Alar."

"He's asking for the rebel named Alar, and he mentioned *oss'stera.*"

Alar glanced at Tove again, then looked toward the rooftops of Richeleau. "Yeah, that's probably me," he said, trying to ignore Tove's snort. The gold cladding on the recently completed dome of the Vollen Church's cathedral glinted in the late afternoon sun. Who could be looking for him? Most of the people he knew were *oss'stera*, and the handful of people who wandered off recently knew better.

"You know Jora, the one who owns the Black Husky?" Lief asked. "He said the guy's acting all secretive, like he's trying to be low key, but all he's doing is attracting attention."

"You get a description?"

"That's why I'm late. I waited around until he came in. Red hair, big build." Lief lifted his hand above his head.

Alar waited, but apparently that was the extent of Lief's description. "Thanks Lief, that helps." Lief nodded, and Alar shared a smile with Tove. They had noticed that Lief seemed to lack a sense of humor, and he apparently had no understanding of sarcasm.

"You think you should go see what it's about?" the boy asked seriously. "I would have talked to him, but I figured you would want to know about it first."

Alar looked up at the sun through the swaying branches of an old oak that clung grimly to the rocky ridge. If he left now, he could be in

Richeleau by evening. "Good idea, Lief. You head on down. Tove got a couple of rabbits yesterday. We saved some for you." As Lief was turning away, Alar added, "Tell Erik to come up and keep watch."

"You sure about that?" Tove asked, watching Lief walking away.

"What?"

"Giving orders to Erik. What with recent events and all … Might not go over well."

She was right, but he noticed Erik and Sten rarely stood their turn on sentry duty anymore, and it was sticking in his craw. "Tove, you're with me," he said and turned his widest smile on her.

Tove went still. "What? Where are we going?"

"Someone is being very indiscreet. We need to find out who."

"We're going to Richeleau?"

Alar started walking, beckoning her into motion. "You worried about going to the big city?"

"Don't you think you should ask Erik or Sten to go with you? Well, maybe not them, but Rolf or Taavi?" After a few quick steps, Tove stopped, forcing Alar to stop and turn.

"Both good choices, especially when it comes to a brawl, but let's hope it doesn't come to that. Besides, between you and me, when a cool head is required, I'd rather have you with me."

Her cheek quirked, a smile arrested before it could make it all the way onto her face. "Cool head, huh?" She fell in beside him as he resumed walking.

"You remember when we liberated that cask of flour in Mirintok and the sheriff came around the corner?" Tove stared ahead, but let a small smile touch the corner of her lips. She peeked quickly up at him and nodded. "Who was it that told him we were the miller's cousins?"

"Can't believe he bought that," she said, chuckling. They stopped at the edge of the ridge and looked down. "Anyone could have done that."

Alar bent over so he could see her face. "Anyone could when they had a chance to sit down and think it over. But it was you who thought of it in the moment." She considered, then gave him a quick nod and sat to ease herself over the edge.

After climbing down, they walked in silence for a while until Tove cleared her throat. "Yes?" Alar asked.

"I'm not really comfortable being around a lot of new people."

"*Ērtsu aku da* (Who are you)?"

She peeked up at him. "*Ērtsa oss'stera.*"

"*O ta?*" Alar said, cupping his hand to his ear.

She lifted her head, letting her face emerge from behind the veil of her hair. "*Ērtsa oss'stera!*" she shouted and gave Alar a wide grin before retreating behind her veil.

"*Otsuna.* And don't you forget it."

"*Otsuna!*"

Chapter 6

Reunion

Alar glanced around to make sure they were alone, then said, "Weapons off," before removing his sword's sheath from his belt. It was illegal for *Alle'oss* to carry swords, and though bows were not outlawed, carrying one in a bigger city like Richeleau attracted attention. They retrieved a deer hide they stashed beneath the roots of an oak that leaned out over a small creek, wrapped their weapons, and hid them away. Resting his hand on the hilt of the knife at his belt, he gave Tove a nod and asked, "You ready?"

She didn't answer, but her face told the story. Her jaws were locked tight, lips working, her face paler than normal.

"You've been to Richeleau before." He started walking, trusting she would follow.

"Yes, but ..." She waggled her fingers in front of her face.

Alar didn't respond, having said all he could on the subject. Tove would have to find her own peace with it, and she wouldn't do it hiding in the forest. "You remember the Black Husky. It's on Karlon Street. It's not in the best part of town, so stay sharp."

Richeleau was the largest city in northern Argren and was the seat of the Imperial government in the district. Fortunately, unlike its counterpart in southern Argren, Kartok, Richeleau clung to its *Alle'oss* roots. Still, the Imperial influence was growing, and it was becoming increasingly uncomfortable for the natives.

They walked in silence until they emerged from the forest onto the road that connected Richeleau to the Imperial Highway, near to the site of their disastrous attack on the slave wagon.

"Um."

"Yes?" Alar asked.

"Why, exactly, am I here?"

"I need you to watch and listen." Alar said. "We don't know who this person is. What he wants. If we meet him, I'll do the talking. You keep an eye out for anything suspicious. He may have confederates."

"I can do that."

Though he couldn't see her face, he grinned as her auburn hair bobbed in time to her nods.

***

It was well past sunset, and the nightlife on Karlon Street was in full swing. The only light was the dim glow from the open doors and windows of the taverns and alehouses clustered in one of the city's rougher neighborhoods. It was late, the crowd boisterous. Rowdy conversations blended with a variety of musical styles into a festive cacophony. They had been standing across from the Husky for three hours. Tove wedged herself between Alar and the brick wall of a pharmacy when they arrived and hadn't emerged. He felt her furtive movements, as she did her best to accomplish the task Alar set her from her hiding place. Lief's description of the man looking for him was useless, as it applied to nearly half the people on the street. Alar was hoping to get lucky, trusting to the fact that Lief said the man was making himself conspicuous. The only luck they had was that they had seen no Imperials.

"Anything?" he asked over his shoulder.

"Nothing."

"Looks like we'll have to go in and talk to Jora." He looked back and found Tove staring up at him, her wide, blue eyes glinting in the low light. She didn't reply, but gave him a nod.

Alar took one last look at the busy street. "Keep an eye out for anyone showing more interest than they should," he said, then stepped into the crowd. Tove took a handful of his shirt and followed so closely, he felt her against his back whenever he slowed to allow someone to pass.

Jora's tavern was one of the smaller establishments on Karlon Street. A handful of mismatched tables were scattered around a room, which was longer than it was wide. Alar spotted Jora behind the battle-scarred bar, which occupied the back half of the right wall. The proprietor, talking to a pair of patrons leaning on the bar, caught Alar's eye and gave him an almost imperceptible nod. Alar stood inside the door and scanned the room. He was happy to see only half the tables were occupied. Much easier to spot a newcomer asking questions. Tove fidgeted, jostling Alar's back. He grinned, imagining her dilemma, caught between her desire to get out of the open door, but unwilling to enter the tavern before him.

Alar wove through the tables, heading for the back of the room. Tove followed, muttering apologies when she tripped over a man's outstretched feet, then ducking behind Alar when he took an unoccupied spot at the bar. She glanced up at him, lips disappearing between her teeth, then leaned out so she could see the room.

Jora appeared, slapping two frothy mugs on the counter. Alar narrowed his eyes at the mugs, then met the bartender's smirk. *Oss'stera* possessed an odd collection of coins, including a few of the iron pennies from the purse he found on the soldier, but they were safely stashed back at their camp, not to be wasted on frivolities like ale.

"On the house," the big man said. He leaned forward and spoke in a quieter voice. "I assume Lief gave you the message."

Alar nodded and took a sip, closed his eyes and swished it around his mouth. A proper *Alle'oss* ale. Bright floral notes followed by a clean finish. He swallowed and sighed. When he opened his eyes, the old man was grinning at him.

"Best ale in Richeleau," Alar said. He set the mug down and surveyed the room. "How's business, Jora?"

"Not complaining, or at least no more than usual." He turned his head to watch a pair of men enter the tavern. "Haven't seen your friend today, but he usually comes in a little later." He looked back at Alar, and added, "Been asking all over town." He gave Alar a significant look and moved off to serve the newcomers.

Alar watched him go, then looked back at Tove. She was staring at the mug, but when she sensed Alar looking at her, her eyes flicked up to him. "Ale?"

"You never had an ale before?"

Her head shook slowly, eyes not leaving the mug.

"Go ahead, try it."

She peeked up at him again, then she seemed to settle into herself, her face taking on a determined set. She took the mug's handle, slid it over to the edge of the bar, leaned down and sipped. When her head came up, foam coated her lip below a wrinkled nose. She considered for a moment, her eyes on Alar, then leaned forward, took the mug in both hands and took a bigger sip. She pulled back, eyes in the distance, mouth working. After a moment, her eyes rotated up to Alar, and she nodded.

Alar turned away grinning, leaned his elbow on the bar and watched the room.

An hour later, he was peering into his empty mug when a commotion near the door drew his attention. The six men filing into the tavern set him on edge. The way they moved, the cut of their hair, their casual dismissal of everyone around them, reminded him of Imps, but these were not like any Imps he ever saw. For one thing, almost all Imperial citizens had black hair. Though it was difficult to discern the exact color of these men's hair in the low lamplight, it was neither black, nor the various red and blond hues of the *Alle'oss*. They were also enormous, taller and bulkier than anyone Alar had ever seen. The men passed empty tables before rousting a pair of *Alle'oss* from a table near the wall. They sat, calling boisterously to Jora's single server. The atmosphere in the room fizzed. Several people rose and slipped out the door. Alar felt the tension coming off Tove at his back. Catching Jora's eye, he nodded toward the newcomers.

"Mercenaries," Jora said. "From the Union." When Alar frowned back at him, he added, "From across the Southern Sea."

Alar looked back at the men. "That's new," he said. "Why do the Imps need to hire mercenaries?"

"Word is the emperor picked a fight with someone he shouldn't have. The Imps need men. This lot has been causing trouble all over town since they got here."

Jora's server, Jena, looked as skittish as a deer as she set mugs in front of the laughing men. Alar, who was leaning on the bar, stood upright and asked, "Hasn't anyone called the gendarmes?"

Jora nodded. "For all the good it did." While he was speaking, one of the men wrapped enormous hands around Jena's waist and pulled her into his lap.

Alar was moving before his better sense could stop him. He felt Tove make a grab for his shirt but kept going. Before he could emerge from the shadows at the back of the room, movement at the door caught his eye. He glanced over and came to an abrupt stop. Ukrit was standing in the door. Suddenly, it made sense. The boy knew Alar was from this area, and as naïve as he was, he would think whispering when he said the word *oss'stera* would keep him safe. It was a miracle he hadn't been arrested.

Alar was still in the darker part of the room near the back when Ukrit's eyes slid across him and settled on the mercenaries. His face clouded when he noticed Jena struggling to escape. Alar watched in horror as the boy crossed the room and tapped the offender on the shoulder. He couldn't hear what Ukrit said, but the men's laughter died in an instant. The big man holding Jena let her go and unwound himself from the chair to stand toe-to-toe with Ukrit. Ukrit was tall for an *Alle'oss,* but he had to tip his head back to meet the man's eyes.

"*Sheoda*," Alar muttered. He stepped aside to allow Jena to pass, then made his way to the table, mind racing. "Ukrit!" he said, taking the boy's arm and dragging him away from the mercenary. "Excuse us," he said to the behemoth, turning his back on him and asking Ukrit. "When did you get into town?" Taking advantage of Ukrit's momentary confusion, he urged him into motion. Alar was just thinking he might extract them both from the situation when the mercenary's heavy hand landed on his shoulder.

"Hold on there, little *I'oss*," he growled. His fingers dug into Alar's shoulder. "Me and this boy are having a conversation."

The words in his gravelly accent ground together, sounding like an avalanche in his rumbling voice. Ukrit pulled his arm free of Alar's grip, but before he could speak, Alar twisted around and looked up at the mercenary. Despite the tense situation, he couldn't help noticing the thatch of hairs jutting from the man's nostrils and the scar that cut across the left side of his face, leaving his eye a milky orb. Forcing himself to look at the good eye, he said, "I just need him for a minute. You can finish up when we're done."

"That's okay," the man said, the grin that appeared doing nothing to soften his face. "I'll just have to finish my conversation with *you*."

Tove was right about Alar's tendency toward recklessness. What she didn't know was that it was the only way he survived their violent life. For months after he joined *oss'stera*, he froze at the threat of imminent violence, an echo of the helplessness he felt watching the Imps butcher his family. Ironically, it was fear that was the root of his recklessness. Fear of what might happen to the members of his new family if he froze at the wrong moment. Turn the brain off and dive in headfirst. It was the only way forward.

As the mercenary's iron-hard fingers dug into Alar's shoulder, the jangly frisson in Alar's mind quieted. In the silence, the spot in his mind, which had remained dormant since Lirantok, hummed, and the lights dimmed. He had to resist the urge to laugh out loud. That was the secret. The spot's song emerged in the icy calm that overtook his mind in the face of violence, just as it had on the hilltop beside the ashes of Ukrit's home. The mercenary's other hand was rising and forming a fist, but Alar had enough time to glance around the room, noting that it wasn't only the man holding onto his shoulder that slowed. His companions were frozen, their faces showing their eagerness. Ukrit's mouth was open, as if he were speaking. Alar looked up at the mercenary's lips pulling slowly back from gray teeth and punched him in the throat.

As suddenly as it dimmed, the light returned, and the world resumed its normal speed. In the stunned silence, the mercenary's gurgling gasps filled the room. He fell to his knees, hands clutching his neck. Alar stepped clear of him, as he fell onto his side. Looking up at Ukrit gaping at him, he said, "We better go."

As he turned, searching for Tove, the injured man's friends finally recovered from their shock. Chairs, mugs of ale, tables were thrown aside in their haste to get at him. He leapt backwards, catching a mug full of ale in the face. Blinking the liquid from his eyes, he shook his head, trying to provoke the spot into action. No use. The men were still coming at normal speed, spreading out to cut off their avenues of escape. Ukrit, facing the front door, backed up and stepped on Alar's foot. Alar jumped backward, prompting a mercenary to slide sideways between him and the back door of the tavern. Soon, Alar and Ukrit stood back to back against the bar.

The mercenary blocking his path to the back door leered down at him, and just as he started to speak, there was a crash and the sound of splintering wood. The man hunched his shoulders and turned around. Tove stood behind him, holding two legs of what used to be a chair. She looked from the man to the remains of the chair and then at Alar.

Alar slid his knife from its sheath, stepped forward, and drove it into the back of the man's thigh. The piercing scream froze everyone in place. Leaving the knife, Alar reached back, grabbed Ukrit's tunic and pulled him into motion. Shoving his way past the falling mercenary, he took Tove's shoulder and pushed her ahead of him. They crashed through the door at the back of the room. Angry shouts followed them down a short hallway, past the privies, then outside into the alley behind the tavern. Tove shook his hand off and took off. Alar followed, letting Ukrit make his own way.

She took the first left, down a narrow space between two buildings. Alar could hear Ukrit cursing behind him, as the bigger man squeezed through. They emerged onto the next street and slowed to a walk.

"I've been—" Ukrit started until Alar cut him off.

"Later."

They heard shouts behind them, but Tove led them through a winding route until they reached the city limits, slipped into the forest and headed north to retrieve their weapons.

"I've been trying to find you."

"I'm aware. Everyone in Richeleau is aware, apparently." Alar stopped and turned to face Ukrit. "I'm sure you know asking about rebels is enough to get you killed."

"I was careful."

Alar snorted and turned away. Ukrit caught his arm. Alar turned on him, but when he saw the anguish on Ukrit's face, he hesitated.

"Scilla is gone."

Chapter 7

Too Tenuous for Hope

For a moment, Alar stared blankly into Ukrit's red-rimmed eyes. Distracted by their narrow escape and the urgency of getting away from the city, he could not place the name. When Ukrit saw his confusion, he deflated. His eyes slid from Alar to the shadowy forest and he mumbled, "You don't even remember her."

And then Alar remembered Ukrit's sister. He glanced at Tove, who was watching the exchange intently, momentarily forgetting to hide her face. Turning back to Ukrit, he asked, "What do you mean, gone?"

Ukrit lifted his hands helplessly. "She was okay for a week after you left. We were making plans, putting our life back together. But then Ulbricht, our older brother, got back from Kartok. I don't know, maybe she thought since I wouldn't be alone ... She started talking about you and the rebels. She asked what good would it do to rebuild, when the Imperials could come take it away on a whim. We argued. I—" He stopped and squeezed his eyes shut. When he opened them, he said, "She left in the middle of the night weeks ago. I assumed she ran off to join *oss'stera*." He spat the last word, anger flickering across his face. Then perhaps remembering he needed Alar's cooperation, he settled himself and said, "I was hoping she was with you?"

"No, sorry, Ukrit. We haven't seen her."

The hope that illuminated Ukrit's face when he asked his question drained away. His head dropped, his shoulders slumped. When he looked up, moonlight glinted on tears on his cheeks. His mouth worked, but no sound emerged.

"But we can help you find her."

Startled, Alar turned around. Tove looked as surprised as he was, but she recovered and gave him a determined nod. When Alar turned back to Ukrit, he saw the same thing he saw on Tove's face the night he found her in a back alley in Kartok. Something too tenuous to call hope. The memory pulled the words from his mouth before he could stop them. "Sure, we'll do what we can, of course." Seeing Ukrit's face transform, Alar bit back the qualification he was about to offer. They would look for her, but if she was missing a month or more, the odds weren't good they would find her.

A dog barking reminded him they were still close to the city. "But first we need to get away from Richeleau." Alar turned and started walking. Tove looked up at him from lowered eyes as he passed, then fell in behind him.

"Where are we going?" Ukrit called after them.

Alar didn't answer. He was remembering Scilla. They spoke little, even while they waited in the forest for the attack to end. She was too worried for her parents, and he was listening for Imps searching for the boy who killed their comrade. Looking as if she had sixteen or seventeen summers, she shared her brother's blue eyes, but her curly hair was the dusky blond the *Alle'oss* called *mania ti dari*. He remembered it flying out behind her as she slid down the steep embankment behind her house. There was fear in her eyes when her face appeared in her window, but no panic. He'd seen the effect on her when he mentioned *oss'stera,* heard the wonder in her voice when she found out some of her countrymen were resisting the Imperial presence. Alar pulled his lips back, hissing a breath between his teeth. It was his fault. He, better than most, knew the effect his words could have in the moments after the Imps killed her parents. He let his anger at Ukrit carry him away.

Behind him, Ukrit crashed through the forest, swearing loudly as he attempted to negotiate the rocky ground in the dark. They arrived at their weapon stash, and Alar splashed across the creek and ducked down to retrieve the bundle.

"What's he doing?" Ukrit asked.

"Shh," Tove answered.

Alar handed her the bow and let his sword hang in his hand. "I don't think we can go back to camp at night, not with …" Tove couldn't see him nod at Ukrit in the dark, but she probably didn't need to.

"Why, how far is it?" Ukrit asked.

"Ukrit, we'll have to blindfold you, and it's a hard enough hike without having to guide you in the dark."

"Blindfold me?" Ukrit said. "I won't tell anyone where it is."

Tove turned and started walking. Alar put his hand on Ukrit's back and guided him after her. "We have a place we can spend the rest of the night." Not that they would need to spend much time there. Alar could only see glimpses of the sky as they walked, but he saw enough to know it was late. Or rather, early.

***

"I don't know why you blindfolded me," Ukrit grumbled. "I have no idea where we are."

"I have no doubt that is true. However, we've found the Imps need only the most innocuous scrap of information to find us." Alar answered. "The type of vegetation, the shape of the surrounding mountain peaks, even the way the forest smells. All of it is useful to the right person." Ukrit lifted his nose and sniffed, prompting Tove and Alar to share a grin. "Careful, I'll stuff your nostrils full of clay. We're comfortable in this place. We prefer not to move, so we're not taking any chances."

It took hours to lead Ukrit over the rugged terrain. Even though they left at first light, it was well past noon when they made it to the base of the ridge.

Tove, one hand propped on a hip, eyed the rocky face. "We'll never get him up there with that blindfold on."

Alar had been worrying at that problem since they set out, but had no solution. "We could go around," he said, without conviction.

"Yeah," Tove said, but the tone of her voice said more than the word about what she thought of that plan.

"Whatever you decide to do, can we get it over with?" Ukrit asked.

Alar had to give him credit. He endured the stubbed toes and barked shins stoically, demonstrating far more patience than Alar expected. And, although Alar could tell he wanted to, he hadn't asked what they would do to find Scilla. That was a good thing, because Alar had no ideas, even after laying awake the rest of the previous night worrying about it. People went missing. It had always been a hazard of living in rugged, mostly wild mountains. *Na'lios* were unforgiving for the unwary and foolish. Scilla may be at the bottom of a ravine, buried beneath an avalanche. She may have run afoul of any of a number of dangerous creatures, or she may simply have become lost. All of this was not uncommon, even before the Empire came. If the Imperials had her, there was little enough hope as to be none.

He turned Ukrit away from him and worked at the knot in the blindfold. Alar could see Tove's face over Ukrit's shoulder. She would be the first thing Ukrit saw when the blindfold fell away from his eyes. She met Alar's eyes, her lips working. Alar lifted a brow, waiting for her to dip her head. Instead, she lifted her chin the smallest amount, a defiant set to her mouth.

Alar pulled the blindfold off. Ukrit blinked and lifted a hand to shade his eyes. "Tove?" When she gave him a tight nod, he put his hand out and said, "Ukrit, nice to meet you, properly."

Tove hesitated, then took his hand and let him shake her entire arm. When Ukrit dropped her hand and turned toward him, Alar glimpsed Tove's surprised expression before Ukrit blocked his view.

"So, what are we going to do to find Scilla?" Ukrit asked.

"We're ... we're climbing up here before we talk about that," Alar said, gesturing toward the top of the ridge. To prevent Ukrit from arguing, he turned away and started up. After the first few feet, he paused and looked down. "Watch what I do, and don't fall or you'll take Tove with you." Ukrit startled, glanced at Tove and nodded.

It wasn't a hard climb, but while perched on the rock face, you were at the mercy of anyone at the top of the ridge. When no one called down a greeting, he worried, but when he pulled himself over the edge at the top, he knew something was amiss. No one was there. He helped Ukrit up, his finger to his lips.

"What's wrong?" Ukrit asked.

Grimacing, Alar held his finger up, then very deliberately placed it to his lips.

"Oh, right," Ukrit said.

Tove rose up beside him, her face showing she was as wary as he was. They crept forward, crossing the spine of the ridge, and peered down into the camp.

In the two months since Alar returned, *oss'stera* had dwindled to ten members. The other eight were arrayed along one side of the fire pit, heads hanging, looking like dogs who chewed their master's favorite boots. Across from them, a woman sat, as relaxed as if she were sitting in front of her own hearth. Other than her having the black hair of an Imperial, there didn't seem to be anything about her that would cause the obvious anxiety in his comrades. The scene gave him the strong impression of a patient mother, about to have a talk with her disobedient children.

He looked at Tove, but she merely shrugged.

"What do you see?" Ukrit, who appeared to be leery of approaching the edge, asked.

They made their way to a spot they could descend out of sight of the fire pit and climbed down. Alar waited at the bottom until all three of them were safely on the ground, then with a glance back at Tove, he stepped into the open. "*Lehasa,*" he called, affecting the same casual cheeriness he always did when returning to camp.

Nine heads snapped toward him. When he saw the woman's face, he froze. Tove made a small sound behind him. A tattoo covered the left side of the woman's face, near the temple. The whorls and dots marked her as a sister of the Seidi, an Imperial witch, a woman capable of killing everyone there with a flick of her fingers. Before he could decide how to react, she spoke.

"*Lehasa*," she said with a smile. "You must be Alar."

Alar was ashamed to admit to himself later, but his first impulse was to turn and run. He didn't know a lot about the Seidi sisters' magic, but he was pretty sure if she couldn't see him, she couldn't hurt him. But before he could urge his legs to act, his eyes flicked to Lief and the fear he saw there galvanized him. Retrieving the grin that fell from his face, he forced himself to approach the witch. He wouldn't be able to pull his sword before she reacted. He brushed his wrist against the sheath of his knife and remembered he left it in the mercenary's thigh. She didn't move and her eyes never left his. He stopped a few paces away, adopting a relaxed nonchalance. If he lunged at her, it might give someone else enough time to kill her.

"Do we know one another?" he asked.

"We have not met." she said. "But I know about you."

It sounded like a threat. He looked up at the top of the ridge, expecting to see a company of Imperial Rangers looking down at him, but the only movement came from high wispy clouds against an azure sky. When he lowered his gaze, she was still watching him patiently, still smiling. "You found our camp," he said.

"Yes, but it wasn't easy. You chose a good spot."

Alar waited, offering her an opportunity to explain what she was doing there. Instead, she looked past him and said, "Hello, Ukrit."

"Who are you?" Ukrit asked.

Alar winced at the blunt tone, but the witch didn't seem to take offense.

"Her name is Ragan," Lief said.

Alar looked at the boy, who lifted his brows, dipped his head and nodded at the witch. When Alar looked back, the woman was giving Lief a proud mother smile.

"Why are you here, Ragan?" Alar asked.

Instead of answering him, she looked past him again and said, "I know where your sister is, Ukrit."

***

Adelbart gazed out the window, allowing the droning voice of the *Alle'oss* representative from the town council to fade below conscious notice. He thought his name was Birger or Bergen, or something like that. No matter. Gerold would relate the pertinent parts later. If there were any. Today's litany was the same as it always was; an endless list of grievances that amounted to disagreements with Imperial priorities. From his resigned expression and rounded shoulders, Adelbart suspected the man finally realized how useless this ritual was. But, Adelbart supposed, the man had to placate his constituents.

"Governor."

Adelbart returned from his musings and turned toward his assistant. Birger, or Bergen, had left, and they were alone. "Yes, Gerold? Anything important, or unexpected, at least."

"No, sir. The usual."

Adelbart sat up, brushing his hands across the spotless surface of his desk. "Excellent! Now, is there anything else?"

"Yes, sir. There is the matter of the *Alle'oss* girl." When he saw Adelbart's confusion, he clarified. "The girl who was removed from the slave caravan for inciting rebellion."

"Ah, yes. Is there any reason to bring it to my attention?" Inciting was a crime. As long as there was a witness, reliable or not, the sentence was death. "The lower courts should handle this."

"Our witness said she mentioned something called ..." He looked down at his notes. "*Oss'stera.*"

"Oss ... An *Alle'oss* word?"

"Yes, sir. We believe so, though no one is sure of the translation."

Adelbart thrust his lower lip out and lifted his brows.

"Lieutenant Manfred, in Intelligence, believes it may refer to an organized resistance group."

Adelbart stared at him, then burst out laughing. When he noticed Gerold smiling blandly back at him, he let his laughter die. "An organized *Alle'oss* resistance group?" Gerold nodded. "Surely, Manfred must be mistaken."

"It could be, but we had reports of someone asking around Richeleau for *oss'stera* and mentioning rebels. The lieutenant doesn't think it could be a coincidence precisely because of the odd nature of the word."

Adelbart leaned back, tapping the top of his desk with an index finger. "I suppose it wouldn't hurt to delve into this."

"No, sir. Should we ask Intelligence to question the prisoner?"

Adelbart considered. Manfred was an ambitious little snot. It was unlikely there really was an organized *Alle'oss* rebellion, but if there was, he wasn't about to let the puffed up little lieutenant take the credit for revealing it. "No. Let the Inquisition handle this. Ship her to Kartok." The headquarters of the Inquisition in Argren had not yet made the move to Richeleau. Adelbart smiled to himself. It was a perfect solution. This way, he would receive the credit for bringing it to the Inquisition's attention.

"Yes, sir."

"Now, is there anything else?"

"No, sir."

"Excellent!" The Governor sprung up, made his way around his desk and turned to allow his assistant to throw his cloak over his shoulders. "Have my carriage brought around." It was Lachlandis evening. Finally. Another benefit of being posted to Richeleau was the cuisine. Adelbart practically smacked his lips in anticipation as he left his office.

Chapter 8

Secrets

Ukrit asked, "Where is she?" and tried to push past Alar.

Alar put his arm out to stop him. An Imperial witch finds their base, apparently on her own, offering the information they need. What were the odds and what did she want? She was watching his face as he worked through his thoughts, but when his lips parted, she sat up straighter, cupped her hands on her knees, gave herself a small shake and adopted an expression of amused expectation. She was mocking him. Alar looked at Tove. She was staring at the woman, a small smile on her face, but when she saw him looking, she coughed and grew serious. He forced himself to take a breath and sigh it out. Suppressing his irritation at the witch's smug smile, he asked, "How would you even know who Ukrit's sister is, let alone know she's missing?" He felt Ukrit fidget beside him, but he kept his eyes on Ragan.

She gave him a small nod and tipped her head to one side, as if she expected the question. "We'll save a lot of time if you allow me my secrets. I won't tell you how I know." When Alar started to speak, she raised her hand to forestall him. "I can only assure you, I have your, and Scilla's, best interests at heart."

"Why would you assume your assurances mean anything to us?"

"I wouldn't assume any such thing. I'm relying on your concern for Scilla to overcome your distrust. At least, initially." The mocking smile faded, and her tone softened. "I know you have no reason to believe me. Let's just say my interests no longer align with the emperor's."

Out of the corner of his eye, Alar noticed the heads of his comrades pivoting back and forth as they followed the conversation. He stared at the tattoo that emerged from the hair at her left temple. "Some stains are not so easily washed away."

She took a breath and whooshed it out, throwing a hand toward the top of the ridge that Alar checked earlier. "I came alone."

Frustration. That was interesting. She had to expect them to be skeptical. If she was already frustrated, it meant she needed them badly and didn't have time to win them over. Alar glanced up again to give himself time to think. Still no Imperial Rangers peering down at them. Not that a sister of the Seidi needed Imps for protection. "Yes, you put yourself at the mercy of a ragtag band of rebels," he said. "Your fear is palpable."

"Which makes my point." She threw a hand toward the members of *oss'stera* seated across the fire, prompting them to scatter. She watched, amused, as they regained their seats, then said to Alar, "Would I need an elaborate subterfuge to eliminate the thorn called *oss'stera* from the emperor's foot?"

Though the sarcasm stung, her point was hard to argue. "Maybe you're hoping to gain our confidence to get information on the rest of the network."

She burst out laughing. When she saw Alar's face, her laughter died, and she smiled apologetically. "I'm sorry. I sympathize with your predicament, and I admire your courage." Her eyes flitted across the ragged members of their band, then returned to Alar. "And your optimism." She lifted her hands and gestured around the camp. "But, trust me, I'm well aware this *is* the network, the entire network."

"Not me," Ukrit stepped forward. "I'm not with oss … whatever. If they don't want to help, I'll help you get my sister."

She brought out the proud mother smile again. "I know you will, Ukrit." Her smile changed when her eyes shifted back to Alar, and the tone of her voice softened. "But we will need Alar's help to rescue your sister."

Alar shifted uncomfortably as all eyes focused on him.

Ragan stood abruptly, sending a startled ripple through the gathering. He heard a soft, "Whoa," from Tove. Alar rooted his feet to the spot, taking slow breaths and forcing his face into a mask as the witch approached him. She stopped a pace away, searching his face and letting him study her in silence. A confusing clash of identities. Black Imperial hair, *Alle'oss* braids falling across the tattoo of an Imperial witch. He didn't recognize the beads, nor did he know the meaning of the screech owl feathers in her braids. When he settled on her eyes, a small smile touched the corners of her lips, and she gave him the smallest of nods.

"Why me?" he asked.

The smile grew, but instead of answering, she looked at Ukrit, who was watching anxiously. "Your sister is being held in the Inquisition prison in Kartok."

Gasps rose from the rebels. A tremor went through Alar, dredging up memories it took him years to bury. Screams, smoke, death and men in white uniforms. But he was no longer that child. He squeezed his eyes shut and willed his mind blank. In the stillness, the spot in his mind hummed a calming note. When he opened his eyes, Ragan was watching him again, the small, knowing smile curving her lips. "Why would an Imperial witch care about an *Alle'oss* girl?" he asked.

"Secrets," she said so low that Alar was sure no one beyond him, Ukrit and Tove heard. She looked up at Ukrit expectantly. When the big man shuffled aside, she slid between them and started walking. "Meet me in Kartok at Manuel's Tavern on Canal Street on the evening of Lachlandis, four weeks from today. Bring Tove, Lief and Ukrit."

Alar called to her retreating back, "Where are you going?"

"I have a task to see to. Don't worry, I'll meet you there." She looked over her shoulder and called. "Don't be late."

***

The silence that descended when the witch disappeared lasted only long enough for them to be sure she was really gone. Then the arguments erupted. Sten was for abandoning their base immediately and moving far from Richeleau. Although he didn't openly accuse anyone of giving the location away, Alar couldn't fault him for being suspicious. It was hard to come up with a scenario in which the sister could find the place on her own.

"Besides," Sten finished his tirade. "If the Inquisition has this Scilla, there's no guarantee she'll be alive in four weeks."

It was a good point, one that had occurred to Alar as well.

"The witch wouldn't ask us to go to Kartok if Scilla wouldn't be alive," Ukrit countered.

Alar wasn't convinced and if Tove's expression was any indication, neither was she.

Erik, for once, disagreed with Sten. Why, he asked, did they call themselves rebels when, in reality, they were just vagabonds, barely surviving on the fringes of society? In a shocking reversal from his usual counsel, Erik was all for attempting the insane rescue. Alar noticed others were as shocked as he was. While it was true o*ss'stera*, by its very nature, attracted misfits, people too reckless, or insane, to live in normal society, not even the most unhinged would consider crossing the Inquisition. He suspected Erik's enthusiasm was rooted in the fact he wasn't involved and Alar was.

Not that any of it mattered. This was his decision, and the only important debate was the one Alar was having with himself. It was partly his fault Scilla was in this predicament. He didn't ask her to run away from home, and he certainly didn't make her ask after rebels where the wrong people could overhear. That was incredibly foolish. On the other hand, with a glance at Tove's disfigurement, he couldn't picture Scilla's determined face without imagining what an inquisitor would do to her. Still, they were talking about breaking someone out of the main Inquisition prison in Argren, and it wasn't just him. The witch asked Ukrit, Tove and Lief to accompany him.

"We're not going," Alar said for the hundredth time, though even he could hear his conviction was wavering.

"You said you would help find her." This had been Ukrit's only argument, uttered with the relentless patience of a mountain stream wearing away bedrock. And it was working.

"We found her, and I never said I would rescue her from an Inquisition prison," Alar said, but his voice sounded to him like someone else was speaking.

"We'll have a Seidi witch on our side," Lief offered.

The boy met Alar's gaze with the same guileless impassivity as always. He hadn't even blanched when the witch volunteered him for this madness. Alar filed that away for later consideration. If there was a later. "Who says she's on our side?" he asked. When Ukrit spoke, Alar overrode him. He gestured around the camp and said, "Think about it. What would a Seidi sister need from *us?*"

"You, apparently," Tove answered.

The murmured side conversations died away and speculative expressions focused on Alar.

In the silence, Tove leaned toward him and asked quietly, "Aren't you a little curious?" When he looked at her, she said, "I mean, a Seidi witch shows up in our camp. She tells us she has the information we need. She offers to help rescue an *Alle'oss* girl she doesn't know, and she says she needs *you* to do it." For once, her gaze didn't waver when he looked at her.

He *was* curious. He would have dismissed it as flattery to get his cooperation, but in his heart, he knew why she singled him out. The spot. During his long walk from Lirantok, alone with his thoughts, he entertained the notion it might be magic. He never heard of any *Alle'oss* capable of wielding magic like the sisters of the Seidi, but after exhausting every other possibility, it was what he was left with. Back home, the very real, practical demands of *oss'stera* pushed the idea from his mind. Though there were fewer of them now, they still needed to eat. They still needed to know what the Imps were up to, and they had relationships with local *Alle'oss* to maintain. Alar found himself pressed into leadership roles Sten and Erik once took as their prerogatives. When the spot remained inert, he began to regard the idea it might be magic as a grandiose fantasy. It was, in part, the embarrassment he felt for considering it that he kept the whole thing to himself.

But the weird time thing happened again the previous night, and this time, he took a moment to look around. It was real, and it had to be magic. There was no other explanation. The trouble was, he had no one to ask about it. How fortunate was he that a Seidi witch wandered into their camp? Could that be a coincidence? He didn't know how their magic worked. The stories about them seemed too absurd to be true. But there was something in the way she looked at him, like she knew. If he could trust her, she might tell him what he needed to know.

He returned from his thoughts to find Tove and Ukrit watching him. The other members of *oss'stera* were being more circumspect, undoubtedly happy they weren't involved. But the moment had arrived. They were waiting for him to decide.

"Okay, we'll go to Kartok," he said.

"Yes!" Ukrit said and slapped Alar on the back so hard he nearly rolled him off the log he was sitting on.

"We'll go, to check it out. See what the prison is like, learn what her plan is." He looked at Tove, seated on his left, and she gave him a nod. He turned to his right and said to Ukrit, "We don't like the way it looks, we walk away."

Ukrit grimaced and started to argue, but shut his mouth after glancing past Alar. When Alar turned back to Tove, she dropped her head. When her eyes flicked up and found Alar watching her, she said, "We better get some sleep. We got a long walk ahead of us."

***

"Any luck?" Alar asked, though he could tell from the way Tove threw herself down next to the fire she hadn't had any. They had been walking for two weeks and were still two weeks from Kartok. They planned to forage while they walked, but they were expecting Tove to feed them. Unfortunately, she could not match her previous success, and hunger was wearing on all of them.

"It's that bow." Ukrit had been giddy the morning they set out, full of optimistic gratitude. But a pampered life left him unprepared for sustained bouts of hunger and sleeplessness. Days of nothing but berries and mushrooms had made Ukrit surly. He annoyed everyone, but Tove seemed especially susceptible to his barbs.

Seeing the effect of Ukrit's comment on Tove, Alar's patience finally ran out, but before he could come to her defense, Lief spoke.

"What do you know about it?"

Ukrit threw his hand toward Tove. "That bow has so much set, it's a miracle it shoots at all. It's no wonder she can't hit anything. Whoever made it had no clue what they were doing." He grumbled to himself. "If this is the best *oss'stera* has to offer, my sister is as good as dead."

Tove's face was hidden behind her hair, but Lief's wasn't, and seeing it darken to a dangerous shade of red, Alar stood abruptly. "Come on, Ukrit." He crossed in front of Lief, catching his eye and nodding toward Tove.

"What? Where are we going?" Ukrit asked.

Alar didn't answer and didn't look back, but after a few steps, he heard Ukrit blundering through the forest behind him. When he caught up, Alar said, "We're near Sherintok."

"So?"

"If I'm not mistaken, today is market day. Let's see if we can find you something to eat." Ukrit didn't seem to notice his sarcasm.

Alar ground his teeth. Ukrit's callousness was sandpaper on his already irritable disposition. Since leaving their base, he had been growing increasingly worried and frustrated. What if this witch expected him to control his magic? If she did, she was going to be disappointed. He lay awake at night, attempting to prod the spot into responding, but it was, once again, stubbornly inert. It only seemed to work when he was in danger or afraid. He could only hope it would respond when he needed it. While he was often reckless with his own life, the idea of gambling his friend's lives on a hope frightened him.

As they stepped onto the road that led to the village, Ukrit said, "I'm so hungry, I could eat a skunk."

Alar stopped. "Ukit, you know, skunk's not so bad if you prepare it right," he said, feeling a guilty satisfaction at Ukrit's grimace. "Especially when you've had nothing but fungus for days. You should try it."

"What's gotten into you?"

"One would think you might be a little more grateful to a group of strangers risking their lives to rescue your sister."

"My sister wouldn't be in danger if it weren't for you."

"I didn't attack your village and kill your parents." Not directly, anyway. "Unlike a lot of us, your sister had a choice." Alar looked him up and down. "And frankly, if the past couple of weeks are any indication of what she had to put up with, I'm not surprised she left."

"What is that supposed to mean?"

"You've done nothing but complain since we left. You think we enjoy walking ourselves ragged day after day with no food and little sleep?" Alar stepped closer and lowered his voice. "She's your sister. At least *you* have a good reason to commit suicide."

Ukrit's fists balled at his side.

"You want to try that again?" Alar asked. When Ukrit hesitated, Alar spun away and began walking.

Ukrit fumed as they walked, but Alar shut out his grumbles as they topped a small hill and the village came into view. He stopped, a kaleidoscope of memories leaving him momentarily disoriented. It looked just like he remembered it, though he hadn't been here in years. He was right. It was market day. The mingled scents of baking bread, roasting meats and the earthy odors of animals rode the breeze, rooting through more ephemeral memories. A child's memories of family, joy, love and a bedrock belief in parents who could make everything right. He told himself he would never return, but Tove and Lief were depending on him. He could do this. He had to do this.

And in the moment when Alar's defenses were in tatters, Ukrit spoke.

"I don't—"

Alar's mind went white. He whirled on Ukrit, brought up his hands to shove the bigger man away, and just as it did on the road to Lirantok, something inside his mind tore. Alar grasped his head, bent at the waist, and screamed.

"Whoa," Ukrit said.

Alar stumbled forward, forcing Ukrit to catch him before he fell.

He straightened abruptly, reeling backwards. Catching his balance, he shut his eyes and looked inward, fearful of what he would find. The spot was still there, but something changed. It was not the tight, distinct otherness it was before. It was still cool and quiet, but where he had been able to delimit the boundaries of that region before, now it blended with the rest of him, so that it was impossible to tell where it stopped and the rest of him began. It hummed softly. He reached for it, as he had been doing fruitlessly for weeks. A bright, pure tone emanated from the spot, flooding his mind with a fizzy rush. Euphoric and energizing, it swept away the accretions of fatigue and hunger, leaving him feeling light and springy. He sucked in a breath, his eyes flew open and he bounced on the balls of his feet. Throwing his arms out to his sides, he beamed at Ukrit. "Woooo!"

Ukrit jumped back, the alarm on his face sliding into fear.

Could he do it again? Was it another accident? Alar's bounces slowed. He held out a hand to Ukrit, closed his eyes and prodded the spot again.

***

Alar opened his eyes. Ukrit's face, framed by red hair and blue sky, hovered above him. When he saw Alar's eyes were open, he said, "What in the Father's name was that?"

Alar was lying spread eagle in the middle of the road. He licked his lips and asked, "What happened?"

Ukrit's eyes shifted to the side, a slight flush coloring his cheeks. He leaned closer and spoke quietly. "I had an uncle that went a little off toward the end. We all loved him, but someone had to babysit him, so, you know, he didn't go for a walk without his pants." His lips pursed. "If you got a problem, it's not your fault, but I'm just saying, since this witch thinks we need you to save Scilla ..." He stopped talking, his brows asking the question he wouldn't.

Alar rolled to his side and got to his feet. "You don't have to worry about me wandering off without my pants on, trust me." He brushed the sand out of his hair. Luckily, the road's surface was soft. He didn't appear to be any worse for fainting, and though his hunger was returning, he still felt better than he had in days. The spot was the same. He would have to be careful, obviously. He couldn't help grinning as he imagined the face of his opponent if he fainted dead away in the middle of a deadly confrontation.

"You say so," Ukrit mumbled.

"Let's go steal some food." Alar threw him a grin and strode down the hill toward the village.

"Steal?" Ukrit called after him.

Chapter 9

Inquisition

Jogging to catch up, Ukrit called, "What do you mean steal?"

Alar stopped and turned, forcing Ukrit to pull up short. "Well, unless you have some coin …," Alar looked him up and down. "You don't, do you?"

Ukrit shook his head. "I spent all I had in Richeleau."

"I was afraid of that," Alar said, turned and kept walking.

Ukrit grabbed Alar's arm and pulled him to a stop. "This is a bad idea."

"You're probably right." Alar looked at the hand on his arm until Ukrit let go. "If we don't get something to eat, we won't be in any shape to rescue your sister. It's been days since we've had anything substantial." He glanced toward the village. "Besides, Sherintok is a big village. People come from miles around for the market, so the village is full of people today. No one will notice us."

Ukrit laughed. "Look at yourself."

Alar glanced down. He had to admit, Ukrit had a point. His clothes were little better than beggar's rags at the best of times. After their journey, mud caked his pants and boots. He rubbed his chin, surprised once again by the patchy, coarse whiskers that sprouted there recently.

"You look like a beggar," Ukrit said, mirroring Alar's thoughts, "and you smell like a goat."

Alar moaned. "Goat!" Smoke and the indescribable scent of roasting meat wafted on the breeze. "My gods, wouldn't that taste good right now?" His stomach rumbled in agreement.

Ukrit snorted, shaking his head.

Alar scowled down at his offending garments, then brightened. "We're trappers come down to the village for supplies."

"Trappers? With a sword? What do we trap?" Ukrit asked. "Besides who would believe someone our age is up in the mountains by themselves, trapping?"

"Just don't talk to anyone." Alar turned and started walking, calling over his shoulder, "Come on, you worry too much." He wouldn't admit it, but Ukrit was right about the sword as well. Technically, it was as illegal for him to carry a sword in Sherintok as it was in Richeleau, but he doubted the local gendarmes would make an issue of it. He considered hiding it somewhere before entering the village, but dismissed the idea. Swords were hard to come by.

As they stepped from the hard-packed surface of the Imperial Highway onto the cobbled street at the edge of the village, the gusty wind settled, unmasking the festive sounds of the market. Alar slowed to a stop and listened. Vendors' hawking their wares, amiable arguments and laughter. A mandolin played the opening notes of *The Lay of Wattana* and was soon joined by a woman's high, clear voice. A tapestry woven from memories of a more innocent time. There was pain and loss in those memories, but he was surprised to discover time had worked its magic, eroding the sharp edges of trauma and exposing treasures he thought lost forever. Reassured, he let the memories of the last time he visited this market loose from where they lay hidden for years. The flood of sweet emotions was so unexpected, tears prickled his eyes and a small grin appeared on his face. Then Ukrit's fidgety impatience intruded.

"Um, you okay?"

Alar opened his eyes and took in the boy's worried expression. Giving him his biggest smile, Alar clapped Ukrit on the shoulder and said, "Better than ever." He laughed at the look of terror on Ukrit's face, turned away and set off on streets that were reassuringly familiar.

When they turned a corner and the market came into view, they stopped and took in the scene. Colorful vendors' stalls dotted the square, emitting familiar scents that watered his mouth and clenched his stomach. Bunting and streamers in the traditional colors of Argren fluttered in the breeze. Shoppers moved among the stalls, dressed in their best come-to-market clothes. The mandolin, joined now by a fiddle and bodhran, played a jig that had people dancing. For a moment, Alar was a child again. He shut his eyes against a swirl of emotions. These were his people. This should have been his life.

Opening his eyes, he scanned the nearby stalls, surprised that so many of the vendors looked familiar. Ukrit shuffled behind him, watching the market over his shoulder. "Okay, what do we do now?"

Alar didn't really have a plan. "We need a distraction."

"Uh-uh. Don't look at me. This is all your idea."

Alar looked over his shoulder. "You want to eat, don't you?"

Ukrit frowned, but nodded.

"Okay. Let's see. We should go stand near one of the food stalls. I'll keep the proprietor occupied, and you steal some food." He peeked once more at Ukrit, then slipped into the crowd, making for a baker's stall. Behind him, Ukrit groaned again, but Alar felt him doing his best to stay close.

Ukrit's assessment of their cleanliness proved right almost immediately. As soon as Alar began elbowing his way through the crowd, people began casting about, noses wrinkled, searching for the source of the offending odor. Soon, a bubble opened around them and before they were within ten spaces of the baker's stall, the bubble burst, giving the proprietor a clear view of them coming. The burly man's eyes narrowed when he caught sight of them. Taking in the state of their clothes and the sword on Alar's hip, he took a protective position behind his counter, arms crossed, and watched them approach.

Deciding it was too late to slink away, Alar sauntered up to the stall, doing his best imitation of a normal customer out shopping in the market. "Morning!" He hooked his thumbs in his belt and gave the man a big smile.

"Morning," the proprietor said slowly.

Alar scanned the table. The freshly baked loaves stuffed with raisins and nuts that were a treat on market day in his childhood drew his attention. "A fine selection you have here, sir."

"It all costs coin."

Alar drew back. "Are you implying what I think you're implying?"

"That's exactly what I'm implying. Now, if you don't have the coin, move along. Your stink is keeping my customers away."

This would be difficult. Ukrit tapped him on his shoulder. Alar, busy returning the bread seller's glare, ignored him. Ukrit tapped him harder and said, "There's something going on down there."

Alar glanced in the direction Ukrit pointed. At the other end of the square, a commotion down one of the side streets was drawing the crowd's attention. Alar turned away from the vendor's stall, trying to understand what he was seeing. Angry voices, still muted but jarring in the festive atmosphere, sent a discordant ripple through the crowd. A cold dread crept up Alar's spine. They needed to get out of here. He glanced at the bread seller who was, unfortunately, still watching them closely.

Then a woman's scream pierced the market clamor, quieting the music and hushing the crowd. Another scream punctuated the silence. The jovial atmosphere fled in an instant. Shouts rang out. The orderly movement of the crowd dissolved into chaos. Parents scrambled to find children. People surging toward the sound of the scream tangled with others fleeing in every direction.

Alar peeked at the bread seller again. Finding his attention diverted, he snatched two loaves, turned and nudged Ukrit away from the stall with his shoulder. In his rush to get away, he wasn't paying attention to where he was going.

"Alar, I don't think this is a good idea," Ukrit said frantically.

Alar tucked a loaf under an arm, took a handful of Ukrit's shirt and pulled him along. They were being pushed by the flow of people when another scream brought the crowd to a halt. Ukrit, panicked now, tugged against Alar's grip. Alar, pushing his way through the throng, looked back at him. "Come on! I got some bre—"

He broke out of the tightly packed mass of bodies into the open. Surprised, he lost his balance and wound up sitting on the hard cobbles staring at a row of legs. He was reaching for the dropped bread when he noticed how unnaturally quiet the crowd had become. Looking around, he saw a sea of hostile glares focused on something behind him. Jumping to his feet, he spun around and froze.

Imperials. But not just any Imperials. These wore the white uniform of brothers of the Inquisition. Two of them circled slowly, keeping the crowd back with drawn swords. A third held the reins of their horses. An inquisitor loomed over the scene from atop an enormous black horse. Alar stared up into the inquisitor's frowning face. *Oh, bless the Mother!* Alar shuffled backward, staring at his toes and pivoting to hide his sword behind his body.

He eyed the loaves of bread at his feet but decided to leave them and follow Ukrit. Before he could turn away, he noticed the two figures huddled on the ground at the center of the clearing. A woman knelt on the cobbles, her face buried in the hair of a young girl she held to her breast. A witch. It must be. The inquisitor wasn't here for him. He was here for the girl.

No, not this, I can't ... His heart fluttered like a trapped bird against the cage of his ribs. He couldn't draw air into his lungs. The part of him that worked so hard to heal the wound he just foolishly exposed was desperate to flee, to escape this memory, but his compulsion to witness the coming tragedy pinned him in place.

The inquisitor's gaze lingered on Alar a moment longer. When he looked away to the assembled villagers, Alar's lungs lurched into motion again.

"This girl is a witch," the inquisitor intoned. "I arrest her in accordance with the decree on witchcraft by Emperor Ludwig, first of his name." He lifted his chin. "Be grateful we don't burn the village to the ground for harboring her."

An angry murmur arose from the crowd, but no one moved to help. Alar scanned the faces, searching for courage, but instead, found more than a few nodding their approval. Behind the inquisitor, a priest of the Vollen Church stood in the front row wearing a satisfied smile. An amulet depicting their vengeful god, Daga, lay on his breast. Anyone in the village could have informed on the girl, but Alar felt sure the priest was responsible.

Alar's sword hung uselessly from his belt, a weighty accusation. Wasn't this what they were fighting for, to stop this type of crime? His hand touched the hilt of his sword, then he locked eyes with one of the brothers keeping the crowd at bay. Empty eyes. Since joining the resistance, Alar had become accustomed to violence. What men were willing to inflict on other men no longer shocked him. Or so he thought. The dispassionate brutality in those eyes was somehow worse than all the mayhem he'd seen men commit in anger. The brother's eyes flicked to Alar's hand, hidden behind his hip, then returned to Alar's face.

"Sergeant, bind her," the inquisitor said.

The big man's eyes lingered on Alar as he sheathed his weapon, then his eyes released Alar and dropped to the mother and girl. In a movement, frightening in its suddenness, he grasped the mother around the waist and lifted her violently away from her daughter. The child tried to follow, but he kicked her away, drawing more murmurs from the crowd. Throwing the woman to the ground at Alar's feet, he turned back toward the accused.

The crowd let out a collective gasp when, in a streak of blue and yellow, the child launched herself at the sergeant, snarling and dragging shallow furrows down his cheek. The sergeant's only reaction was to turn his head away and grasp her wrists. She struggled uselessly as he casually jerked her off the ground with one hand, wiping the blood from his cheek with the other.

One of the other brothers laughed, the sound a jarring contrast with the mother's quiet weeping. When Alar turned numbly to stare at him, he realized he knew him. Bright red hair, unusual for an Imperial, made this one instantly recognizable. *Oss'stera* had encountered him before, and it hadn't gone well. Alar turned his face away, but couldn't help watching the scene out of the corner of his eye.

The sergeant kicked the struggling girl's feet out from under her, dropping her onto her back. The impact forced the air from her lungs, leaving her gasping, her eyes unfocused. He stood over her, gazing down, fingers tracing the scratches on his cheek. When she didn't stir, he retrieved manacles from the saddlebag of his horse, and knelt, a knee on her chest while he attached them to her wrists.

Alar let his gaze fall to the woman at his feet. She lay on her side, facing away from her daughter, apparently unable to watch. Glancing around, he noticed the villagers studiously ignoring her. Hot prickles climbed his back. *She's from this village. Don't they see her pain?* He started to lower himself to her side when a man burst out of the crowd, shoving Alar aside. The man set a crying boy beside the woman, stood, fists clenched, and took a step toward the sergeant and the girl. The brother with the red hair intercepted him, dug the tip of his sword into the man's chest, wagged a finger and shook his head.

The man hesitated, looking from the smiling inquisitor to Red. *Don't do it.* Alar tensed, readying himself to reach for the father if he made the foolish choice. And then the man's shoulders sagged. It was the moment he said goodbye to his daughter, a moment he would regret the rest of his life. But at least his son would have a father.

The girl's eyes focused on her father's face as the sergeant, oblivious to the family's anguish, pulled a leather hood over her head. He lifted her to her feet, handed her off to the third brother, and mounted his horse. Once settled, he reached down, grasped the back of her dress, and lifted her to sit in front of him. The other brothers mounted their horses, and the group pushed through the crowd toward the other end of the village.

The Inquisitor waved his hand lazily and said, "May Daga watch you and keep you." Glancing once more in Alar's direction, he turned his horse and followed the others.

Alar stood, stunned, a flood of memories leaving him insensible to his surroundings. People jostled him as they dispersed, but he barely noticed. Agitated conversations broke out all around him, but he heard only the weeping of the family huddled at his feet. Slowly, he became aware of Ukrit shaking him by the arms and saying his name.

"Alar, what's wrong?"

Alar focused on Ukrit's face. "We have to rescue her."

Chapter 10

A Simple Plan

Ukrit took a step back. "What?"

Alar retrieved the trampled bread, tucked one of the loaves under his arm, and pulled Ukrit into an alley. "Didn't you see what happened?"

"Yes, I saw it. They arrested that girl." He glanced at the entrance to the alley. When he looked back, uncertainty clouded his features. "Why would they arrest a girl that age? What could she have done?"

"She didn't do anything," Alar spat. "They arrested her because they think she's a witch."

Ukrit gave him a blank look. "What, you mean like that Imperial woman, Ragan?"

"Yes. No. I don't know if it's the same." Alar leaned his back against the wall of the building at the side of the alley. "The point is, she did nothing other than being born different. They take them away to … somewhere."

"But … she must have *done* something. Broken some law."

"No! You saw her! She's seen, what, ten summers. What could she have done they would kill her for?"

"Kill?" Ukrit looked at the people passing the alley in the street. The mandolin player started playing again, his bright tune now seeming indecent. "There will be a trial, surely."

"No, Ukrit. Somehow, you've managed to live your life with your eyes closed." Ukrit looked as if Alar had slapped him. Alar sighed. "I'm sorry. You're lucky to have such a fortunate life. It's not your fault. But most of us live in a world where inquisitors can snatch little girls from their parents with impunity." He paused and waited until Ukrit, who was gazing at the alley entrance, looked at him. "You saw it. No one lifted a finger to stop them. No one ever does. They're used to it."

Ukrit looked down. He started to speak, stopped, then looked at Alar again. "*You're* fighting back."

Alar barked a laugh, pushed himself off the wall and spread his arms. "Look at us, Ukrit. We're filthy, starving." He shook the loaves. "We're stealing bread from our own people." Leaning closer to Ukrit, he said in a calmer voice, "If the *Alle'oss* wanted to fight back, they would, at least, feed us."

The sounds of the market resuming filled the silence. "You're upset because of what you saw," Ukrit said. "Give yourself some time to settle down. You'll come around." He planted his hands on his hips. When he spoke again, he put some iron in his voice. "We have to be in Kartok in two weeks. We need to leave now."

Alar took a breath and sighed it out, bracing himself for what he knew Ukrit's response would be. "No. I'm going to save the girl."

It was Ukrit's turn to laugh. "What? How are you going to do that?" He waved an arm toward the street. "There were three soldiers and the, what'd you call it, the inquisitor? What are you going to do, become an Imperial witch all of a sudden?"

"I don't know what I'll do, but I'm going to save her. I'm tired of fighting for nothing." He offered the loaves to Ukrit.

Ignoring the bread, Ukrit shook his head and said, "You'll never catch them. They're on horses and have a head start."

Alar let his hands drop to his side and studied the thin patch of sky visible in the alley. "It's late in the day, so they'll have to stop for the night soon. They'll probably stop at the top of Eagle Pass. It's too dangerous to go down the other side in the dark. I'll go through the forest and meet them there. I grew up not far from here. I know this country."

"And then what?"

"I don't know. I'll come up with something," Alar said through clenched teeth. A voice in the back of his mind was telling him this was reckless, even for him. He needed to go before Ukrit's common sense prevailed.

Ukrit looked at his feet. When he looked up again, his lips were pressed into a tight line. He held up a placating hand and said, "Alar, I respect your noble impulse, but that Imperial witch said, for whatever reason, she needed you to rescue my sister. If you run off and get yourself killed, Scilla is as good as dead. Is this girl worth that risk?"

Alar stared at him. He looked at the loaves of bread in his hands, lifted them, as if weighing them on a scale. If it had happened somewhere else, somewhere other than Sherintok. But it didn't. How could he explain to Ukrit, it wasn't a weighing of Scilla's life against the life of some unknown girl? The scales were tipped the day an inquisitor took Alar's sister. He lifted a loaf, took a bite, then handed the rest to Ukrit. "Here, take these back. Tell Lief and Tove I'll meet all of you at *honua* in two days. They'll know what it means."

"No," Ukrit said, taking a step back and ignoring the bread. "If you go after her, you're condemning my sister to death. They'll kill you."

Alar let the bread fall. "I'm sorry, Ukrit."

Ukrit took a step to block Alar's path. "I can't let you do this."

"You think you can stop me?"

Uncertainty softened the hard lines of Ukrit's face, but he set his feet and said, "I have to try." They stared at one another for a moment, then Ukrit's face crumpled and he lifted a hand in supplication. "She's my sister, Alar."

Alar had to go before second thoughts melted his resolve. "I'll meet you in two days." He tried to squeeze past, but Ukrit reached up to grip his shoulder. Ukrit was a bigger man, hardened by physical labor, strengthened by a life free from want, but Alar had been fighting for whatever he could pull from life's stingy fingers since he had eight summers. He responded without conscious thought. Catching the wrist of the hand on his shoulder, he brought his other hand up against the elbow and used the leverage to swing Ukrit into the brick wall at the side of the alley.

Letting go, he stepped back, hands up. Ukrit put his back to the wall, wiping blood from his upper lip.

"Two days." Alar ducked away to avoid Ukrit's wounded expression and sprinted toward the alley mouth.

"Alar!"

The anguish in the boy's voice almost brought Alar to a stop, but when he reached the street, he sprinted after the inquisitor. Once he outran his doubts, he prodded the spot carefully, wondering if he would wake up sprawled across the cobbles. Instead, he was rewarded by a pure tone and a burst of energy that seemed to flow from his mind into his limbs, leaving his muscles springy.

Nearing the edge of the village, he caught sight of the priest standing with a small group of men. They were laughing, probably congratulating themselves, untouched by the pain they caused. The priest's smile faltered as he watched the angry young man pass.

The road exited the village, then curved to the west. A mile or so on, it curved back to the south and began a long, gradual climb to the top of Eagle Pass. The pass, which cut through a precipitous ridge, was the only way from Sherintok to the Imperial Highway and on to the Inquisition headquarters in Brennan.

Alar turned off the road onto a path that climbed straight up the ridge. Though the climb was steep, he should easily beat the brothers to the top of the pass. Or at least, he should if he were at his best. But he was far from his best. Weakened by hunger and lack of sleep, he was soon staggering on wooden legs. Whatever the spot did to him to give him energy, it didn't last long. He stumbled, catching himself against a tree, leaned over and vomited the bread onto the ground. He stood unsteadily, wiped his mouth with the back of his hand, and peered up the hill through the trees. The top was nowhere in sight.

It was years since he climbed this hill. Then, as now, the leaves, in their summer glory, rustled in a cool breeze, setting sunlight dapples dancing on the forest floor. His family was returning home after a long day at the summer festival. Alar smiled, remembering his sister's excited recital of the day's events. His parents listened patiently, exclaiming at all the right places, though they were there when it happened. The young Alar trailed behind, worn out by the day's excitement, complaining bitterly about the climb. Done with her recitation, his sister set to encouraging him.

"You can do it, Alar. Think of the great heroes like Sigard in Papa's stories," she said. "Sigard overcame all obstacles, even when he didn't think he could."

With his sister's encouragement, he made it to the top, a hero in his own imagination. He had seven summers. If he made it then for his sister, he could make it to save this girl from his sister's fate. He focused on the spot, listening to its song. He considered prodding it again, but decided it was too risky. If he fainted, he might never catch them. Groaning, he stumbled on.

When he finally reached the top, heart thudding, he fell to his hands and knees. He would have vomited again, but had nothing left to give. Closing his eyes, he prodded the spot carefully and focused on the wave that infused his mind. It was like *pulling* a fizzy breeze from the spot into his head, as refreshing as glacier cooled breezes in summer. With no better name for it, he thought of it as pulling. There was still the emptiness at his core. Pulling didn't erase his hunger. But like a surge of adrenaline, it tamped down his hunger pains, focused his mind and set his limbs tingling.

He stood unsteadily and examined familiar surroundings. To the left of the path, an outcrop jutted out above the pass. The vista that stretched out before him brought him back to that day years ago, reminding him why he loved his country. A patchwork of nature's summer palette cloaked the nearby mountains. The sun dipped toward the horizon, leaving the sky a deep blue, dotted here and there by puffy, white clouds. A cool breeze lifted his sweat-soaked hair and raised goose bumps on the back of his neck.

As a child, he stood on this cliff, a hero having conquered the hill, confident his father's strong arm wouldn't let him fall. Now, his confidence worn away by life's rough handling, he shuffled carefully to the edge and leaned out until he could see the road where it topped the pass. Travelers often used the flat clearing directly beneath him to stop for the night. Opposite the clearing, the road bordered a deep gorge. The precipitous drop into the gorge was the reason few descended the far side of the pass at night. The road narrowed on the way down, and a single misstep could send a horse or a person plunging to their death. Alar watched the road in the failing light. Was he too late?

The plaintive song of a whip-poor-will heralded the night, and Alar had nearly given up hope when the Imperials finally came into view. "Please stop," he murmured. When the inquisitor pointed to the clearing, and they turned onto it, Alar threw his hands into the air. "Yes!"

Now what? His arms dropped limply to his side. He needed a plan. A plan that would allow a malnourished, barely trained, sixteen-year-old to save a girl from three Imperial brothers and an inquisitor. He thought back to the last time *oss'stera* encountered the red-headed brother. The rebels happened upon an inquisitor and his escort on a lonely road, likely on their way to ruin the lives of a family in a village high in the mountains. Delighted at their luck at finding the small group alone, confident in their superior numbers, *oss'stera* attacked on impulse. Four members of their group paid with their lives for that miscalculation, and several others nursed wounds as they fled into the forest. The red-headed demon, cackling gleefully as he swept through Alar's companions, featured in his nightmares ever since.

"What exactly was I thinking?"

Ukrit was right. This *was* reckless, even by Alar's standards. While he was working up the courage to turn away, the sergeant dismounted, dragged the girl down and dropped her on the ground. Stepping over her, he led his horse to the edge of the clearing, where he removed the saddle and brushed the animal. Alar pressed his lips together, the fetters of fear and doubt falling away to expose a molten anger. *They treat their horses better than they treat the* Alle'oss.

Gazing down at the brothers making camp, Alar relished the danger of pulling with his toes on the edge of the cliff. "Sten always said a simple plan is the best plan."

Chapter 11

A Tale Worthy of Heroes

A full moon cast a pale blue light over the encampment as he approached. The inquisitor was already under his blanket. While they cleaned their utensils, the brothers traded crude jokes. The girl, still hooded, huddled without a blanket near the horses, the chain of her manacles looped around a sapling.

Alar crouched behind a tree just off the path, watching them argue over who would take the first watch. Eventually, the sergeant sat on a log by the fire while the others went to their bedrolls. Alar waited. His plan was simple. He would rush the sergeant from behind and kill him. Quick and silent. Next, he would kill one of the other brothers in their sleep. If he was quick, he could kill the third before he disentangled himself from his blanket. That would leave the inquisitor. How hard could that be?

It was a feeble plan. More a hope, really. Alar winced and settled in to wait.

An hour later, he slipped from his hiding place and edged onto the path. He drew his sword and crept toward the sergeant. Stepping from the path into the clearing, he paused and studied the ground, choosing his steps so he could cross the space silently. The crickets' night songs hushed, leaving the sergeant's tuneless humming to fill the silence. The big man sat motionless, his back to Alar. Hefting his sword, Alar took a breath and before second thoughts could intrude, he sprinted toward his quarry.

The sergeant didn't move as Alar approached, and with a rising sense of excitement, he began to think the plan might get off to a good start. He drew his weapon back, closed his eyes and swung with all his strength at the back of the brother's neck.

Having never cleaved anyone's head from their shoulders, he wasn't sure what to expect. He imagined the spine would offer some resistance, so when the blade swung freely, it came as a shock. Before he could stop himself, his momentum spun him around. His heel struck the log, launching him into the air. He landed on his back in an explosion of sparks in the dying campfire, rolled and came to his feet on the far side.

Forgetting the brother for a moment, Alar batted frantically at his hair until he noticed his spotless blade on the ground at his feet. How did he miss? He looked up and found the sergeant, a stick in his hand, leaning forward, frozen in the act of poking the fire. Alar watched in horrified fascination as the sergeant dropped the stick, wrapped an enormous hand around the scabbard of his sword, propped against the log beside him, and rose slowly. Apparently in no hurry, the man rolled his neck, producing a series of improbable crackles, then drew his sword and tossed the scabbard aside. "You just made a big mistake, son." He nodded at Alar's weapon. "You might want to pick that up." Then he stepped across the fire.

Alar scrambled after his sword, scooped it up, and nearly dropped it when he tripped over another log. He shuffled backwards, his feet tangling as he tried to assume a ready position. The brother laughed, set his feet and brought his weapon up.

Glancing over his shoulder, Alar was trying to decide if it was too late to run when his opponent lunged toward him. He just managed to raise his own weapon in time to deflect the blow to the side. The brother laughed and let Alar retreat out of range before following at a leisurely pace.

The sergeant's attack lacked finesse. He followed Alar across the clearing, taking long, hard swings like he was chopping wood. Though Alar could see them coming from a mile away, it was all he could do to hang onto his sword with each teeth rattling blow. *Vo kustak.* The big ogre was toying with him.

Unfortunately, anger was no compensation for lack of skill, and Alar was tiring. He backed away on unsteady legs, needing both hands to keep his weapon aloft. Seeing his prey fading, the big man paused and gazed at Alar with the dead eyes that had so frightened him in town. The game was over. Taking a moment to relish his impending victory, the sergeant rolled his shoulders, adjusted his grip on the hilt of his sword, and grinned back at his jeering companions.

Granted a momentary reprieve, Alar let his leaden arms drop and rested the tip of his sword in the dirt. Having danced with death for years, he had more than his share of narrow escapes. But tonight, Alar's spirit's luck had finally run out. He couldn't defeat this monster, and he was too exhausted to run away. He regretted Tove would not know what happened to him, and he hated that Urkit was right and Scilla would suffer because of his rash decision. But he wasn't surprised to discover he was at peace with his fate. Compared to all the foolish ways he might have met his end, at least this was for a noble cause.

And in the serenity that settled over his mind, his song emerged, soft and pure. He tensed, hope flickering to life. In the frantic scramble to stay alive, he forgot about the spot. But before he could pull, an image of himself fainting dead away while the sergeant and his cheering companions looked on popped into his head.

The sergeant's head snapped around at the sound of Alar's laughter. When he saw Alar grinning, his face twisted. "You think this is funny, you little *l'oss?*

Alar's smile widened. He lifted his chin, thumped his chest with his fist, and said, "*Ērtsi* Alle *'oss,* you big *wota.*"

Confusion flickered across the man's face, then he bellowed, sprang forward, and brought his sword around in a sweeping blow, aimed at Alar's neck.

Alar's moment of bravado cost him the time he needed to prepare for the attack. He couldn't get his feet to move, and he would never get his sword up in time. He closed his eyes, pulled hard, a collage of all the places he would rather be flashing through his mind.

Instead of the agony he expected, there was only a slightly unpleasant twist behind his eyes, then all sound—the sergeant's bellow, his companions jeers, the wind in the trees—all of it cut off, as if snipped by shears.

All sound, except for his song. Normally, soft and ethereal, it swelled, lush, textured and so beautiful it sent shivers down his limbs. *Am I dead? That wasn't so bad.* He eased his eyes open and gaped. The sergeant stood frozen in mid-swing, the edge of his sword poised inches from the spot where Alar's neck met his shoulders.

Alar jumped back. His opponent didn't move. In fact, nothing was moving. He turned in place, gaping at the thin, roiling mist that obscured everything. At least it looked like mist. He waved a hand in front of his face, then rubbed a thumb and finger together. It wasn't wet like mist. Walking around behind the brother, he tried to remember exactly what happened. He had been about to die, that was sure. He closed his eyes, pulled hard, and wished he was somewhere else. With a chuckle, he mumbled, "Wish granted." But where was he?

Distant wails and moans, so faint he hadn't noticed them before, drifted eerily out of the mist, triggering a memory from his childhood. He knew this place. Every *Alle'oss* child heard the stories the lore masters told in taverns on dark, winter nights. How often did he sit on his father's lap, clutching his older sister, captivated by the tales of heroes brave or foolish enough to venture into the underworld? He was in the realm of the dead.

He peered into the murk, listening to the wails growing louder. If this *was* the underworld, those were the *sjel'and*, the spirits of the dead, serving their penance before passing on to other realms. In the stories, the spirits were not kind to trespassers.

Noticing he had brought his sword up into a ready position, he laughed and forced himself to relax. It was ridiculous. Absurd. They were just stories. Tales of heroes adults told children to shield them from the harsh realities of a cruel world, to let them believe evil could be defeated if one was brave and honorable. As young as he was, Alar had seen far more of the world's ugliness than anyone should have to. He knew evil usually won and heroes like Sigard didn't exist.

And, yet …

If this *was* the underworld … He turned slowly, taking in the scene. The inquisitor, watching with a smug smile. The villain. The other brothers, their faces showing delight at the spectacle of Alar's impending death. The minions. The enormous sergeant, his face twisted in rage, frozen in the midst of his killing blow. The evil ogre. In the middle of it all, the small figure of the girl, taken and chained against her will. The innocent victim. All the story needed was a hero. A slow grin played at the corners of his lips. Maybe the old stories weren't so crazy, after all. Unfortunately, it was so long ago, Alar couldn't remember why the heroes entered the underworld. Or how they got out.

He studied his opponent. Maybe if … Lifting his sword, he thrust it into the sergeant's back. Nothing. It left no mark. Reaching out tentatively, he touched the brother. His fingers sank to the second knuckle, and his fingers went instantly numb, like they had fallen asleep. He jerked his hand back and flicked the tingles away.

Now what? He walked all the way around the sergeant until he stood behind him again. He got here by pulling. Maybe if he … He lifted his sword, shut his eyes, concentrated on being back in the real world and pulled. There was the unpleasant twist behind his eyes, followed by gasps and shocked yells behind him and a grunt of surprise from the sergeant. He opened his eyes and found the world unveiled and moving again.

When his target disappeared, the sergeant stumbled forward, out of Alar's reach, then began casting about for his missing opponent. Alar closed the distance, but before he could strike, the sergeant, alerted by his companion's warnings, whirled around. Alar leaned away, letting the tip of the sergeant's sword pass below his nose, then he lunged and thrust his blade into the man's unprotected neck.

The sergeant clutched at his throat and fell to his knees, shock finally illuminating his dead eyes. Alar stepped back, drew his sword free, and watched the ogre fall. If he was honest with himself, he never expected to get this far. He turned to face the others, his smile stretching when he took in the shock on the remaining brothers' faces.

"Kill him." The inquisitor's shout sent his minions scrambling for their swords. Alar assumed a much more confident ready position and waited.

The two Imps approached warily. The demon with the bright red hair took the lead, followed by his hulking companion.

Red smirked at Alar, then motioned to the giant behind him, saying, "Watch my back." He stopped two paces from Alar and peered at his face with narrow eyes. "Have we met before?"

Alar swallowed and shook his head, suppressing the memory of screams, maniacal laughter, and his friends' crimson blood spattered across a white uniform. Red shrugged and glanced at his opponent's feet. Alar's eyes flicked down to his stance uncertainly. Red smiled, crouched, lifted his sword, tracing small circles with the tip. After a brief pause, he exploded forward.

His strikes were not the unsophisticated hammer blows of the sergeant. He attacked with purpose, displaying the grace and flair of a truly devoted swordsman. Alar barely parried the first thrust and managed to back away without tangling his feet. A smile on his face, Red drove him toward the gorge, thwarting his every attempt to shuffle sideways. Alar, blocking desperately, couldn't focus enough to pull.

And then he stepped back into air and nearly plunged off the edge. He caught himself, but with both feet on the rim of the gorge, it was all he could do to block Red's downward chop with two hands on his hilt. The blow drove him to one knee and sent his sword spinning into the gorge.

Rather than immediately finishing Alar off, Red took a step back, finally letting the smile fall away. "Say goodbye, little *l'oss*," he said, then lunged forward and swung his blade at Alar's head.

Desperately, Alar reached for the spot behind his eyes and pulled. There was the twist behind his eyes, then his song swelled as before. Still, he was so sure he was about to die, he waited, his entire body clenched against the blow. When it didn't land, he let his eyes open a crack. Red was frozen in the middle of his downward swing. Carefully, Alar looked down. One foot and one knee perched precariously on the rim of the gorge. Could he fall into a gorge in the underworld? He didn't know, but, unwilling to risk it, he shifted carefully to the side. When he was clear, he stood and threw his arms above his head. "Woohoo!"

The mist swirled this time, and the howls of the spirits were much louder. Alar hurried around behind the giant, who was standing behind Red, and studied the situation. When he was ready, he pulled carefully, and let the world resume.

Red swung at air. Thrown off balance, he teetered on the edge of the gorge. The giant grasped the collar of Red's mail shirt, just as Alar lowered his shoulder and slammed into his back. He bounced off, arms flailing. It didn't feel like the man even noticed he was there. But the giant took the smallest step forward, just enough to push poor Red off balance. He swayed once, rising up on his toes, then his feet slipped off the edge and he dropped, feet first, into the gorge.

The giant, his hand tangled in Red's mail shirt, was yanked forward. He let go before Red's weight dragged him over, but he balanced on the edge, his sword flying into the night, arms windmilling. Alar jumped to his feet, put his foot on the giant's backside, and shoved him headfirst after his sword. He stepped up to the edge and looked down in time to see the brother's disgusted grimace before he disappeared into the dark.

"You're a witch!"

Turning, Alar found the inquisitor pointing and gaping at him. Alar chuckled and sauntered toward the man. "That's right. I'm a witch, a *real* witch. Let's see how tough you are without your thugs."

The inquisitor drew a knife and glanced down at the girl lying at his feet.

"Uh-uh, I wouldn't do that," Alar said, wagging his finger.

The inquisitor hesitated, knife poised above the prisoner, then he dropped the knife and dashed for his horse. Yanking the tether free, he hauled himself up. Alar started running, but had to leap aside as the horse galloped past. When they reached the road, the inquisitor dug his heels in, urging the horse down the far side of the pass. Without a saddle, the horse's abrupt surge left the rider flailing, his hands flying out to his sides. As the inquisitor struggled to regain his seat, the horse bucked, sending his rider cartwheeling out over the gorge.

Ignoring the inquisitor, Alar watched the horse disappearing down the road. "That's unfortunate."

Leaves rustled in the light breeze. The crickets slowly resumed their songs. An owl hooted mournfully. Alar stared at nothing, so surprised to be alive, it left him numb. Giddy laughter bubbled up out of him, then a wave of dizziness forced him to bend over and catch himself with his hands on his knees. He pulled carefully to settle his stomach and still his breath. "You are one crazy *pashak*, Alar," he murmured, imagining Tove saying the words.

When he felt confident he was past fainting, he straightened and ran his fingers through his hair, pulling it away from his sweaty face. "Spirit's luck," he murmured, and approached the girl. As he neared her, the song in his mind swelled. Stopping, he turned his head from side to side and noticed the song rose when he was looking directly at her. He filed that away for later consideration. She hadn't made a sound through the entire ordeal, at least not that he heard. Ether brave or unconscious. Kneeling, he retrieved the inquisitor's discarded knife and reached for the leather thong that secured the hood. She jumped.

Not unconscious then. He gently drew the hood off, revealing wide, frightened eyes.

"Hello, I'm Alar." He helped her sit up. "What's your name?"

"Ecke," she said.

"Ah, that means queen. Did you know that?" he asked, examining the knife.

"Yes. My mother named me." She stared around the clearing. "Where are they?"

Alar glanced at the sergeant's body. "They, uh, had to go." He inserted the knife into the sheath on his belt, then went to search the body and was relieved to find a set of keys on a ring attached to his belt. He picked up the sergeant's sword. It was a beautiful weapon. Longer than his own, but lighter, due to a wide fuller on both sides of the blade. The edge was pristine, despite the punishment it just endured, and the balance was perfect. How much *Alle'oss* blood had this sword drunk? Alar shrugged. Good steel was good steel. He cut the keys free and carried them back to the girl.

While he unlocked the manacles, he asked her, "Have you ever ridden a horse?" He glanced at the sergeant again and added, "Willingly?"

"No," she said vaguely, rubbing her wrists. "I've always wanted to."

"Today's your lucky day, then."

He stood and set about preparing to leave. They ate their fill of the soup left in the pot by the fire. He dragged the body to the gorge and tipped it over the edge. More Imperials would come searching for the missing party. No need to make it easy for them. Rummaging through their belongings, he found warm cloaks, blankets and enough food and money to arm and feed all of *oss'stera*.

Ecke regained her wits while Alar saddled the horses. "Can I go home?" she asked.

Alar turned to face her. "I don't think that would be a good idea. Someone in that village betrayed you to the Inquisition. It won't be safe for you or your family if you were to go back now. We'll find a way to send them a message, and maybe, after some time, you can visit." She nodded, and he turned back to the horses.

"Where are we going?"

Alar smiled. "Kartok."

Having finished his preparations, he turned to Ecke and asked, "Are you ready to go?"

She pressed her lips tight and turned toward what was probably the only home she had ever known. Alar's heart sank when she sagged. Then she seemed to gather herself. Straightening her shoulders, she turned back to him and said, "Sherintok hasn't felt like home since that new priest arrived. Maybe they'll leave my family alone after I'm gone." She nodded and said, "I'm ready to go."

Alar smiled. "Well then, little sister, let's go."

Chapter 12

Honua

It wasn't far from Sherintok to *honua*, the shelter. Two days would have been plenty of time if they took the Imperial roads, but as they were riding stolen Imperial horses and Ecke was a wanted witch, Alar took a roundabout path. As two days stretched into the fourth, he could only hope Tove and Lief could convince Ukrit to wait. One benefit of the extra time was he had a chance to get to know Ecke.

She was remarkably independent for having only ten summers, even for an *Alle'oss*. She mounted the big stallion with a minimum of fuss, grasped the reins without hesitation, and followed Alar's instructions confidently. When she saw they were heading toward her home, she grew pensive, but when Alar guided them onto a path that bypassed the village, she relaxed. When they were safely past the village, the reality of her deliverance sank in. She perked up, chatting about small things and laughing at their fumbling efforts to manage their mounts. That lasted until they stopped for a short sleep.

When they resumed, he noticed her watching him when she thought he wasn't looking. He knew what was coming, but he wasn't ready to explain what happened to her captors. To put her off, he regaled her with tales of his life in *oss'stera*. Alar knew how to read an audience, and it wasn't long before he had Ecke exclaiming in wonder. He wished Tove was there so he could see her eyes roll at his exaggerations. Still, even Tove would have to admit, his eloquence merely gilded the edges of real events. There was plenty of adventure to life in *oss'stera*. There was also hunger, fear, anxiety and boredom, but those were not what good stories were made of.

"What will become of me?" she asked after he fell silent.

Alar had been worrying at that problem as well. Unfortunately, whatever changed to make a girl a witch, it was impossible to hide. Though Alar had never felt it, he heard people say when a witch was nearby, it felt as if their brain was twisting. It was painful and unnerving, which made it easy for the priests to paint them as monsters. How many of the remaining members of *oss'stera* would suffer from Ecke's presence? There was also the fact that, despite Alar's bravado, life in *oss'stera* wouldn't be anyone's first choice. But faced with her worried expression, and with no other ideas, he said, "You're welcome to stay with us."

To distract her from that troubling prospect, he asked her about life in Sherintok. It surprised him how familiar it all sounded. He knew the names of many of the prominent citizens. The festivals were the same. He laughed when she described the tavern where the same lore master told tales of heroes and the underworld. But why shouldn't it sound familiar? Village life changed only begrudgingly, and it was only six years past that he left Sherintok. When she suddenly fell silent, Alar left her to her thoughts and tried to imagine the life he might have had. He looked at Ecke, swaying with the gait of her horse, staring into her memories. If he was still that boy, if the Inquisition had never come for his sister, what would have become of Ecke?

It wasn't until late on the third day that she described the persecution she suffered at the hands of her neighbors. Other than his sister, Ecke was the only *Alle'oss* witch Alar had been around. As far as he knew. Having only eight summers when his sister changed, he was too young to understand what was happening. All he knew was one day his parents became anxious and sad. His sister disappeared behind closed doors, and when he did see her, tears streaked her face.

He never had a chance to ask her what was wrong. Not before the brothers came. He listened to Ecke's haunting story, barely breathing, her words daubing details onto the gauzy memories of his sister's torment. As she trailed off, he found his hand resting on his tunic above his sister's painting.

No one knew why some girls became witches. Alar's sister had ten summers when she changed, but it often happened as early as eight summers. The Imperial Church taught that witches were abominations and worked through the Inquisition to arrest them. Alar found it suspicious that the Empire worked so hard to eliminate witches. What were they afraid of?

He might never know how the Inquisition found his sister. They simply showed up at their door one rainy day. His father, unlike Ecke's father, fought for his daughter. The brothers had been so incensed, after killing his father, they killed his mother as well. Alar guessed the only reason they left him alive was simple cruelty. Though most of his memories of that day were softened by the shock that descended on him afterwards, one of the few clear images he retained was the brothers' laughter as they rode away, leaving him sitting in the mud next to his parents' bodies.

During his long walk home from Lirantok, it occurred to him he might be a witch. He never heard of a male witch, but most of what people knew to be true about witches was rumor or Imperial propaganda. But no one showed signs of discomfort when he arrived home from Lirantok. Whatever he was, he was no witch. He wasn't sure whether he was relieved or not. Still, his experience with Ecke made him think it might be a related phenomenon. His song responded to her presence. If she was nearby, he could close his eyes and know exactly where she was. He didn't remember experiencing the same thing with his sister. Another question for Ragan.

On the afternoon of the fourth day, they were forced to take the Imperial Highway over the last few leagues. Ecke kept to herself while Alar watched warily for other travelers. Late in the afternoon, he stood in his stirrups, shading his eyes from the sun, low on the western horizon. The only living thing in sight was a family of elk crossing the highway in the distance. With the groan of a much older man, he swung his leg over the back of his mount and dropped to the ground. It was years since he rode a horse. Fortunately, the big Imperial horses were well trained and surprisingly patient with their inexperienced riders. Taking a moment to steady himself on aching legs, he dug his fingers into the taut muscles of his lower back and glanced up at Ecke's hopeful face. "We're here," he said.

Though she was tall for ten summers, she still had to stand in the stirrup, gathering herself, before leaping backward to dismount. Landing awkwardly, she sat heavily, flopped on her back in the tall grass beside the road, arms outstretched. "Thank the Mother." The horses, free from their burdens, pulled up tufts of grass at the side of the road.

He took Ecke's hand and pulled her up to stand unsteadily, bent over slightly as if she were as old as Alar felt. He hobbled after the horses and retrieved their reins. Handing one to Ecke, he took another, and trusting the third would follow its companions, he motioned toward a narrow opening in the tree line. "This way."

He stumbled on *honua* a few years before, during one of his few trips to Kartok. The clearing, set back from the road, was sheltered from the weather by a towering granite outcrop. It was one of the few places they felt safe in this part of Argren. The last thing they wanted was to alert others to its location, so he wasn't happy to hear raised voices when he was among the trees. He wasn't surprised to hear Ukrit shouting, but the other voice was a surprise. He wasn't sure he ever heard Tove raise her voice.

"We've waited long enough. Too long!" Ukrit shouted. "We'll never make it to Kartok in time."

"If he said he would be here, he'll be here," Tove answered.

Alar smiled, touched that her voice betrayed not a note of doubt.

"Lief," Ukrit said in a softer tone. "What do you think?"

Alar stopped, curious to hear his response.

"It's late. We wouldn't get far today, anyway. We'll decide in the morning."

There was a pause. When Ukrit spoke, it was so low, Alar could barely hear him. "You can do what you want, but I'm leaving at first light."

"Good luck rescuing your sister," Tove said.

One of the horses behind Alar snorted, silencing the voices in the clearing. "*Lehasa*," Alar called and was answered by a squeal. He stepped into the clearing, bracing himself for what had become a familiar ritual. Tove raced toward him, but before she could wrap her arms around him, the horse poked his nose over Alar's shoulder, forcing Tove to pull up short.

"Where'd you get that?" she asked.

Alar gave her a smile, "Love you too, Tove." He edged forward, forcing her to back into the clearing.

"*Lehasa*, Alar," Lief said, a rare smile on his face.

"*Hasa*," Alar answered and winked at Ukrit.

When Ecke appeared, Ukrit blurted, "You got the girl. How did you do that?"

"*And ti su* (spirit's luck)" Alar said and winked at Tove. He led the horses to the side of the clearing and began to remove their saddles.

"Huh?" Ukrit said.

"No, it's a good question," Lief asked. "How did you do that?"

"The *girl's* name is Ecke, by the way," Alar said. "Ecke, this is Tove. The big man is Ukrit and the young one is Lief."

Tove backed away from Ecke. "She's a witch," she said, putting her hand to her temple.

"She's a what?" Ukrit asked.

Tove wrinkled her nose. "You can't feel that?" she asked Ukrit.

Noticing Ecke's discomfort, Alar interrupted Ukrit's response. "Yes, Ecke is a witch. You'll just have to keep your distance." When Tove looked uncertainly at him, he added, "Maybe Ragan knows something about it." Her face cleared and she nodded. Alar turned back to the horses.

"Wait. What are you doing?" Ukrit asked. "We should leave."

Alar tossed a saddle bag to Tove. "I don't know about you, but I could use a good meal."

Tove opened the bag and peered inside. Her eyes widened, and she held it out for Ukrit and Lief to look. On a few occasions, over the years, they had been able to steal from the Imps, and had concluded the Inquisition had the best rations. He and Ecke only nibbled some biscuits and dried beef during their trip, but the brothers carried much better than that. Tonight's meal would be the best any member of *oss'stera* had eaten in months.

"Beans and bacon," Tove whispered.

"Shouldn't we get going?" Ukrit asked, but with less conviction.

"Wait a minute," Lief said. "Let's get back to how you're alive." He looked at Ecke, who shrugged.

"I've been asking the same question for the past four days," she said. "All I know is when he took the hood off, one of them was dead and the others were gone."

"One of the brothers?" Ukrit asked.

Ecke nodded, and everyone's eyes focused on Alar. He ignored them, busying himself with the horses.

"Got a new sword, I see," Lief said. "Again."

Alar looked up at the bits of sky visible through the canopy. It would be dark in two hours. He turned to face everyone. "Listen, Ecke and I had a rough time getting here. I don't know about her, but I'm going to be asleep soon. I would love to do it on a full stomach." When everyone stared, he added, "I'm not going to explain." Noticing Tove's hurt expression, he gave her a significant look and added, "Not yet."

Tove let her eyes drop and turned away. She and Lief set about preparing a meal. Ecke sat on a stone on the edge of the clearing, watching them. Ukrit stared at Alar. Alar gave him a big smile and returned to the horses. He wanted to tell Tove, but he wasn't up to questions he couldn't answer from Ukrit and Lief. They wouldn't believe him. Of course, he could always give them a demonstration. He tried to guess their reactions if he were to disappear. Somehow, he thought Lief would take it in stride, but he wasn't at all sure what Ukrit would do. Besides, he was hungry, exhausted and wasn't sure he understood the full ramifications of what happened to him. He needed to talk to Tove, alone. She would help him figure it out.

Chapter 13

Kartok

Warm sun, combined with the gentle sway of his horse, lulled Alar into a comfortable drowse. Birds, going about the business of raising their broods, provided a counterpart to Ecke's soft humming in the saddle behind him. Ukrit and Tove weren't quarreling for a change. A pleasant moment before they arrived in Kartok. He was idly trying to place Ecke's song when Tove broke the spell.

"What should we do about the horses?"

Alar sighed and glanced at her. It was a good question, one he had been worrying over since they left *honua*.

"What do you mean, what should we do with them?" Ukrit, sitting behind Tove, asked. Because of the discomfort Ecke caused Tove and Lief, she had to ride with Alar. That meant Ukrit had to take turns riding with Lief and Tove.

Tove and Ukrit couldn't seem to leave one another alone, and it was worse when Ukrit was riding with her. Wanting to head off Tove's caustic response, Alar hurried to say, "Not only are these Imperial horses, they wear the Inquisition's brand." When Ukrit looked at him blankly, he added. "We can't stable them or sell them without attracting unwanted attention, especially in Kartok."

"Just riding them would get us arrested," Tove said sharply.

"We could let them go," Lief suggested. "Though it would be nice to have a ride back when we're done here."

Alar shared a grin with Tove. Though Lief didn't seem to have a sense of humor, he had a stubborn optimism Alar and Tove found refreshing. Alar wasn't at all sure they would leave Kartok alive, and he could tell Tove shared his pessimism. "We can't let them go," he said. "Someone, maybe the wrong someone, will find them and start asking how they got here."

"And they'll guess the riders must have been traveling to Kartok," Tove said.

"Whatever we decide, it has to be soon," Alar said, pointing to a gray smudge rising into the blue sky to the west. Smoke from the cook fires and forges of Kartok. Alar let his hand drop as a wagon rounded a bend in the road. Noting the red and blond hair on the two occupants, Alar said, "They look *Alle'oss*. Must be coming from Kartok. Let's ask them for news."

They edged over to the shoulder of the highway when the wagon drew near. Alar waved and called, "*Lehasa.*"

"*Hasa,*" the driver responded, pulling the wagon to a stop.

"You coming from Kartok?"

"We are," the man answered. A boy who looked enough alike the man to be his son sat beside him.

Alar noted the boy's interest in the horses, but ignored it. "What news?"

A flurry of negative emotions crossed the man's face, before he said, "Nothing particular." The boy nudged the man, whispered something to him, and nodded at Alar's horse. The wagon driver glanced at the horse and said, "I see it, Tamas." He turned to Alar and let his smile widen. "Empire's tightening its grip, even more than the last time I was here." His brows twitched up.

Alar glanced at Tove, who nodded. "You wouldn't be in the market for horses, would you?" he asked.

"Might be. For the right price."

"What's the right price to you?"

"Well, there's all kinds of ways of paying." The man's smile slid into a smirk. "For instance, keeping secrets is as valuable to some as hard coin."

Alar returned his smile. "Sometimes quite a bit more."

***

"I still say you should have asked for more," Ukrit grumbled.

"Needs must," Alar mumbled, his attention focused on the tavern across a plaza from the small park where they gathered. It turned out the father and son who took the horses off their hands were from a village none of them ever heard of. The man said Fennig was on the back end of nowhere, and no one there would care a whit where the horses came from.

"Huh?" Ukrit asked.

Alar cast an irritated glance at Ukrit. "Ukrit, if you want to hang out with *rebels,* you need to start developing the right mindset." He turned his attention back to the tavern and mumbled, "Or you're going to get us all killed."

"Not planning on hanging out with *rebels,*" Ukrit said under his breath. "Once this is over, Scilla and I are going back to Lirantok. If I never hear of *oss'stera* the rest of my life, it will be too soon."

Alar rotated his neck. Ukrit had a way of spitting the word *oss'stera* that needled Alar's naturally buoyant disposition. He blew out a slow breath through parted lips and studied the buildings surrounding the plaza. Even though the emperor moved the district capital to Richeleau, Kartok was the heart of Imperial influence in Argren. In the years since he was last here, the Empire had begun to stamp its rigid aesthetic on the city. They paved over much of the green space the *Alle'oss* revered, or replaced it with their blocky, stone buildings. He couldn't deny the wealth evident in this small section of the city, but from his limited experience with Imperial cities, the rise in wealth here meant a new *Alle'oss* ghetto somewhere in the city. The black hair of the citizens passing through the plaza showed they were predominantly Imperials.

Standing in the shadow of an ancient elm, one of the few left in this part of the city, he focused on the two-story brick building across the plaza. It was Manuel's tavern, where Ragan told them to meet her. "Wonder why she picked this place?"

"You see Tove?" Lief asked at his elbow.

When the words registered, Alar felt a jolt of alarm. They waited in the park at the side of the crowded square to minimize the chance someone would notice Ecke, who sat pensively on a bench at the back of the space. Tove was taking a closer look at the tavern. Alar intended to send Lief, but Tove surprised him by volunteering. Knowing Tove's reticence in crowds, not to mention her history in this city, he nearly declined. But when he saw the determination on her face, he relented but told her to stay in sight. It was near noon and bankers and merchants visiting the vendor stalls for a midday meal crowded the plaza. He leaned out and peered around the trunk of the elm, hoping to see a splash of Tove's auburn hair.

Ukrit leaned over a wide boxwood hedge, searching the near corners of the plaza.

"Freeze, *l'oss*!"

Ukrit launched himself into the hedge. One minute he was beside Alar and the next, all Alar could see were his boots kicking frantically in the air. Alar whirled around, drawing his knife, heart hammering. Instead of Imperial soldiers, he found Tove, head up and grinning from ear to ear, enjoying her joke. Ecke, hand over her mouth, shared her mirth.

Alar gaped at Tove. The sly grin she gave him was an expression he'd never seen on her face. The scar pulled at her lips, revealing a glint of white teeth, but rather than dipping her head when he glanced at it, she planted her hands on her hips, hitched a brow and nodded toward Ukrit's boots. Alar followed her gaze, sliding his knife into its sheath. It was Ukrit. He watched Tove smirking at Ukrit's struggles. Something about the boy brought out the demon in her.

"Gods, don't do that anymore! I mean it," Lief said.

Alar knew he shouldn't play along, but listening to Ukrit swearing as he struggled to extricate himself from the hedge, he couldn't help himself. A small grin curved his lips. Ukrit finally rolled backward out of the hedge. Leaping up and finding himself on the wrong side, he glanced around, tried to jump back across the bushes, tripped and landed awkwardly at their feet.

When he managed to stand, he took in their grins and said, "Very funny! No, I mean it. Is mockery and creating a spectacle part of the *right* mindset for being a rebel?" He turned his back to them and crossed his arms.

Alar leaned over and whispered in Tove's ear. "He's got a point."

She pushed out her lips and shrugged.

"What'd you find out about the tavern?" Lief asked.

Alar, who was about to ask the same question, snapped his mouth shut. Of course, Lief was the one attending to business, ignoring their japes.

"Looks legit," she said. "Nothing unusual, except that there are a lot of *Alle'oss* in there. For this neighborhood, I mean."

Alar nodded, his question about why Ragan chose the tavern partially answered.

"Found out something that might be important."

Ukrit, along with everyone else, turned toward Tove. "What?" Lief asked.

"Saw a couple of Inquisition brothers."

Lief swore softly.

"They were leaning close, like they didn't want to be overheard, so I followed them."

Alar swore.

Tove's eyes narrowed.

"Sorry, what did you find out?" Alar asked.

"You remember the Inquisition building? Not the prison." She paused, focusing on Alar.

She didn't have to say the name. He read it in the scar that disfigured her face. "*Zhot ti lios,*" he said.

Tove gave him the smallest of nods.

"House of ... death?" Lief asked.

Alar nodded absently. The house of death was what the *Alle'oss* in Kartok called the Inquisition headquarters. *Zhot ti lios* or *Zhot ti* for short. He looked up at the towering elm. The tree's branches hung limp in the still air, as if it was listening breathlessly to their conversation.

"They mentioned they got a sister in one of the cells," Tove said.

"What, Scilla?" Ukrit asked.

Tove didn't look at him, but she shook her head and said, "A sister of the Seidi."

"A sister?" Alar asked. "Our sister? Ragan?"

Tove shrugged. "Didn't say a name. They're keeping her there instead of the prison." She caught Alar's eye, but she spoke to the group. "It's where they keep you while they work on you."

Alar gazed at the tavern. Thanks to the horses, they arrived a day early, so they wouldn't know if Ragan ran into trouble until the next evening.

"Work on you?" Ukrit asked.

"Torture," Lief said.

Ukrit finally worked through the implications. "If they have Ragan, we'll never rescue Scilla."

The group fell silent. They didn't owe Ragan anything, but Ukrit was right. Without her, Scilla would suffer horribly at the hands of the Inquisition's torturers.

"Wouldn't hurt to go check out the neighborhood," Tove said.

"Might overhear something," Lief added.

"Good idea," Alar said. He lifted a small leather bag and shook it, jingling the coin he took from the brothers. "There are some reasonable inns not far from the river there. We'll get a room, then check it out."

***

Adelbart, uncharacteristically focused, watched the Union mercenary commander warily. How was it the Union mercenaries were all such hulking specimens, and their leader was this squat worm of a man? One of many mysteries that swirled around Chagan Koutman. The governor had Gerold investigate the man before he made his proposal, of course. For all the good it did. Time was too short for a thorough investigation, and besides, the Empire never fully penetrated the Union's murky politics. As near as they could tell, he was some sort of underworld boss, though who could tell what that meant in the Union? The only thing Adelbart knew for sure, besides the man being repugnant, was Chagan's mercenaries were his last resort. He could never have used Imperial troops for this task.

Chagan turned away from the window, glanced at the painting above Adelbart's desk, then turned a predatory gaze on the governor. A traitorous bead of sweat made its slow way down Adlebart's temple. Chagan grinned.

"This service," Chagan said, "you request is not covered by our contract with your emperor."

"Yes," Adelbart said. "I'm aware of the terms of your contract."

"So, you are aware how much the emperor paid."

Adelbart nodded impatiently. "Yes, yes." He glanced out the window. It was already noon. Time was growing short. "Let us skip ahead to where you tell me how much it will cost me."

"Since you are talking to me instead of your Captain Brennerman, I assume this is a personal matter, which you wish to keep from official Imperial notice." Chagan wiped a tear from the corner of a rheumy eye with a pinky. "Discretion is not inexpensive. Then there will be an additional fee to expedite the planning of this endeavor—"

"I thought we were skipping ahead," Adelbart said. "You may leave an itemized invoice with my assistant later. But as you said, time is short and growing shorter."

Chagan's grin widened. "Of course."

The price the mercenary uttered left Adelbart speechless. "But ..." Adelbart's gaze rotated to his office door. Gerold warned him, had argued vehemently against using the Union mercenaries. But what recourse did Adelbart have? It was all well and good to say it was a bad idea, but in the absence of an alternative, a bad choice was at least a choice. He looked at Chagan, who was watching him with a knowing grin on his face. "Agreed," he said, his voice barely above a whisper.

"Excellent, your excellency." Chagan chuckled at his joke. He rubbed his hands together, producing a sympathetic quiver in his jowls. "Now, since secrecy is paramount, we will dispense with the formalities of an invoice or contract."

Adelbart nodded, ignoring the distant alarm bells sounding in his befuddled mind.

Chapter 14

Zhot ti Lios

After procuring a room in a nearby inn, Alar, Tove and Lief left to case the prison. Ukrit wasn't happy staying behind, but Alar convinced him it was dangerous for Ecke to roam the busy streets. Fortunately, unlike Tove and Lief, Ukrit didn't suffer in Ecke's presence, so it wasn't hard to convince him he was the right one to stay with Ecke. It was a convenient excuse to be free of the boy's annoying presence.

As they made their way toward the Inquisition building, Alar kept an eye on Tove. Though she never shared details of her traumatic childhood, he knew she was intimately familiar with *Zhot ti*. It surprised him when they arrived in Kartok at how lighthearted she appeared, and the prank she pulled on all of them seemed to confirm she was okay. But as they entered more familiar neighborhoods, he could see the struggle playing out on her face. Now, as they gazed at *Zhot ti* across a busy street, he saw something else in her expression, something he was happy to see. Hatred was a dangerous emotion. Allowed to fester, it poisoned one's soul and made one reckless. But in their world, hatred was far safer than despair.

"It could be worse," Tove said.

Alar gave her a skeptical look. "How?"

She shrugged, started to speak, thought better of it, and shook her head.

"It could be in Brennan," Lief suggested.

Brennan was the Imperial capital. Alar had never been there, but everyone heard about the Inquisition's fortress, and he had to concede Lief's point. For what it was worth.

There were more *Alle'oss* than Imperials on the street in the working-class district around *Zhot ti.* The aroma wafting from the street vendor's stalls was a heady mix of the herbs and spices the *Alle'oss* loved. Using a hard penny from his stash, Alar bought a handheld pie, split it in two, and handed the pieces to Tove and Lief. To their questioning looks, he said, "So we blend in." What a marvel to be able to feed oneself so easily. It was remarkable what a difference a few tiny bits of metal made.

They took two slow passes across the street from the prison. What they found wasn't encouraging. The three-story building housed the mint when Argren had its own currency. That was long before any of them were born. Alar didn't know what the building was used for in the years after the Empire came, but at some point, the Inquisition took it over and converted it into their headquarters in Argren. It was a good choice. A high wall topped by iron spikes surrounded the stone building. Large double doors in the front were the only entrance, and there were no windows on the first floor. There were fewer brothers than he expected, but Imperial soldiers patrolled the streets around the prison and examined the credentials of everyone entering.

Having seen enough of the front, Alar directed them down a side street two blocks north of the prison. They headed east until they encountered the river, then turned south, strolling along the boardwalk that wove among stands of mountain yew on the shore. Apparently, the Imperials hadn't figured out how to build at the very edge of the river. The scent of evergreen almost eclipsed the fetid odors of the city. The river narrowed in the city, tumbling over the pink granite boulders found in this part of the mountains.

Alar stopped and rested his hands on the railing overlooking a small cascade. He glanced at Tove. She was licking her fingers, seemingly entranced by the motion of the water. "I've heard yew is a good wood for making bows," he said.

She didn't respond at first, but when his words penetrated her thoughts, she cut her eyes to him, scowled, and wiped her hands on her tunic. "Let's go," she said, and started walking.

Though most of the people they encountered were *Alle'oss*, they attracted a lot of curious stares.

"We need some new clothes," Lief said.

"A bath wouldn't hurt either," Tove said.

Alar touched the bag of coins at his belt. New clothes would be nice, but *oss'stera* had many other, more pressing, needs. "A bath would be a good idea," he said and pointed down a street. "Here I think."

A few minutes later, they stood on a street corner studying the back of *Zhot ti.*

"This has some possibilities," Tove said.

The street behind the building was narrower and quieter than the one in front. The side of the street opposite the building was lined with trees that would provide some cover for them to approach the wall.

"Those must be the cells," Alar said, nodding to the rows of barred windows on the top two floors.

"We're not getting through those bars. Not easily, anyway," Tove said. "Getting through the doors to cells won't be any easier."

Alar nodded. "Anyone ever escape?"

She hesitated, her mouth working, then she gazed up at him and said, "Only one."

He held her gaze. "One problem at a time," he said and looked away. "First, we need to find out if our sister is in one of those cells."

Lief grunted his agreement. "You think you could climb that?" He pointed and said, "That detail on the corner there. Like a ladder."

Alar grinned at him. "Me?"

The boy nodded solemnly, gazing up at the building.

Alar waggled his head and pushed his lips out. "Maybe." A series of flat, triangular stones protruded from the corners. One vertex of the triangle lined up with the building's corner, and the two sides extended a few inches on either side. "That would be a tough climb."

Ignoring his comment, Tove said, "Then you hang on to the bars and work your way along those ledges underneath the windows." When Alar looked down at her, she lifted her hand, walking her fingers as if walking up the wall. "Then you go up the next corner and back across."

"As easy as that, huh?" Alar said, mimicking her walking fingers.

"Should be a piece of cake for a man who can take care of an inquisitor and his escort alone," Lief said.

Tove lifted her hand toward Lief, arched her brows, and gave Alar a nod.

Looking back up at the cells, he said, "You two should be in a mummer's show." Still, though they didn't know the reason, they had a point. He hadn't tried entering *annen'heim* since the night he rescued Ecke, but nothing changed in his mind that would suggest he wouldn't be able to. If someone caught him, he could simply disappear. Remembering his fingers sinking into the sergeant's back, he shivered. What would happen if he was hanging onto the bars in the windows when he entered the underworld? Would his hands simply pass through? Then what? Could he fall in the underworld? If he fell, would he sink into the ground? It would be best if he didn't have to find out.

A pair of Imps appeared at the other end of the block, and the trio retreated out of sight.

"What's the timing on the patrols?" Alar asked as they strolled toward the river.

"I counted nine hundred," Lief said. "Fifteen minutes."

"Might be different at night," Tove said.

"Okay, we'll come back this way at midnight. Check it out, and if it looks good, we'll see what we can see."

***

"How do you know she's even in one of those cells?" Ukrit asked for the fourth time.

Alar shook his head and smiled. "Ukrit, that's why we're here; to find out." Ukrit refused to be left behind this time, and since it would be easier for Ecke to move about the city at night, Alar relented. A waning gibbous moon painted the back of the building in pale light. The five of them stood in the shadows of a narrow alley where they could remain unseen by the guards.

"And if you don't find her?"

"We'll have to come up with another plan."

"How are you getting the rope on the roof?" Ukrit asked.

"The rope isn't for climbing the building you *wota*, it's for getting over the wall," Tove said.

Ukrit's head rocked back and his eyes unfocused for a moment. "Wota? What—"

"Twenty minutes," Lief interrupted the argument.

Alar followed his pointing finger to a pair of soldiers who had just rounded the corner. He gestured to bring everyone in close and spoke in a low tone. "As soon as the Imps are out of sight, I'll go. Once I'm over the wall, I'll wait until the next patrol passes before climbing. Give me a signal when it's okay to go."

"You mean, like an owl's call?" Tove asked.

Ukrit snorted. "An owl? In the city?" He looked thoughtful. "Maybe, a pigeon."

"Cooo, cooo?"

Ukrit stared at her, then looked at Alar. "What if we bark like a dog? There's lots of dogs in the city."

Alar rolled his eyes. "An owl will be fine." He pointed at Ukrit. "Keep an eye on me and be ready with the rope when I come down. I'll be waiting behind the wall opposite this end of the building." Ukrit nodded. "If something goes wrong ..." He shrugged. "We'll meet back at the inn." There were nods all around.

As Alar turned away, Tove caught his arm. She looked up at him, her face lost in shadows. He leaned down, putting his ear near her mouth.

"*Andsutra*," she whispered.

Alar pulled her into a quick hug, grinning as she tensed in surprise. He squeezed her arms, then jogged toward the wall where Lief was waiting, having thrown a lasso over two of the iron spikes on top of the wall. Once he was standing on the top of the wall, Alar lifted the rope free of the spikes, and dropped it, then holding onto the spikes, he eased himself down and dropped to crouch at the base of the wall and waited.

Though Alar hadn't gone into the underworld after the first time, he had explored the pleasures and dangers of pulling. Having only fainted once more, he now felt he understood his limits. While he waited, he pulled shivery waves of euphoria through his mind and approached the corner of the building.

Moonlight, filtered through wind-tossed branches, danced across the scrubby grass between the wall and building. He peeked around the side. It was unoccupied, and a locked iron gate spanned the space. He examined the stones he would use as a ladder. They were spaced a foot apart but extended less than an inch from the wall. This would be much harder than it appeared from a distance. Putting his back to the wall, he sank to the ground and waited.

It seemed like much longer than twenty minutes before he heard the guards passing by on the other side of the wall. Standing, he turned to face the building and looked up at the cells five paces above his head.

"What was her name?" a deep voice asked.

"Lorna or Laura, something like that," another voice answered.

"And you met her at the Hog's Breath?"

"No! I met Moira at the Hog's Breath. I met Lorna, or whatever, at the Rusty Nail."

The voices faded until they were beyond hearing. Alar waited until he heard Tove's screech owl warble, then he squeezed his fists, shook out his hands, put the tips of his fingers to the stone and started climbing. The corner pointed at his chest, his right hand and foot on the back wall, and his left hand and foot on the side wall. He had only made it halfway to the second-floor cells when he realized this was a bad idea. Though the rough stone was easy to grip, only his fingertips and toes supported his weight. By the time he got to the second floor, his hands and feet were cramping and his fingers were scuffed.

Reaching out with his right leg, he settled his foot on the ledge below the first window, counted to three, then made a grab for the bars. Just as his right hand closed around the bar, the fingers of his left hand lost their grip. He swung away from the building, his right foot slipping off the ledge, leaving him hanging by one hand. Heart hammering against his ribs, he managed to get a grip with his left hand and pull himself up.

"*Vo Kustuk*," he said under his breath. "That was close."

The ledge was narrower than it appeared from the ground, not quite wide enough to accommodate the balls of his feet. He stood on his toes, hands locked on the bars, and peered into the cell. Moonlight and light leaking through the small window in the cell door weren't enough for him to make out details, but he could tell the cell was unoccupied. It was small, maybe four feet wide and three paces long. The only furnishing was a narrow cot along one wall. He glanced toward the far end of the building, then shuffled sideways to the next cell.

Some of the cells were occupied, the prisoners asleep, or unconscious on the cots, but he was confident when he reached the last cell he hadn't seen Ragan. Before attempting to climb to the third floor, he lifted one foot at a time, shaking them to loosen the painful knots in his calves. He didn't know how much of his twenty-minute window he used up, but the thought of having to return to the ground and climb back up was not appealing. He would need to hurry. Taking a breath, he whooshed it out and reached for the corner.

He was halfway to the next floor when he realized he made the wrong choice. His arms trembled. His fingers were chafed bloody by the rough stone. The muscles in his calves were spasming and his toes were numb. He would have pulled to revive his failing muscles, but was afraid of fainting while hanging onto the side of the building. For one moment, he considered climbing down, but the relative safety of the third-floor ledge and a firm grip on the bars was closer, so he kept climbing.

Somehow, he made it safely onto the third floor ledge. He hugged the bars with trembling arms and pressed his forehead to the cold iron. Sighing, he sagged, letting his weight stretch the knots in his calves.

"Who's there?"

Alar's toes slipped from their precarious perch. He nearly lost his grip on the bars when his knees struck the sharp edge of the ledge, but he held on. While he scrambled to get a foot back on the ledge, hands extended through the bars and closed around his arms. He looked through the bars and found a familiar face looking back at him.

"Scilla?"

She leaned closer and searched his face. "Alar?" she asked, astonished. "What are you doing here?"

"Rescue mission," Alar said, smiling weakly. Together, they got him situated on the ledge again, but before he could explain, they heard a guard's laughter. It sounded as if the guards were rounding the corner onto the street beside the prison. "Listen Scilla," Alar whispered. "I would love to chat, but I've got to hide before the soldiers come back around."

He looked up. A series of gargoyles, drains for the flat roof, protruded from the wall. If he could get high enough, he could reach the one above Scilla's window. Gritting his teeth, he gripped the iron bars and pulled himself up. He was going nowhere until he got his feet on the windowsill. After gathering himself, he pushed off and pulled himself up. His foot landed on something shaky, Scilla's hand as she tried to push him up. With her help, he got his fingers around the gargoyle's spindly horn. He got his foot on top of the narrow ledge above the window, then jumped and got his other hand on the small parapet that bordered the roof. For a panicked moment, he was afraid his quivering arms would fail him, but scrabbling with his feet against the wall, he found enough friction to push himself up and get a knee on the gargoyle. From there, he threw an arm over the parapet. Sighing, his entire body shaking, he sagged, crouching with both feet on the gargoyle, the side of his face resting on the top of the wall.

"Alar."

He opened his eyes to a woman's face, filling his vision. In the moment before his exhausted body reacted, he noted her pale face, her tattoo, a finger held to her lips. When his body finally got the message his startled mind sent, it launched him backward.

"What?" he blurted, arms and legs flailing.

The woman reached for him, but her fingers merely brushed his shirt before he fell out of reach. He was falling backward, from three stories in the air. This wouldn't end well. On instinct, he opened the portal to the underworld and fell through.

The world retreated behind its veil, coming to a halt, as it did before. The woman, frozen in time, stared down at him. Her right index finger held close to her lips, her left hand extended in her failed attempt to catch him. It was difficult to make out her face now, but there was no doubt it was Ragan. What was she doing on the roof? Was she escaping?

He glanced to the side. At least, now he knew whether he could fall in the underworld. He couldn't. He hung, suspended horizontally, looking up. The moans of the *sjel'and* sounded far away, fortunately. Though he couldn't remember what the *sjel'and* did to the heroes who trespassed in their realm, he knew it wasn't good. He guessed when he heard the stories as a boy, his face was buried in his sister's shoulder, and he was trying not to listen. Who could have known that information would prove useful one day?

He tried to turn over, but with no leverage, all he could do was twist ineffectually. What a ridiculous situation to find himself in. Letting his head fall back, he could see the top of the wall was still below him. He was too high to return to the physical realm, but in trying to see the ground, he found that by twisting at the waist and swinging his outstretched arms repeatedly, he could turn himself. With a mighty effort, he turned so he was facing the ground. Four feet below him, a branch from a tree across the street extended beyond the wall. Positioning his hands above the branch, he took a deep breath, opened the portal, and dropped into the world. The branch slipped through his hands and smacked him on the face. He hugged it to his chest, riding it down until it struck the top of the wall. The branch snapped, then pivoted and slammed him into the wall. When he opened his eyes, he lay on his back, gasping for breath, not quite believing he was alive. He looked up in time to see the woman's head silhouetted against the moon before she disappeared behind the edge of the roof.

"What in the otherworld?" It was the deep voice of the soldier he heard before.

"Someone's inside the wall! Come on."

They saw the branch as he rode it down. Alar staggered to his feet, listening to the soldiers' footsteps receding. Everything hurt, but he had no time to catalog his injuries. He hobbled toward the other end of the wall. "Ukrit. Rope."

There was no response. He was about to call again when something dropped onto his head. His entire body clenched in surprise. The resulting agony forced a choked scream from his throat. Heart thrumming, he reached up, swiping frantically at the object wrapped around his head. It was the rope. He gripped it and pulled uselessly, too exhausted to reach the top of the wall. The rope began to rise. He gritted his teeth and hung on. When he reached the top of the wall, he pulled himself up, balancing precariously above a rusty spike.

"Hurry, unlock it!" The Imps at the locked gate in the side yard.

"Give me a second." Another voice. A jangle of keys.

The squeal of a rusty gate sent Alar diving blindly from the top of the wall. Ukrit caught him, and they tumbled to the street. Alar rolled onto his back and suddenly Tove was there, pulling him up. They ran, chased by footsteps in the street beside the prison.

Chapter 15

All the Sisters

Alar fended their questions off until they sat at a corner table in the common room of their inn. It took several judicious pulls and half a tankard of ale before he could sit comfortably with his various injuries. He took another sip, set the tankard down, and looked across the table at a trio of scowling faces. Everyone but Ecke, who sat in the shadows against the wall behind him. Though there were few patrons in the inn at this hour, it was more comfortable for Tove and Lief this way.

Tove leaned forward, lips pursed, elbows on the table. "You found her." It wasn't a question.

"Both of them," he said and took another swallow.

Tove, Lief and Ukrit exchanged confused looks. "Both of who?" Ukrit asked.

"Your sister, our sister. All the sisters, related and otherwise," Alar said with a grin.

"Alar, it's late. We're exhausted. Don't make us have to pull it out of you," Lief said.

Alar cocked a brow at the boy and tried, unsuccessfully, to catch Tove's eye. After another sip, he said, "Scilla, *your* sister," he pointed at Ukrit, "is on the third floor. The cell on the southern end. We had just said hello when the guards appeared. I decided to hide on the roof, where I found Ragan, *our* sister, shushing me."

"You spoke to Scilla?" Lief asked.

Surprised that it wasn't Ukrit, Alar said, "Yes." Before Ukrit could ask, he held up a hand toward him and said, "She's fine. Or seemed to be."

Ukrit drew in a sharp breath. He planted his elbows on the table and buried his face in his hands. His shoulders shook, though he made no sound.

Alar looked away and found Tove was staring frankly at Ukrit.

"The witch was on the roof?" Lief asked.

Before Alar could answer, Tove asked, "And she was shushing you?"

Alar lifted his hands and shrugged. "I know how that might sound, but it's the truth."

They shared a skeptical frown.

Alar looked from one to the other. "You didn't see anyone on the roof?"

Lief shook his head. "We were keeping lookout. I just happened to look up when you jumped."

"Yeah, what was the idea of jumping off the roof?" Tove asked.

Before Alar could answer, Lief asked, "And how is it you're still alive?"

Silence fell and everyone focused on him. Ukrit dragged his hands down his cheeks, wiping away moisture. Ecke pulled her chair around so she could see Alar's face, forcing Tove and Lief to scoot backward. "Sorry, I want to hear this, too."

Alar took in their faces. He didn't really care what Ukrit thought, but Tove and Lief had a right to expect more from him. He had a feeling the truth would come out when they met Ragan. It was time to explain. The problem was, the conversation he imagined with Tove was different, more personal, than what he would have with the others. To give himself a chance to gather his thoughts, he let his gaze drop to his tankard when a shadow fell across the table. A figure wearing a long coat, the hood obscuring their face, stood next to the table, blocking their view of the hearth.

Alar frowned. "Excuse me, this is a private conversation."

Ignoring him, the person pulled a chair out and sat between Tove and Ukrit.

Alar leaned across the table and peered at the face, then sat back and asked, "What were you doing on the roof?"

Ragan chuckled and pulled her hood back. "Gave you a bit of a scare, didn't I? Sorry about that. I wasn't expecting you to jump."

"Ragan," Tove said. "Nothing at all creepy about this woman," she added under her breath.

"You were on the roof," Ukrit blurted. "How did you get on the roof? Did you fly?"

"Fly?" Tove asked.

"You don't know," Ukrit said. "She's a witch, right?"

Tove opened her mouth to retort, then turned thoughtful. She, along with everyone else, turned expectant expressions on Ragan.

"Fire escape," she said. "On the southern end of the building."

An uncomfortable silence settled on the table until Lief chuckled and said, "Fire escape. Of course. Why didn't we think of that?"

Tove snorted. "But how much fun would that have been?"

"Ha," Ecke blurted, sending bright ripples through the song in Alar's mind.

Ukrit chuckled, then all of them were laughing. All except Ragan.

"What were you looking for tonight, Alar?" she asked. "Who were you looking for?"

Alar's laughter subsided. He waited until the others quieted and said, "As a matter of fact, we were looking for you." When she gave him a blank look, he said, "Tove heard a couple of brothers talking about a sister they had in custody. We were afraid it was you." No surprise in her expression. "Who's in *Zhot tl*? She a friend of yours?"

The first crack in her confident facade appeared for a moment, then was covered over. "Yes, she's a friend of mine."

Ukrit was staring at her, his brow furrowed. "How do you even *keep* a witch in prison?"

"Witchbane," she said impatiently. "It's an herb that grows in the Northern Mountains. A hallucinogen. Makes it impossible to focus enough to access the spirit realms." When they all stared at her, Ragan added, "We can't use magic." While they were considering this, she said, "Besides, we can't all produce fire and lightning. Gallia has very unique gifts."

"Why don't *you* just burn the place down?" Ukrit asked.

She gave him a level stare and said flatly, "Not every sister can create fire." She waved a hand and said, "Besides, it's not just brothers in that building, and the goal is to get her out safely and escape. That's not a sure thing with the place on fire."

Ukrit arched an eyebrow. "What *can* you do?"

She froze, dropped her eyes to the table, then peeked up at the faces turned toward her. "I ... well ... it's—"

Alar interrupted her stammering response. "You need our help to get your friend out. That's why you came to us."

Still flustered, Ragan waved her hands and said, "I came to *you*. You can enter *annen'heim*."

There it was. As everyone's attention returned to him, he thought back. *Annen'heim*, that was the name the lore master used for the underworld. But how did Ragan know he could enter that realm? She must have seen it as he fell from the building, but she came to their camp before even he knew he could do it.

"Anne — What is she talking about?" Tove asked.

Ragan, who used the momentary lull in the conversation to regain her composure, stared at Alar when she answered. "You must have heard the myths as a child. *Alle'oss* heroes like Sigard and Ulfson, who could walk in the realm of the dead." Her eyes flicked around the table. Everyone was watching Alar, but their expressions were thoughtful now, replaying childhood memories.

All except Tove. "There were no heroic stories in my childhood," she said. "Maybe someone can tell me what you're talking about."

Alar had been desperate to tell her. He was just waiting to get her alone, but she couldn't know that. He tried to catch her eye, willing her to understand, but had to look away from the hurt expression she turned on him. Before he could explain, Ragan interrupted him.

"The Imperials call them realm walkers," she said. "They can enter the realm of the dead and return. The only known realm walkers were Imperial women, but they lived hundreds of years ago. I've never heard of an *Alle'oss* realm walker."

Lief, who was staring at her with an intensity Alar had rarely seen on his face, said, "Sigard and Ulfson." He looked at Alar. "And Alar, apparently."

Tove rose. "I'm going to bed." Lief hesitated, then followed her. Ukrit gave Alar a funny look, then followed.

"Tove," Alar called after her. "I can explain." When she didn't stop, he focused on Ragan.

"Sorry," she said. "I assumed they knew."

Alar took a sip, set the tankard down, and nudged the base with the tips of his fingers. "I can't figure you out, Ragan. You have the mysterious, all-knowing sister act down. And there's no doubt you know things you have no business knowing. But what worries me is you seem to know less than you think you do. You want to keep your secrets. Fine. But when your secrets hurt the people I care about, we have a problem."

An uncomfortable silence settled on the table. Ecke rose and edged toward the exit. "I'm just going to—"

"No, you stay here," Ragan said. "We have something to discuss." To Alar, she said, "You should get some sleep. We have a big day tomorrow."

Alar looked at Ecke. She gave him a small nod and returned to her seat. He would have objected to leaving her alone with the sister, were he not exhausted, sore and dispirited. Suppressing a groan, he rose and walked stiffly to the stairs that led to the inn's rooms.

The regular breathing coming from Lief and Tove when he arrived in their shared room was intended to sound like they were sleeping, but Alar had heard them sleep enough times to know they were pretending. Ukrit didn't bother pretending. He lay on one of the thin straw mattresses, staring up at the low ceiling. Alar eased himself down onto his stomach, breathing in the mingled scents of musty canvas and fresh straw.

"That's why you beat me," Ukrit said in a low voice. "You used some kind of magic."

Despite everything, Alar couldn't help grinning into the rough fabric.

Chapter 16

She's Way Too Pretty to Be a Boy

Alar was alone when he woke. His best guess was they retired to their room at four the night before and, based on the gray light leaking through the single window, it wasn't much past that. He rolled onto his stomach, struggled to his feet, and stared blearily around. Bending over, he scrubbed at his face, then swept up and ran his fingers through his tangled hair. After pulling to clear his head, he stumbled out the door. Pulling loosened his stiff back and eased his many aches, but though it tamped down his hunger pains, it couldn't fill his empty stomach.

He was disappointed to find there was no breakfast waiting for him in the common room. Only Lief was there, nursing a small beer. The boy rose without comment and motioned for Alar to follow. Out on the street, Alar squinted at the sun peeking between two mountains visible above the rooftops. It must be between six and seven. It soon became apparent Lief was leading them toward the scene of their previous night's adventure. It wasn't until they were nearly there, that Lief pointed ahead and spoke. "Ragan has the others at a cafe where we can see *Zhot ti.*"

Tove's red hair was the first thing Alar noticed, but everyone else was present as well, arrayed around the tables on the walkway beside the street. The remains of a hearty breakfast littered the tables. Tove glanced up as he and Lief approached, then looked away. Lief took the chair beside her, leaving Alar standing and gazing at their target.

"Want some breakfast?" Ragan asked. "I'm buying."

Alar glanced at her, scooped up a half-eaten muffin and took a bite. Noticing Ecke sitting quietly, he froze. It took a moment to understand what was odd about her, but then he realized he didn't sense her presence. He looked from her smirking face to Tove and Lief sitting comfortably, then at Ragan. "That's why you wanted to talk to her last night," he said around a mouthful of muffin.

Nodding, Ragan said, "Ecke can hide herself now. Much safer this way."

He stared at her. "Would have been nice for her to know that before—" He clamped his mouth shut and looked away from her. Ragan wasn't responsible for the Inquisition's crimes. Besides, there were more pressing problems to worry about right now. Dropping into a chair across from Ukrit, he asked, "What are we thinking?"

"Not much, so far," Ukrit answered.

"We've been waiting for you," Tove said, a note of accusation in her voice.

Alar swallowed his irritation, reminding himself she had a right to be angry. "You could have woken me."

She slouched in her seat and looked away. Dark crescents cradled her blue eyes. He scanned the others, noting the marks of exhaustion on all their faces. Not the best time to be concocting a rescue plan that was bound to be crazy under the best of circumstances.

"As I see it, we have three problems to overcome," Ragan said.

"Only three?" Alar asked, taking a sip of Ukrit's caf. Wincing at the beverage's bitterness, he set it down. Must be an acquired taste.

"You can get *into* the building while in *annen'heim*, but you'll have to return to the physical realm to get Scilla and Gallia out of their cells." Before he could ask, she said, "You can't take them into *annen'heim* with you." She lifted a finger, ticking it off with the index finger of her other hand. "So, we need to give you time to get in, find

Gallia, and get both of them out of their cells." She ticked off another finger. "We need to clear the building and the street of guards so you can get them out and away from the building." She dropped her hands to her lap. "Then we need to get safely out of the city."

Alar plucked a sausage link from Ukrit's plate and took a bite of the salty treat. When was the last time he had sausage? Years. Swallowing, he asked, "So, you don't know which cell Gallia is in?" When Ragan shook her head, he pointed to *Zhot ti* with the sausage. "But you know she's in there?" When Ragan nodded, he said, "I didn't see her on the second floor." He popped the sausage into his mouth, wiped his hands on Ukrit's napkin and picked up slices of cheese and apple. "Do you have any idea how many brothers we're talking about?"

"There is a full company stationed in Kartok."

"So, about a hundred," Tove said.

"A hundred?" Ukrit blurted.

"But most of them will be in their barracks at night," Ragan said.

"Then there are the soldiers," Lief nodded to the four who had just come into view in front of the building.

"Four instead of two," Tove said. "Must be because of last night."

"Another company of Imps," Ragan said. "But most of *them* will be in their barracks."

"In *Zhot ti*? At night?" Alar asked, pointing at the building.

Ragan popped her lips, eyes narrowing slightly as she considered. "Five, probably, maybe as many as ten. Plus the soldiers at the gate and on patrol."

"Not so bad," Ukrit said.

Alar gave him an incredulous look. "Not so bad?" Before Ukrit could answer, Alar said, "Assuming, for a moment, I can get them out of *Zhot ti*, it's unlikely I can do it without someone raising an alarm. Scilla looked well last night, but there's no telling what shape Gallia is in. I might have to carry her, and we could have two hundred angry Imperials chasing us within minutes." He looked at Ragan. "It seems to me, that third problem—the getting away bit—that's the key to the whole thing."

"So we need to keep them busy," Tove said.

Alar looked at her, and this time she didn't look away. "Right," he said, "and away from here."

They all turned and looked at *Zhot ti lios,* just as the sun rose high enough to illuminate the front of the building.

"What would keep a bunch of Imperials busy?" Lief asked.

"What they hate most in the world," Alar answered. He looked at Ecke. "A witch."

Her face reddened.

"That's an idea," Ragan said.

"Hey!" Ecke and Tove chorused.

"We might just end up having to rescue three instead of two," Lief said.

"They don't have to actually see her," Alar said.

"Just feel her nearby," Ragan said, nodding.

"Still," Ukrit said. "If someone sensed a witch, would that be enough to send all the brothers scurrying after her?" He glanced at Ecke. "It only took four brothers in Sherintok."

They fell silent, until Tove said, "It might, if the person sensing her was someone who could get the Inquisition's attention."

"The bishop," Alar said. Tove looked away when he grinned at her. Kartok was the seat of the diocese of Argren, the home of Bishop Anders Vinton.

"He would certainly get their attention," Lief said. "I hear he hates witches."

"That's good," Ragan said. "But it's not enough. They would just send brothers from the garrison, not from the prison."

"If they thought they were under attack, they might pull some of the guards from the prison," Tove said.

"Would get the Imps in the barracks involved as well," Alar said.

"So, the bishop reports a witch." He looked at Ragan and lifted two fingers. "Two witches?" When she nodded, he filed that away for later consideration. Were Seidi sisters and *Alle'oss* witches the same? "Then a fire—make that fires, big fires—break out, somewhere a long way from here, on the edge of town."

"Course, that could just be a fire. It doesn't necessarily mean they're under attack," Lief said. "It might only attract the fire brigade. Plus, there's no guarantee they would pull brothers from the prison, even if they were under attack."

The group fell silent. Alar took a roll from Ukrit's plate and chewed the yeasty bread, gazing at *Zhot ti*. A boy appeared and approached the front gate. The guards waved him through without checking his credentials. "What was that?"

"What?" Ragan asked.

"That boy, the one the guards let through."

"Messenger," she said.

Alar watched the boy exit the building. "So, the bishop reports witches in the city."

"Then fires start on the edge of town," Lief said.

"A messenger arrives at the prison with an urgent message that the city is under attack and requesting reinforcements," Alar said.

"An attack by *Alle'oss* rebels," Tove said.

They sat silently for a time.

"Might draw some of them out. Give you enough time to get them out of their cells. Maybe," Tove said. "But there's still the problem of escaping and it won't take them long to figure out there aren't any rebels."

"If you find Gallia, she can help you get out of the prison," Ragan said.

"You said she was drugged with this witchbane," Lief said.

"There's an antidote," Ragan said.

"Is there anything *you* can do?" Ukrit asked Ragan. When everyone looked at her, he added, "You *are* a witch, right?"

She hesitated, taking in the faces pointed in her direction. A spasm, so quick Alar might have imagined it, rippled across her face. Was it fear? "I will do my part to enhance the illusion the city is under attack."

Before anyone could ask what that might entail, she said, "As for getting out of the city, I know a place we can hide for a few days. Safely. When the situation cools down a bit, we sneak out of town."

"They'll turn the city inside out," Alar said.

"They won't search this place," Ragan said. When Alar lifted his brows, she said, "The Seidi house."

"What's a Seidi house," Ukrit asked.

"It's a place for sisters to stay when they are in town. There are Seidi houses in all large Imperial cities."

Alar stared at her. It wasn't that it was a foreign concept. Everyone in *oss'stera* knew of the Inquisition houses for brothers in Richeleau and Kartok. It made sense there would be the equivalent for the Seidi. It was hearing Kartok referred to as an Imperial city that caught Alar off guard. He looked at Tove and saw the same shock on her face.

"The Inquisition wouldn't dare search it," Ragan said, either ignoring or unaware of their reaction.

"Maybe so, but it might be a bit crowded, what with the Imperial witches about," Lief said.

"We can hide in the cellar. No one will know we're there. No one except an old friend of mine who tends the house," Ragan said. "She'll hide us if Gallia or I ask."

"Where is it?" Lief asked.

"On the northern end of the city, beside the river," she said. "The boardwalk will take us there."

Alar returned her gaze, trying to read her carefully controlled face. He had no reason to trust her, and hiding in an Imperial safe house put them completely at her mercy. She could betray them once they helped her friend escape. But he couldn't see how she would do it without giving herself and Gallia away, as well. There had to be a reason her friend was being held by the Inquisition. "This sister will be fine with," he glanced around, "five *Alle'oss* showing up at her door in the dead of night, with the city under attack?"

"She will if you're with me. I know she will."

Alar exchanged uneasy looks with his companions.

"Okay," Lief said. "So. The plan is to scare the bishop into alerting the Inquisition." He paused, lifting a brow at Ragan. When she looked away, he continued. "They're nervous, so when we start some fires, some *big* fires, they'll believe it when a messenger boy arrives with news the city is under attack." He looked around. "Alar goes into a *mostly* empty house of death, gets the prisoners out of their cells and brings them out with the help of Gallia's unique gifts. Then we run along the river and hide in the Seidi house, where we stay under the protection of an Imperial sister. We hunker down while the Imps tear the city apart looking for us, then we sneak out of the city."

Into the silence, Tove said, "Well, when you say it like that …"

Lief shrugged, swirling some spilled caf on the table with his finger. "I'm just saying, there are a lot of moving parts. Maybe if we had a month to nail the plan down …"

Alar was staring at Lief, wondering if he was truly as young as he looked, when Ragan spoke.

"Tonight."

The group became very still. Alar blew a breath out. "Ragan, this might be a good plan if we have some time to work out the kinks. We'll have people all over the city. Somehow we have to coordinate all these pieces, make sure no one gets hurt in the process, then everyone has to get to safety. The timing has the be perfect. People have to have their routes down cold. There have to be contingencies." He shrugged. "Even then, it would be dangerous."

Ragan didn't so much as sag as settle into herself. For the first time, Alar noticed how exhausted she looked. "I know you have taken a lot on faith to come this far," she said. "I'm asking you all to go a little farther. I can't tell you how I know, but tomorrow will be too late. The Inquisition has sent an inquisitor to take charge of this case. He'll be here tomorrow with reinforcements and two powerful sisters."

"Scilla will be dead if we wait," Ukrit said. He waved his hand at *Zhot ti.* "There's a reason she's in there. You said it's where they 'work on them'."

Alar exchanged looks with Tove and Lief. He could see on their faces what he was thinking. Even *oss'stera's* most carefully planned escapades tended to end in disaster. "Does anyone have a better plan?" he asked.

Their silence was the only answer he received.

Alar lifted his brows to Tove and Lief, giving them an opportunity to object, but when they didn't, he said, "Now all we need is a messenger boy."

"I'll do it."

Alar, who had turned to look at the building, recognized the voice, but he had to turn around to be sure.

Tove was looking at him defiantly.

"The messengers are all boys, Imperial boys," Ragan said, doubtfully.

Tove gathered her hair in one hand and held it up. "Chop it off. I used to pass for a boy … before." She met Alar's eyes briefly before looking away. "I can do it."

"But your hair is red," Ukrit said. "Even with the cap—"

"I'll dye it."

"What?" Ukrit asked, glancing around at the stunned faces.

"Tove, are you sure?" Alar asked.

"Why, what's the big deal?" Ukrit asked.

Lief cleared his throat, but it was Ragan who answered. "There are some among the *Alle'oss*, especially in Kartok and Richeleau, who dye their hair black and darken their skin. It's a way of trying to fit in with the Imperials."

"It's a betrayal by cowards," Lief spat.

"Not everyone who is afraid is a coward," Ragan said. "They may have families to protect."

Alar spoke quickly to forestall Lief's angry response. "They may fool themselves, but they won't fool the Imperials. They'll never be accepted. The Imps let them inhabit the edges of their social circles, but they would turn on them on a whim. Pretending to be Imperial won't protect them. They betray their own culture for nothing."

Ragan pursed her lips but didn't argue further.

"I don't see what the big deal is," Ukrit said. When Alar scowled at him, he said, "It'll grow out. The bigger problem is, no one will believe it." When Alar looked doubtful, Ukrit threw up his hands. "She's way too pretty to be a boy."

Alar couldn't help grinning at Tove's expression. Though she had been what could be generously called bashful since he found her, he had never seen her blush so deeply. Her scar stood out on darkened cheeks, but she was too shocked to look down. He leaned toward her so that he could block everyone else out and caught her eye. "Are you sure, Tove?" he asked. "Can you go back in that building?"

She stared at him, started to speak, then the hatred he glimpsed on her face the previous day flickered across her features. Dropping her head, she mumbled, "Like the *wota* said, it will grow out."

Before Alar could tell her that wasn't what he meant, she looked up and gave him the answer he needed.

"It's for *oss'stera,*" she said in a quiet, but firm, voice.

"*Otsuna,*" Alar and Lief said softly and were rewarded with a small grin.

"We still need a uniform," Lief said. "One of those messenger boy uniforms."

"Leave that to me," Ragan said, and rose. "Ecke and Tove, come with me."

Alar stood as well. "Ukrit and Lief, let's go scout potential fire hazards. We meet back at the inn at noon."

Chapter 17

Andsutra ta Jilosa ti Mea

The well-dressed Imperial man leaned his shoulder into Ukrit as he passed, shoving him into Lief's path. "Watch where you're going, *l'oss.*" Noticing Alar's hard stare, the man smirked.

Ukrit gaped at the man's retreating back. He took a step in pursuit before Alar caught him.

"Did you see that?" Ukrit asked indignantly, pulling his arm free. "He went out of his way to run into me. And what does he mean by *l'oss?*"

"Yes, we saw it," Lief said.

"Welcome to the Empire, Ukrit," Alar said, shaking his head.

"*L'oss?* I've heard that before. What does it mean?" Ukrit asked.

"*Alle'oss, l'oss,*" Lief said. When Ukrit stared at him uncomprehendingly, Lief added, "It's a slur."

Alar watched Ukrit's face redden as he worked through this information. Ukrit had always struck Alar as simply naïve, the result of a sheltered life growing up in Lirantok. But his steadfast refusal to see the truth forced the boy into such extreme mental acrobatics, Alar was beginning to suspect it wasn't that simple. "Ukrit, you travel to Richeleau. Have you ever been to Kartok?" he asked.

Caught off guard, Ukrit hesitated. "Yes. I've come with my brother."

Before Alar could ask his next question, Lief interrupted him.

"I could understand your ignorance if you never left the Ishian River valley, but you've traveled," he said. "How is it you're constantly surprised by what the Empire is like?"

Alar watched the big man's face carefully, catching the hint of emotion before his expression closed. "I keep to myself," he mumbled, turned and walked away.

It was only a moment, but it was revealing enough that Alar thought he might finally understand. He had seen people like Ukrit before, people who navigated life, avoiding anything that challenged their comfortable illusion of a safe world. It was understandable for those *Alle'oss* living in remote villages. Rumors of the Empire's atrocities, passed about in the village tavern, were easily dismissed when the world looked as it had your entire life. But remaining ignorant in the larger cities, where the Imperials held sway, took effort. Even Kartok had *Alle'oss* neighborhoods. If you were careful, kept to yourself, you might avoid Imperial unpleasantness. For a time.

Lief, Tove, and the rest of *oss'stera* condemned such people as cowards. Alar suspected that was really the root of their annoyance with Ukrit. But Alar thought it was more complicated. Active resistance required a courage that most people didn't possess, especially for those who had something to protect. It was much easier when you had nothing left to lose. Would he have left his simple life on the farm to join *oss'stera* if the Inquisition did not murder his family? He couldn't honestly say. Still, though not everyone could join them, willfully remaining ignorant was unforgivable.

Alar had been so preoccupied with his own problems, he dismissed the big man too easily. It took courage for Ukrit to leave his home to search for Scilla. The problem was, it forced him into the Imperial world, where ugly truths were impossible to deny. Ukrit's increasingly convoluted rationalizations allowed him to believe he could return to his previous life. Not that it would do any good. Alar had glimpsed Ukrit's tender heart. Whether or not he admitted it, what the boy had seen changed him, and even if Scilla lived through the night, she would never be the person Ukrit remembered. One way or the other, there was no going back for either of them. Alar watched Ukrit, walking ahead of him, hands in his pockets, shoulders slumped. He and Scilla would have choices to make, and Alar would make sure *oss'stera* offered an alternative. If they wanted it.

***

"You ready?" Alar asked. He, Lief and Ukrit were alone in the common room of the inn, finishing a light meal. Earlier, after finalizing the details for the plan, Ragan, Tove, and Ecke left to complete Tove's transformation.

Lief responded by standing up and giving Alar a firm nod.

Ukrit, who had been very quiet since they returned to the inn, stood slowly. His eyes flicked up to Alar, then dropped. "Yeah. Let's go," he mumbled.

Alar caught Lief's troubled look and couldn't help sympathizing. The boy's fate might very well depend on Ukrit before the night was over. When Lief looked at him, Alar gave him what he hoped was an encouraging smile, then headed toward the door.

The sun disappearing behind the hills west of the city cast long shadows, as they turned onto the street that ran in front of *Zhot ti*. Alar's attention was on a guard lighting the lamps that illuminated the front gate, when he collided with Lief.

Lief glanced over his shoulder, pointed ahead and asked, "Who's that with Ragan and Ecke?"

Alar peered ahead, but Ukrit, who continued walking, unaware they stopped, blocked his view of the person Lief was talking about. "Let's go see," he said, just as Ukirt stepped out of the way.

Lief leaned toward him and whispered, "Is that Tove?"

It *was* Tove. Her hair was still damp, but it was cut short and dyed black. The girl who slouched within herself, hiding from the world, was gone. In her place, a boy stood confidently, shoulders back, arms hanging nonchalantly at his sides. Ukrit said something she must have found funny, because she grinned at him. Alar glanced at Lief, who was staring incredulously. "Come on, let's go," he said.

"Everyone know the plan?" Alar asked as he arrived. When they all nodded, he said, "Remember, safety first, no unnecessary risks. As soon as your part is done, get to the Seidi house and wait for Ragan."

"*Andsutra*," Lief said, turned without saying anything to Ukrit and walked away.

Ukrit met Alar's eyes. "Good luck," he said and followed Lief.

Alar watched them for a moment, then asked Tove, "Got the uniform?"

She nodded to the bundle under her arm.

"Looks good," he said, grinning. He reached up and flicked a lock of her hair.

When she looked at him, a small smile on her face, the sunlight glinted in her blue eyes. "Remember, don't look anyone in the eye," he said. "Maybe, keep your hat brim pulled low."

She nodded, gave Ragan and Ecke a wave, and said, "*Andsutra*."

Alar watched her walking away.

"I want to have a word before we leave," Ragan said.

"So do I," Alar said. He pulled a small vial from his pocket. "Assuming I get to your friend and pour this into her mouth, how long before she's coherent?"

She shook her head. "Hard to say. I don't know what kind of dose they've given her. Let's say ten minutes to be safe."

Alar stared at her. "So, in addition to finding the keys and finding her cell, I'll have to wait around for ten minutes?" He looked toward *Zhot ti* and said in a low voice, "Didn't mention that before."

"You didn't ask," she said. "Besides, what would you have done if you knew?"

"Worried more," Alar said. He gave her a rueful smile and asked, "What did you want to talk about?"

"I assume you have only recently discovered this ability to enter *annen'heim?*"

"You mean you don't know?"

Ignoring his sarcasm, she said, "The realm of the dead is a very dangerous place."

Alar looked away. "Seems like I remember something like that from the stories."

"I hoped to have more time to explain, but events have overtaken us." She reached up and tapped him on the forehead, getting his attention. "Every person has a spirit."

He leaned his head away from her finger, his nose wrinkling. "What, like the spirits in *annen'heim?*"

"Exactly like those spirits." She pinched his bicep. "Your spirit is bound to the physical realm by your material essence, your body. When the body dies, the spirit is freed to travel to *annen'heim.* There, it will linger until it sheds the burdens it accumulated in life." She eyed him speculatively. "You seem like a good person, but being in *oss'stera,* I'm sure you have much to atone for." Ignoring his snort, she said, "When the gods allow, your spirit will pass onto the other realms."

"Other realms?" Ecke asked.

"Gods?" Alar asked at the same time.

Ragan looked at Ecke. "Yes, there are eight realms, each inhabited by different spirits. We will speak on this later." She turned back to Alar and, ignoring his question, spoke quickly. "Our magic," she indicated herself and Ecke, "is born of the spirits we channel into this realm, the physical realm." She raised her arms and gestured around them. "Each type of spirit manifests differently here. Fire, lightning, fog, and many others. These are the spirits the *sjel'and* will become one day."

She was about to continue when Alar interrupted her. "How are realm walkers different from witches?"

She gave a small shake of her head, her brow furrowing. "I assume, when you enter *annen'heim,* you follow the same path your spirit will when you die."

"So ... I die?"

"Metaphysical questions are best asked of the priests. But it is the opinion of a great *saa'myn* I know," she said, then added before he could ask, "An *Alle'oss* witch. She believes the spirits of realm walkers are only tenuously tied to their bodies. Your spirit can enter the realm of the dead because it is not so tightly bound here. Fortunately for you, your spirit is not entirely free, so it drags your body along with it. If it didn't, your spirit would remain in the underworld. You would die."

Alar stared at her, then looked at Ecke, who was staring wide-eyed back at him.

"When you enter *annen'heim,*" Ragan continued, oblivious to their shock, "you are not entirely material, but neither are you a spirit. At first, you can't move through the realm as a spirit would, but unlike the *sjel'and,* you can interact with objects in the material realm, after a fashion."

Alar flicked his fingers, remembering how they grew numb when they sunk into the brother's back.

"Listen, this is very important," she said. "The *sjel'and* covet what they lost and long for their deliverance from the realm of the dead. They are drawn to places where there is death or where a sister or witch is channeling the spirits. There will likely be both tonight, so you should not linger in their realm."

"Good to know," he said with a weak grin. When he noticed her grim expression, his grin fell away. "Um ... what exactly will they do to me? If they catch me?"

"There is some debate about that, or there was when the realm walkers lived. All we know for sure is that some who ventured into *annen'heim* never returned. The prevailing opinion is that the spirits rip your soul from your body."

Alar stared at her.

She met his gaze and said, "You shouldn't stay in *annen'heim* for long."

Alar chuckled. "I'll try to remember that."

"I ... can help tonight. I'll try to keep the spirits occupied, give you a little extra time."

There was no mistaking it this time. Her voice was thick with fear. He looked down at her and found it reflected in her expression.

"*Andsutra*," she said, then turned away.

Ecke gave him a worried frown, then said, "*Andsutra*," and followed Ragan.

Alar watched them, until they disappeared into a side street, then strolled toward *Zhot ti* until he found a shadowy doorway from which he could watch the front gate. "*Andsutra ta ji losa ti mea*," he muttered.

Chapter 18

Payback

Though it was technically still late *alāla,* the warmer months, *dōnag* made its presence known early in Argren, even at the lower altitudes in Kartok. As the sun ceded the sky to her sister, the moon, the temperature dropped. Alar blew into his cupped hands, rubbed them briskly together, then tucked his fingers under his armpits. Whatever Ragan was supposed to do to get the show going, it should be soon. She wouldn't reveal what it was, but she assured them it would be unmistakable.

When it came, it started in an entirely unexpected way. Dogs were common in the city. Their constant presence was such a normal part of the city soundscape, they faded from conscious notice. But as Alar stepped away from the wall, bouncing lightly to warm his legs, every dog in the city started barking at once. A frantic, growling, yipping chorus of frightened animals.

Alar crouched, his hand resting on the hilt of his sword. Goose bumps rose on his arms and raised the hairs on the back of his neck. Something deep inside him, a primitive sense of self-preservation, whispered warnings. His legs, listening to the warnings, took a step before he got control of himself. "It's just dogs," he said out loud, reassuring himself. "Many. Terrified. Dogs."

And then, from below the level of the dog's howls, another sound emerged. It started low, as if clawing its way from below the surface of hearing. It paused, a rumbling so deep it was almost a vibration, before surging suddenly in volume, forcing Alar to clap his hands to his ears. Then it soared up through octaves, thinning into a keening howl that knifed through the hands pressed to his ears. The song that emanated from the spot in his mind responded. And just before passing above the range of hearing, the unearthly howl stopped, as if cut with a knife.

The silence that descended was a held breath. Even the dogs' howls trailed off, as if they too were listening, hoping the beast that visited their city left them unscathed. Alar straightened, lifting his hands, tentatively, from his ears. When there was no recurrence of the sound, he dropped his hands, walked to the center of the street and stared in the direction of the cathedral from which the sound emanated. Though Alar had not been in *annen'heim* often, he recognized the call of the *sjel'and.* Did Ragan channel a soul spirit into their realm? The thought of one of those phantoms loose in the world frightened him more than any human conjured terror. He wiped sweaty palms on his shirt, took a breath, sighed it out in a cloud of mist and pulled carefully to slow his heart.

Peering around at suddenly sinister shadows, he returned to the doorway and waited. Whatever Ragan did, it had the desired effect. The citizens of Kartok emerged into the night, shouting to one another excitedly and gathering on street corners. The six Imps guarding *Zhot ti* stood in the street, talking excitedly and gesturing toward the cathedral. As Alar watched, four brothers exited the building and joined them.

If Lief and Ukrit were on schedule, the second act should start soon. And as if on cue, one of the guards pointed to a glow on the northeastern horizon. The fires, right on time. Earlier in the day, they found a large lumber yard, far enough outside the city limits that the fire was unlikely to spread quickly. With the guards' attention on the fires, Alar slipped out of the doorway and edged closer to *Zhot ti.*

A half hour later, the glow above the rooftops to the northeast was unmistakable, and the mood in the city fizzed. Large groups of people, carrying a variety of improvised weapons, roamed the streets. Alar was relieved to see *Zhot ti's* reputation kept them away from the building. He watched a pair of *Alle'oss* race past, pursued by a gendarme. When he looked back, Tove, dressed as a messenger boy, entered the pool of light in front of the jail. The guards, still standing in the street looking toward the glow, barely glanced at her as they waved her through the gate. She ran up the steps and disappeared through the door. Alar drew his sword, slipped from his hiding place, and crept toward the building. Tove was supposed to deliver the message and leave immediately. When she didn't appear, he stepped behind the corner of the wall that surrounded the building, debating what to do. Should he wait until she was out of danger, or go looking for her? He was leaning out, trying to get a good view of the gate, when a large group of brothers burst out of the building and sprinted toward the fires. After a brief hesitation, four of the Imps standing in the street followed, leaving only two guards at the gate. It couldn't have worked any better.

"Come on, Tove," he muttered. "Time to leave."

But she didn't appear. Deciding he couldn't wait any longer, Alar swore quietly and stepped into *annen'heim.*

A jittering cacophony of moans and wails assailed him. He never heard so many, so close before. He crouched, peering into the murk, feeling an urgency to get moving, but afraid of blundering into a spirit. Dark shifting shadows roiled the mist. Remembering Ragan's promise to keep the *sjel'and* occupied, he muttered, "Hope you're doing your thing."

Moving as fast as he dared, he approached the gate, slipped past the frozen guards, and entered the building. The foyer was a large room with a high ceiling. There were four exits, a closed door on each side wall and two doors that entered hallways on the back wall. A brother, sitting behind a high desk facing the door, was the only person visible. Tove was not there. Now what? Should he look for her or get the prisoners? He hesitated, then, trusting Tove to take care of herself, he decided to find the prisoners first.

He entered the left hallway on the back wall, then returned to the physical world, relieved to be leaving the *sjel'and* behind. A flight of stairs led up and to the left. He climbed the stairs to a landing on the second floor, then peeked around the jamb of the door into a hallway that ran the width of the building. The cells he peered into from the other side the night before were across the hall, behind heavy oak doors. A guard sat at a desk at one end of the hallway. Ragan assured him the guards on each floor would have the keys to the cells. He continued up the stairs.

The third floor was identical to the second, except there was no guard on this floor. Perhaps he was one of the brothers who left to help repel the rebel attack. He jogged to the desk, sheathed his sword, and began pulling out drawers. No keys. Now what? Kneeling, he thrust his head under the desk, searching the floor.

"Looking for these?"

He jumped, banging his head on the underside of the desk. Scrambling backwards, he shoved the chair out of the way, jumped up, and drew his sword. Tove was standing on the far side of the desk, a wide smile plastered across her face.

"I told you to stop doing that!" he said, leaning against the wall, hand over his heart. Tove shrugged and lifted a finger on which a large keyring dangled. Alar pushed himself upright and sheathed his sword. "Where did you get those?"

Tove smirked and offered him the keys. "Found 'em."

Alar's eyes narrowed. "Found them? Just lying around?"

"Not *just* lying around. Someone dropped them."

"Alar, is that you?"

It was Scilla's voice.

Alar took the keys off Tove's finger as he hurried past. Scilla was looking through the bars when he arrived in front of her cell. "Told you, rescue mission," he said with a grin.

He found the key on the third try, unlocked the cell, and pulled the door open. Scilla stepped into the hall. She looked thinner than Alar remembered. Her face was gaunt and her hair hung lank, but she looked well considering.

"You okay?" he asked.

She rubbed her hands up and down her upper arms and nodded. "I could eat, but they haven't done anything to me yet."

"She's in here, I think."

Alar turned around. Tove was standing next to a cell halfway down the hall. "Scilla, this is Tove," Alar said as he joined her.

"Hello," Tove said. "Your brother has been a right pain in the ass."

"Ukrit's here?" Scilla asked, surprised. When Alar glanced up from the keys, she asked again, "Ukrit? My brother, is here?"

"Well, not *right* here," Tove said. "But yes, he's out there, somewhere." She waved her hand toward the front of the building. "Came looking for us when you ran off."

Alar found the right key and pulled the door open. "Keep watch," he said to Tove. He started to enter the cell, then turned back. "And don't sneak up on me again."

The woman, Gallia, he hoped, was lying on the bed, unconscious or asleep. He rolled her onto her back, noting the tattoo on her face, then removed the vial from his pocket, uncorked it and got ready to pour it into her mouth.

"Wait," Scilla said, coming into the cell. When Alar looked at her, she said, "She'll choke. Here." She nudged Alar out of the way, sat on the edge of the bed, and lifted the woman into a sitting position.

Alar trickled the contents of the vial into her mouth, then stepped back. He wasn't sure what he was expecting, but was slightly disappointed when there seemed to be no effect at all.

Scilla let the woman down and stood next to Alar. "What's supposed to happen?"

"She's supposed to wake up."

"Who is—" Scilla said before Tove interrupted her.

"Well?" Tove asked from the cell door.

Alar shrugged. "Nothing. I guess we wait."

Tove's lips tightened. She nodded and disappeared.

"She's a sister," Alar said. "Of the Seidi. An Imperial witch."

Scilla's eyes widened. She looked down at the woman and leaned over to peer at the tattoo on her face. Straightening, she frowned and was about to speak when Alar interrupted her.

"It's complicated." He bent over and put his ear to Gallia's mouth, listening to her breath.

"I can't believe Ukrit came after me," Scilla said.

"Been worried sick," Alar said, straightened and stepped into the hall. Tove was standing in the center of the building, staring into an unoccupied cell. "Tove?"

She looked at him, a strange expression on her face.

"You okay?" he asked.

She nodded slowly, turned away, and stepped into the cell she had been gazing into. Alar was about to follow when he heard a woman's voice behind him.

"Who ... are ... you?"

When he reentered the cell, Scilla was helping Gallia sit up on the edge of the bed.

"We're friends of Ragan," Alar said. "We came to rescue you."

The woman raised her head, looked blearily from one to the other, then bent over and vomited on the floor. Alar and Scilla jumped backwards. They waited while Gallia wiped her mouth with the back of her hand and looked them over.

"A little young for this sort of thing, aren't you?" she asked.

Tove, standing in the cell door, cleared her throat, but before she could retort, Alar said, "We're precocious." He grinned at Tove's frown.

The woman tried to stand, then settled back onto the bed. Alar stepped around the pool on the floor, took her arm and helped her up. "We should move along," he said.

"How are we getting out?" she asked.

"Ragan said you would help with that," Tove said.

Gallia snorted. "In other words, you have no plan."

"We got a plan," Tove said, "and the plan is you help us get out."

"How many guards are there in the building?"

"At least three," Alar said.

"None," Tove said.

Alar stared at her.

Her brows rose. "What?" When Alar just looked at her, her expression hardened. "Payback," she said.

Alar nodded. "Good." Glancing at the others, he said, "Right, let's go."

Minutes later, they were back on the first floor. The brother who was sitting at the front desk when Alar arrived was laying in a pool of blood behind the desk. Alar lifted a brow at Tove. "Someone you knew?"

"He had the keys," she said.

They crossed the room, and Alar peeked out the front door. If anything, the city was even more chaotic than before. Fortunately, except for the two Imps guarding the gate, the street in front of the building was empty. "What should we do about the guards?" he asked.

Gallia gave him a scathing look.

"What I mean is, are *you* going to do something, or is this on me?" Alar asked. When Gallia looked past him toward the gate, Alar rolled his eyes at Tove, who grinned.

"It's not really my kind of thing," Gallia said.

Alar stared at her. "Right." He drew his sword. "Be right back," he said and stepped into the underworld. Moments after he entered *annen'heim*, the calls of the *sjel'and* changed, rising in pitch and cadence. He had a bad feeling they detected his presence. Seeing no dark shapes between himself and the guards, he hurried down the short walkway. One of the Imps stood in the center of the gate, blocking his path to the second. He considered for a moment, hefted his sword, and returned to the physical realm. Immediately, he thrust his sword into the brother's back, eliciting a grunt from his victim and a surprised shout from his companion. Alar pushed the man with his free hand, pulling his sword free, expecting the man to fall. Instead, he stood, swaying side to side. Alar couldn't get to the other brother as long as this man was standing in the gate. He lowered his shoulder, intending to push the bigger man aside.

As he pushed, the wounded man's legs gave out and he dropped. When the expected resistance vanished, Alar stumbled over the body and fell forward, becoming entangled with the remaining brother. He heard Tove and Scilla shout. Before he could bring his sword up, the brother clamped his hand on the wrist of Alar's sword arm. Alar stepped back and tried to jerk his arm free, but only managed to wrench his shoulder. Snarling, the brother reached for his own sword with his free hand. Alar punched him, but only grazed his cheek.

When the brother pulled his sword free of the scabbard, Alar stepped into *annen'heim.* His wrist passed through the brother's hand, numbing his arm from his fingers to his elbow. He spun around, searching for the sword he dropped, when his eyes fell on the body of the first brother. Ragan said the *sjel'and* were drawn to death. He backed away, deciding whether he should return to the physical realm, when he noticed his sword. Bending over, he attempted to retrieve it, but could only paw at the hilt with numb fingers.

Dark shapes swirled around him. Just as he scooped up the sword with his weaker hand, the darkness fled, chased by a brilliant light. Alar shied away, hand up to shade his eyes. A glittering ball of light appeared above the dead brother's body. It rose, blindingly bright, then, as the dark shapes coalesced around it, it dimmed until it turned dark and writhed as if in agony.

Terrified, Alar fled across the boundary. The brother's sword swept past his head.

"What—?" the brother got out before Alar swung his sword awkwardly with his weaker hand, burying it in the man's forehead. He watched the Imp fall backwards, jerking the sword from Alar's hand. "What in the Father's name was that?" He looked down at the body of the first Imp, his heart galloping painfully in his chest. Did he just see the man's spirit enter the realm of the dead?

"Smooth."

Alar looked up at Tove's wide smile. He ran his fingers through sweaty hair, giving himself a moment, then he forced a smile onto his face, and said, "It will be much more impressive in the stories."

The sound of running feet interrupted them. Alar looked up as ten brothers rounded the corner at the end of the block. He took Gallia's arm and pulled her in the opposite direction, but she resisted. When he looked at her, her eyes were closed, her face serene. "Come on!" he shouted.

Then, suddenly, his song rose, like it did in Ecke's presence. She shuddered, and the world dimmed. He glanced around, thinking he might have fled into *annen'heim* in his panic, but the brothers were still closing in and the thickening mist obscuring the street was wet. It was fog. He took her arm and pulled her away from the approaching brothers.

"Alar?"

It was Tove's voice. She was standing only a few feet away, but already, she was only a shadowy outline in the fog.

"Spread out, don't let them get past." A man's voice, but from which direction was difficult to tell in the fog.

This is what Ragan said Gallia could do to help them escape? How were they going to escape when they couldn't see six inches in front of their faces? "Tove," he shouted, reached out and took a hold of someone's arm.

Then, from out of the fog, an ethereal note rose. A voice, a woman's voice, singing. Alar stopped and stood transfixed. It felt as if the woman's voice was burrowing into his mind, searching for something. And then his song joined the voice. Not with the ethereal notes he heard before, but a voice that added a beautiful harmony to the song. The lyrics were in a language he didn't know, but somehow the voice inside him did. He stared into the fog's ghostly canvas at half-formed images. The voices swelled, teasing swirling tendrils of light and dark into a memory of a man and woman, facing one another across a tumbling mountain stream. A memory of something Alar never experienced. Love, betrayal, bitterness, emotions he never knew, overwhelmed him, and he wept, his tears mixing with the mist condensing on his cheeks. The man turned away from the woman. Alar wanted to shout at him, to warn him of the mistake he was committing, then a face swam out of the fog, a face with a tattoo. The person standing in front of him took him by his shoulders and shook him. He grasped after the memory, but it fell to tatters and dissolved. Slowly, he became aware of the words the woman was yelling above the song. "Alar, Alar, wake up. We have to go. She can't keep this up much longer." It was Ragan. She slapped his face, and the sting finally pulled him out of the song's spell.

Alar shook himself and nodded. Allowing Ragan to take Gallia's arm, he felt around for Tove. "Tove. Scilla," he shouted. Tove's strangled voice came from his right. Her hand groped out of the fog and closed on his arm. He took her hand, pulled her close, and found Tove was holding Scilla's hand. Alar gritted his teeth against the pull of the song and led them stumbling through the fog in what he hoped was the right direction. He was in such a hurry, he nearly ran into a brother. The man, lost in the song, stared ahead at something Alar couldn't see. They hurried past the man and kept going.

The fog thinned and the song stopped. Tove pulled her hand free. He looked back and found her helping Ragan, who was trying to support a swooning Gallia. Ragan looked at Alar and said, "Help me."

Alar took a step toward them, then Ukrit pushed past him and caught Gallia before she fell. He picked her up and carried her down the street, Ragan at his heels.

Although the fog was nearly gone, the shouts of the brothers behind them were still confused. Lief rushed past, joining Tove and

Scilla, following Ukrit. They were going to make it. Despite the odds, the slapdash plan, the brothers returning at an inopportune moment, they were going to make it. He looked back once more, checking for pursuers, then followed the others.

They were approaching the intersection where they were supposed to turn west, toward the boardwalk, when horses appeared in the street ahead of them. Even in the dark, the white uniforms of the riders were unmistakable. Brothers.

"The inquisitor," Ragan yelled. She reached out and grasped Ukrit's arm. Ukrit stumbled, dropped Gallia onto the cobbles, and dove to avoid stepping on her. Tove's hand locked onto Alar's left wrist, sending fiery tingles through his still numb arm. Alar pulled away from Tove and hurried forward to help Gallia stand. The brothers on horseback were approaching. Alar squeezed his left hand into a fist and reached for his sword before remembering he left it behind.

"They're getting organized back here," Tove yelled.

Alar didn't bother looking. As the brothers in front of them neared, he saw two women accompanying them, elaborate tattoos on the left side of their faces. Sisters. He took a deep breath, whooshed it out and prepared to step into the underworld.

"WooOOooOOooO UF UF UF!"

The last huffing grunts were so deep and powerful, he felt them in his chest. He fell to his knees. Screams of men, women, and horses erupted around him. Lifting an arm protectively above his head, he peered up. He was terrified, but needed to see the twisted, shadowy form towering above them. A *sjel'and.* Alar was not a stranger to fear. In fact, it was an emotion he was well acquainted with. But the pure horror he felt, looking up at that monstrous spirit, stole his reason.

Driven by a primal need to survive, he fled, chased by screams, the clatter of horses' hooves on cobbles, running feet, the animal sounds of panicky terror, and above it all, the fury of the *sjel'and,* battling to escape Ragan's hold. He ran, only dimly aware he was screaming. The spirit's wails intensified, becoming more frantic and menacing, until they rose in a shriek before falling silent. Still, Alar ran until he stumbled and fell, bruising his knees on the stone cobbles. Like frightened prey, he froze, listening for the spirit above his heaving breaths and thudding heart.

There were screams, but only the earthly screams of frightened humans. Even the dogs had fallen silent, terrified of what found its way into their city. Alar got to his feet, bent over, resting his weight on his sore knees.

He lurched upright at the sound of running feet. Wiping his mouth with the back of his hand, he backed away, once again feeling for a sword that wasn't there. As the man neared, Alar recognized Ukrit. He reached out and snagged his arm as he passed. Ukrit shouted and turned panicked eyes on Alar, fighting to free his arm.

"Ukrit! It's Alar."

Ukrit struggled for a moment more, but when he focused on Alar's face, his panic subsided. Pulling his arm free, he pointed back the way they came. "What in the Father's name was that?"

"*Sjel'and*," Alar said. "Ragan must be able to summon them into the physical realm."

"Summon …" Ukrit stared at Alar in horror. "Why would she do that?"

"Well, you did ask her if there was anything she could do."

Ukrit frowned at him, then his face cleared. "In the Mother's name, if I'd known such things existed … Remind me to keep my mouth shut, next time."

Alar chuckled weakly. "Let's hope there isn't a next time. Besides, it worked. We got away." He looked back the way they came. "I'm guessing everyone scattered. There's a good chance everyone got away."

Ukrit followed his gaze. "That inquisitor and his friends sure took off," he said. He paused, his eyes cutting to Alar. "Should we go look for the others?"

Alar considered. "No, there's no telling which direction everyone went. We just have to hope they made it to Ragan's safe house."

"Then what do we do?"

"We hide," Alar said. "That's what Tove and Lief will do. The Imps aren't going to be happy about this. They're going to turn this city upside down. The question is where. We ran the wrong way. The safe house in that direction." He pointed back the way they came.

"I know a place," Ukrit said.

"*You* know a place?" Alar asked. Ukrit nodded. "Well, lead on, then."

Chapter 19

The Toughest Person I Know

Smoke from the fires, carried by an eastern wind, drifted and swirled through the streets Alar and Ukrit walked through. The fire's glow, visible over the rooftops, cast the scene in nightmarish red hues. It reminded Alar of a description he read of the Otherworld, where the Imperial god, Daga, held sway. As they set out, the city was quiet, the citizens frightened indoors by the appearance of the second *sjel'and.* But it wasn't long before they emerged. The *Alle'oss* were not generally superstitious. A century of Imperial indoctrination submerged most of their own mythology. Stories of fairies and spirits were only childhood memories for the old. And while it was impossible to avoid the Imperial religion, to most, the lurid warnings of demons and angels were more amusing than frightening.

But the soul spirits represented a horror buried deep within the cultural memory. It was why the stories of *annen'heim* alone survived while Imperial dogma eroded the rest of the *Alle'oss's* rich cultural landscape. No one could help hearing the spirit's chilling howl, and though few saw the spirit towering over the city, news of its appearance spread faster than Alar would have believed. Crowds gathered in the streets, seeking comfort in the familiar and the collective. It was an illusion. The pitchforks, axes and bows they brandished would amount to nothing if Ragan had lost control of the *sjel'and.* He shuddered, imagining that dark specter sweeping through the city. He would like to think that wasn't possible, that the sister was in total control, but her fear and reluctance to explain what she planned suggested otherwise. She took an awful risk to allow them to escape.

Alar expected the Imperials to react quickly, but as they neared the *Alle'oss* commercial district that hugged the eastern edge of the city, they'd seen no sign of them. He was about to suggest they keep going and slip into the forest that pressed up against the city when the first Imps appeared.

"Ukrit," Alar said through clenched teeth.

"It's here, hurry," Ukrit said. They ducked into a side street, then ran along a large one-story building until Ukrit stopped beside a door on the building's side. The door was wide enough to admit a wagon and hung from a track so that it could be slid aside. Ukrit pounded on a small door set inside the larger door. The door opened almost before Ukrit finished knocking.

The man who peered through the narrow opening squinted at them in the light of a small lamp. Through the gap, Alar saw bushy whiskers, more gray than red, and one narrowed eye.

"Hera Gundar," Ukrit said. "It's Ukrit Woodsmith. I've been here on business for my father, Bo Woodsmith." Ukrit gestured at Alar over his shoulder. "This is my friend, Alar."

"Ukrit?" Gundar asked and pulled the door open wider. "What are you doing in Kartok? Out on a night like this?"

"Can we come in?" Despite how much Ukrit assured him Gundar was a good friend, Alar could hear the relief in his voice when the man recognized him.

Despite his obvious fear, Gundar hesitated only briefly, before he pulled the door open and said, "Yes, of course. Come in."

The harsh voices of soldiers confronting other residents in the district cut off when Gundar closed the door. The inside was an immense open space, as wide as the front of the building. The back was lost in shadow, but Alar thought he saw doors, suggesting there were other rooms. While Ukrit shook hands with Gundar and made some awkward small talk, Alar studied the room. It appeared to be a woodworker's workshop. Tools were neatly arranged along the walls. Workbenches and projects in various stages of completion occupied the center of the room. The scent of freshly cut wood permeated the air. A variety of bows were stacked against one wall. There were longbows, recurve bows, and other types he couldn't identify. Thinking of Tove, he returned his attention to Gundar, who was looking uncomfortably between Ukrit and the door.

"So, you see, Hera Gundar, we need a place to hide. Just until things blow over," Ukrit was saying. Gundar hesitated, but Ukrit rushed on before he could speak. "Not that we *need* to hide. For anything in particular. It's just that, not being from the city, we're worried they might take us in, just because … of that."

Alar rolled his eyes. "We'll be out of your hair as soon as possible. We just need to wait until the Im … the soldiers move on."

For a moment, it looked as if Gundar would refuse, but then he nodded his head toward the interior of the workshop and said, "This way." He led them to the center of the room. "Wait here," he said and moved off toward the back of the shop, leaving them in relative darkness. When he returned, he carried a thin iron bar with a slight bend on one end. He handed the lamp to Ukrit, nudged him aside and inserted the rod between two planks in the floor, then lifted a section of the floor up. Holding the trapdoor open, he gestured to the dark space below. "Be quiet and no one will know you're there."

"Thank you," Ukrit said and followed Alar down the steep steps, carrying the lamp.

The room below appeared to be another, smaller workshop. A similar set of tools hung from pegs on one wall. Lumber was stacked along the other walls. A small bench sat beside the stairs.

"Who is this man?" Alar asked after Gundar closed the door.

"His name is Frode Gundar. My fa—" Ukrit looked up at the door, swallowed, then tried again. "Our family has done business with him for years."

"You trust him with your life when the Imps arrive?" Alar glanced around. "We're trapped like rats in here."

Ukrit snorted and gave Alar a sick smile. "I'm trapped like a rat. You can just escape into *annen'heim*."

He *could* escape into the underworld, assuming the spirits allowed it. But could he abandon Ukrit? He looked up and found Ukrit watching him.

Ukrit must have read the uncertainty on Alar's face because he looked away and spoke in a flat tone. "Yes, I trust him."

Alar wasn't so sure. The man's reluctance was palpable. He felt again for his missing sword, then cast around for another weapon. Crossing the small workshop, he picked up one of the thin, wooden staves stacked along the wall. Hefting it, he tapped it against the palm of his hand, eying the trapdoor.

Frode's boots thunked on the planks above them as he moved about the workshop. Alar followed his progress by the lamplight leaking between the wooden planks. A loud knock on the front door brought the footsteps stuttering to a stop. The knock came again, more insistent, followed by a muffled command to open the door. Alar snatched the lamp from the workbench where Ukrit set it and shoved it into a cabinet, leaving the small space lit only by the light filtering from above.

Alar followed Frode's steps as he hurried to the door. There was a slight pause, then the sound of the latch being lifted and the creak of the door swinging open.

"Sergeant Witten." Frode's muffled voice. "What can I do for you at this late hour?"

The Imp spoke, but his voice was too low to make out the words. More footsteps on the planks as someone entered the workshop, these accompanied by the click of hobnails, then a voice asked, "Surely, you've noticed the city is in chaos?"

"Lieutenant Borne," Gundar said. Alar was wondering about the edge that crept into his tone, when he spoke again. "Ayuh. I did, at that. Hear the disturbances, that is. That's why you find me awake." Frode sounded calmer than Alar would have given him credit for. "My question should have been, what does this have to do with me or my shop?"

"We need to search your premises."

Alar winced as Frode hesitated. Lifting the stave, he glanced at Ukrit. The big man was looking up, but when he sensed Alar watching him, he lowered his gaze. One blue eye glinted in a thin strip of yellow light that fell across his face.

"Maybe if you could tell me what you're looking for, I could save you the trouble."

"A band of rebels invaded the Inquisition headquarters tonight. Several prisoners escaped."

After a slight hesitation, Gundar responded, a note of amusement in this voice. "You think I'm harboring fugitives?"

"Sergeant." The lieutenant's voice.

Moments later, the thuds of many boots echoed in the small space. Alar watched the shadows cast by the Imp's lanterns spreading out through the room above. Ukrit let out a small sound when something heavy crashed to the floor, dislodging a cloud of dust that swirled in shifting shafts of light. The crash was followed by others, as the Imps dismantled the shop. For what reason, Alar couldn't imagine. The workshop provided few places to hide fugitives.

Alar stood at the base of the steps, tapping the bottom tread with the tip of the stave, watching men's shadows pass overhead. He glanced over and found Ukrit watching him with an odd expression, a stave dangling from one hand.

Though it felt as if it lasted hours, Alar guessed it only took minutes for the Imps to destroy Frode's workshop. He imagined the proprietor standing aside, his face wearing the expression *oss'stera* called *ot'jorla*, Imp face. It was the carefully blank stare people adopted when confronted by Imperial violence, like rabbits, huddling, motionless in hopes the wolves would move on without noticing them. The workshop could be replaced. At a cost. The man's life and the lives of his family could not. When the crashes subsided and the men filed out, Alar blew out a breath.

A moment later, the trapdoor opened, and the artisan peered down into the cellar. Alar stared at him. Unable to imagine words that could express how sorry and grateful he was, he merely said, "*Tok.*" The man gave him a weary nod and let the door close.

Alar retrieved the lamp from the cabinet. "You were right about him," he said. "Somehow, we'll have to find a way to repay him."

"I can't believe it." Ukrit was looking at his feet, shaking his head.

"What?"

Ukrit looked up. "He didn't do anything. Didn't say anything. They could have searched the place without destroying it."

Alar watched Ukrit's face as he struggled to fit this truth into what he believed the world to be. "It wasn't just about finding us," he said. "We embarrassed them tonight. This was about retribution."

"But why Gundar? They knew he wasn't part of what we did. They didn't even accuse him of anything."

Alar couldn't say why they chose Gundar. It might have been random, or there may have been a history between the lieutenant and the artisan. The reason didn't matter, and Gundar was almost certainly not the only one who would suffer because of what they did. It was part of the price the Imperials exacted for resistance. Like the innocent residents of Lirantok, brutalized by Imp cavalry because of *oss'stera's* botched attack on the slave wagon. It was a familiar moral dilemma. What was an acceptable price to pay for freedom? Most of *oss'stera* would say no price was too high, but Alar wasn't so sure. He doubted whether Gundar would agree, either.

Ukrit was still watching him. Alar was surprised he hadn't retreated behind the closed expression he used when he didn't want to hear something. Sensing the critical moment had arrived, Alar asked, "You've been to Kartok before, right?"

Confusion, before anger swept it away. "I already told you, I have. What's your point?"

When Alar didn't respond, Ukrit took a step toward him, his hand curling into a fist. When Alar didn't react, Ukrit hesitated. Alar watched a variety of emotions cross his face, curious about which one would win out.

"I …" Ukrit turned away and dropped onto the small bench, his eyes roving vaguely around the cellar. "My father or my older brother always dealt with the Imperials. My brother, he's the one who knows the business. Scilla and I … we're … My father just sent me to meet with *Alle'oss,* like Gundar." He was quiet for a moment. When he spoke again, it was with a bleak tone. "I've never been out of this side of the town." He looked up at Alar. "He didn't want me to know. He was protecting me. Me and Scilla." He let his head drop. "I knew it and was happy for it."

His voice was so low, Alar barely heard him. He watched Ukrit for a moment, then turned away and returned the stave to the stack. There were dozens of them. They appeared to have been roughly split out of larger logs, the bark still on the curved side. They were too narrow to be used for lumber. "What are these?" he asked.

Ukrit looked up to see what Alar was referring to. "Bow staves."

"*Bow* staves? They're used to make bows?"

"Yeah," Ukrit said, standing and coming over to stand beside Alar. He added the stave he was holding to the stack. "You have to season the wood before you make a bow. Otherwise, it will retain its set." When Alar looked at him blankly, he said, "After a while, wet wood will stay bent when you remove the string. It loses its power." He snorted. "Like that pitiful bow Tove was using."

Alar spun to face Ukrit, taking the bigger man by the arm and pulling him around. "You know, Ukrit, you may know a lot about wood and bows, but you don't know *sheoda* about people." Ukrit's hurt expression only fueled Alar's anger. "Tove made that bow."

Ukrit rocked back. "I didn't—"

"She's never made a bow. Never made anything, as far as I know. We needed a bow to feed ourselves, so she took it on herself to make one when no one else would. No one taught her how to do it." Alar pointed to the tools on the opposite wall. "I assume you use those with these." He pointed at the staves. "Tove used a hunting knife." Ukrit tried to speak again, but Alar waved his hands around the room and overrode him. "We don't have a place we can season wood."

Ukrit waited to be sure Alar was done, then he said, "She made that bow with a hunting knife? Just carved it?"

"And fed us for weeks with it." Alar nodded, his anger draining away. "That girl has already survived more trouble than most people see in a lifetime. Somehow, she gets up every day and keeps going." He looked away and lowered his voice. "She's the toughest person I know."

They were silent for a while and then Ukrit said, "I didn't know."

"Well, you could have if you took an interest in anyone other than yourself."

They jumped as the trap door opened. Frode came partway down the steps and said, "The soldiers have moved on. If you hurry, you should be able to make it to the edge of town in the chaos." The words were a suggestion, but Alar heard the plea in his voice.

Chapter 20

An Excellent Plan

Alar crept down the path, listening for voices. He smelled smoke. Someone was using *honua*. It might be Tove and the others, but it paid to be careful. Ukrit followed, quiet for once.

After leaving Gundar's shop, they survived a handful of close shaves escaping Kartok, then came straight to the shelter. It only took them two days to work their way through the bread and cheese the old man gave them as they left his ruined shop. They had only a few mushrooms to eat since. Alar thought, longingly, of the provisions he stole from the brothers the night he rescued Ecke. Ragan secured all of it in the Seidi house before the rescue. For a few brief days, he lived like a normal person, free from hunger. It was surprising how quickly one became accustomed to having a full stomach.

"You think it's done?"

Alar grinned. The voice was Tove's. He straightened and strode into the clearing, throwing his arms wide. "What's for supper?"

Tove, Lief, and Scilla leapt up from their spots around a small fire. He just had time to brace himself before Tove threw herself at him, wrapping her arms around his chest. He hugged her, rocking side to side, until she pulled away and punched him on the shoulder.

"Hey, what was that for?" he asked with a grin.

"That was for scaring me!" Tove said.

Alar pulled Lief into a hug. When they separated, he glanced at Ukrit and Scilla tearfully greeting one another and asked, "Ecke?"

Tove and Lief exchanged a look and shook their heads. "Ragan nor Gallia, either," Tove said. "When that … thing appeared, everyone scattered." She waved her hand at Lief and Scilla. "We just happened to head in the same direction. We ran until we hit the river. We were heading toward that Seidi house until some Imps showed up and we had to jump in the river."

"Rode the rapids until we were out of the city," Lief said.

"You were in the river?" Alar asked. When they nodded, he said, "It was awful cold that night."

For the second time in the past week, Alar was surprised by Tove's blush. He looked from her to the others and found them all blushing.

"We stayed in the river until we found a sheltered spot," Scilla said, finally. "Then we built a big fire, and …"

Alar looked from her to Tove, who shook her head.

"We took our clothes off so they would dry," Lief said.

There was a moment of silence. Lief stared back at him with his usual impassivity, but his pink cheeks were a clear sign there was more to Lief than he let on. Feeling a silly grin growing on his face, Alar looked from Lief to Tove's challenging expression, and laughed. When he glanced at Scilla and found her peeking at him from lowered eyes, his laughter died. Cheeks warming, he coughed. "Yes, well, that was probably wi—"

"You were naked?" Ukrit blurted.

Tove thrust her chin forward and said, "It was warmer than wearing wet clothes. You would prefer we die of hypothermia?"

"Well … no, I just mean …"

"What's for supper?" Alar asked, grinning at Tove and putting his arm around her shoulders to steer her toward the fire.

"Not so fast," Tove said, shrugging his arm away. "I think you have something to explain."

Alar scanned the expectant expressions. "Okay, let's …" He took in the pair of rabbits on spits above the fire. "Let's sit, have some supper, and I'll tell the tale."

Alar told the story of the night he rescued Ecke. His audience showed their appreciation, laughing and gasping at the appropriate places. Alar had to admit, it was a heroic tale, worthy of the lore master's attention. He barely had to embellish at all.

Tove, who listened to his stories often enough to distinguish the truth from the lies, stared at him speculatively when he was finished. "I believe you may be telling the truth. Or enough of the truth, anyway."

Ukrit and Scilla, who listened raptly, unfamiliar with the ritual, frowned at them. "But I saw him do it," Scilla said.

Alar lifted a hand toward her and nodded at Tove. "So did you," he said.

"I haven't seen it," Lief interrupted her response.

Alar gave everyone his widest smile, then stepped into *annen'heim*. Remembering the terror he felt watching the brother's spirit leave his body, his grin fell away instantly. He rose to a crouch and peered into the murk. No shadows. No sounds. He hurried around behind Lief and returned to the physical realm to gasps and applause. Taking a bow, he reached out and gave Lief's ear a light flick.

"That could be useful," was the boy's only comment.

Alar returned to his spot and looked at Tove, who was watching him from across the fire.

She grinned and said, "I always knew you were a little off."

"What do you mean, 'a little'?" Ukrit asked.

Tove stared at him. "Is that a joke, a quip, a sign of a sense of humor?" When he blushed, she said to Alar, "Not the only one with revelations tonight."

Once they were satisfied with Alar's explanation of his own abilities, the conversation turned to Gallia and Ragan.

"What was that, anyway?" Tove asked.

"The *sjel'and?*" Alar asked. He was prepared to launch into an explanation when Tove interrupted him.

"No, the song and the fog," she said and shook herself. "It made me see things, feel things. Things I never thought about before."

"Unique gifts," Ukrit said quietly. "That's what Ragan said."

They all sat quietly, each with their own thoughts. It occurred to Alar they might not have all seen the same images. "What did you see, Tove?"

She looked up, then her gaze fell away. "I don't want to talk about it."

"Was it bad?" Ukrit asked.

Alar was staring at Ukrit when Tove stammered an answer.

"No, it was … I don't know what it was," she looked up at Alar, her eyes begging him to change the subject.

"Ragan said the sisters bring spirits into the world," he said hurriedly. When everyone turned away from Tove, he added, "That's where their magic comes from. Spirits."

"Like that *sjel'and* thing?" Lief asked uncertainly.

"That thing was awful," Scilla said. "If I knew those things were real and could leave *annen'heim*, I would have stayed home." She caught Ukrit looking at her and added, "Under the bed."

Alar was waiting for Ukrit's anger, but was surprised when he grinned.

"Well, they're not all that bad," Alar said. "The spirits, I mean. That thing Gallia did, I wouldn't mind doing that again. I mean, when there isn't the risk of sudden death and all." He threw an apologetic expression at Tove and asked, "Did anyone hear a voice, I mean, in their mind?"

A chorus of agreements answered his question.

An hour later, the conversation lapsed. Alar looked up and met Scilla's eyes. She grinned. "Thank you," she said, then looked around at all of them. "Thank you for rescuing me."

When her eyes returned to him, Alar felt his cheeks warm again. "It's what we do," he said, gesturing grandly. "Risk life and limb to …

you know … rescue fair …" His gaze fell on Tove. She was staring at him, mouth hanging open. "What?"

She shook her head, snapped her mouth shut, and looked away.

"I don't know about all of you, but I'm worn out," Lief said into the awkward silence. "Rescuing … fair … you know … It's hard work. Now that we're all safe, I'd like to get a good night's sleep."

Alar narrowed his eyes at Tove's smirk as everyone rose and found places around the fire. Scilla lay down, leaving a gap beside her. Alar looked up to find Tove lifting her brows and glancing at the spot. "Um … I'll take the first watch," he said. "Someone has to stay up and keep the fire going." Tove gave a soft chuckle and found a spot to lie down.

***

Despite laying on the cold ground with no bedding, Alar slept better than he had in weeks. Even so, the next morning came too fast. He was gazing into the dying embers of the fire, sucking on a rabbit's leg bone, when he looked up at Tove, who was watching him from across the fire.

"Now, what?" she asked.

"Hmmm?" Alar looked around and found everyone watching him. He tossed the bone into the woods and jingled the late inquisitor's money bag, still tied to his belt. "We go home." He looked around. "I'm thinking it's time for *oss'stera* to become more than a gang of vagabonds."

Lief nodded toward the money bag, and said, "You think you should let Sten and Erik decide what to do with that?"

Noticing Tove shaking her head, Alar grinned. "No, let's save everyone the mother of all arguments, and make the decisions on our own. An inner circle, as it were."

"What they don't know …," Tove said, and Lief shrugged.

Alar looked at Ukrit. "What about you two?"

Scilla spoke first. "I'm coming with you. I mean, if that's okay. That's what I was trying to do when they arrested me." She gave Ukrit a sideways look and said, "They told me some others in *oss'stera* were being careless. Asking about rebels around the wrong people? That's how they caught me."

A frown crawled slowly onto Ukrit's face as he worked through her implication. "Me?" he asked, pointing at his chest.

"It wasn't one of us," Tove answered.

Ukrit took in the accusing expressions pointed his way, and looked at his feet. When he looked up, Alar expected a defensive response, but he said, "I'm sorry. I know better now."

Alar clapped him on the back. "No harm done." Taking in Scilla's and Tove's incredulous expressions, he added, "Ultimately. We're all here, right?" Changing the subject, he said, "You're welcome to come with us, Scilla, as long as don't mind living the *oss'stera* life; outcast, hungry and exhausted. What about you, Ukrit?"

Ukrit looked startled. His cheeks reddened. Shuffling his feet, he cleared his throat, and said, "Well, I was thinking Tove and I could go by Lirantok."

It was so unexpected, the clearing fell silent, but for a crow grumbling to itself high on the granite edifice above them. "What would I do that for?" Tove spluttered.

Ukrit's mouth opened, but no words came. He looked helplessly at Alar.

"I think we found a bowyer for you, Tove," Alar said. "Ukrit is going to teach you how to make a bow."

Tove stared at him, then her head pivoted to stare, open-mouthed, at Ukrit.

Ukrit hitched his thumbs in his belt and shifted his weight. "We have some seasoned staves. Our workshop survived the fire. We have the tools and the materials." He met her eyes, his voice gaining strength. "We'll go make some bows together. Sort of an accelerated apprenticeship. Then we'll come back." He glanced at Alar and waved a hand at his sister. "Scilla and I, we'll teach *oss'stera* how to shoot."

"That sounds like an excellent plan," Alar said. "Tove, what do you think?"

Tove nodded without speaking.

"Well then, let us be off," Alar said.

Chapter 21

Chasing Geese

Novice Harold Wolfe stood erect, right hand planted on his hip, his sword dangling from his left hand at his side. The enormous room was silent, save for his opponent's heavy breaths. Harold gazed at the rivulet of his own blood, trickling down his blade to patter into the sand of the practice arena. It was only the latest of his many tithes to what had become to him, hallowed ground. He wanted nothing more than to sag, sucking in deep breaths, but he wouldn't give them the satisfaction.

Sergeant Halder, the Inquisition Academy's weapons instructor, took his position as the judge of the bout. "Right," he said, not even trying to hide his frustration. "That's enough rest." He stabbed his finger toward the center of the ring.

The sergeant, a man who wore his scarred face like a threat, had tormented Harold since he arrived in the Inquisition Academy. The man took one look at Harold on that first day, an alley rat fresh from the streets of the Imperial capital, and decided it was his mission to chase him back where he came from. But with only a short, cruel life to look forward to if he left, Harold arrived with a monumental chip on his shoulder and a burning desire to prove he belonged.

On his first day of combat training, Harold, scrawny from a life of want, stood alone, his much taller classmates peering at him as if he were a wild animal. Halder brought Harold to the middle of the training floor and handed him a practice sword. Harold awkwardly tried to mimic the instructor's ready stance, the heavy hickory sword dangling from his hand. He watched the sergeant warily as he circled, using his own wooden sword, made iron by age, to forcefully point out the flaws in Harold's stance and grip. His classmates, appalled to find someone from the lower caste among them, snickered and hooted.

Unfortunately for the sergeant, Harold possessed an alley rat's cunning. When the big man suddenly sprang at him, Harold darted under the textbook lunge, and swung his weapon, two-handed, like a club at his tormentor's ankle. It may not have been proper form, but its effectiveness was undeniable. The crack of the man's ankle breaking echoed in the sudden silence. Harold had no idea how he survived the resulting storm, but in the years that followed, Halder ensured he paid for his momentary triumph in spades. Harold suspected the sergeant had a ledger somewhere, in which he cataloged the injuries he inflicted on Harold's body: contusions, scrapes, cuts, broken bones. In Harold's opinion, he had long since balanced the scales.

Whatever the sergeant's intention, his special attention was just the thing Harold needed. Unlike his upper caste classmates, Harold never held a sword before arriving at the academy. Nevertheless, with the unwitting assistance of the instructor, it wasn't long before Harold could stand toe to toe with any of them. Harold's growing skill forced the sergeant to resort to using proxies. The man standing before Harold now, the Inquisition's top-ranked swordsmen, was only the latest. Anticipation of Harold's humiliation drew a crowd. His fellow novices, academy instructors and even an inquisitor, hovered silently in the bleachers like vultures. Harold flexed his forearm, pulling at the drying blood. More stitches, but he didn't mind. The scars decorating his body were the trophies the Inquisition would never award him.

Reminders of victories earned through his own skill, perseverance and a pugnacious belief in himself.

He settled into a ready stance, lifting his sword and giving his opponent a wolf's grin, amused by the flicker of uncertainty that crossed the man's face.

***

Harold stripped to the waist, prodded at the cut in his forearm, and decided two stitches would be enough. He could trace his growing skill with a needle and thread in the scars on his forearms. Running his thumb over the ragged, puckered track near his left little finger, he smiled. It was the first, and it was obvious. To be fair, he was stitching himself, one-handed, with his weaker hand. Bending over, he retrieved a towel and wiped the sweat dripping down his torso. The Inquisition's champion swordsman gave a good account of himself. Halder declared him the winner, but the cheers that rose from the crowd were forced, and the procession filing out behind their champion was as silent as a funeral.

"Novice Wolfe."

Surprised, Harold turned toward the voice and snapped to attention. It was the inquisitor who watched the bout. Inquisitor Hoerst. A man altogether more subtle and dangerous than Halder. Trailing along behind him was one of Harold's classmates, Stefan Schakal, and another brother Harold didn't recognize.

"Yes, Inquisitor," Harold said.

Hoerst came to a stop two paces in front of Harold, leaving him at attention and smiling placidly. "Very impressive." He waved toward the arena. "For a half-breed. Who would have thought you would have come so far, no?"

Harold nodded, ignoring the sneer on Stefan's face. "Thank you, sir."

"Novice, let me get right to the point."

Harold interpreted this to mean he wanted to spend as little time in Harold's presence as necessary, but the feeling was mutual.

"You heard the news from Kartok?" Hoerst asked.

"Yes, sir. Two prisoners escaped from the Inquisition headquarters. The means of their escape is not known."

"Yes, that is correct, except regarding the means of their escape." Harold's brows rose.

"One of the prisoners was a novice of the Seidi, a runaway, and apparently she had the assistance of other runaways."

Runaway novices from the Seidi? Harold never heard of such a thing. He studied Hoerst's face for any sign he was having him on. It wouldn't be the first time. But whatever was going on, the inquisitor appeared to be serious. "Runaways, sir?"

"Yes, I know. I had the same reaction. But then, there you are," Hoerst said, his smile widening without making him appear friendlier. "Novice Schakal and I are accompanying some sisters to investigate in Kartok." He fell silent. It was one of his favorite games, a game Harold no longer played. He wanted to lead Harold along, forcing him to ask a string of questions to get the answers he needed. They stared at one another. Harold noticed the brother standing at the back, growing increasingly uncomfortable as the silence drew out. Harold suppressed a smile, wondering what would win out; Hoerst's desire to humiliate him or disgust at being in Harold's presence?

Finally, a flash of irritation troubled Hoerst's smile. "There is a report the novices had the assistance of a rebel group." He hesitated, then half turned to Stefan.

"Oh stera, sir," Stefan said.

"Ah, yes." The inquisitor looked at Harold, the placid smile back on his face.

"An *Alle'oss* rebel group, sir?" Harold asked.

"Yes, apparently Governor Adelbart captured a member of this group in Richeleau. He thought it important enough to render her into our care in Kartok. Before we could question her properly, she escaped with the novice."

When he settled into silence again, Harold's curiosity got the better of him. "What does this have to do with me?" Hoerst's grin widened, but he didn't speak until Harold added, "Sir."

"Novice, I wish you to go to Richeleau to investigate these rebels. Let us see what the Academy's top ranked novice can do to uproot this threat to the Empire." He turned and gestured to the brother standing behind him. "Take Brother Henrik with you and see what you can find out." He waited, the placid smile replaced by a predatory leer he reserved for heretics and Harold.

"Yes, sir," Harold said. "We will leave immediately."

"Of course," he said. "You will report to the local Inquisition commander and make sure you pay a courtesy visit to Governor Adelbart. He would not be happy to have the Inquisition investigating in his neighborhood without his knowledge." He held up a hand and Stefan placed an envelope in it. He handed it to Harold and said, "Here are your orders." After Harold took the envelope, Hoerst looked him up and down, his eyes lingering on Harold's gray eyes, the only outward evidence of his half-blood status. Without another word, he turned and walked away.

Harold and Henrik studied one another with guarded expressions. The brother was a companion-at-arms, what amounted to regular soldiers for the quasi-militaristic Inquisition. Harold's past relationships with these brothers had been complicated. Most of them were from the upper caste and grew up considering themselves superior to people like Harold. The upper caste were within their rights to abuse those below them in any way up to physical assault, which was technically illegal. It was a technicality without meaning for many in the lower castes, who often found the Imperial courts unsympathetic. Outright murder was frowned on, especially in front of witnesses, but a well-placed bribe could make even that charge go away. The problem the rank and file brothers had was Harold outranked them. Not knowing what to make of him, they usually settled on a sullen diffidence, falling just short of outright disobedience.

As he and Henrik studied one another, Harold saw something different in this brother's expression. Not respect perhaps, but something other than contempt.

When Harold didn't say anything, Henrik ventured, "Oh stera, sir?"

"Brother Henrik, have you ever heard of rebels in Argren, *Alle'oss* rebels?"

"No, sir."

"Have you ever heard of a novice and a companion-at-arms venturing into the field without an inquisitor to supervise them?"

"No, sir."

Harold gazed up at the ceiling, wondering at the game Hoerst was playing, but coming up with nothing. Not that he wouldn't mind being away from Brennan without supervision.

"Sir?"

Harold looked at Henrik and prompted him. "Yes?"

"Are you going to the infirmary to get that stitched up?" He pointed to Harold's forearm.

Harold glanced down, chuckled, then held his right hand up and showed Henrik the ragged scar near his pinky. "I stopped trusting them when they wanted to lop off my hand for this one."

"Ah," Henrik said, as if this made perfect sense. "You want me to do it?"

Surprised, Harold looked at the cut for a moment, then said, "Yes, that would be much appreciated."

"No problem, sir."

Harold bent over to collect his gear. When he stood, Henrik reached out and relieved him of his burden and gestured toward the exit. "You ever been to Richeleau, Brother Henrik?" Harold asked.

Henrik fell in beside Harold as they made their way to the exit. "No, sir. I've only ever been in Argren once before, and that was to Kartok."

"That makes two of us. Well then, brother, let us chase some geese, shall we?"

***

Stefan watched Harold and the brother exit the combat arena. "You sure this will rid us of that blight?" he asked Hoerst. When a small frown flickered across the inquisitor's face, he added, "Sir."

"Nothing is sure. However, the situation in Richeleau is complex. Harold will find ample opportunities for his curiosity and impertinence to land him in trouble."

"Oh stera?" Stefan said, sounding doubtful.

"Oh, I have no doubt this oh stera are little more than garden variety hooligans. No, there are much larger forces at play there."

Chapter 22

A Horrible Fascination

Ragan opened her eyes and gazed at dust motes drifting lazily in sunlight leaking past the curtains in her bedroom. Still daylight. She looked down and was surprised to find her journal cradled in her lap. Laying it aside, she padded over to the window and pulled the curtains aside. The sun peeked through the trees, limning leaves in their autumn glory. "Late afternoon," she whispered. She sighed, pulled the curtain open, and gazed out the window. It was noon when she called the *sjel'and*. Even when she was home in Fennig, she was rarely entirely present. Hearing a noise behind her, she turned to find Gallia standing in the doorway, a familiar frustrated frown on her face.

"What's wrong, Ragan?"

"Something's happened." Ragan said. She crossed to the bed and sat. "I don't know what. Months of work ..." She picked up the journal, leafed idly through the pages, then placed it on the small table beside the bed. She pasted a smile on her face, looked up at Gallia, and patted the mattress beside her.

Gallia hesitated, then came into the bedroom and sat beside her friend. "Maybe, if you told me what you're doing," she said. Her hand lifted from her lap, gesturing vaguely. "I don't know what I can do, but it might help to talk about it."

"I ...," Ragan caught Gallia's hand and pressed it between both of hers. "You don't have to stay. I want you to know I appreciate it, but I know you're anxious to leave the Empire."

"I told you I would stay until the baby comes," Gallia said, squeezing her hand.

Ragan looked down. She pressed Gallia's hand to her swelling stomach.

"Oh," Gallia exclaimed. "It's moving."

"She," Ragan corrected gently. "She's always active when I ..." She glanced up at Gallia and looked away.

"Maybe, if you would just tell me what you're trying to do."

Ragan looked into the other woman's eyes. It would be nice to have an ally. Someone she could confide in. Making a sudden decision, she asked, "You remember what they taught us at the Siedi about prophecy?"

Caught off guard, Gallia looked away, her lips taking on the twist Ragan knew meant she was concentrating. She couldn't help a small smile. It was one of the first things she noticed about Gallia when they entered the Seidi together at eight years-old.

"Yes," Gallia said, her voice quiet as she rummaged through dusty memories. "Long ago, a few sisters were chosen by Daga, and granted a gift that allowed them to see the future, or possible futures, anyway." Gallia frowned and searched Ragan's face. "But we know that isn't true. There is no god named Daga. The spirits grant our gifts, right? *You* told me that. It's one reason we left the Seidi." When Ragan merely looked away, she asked, "It's just a myth, right, prophecy? No one can see the future."

If only that were true. "There is a woman here, in Fennig, a *saa'myn.*" Ragan glanced at Gallia and noticing her confusion, she said, "The *saa'myn* were once the shaman of the *Alle'oss* people. They were spiritual leaders, healers, counselors. They understood the spirits in a way that no sister of the Seidi ever has."

"How is it I never heard of them?"

"You know what the Church does to anyone with knowledge of the spirits. The Empire exterminated the *saa'myn*. I can only assume Beadu is the very last of her kind. I have found no others, though I have searched." Ragan hesitated. "I would have told you about her already, but we've been so busy since we got back, and—"

Gallia waved her explanation away. "Where is she?"

Ragan looked at the square of sunlight crawling slowly up the wall, then pushed herself upright and took Gallia's hand. "Come on." She led the other woman into the empty common room, pulled on her boots, then she and Gallia threw cloaks over their shoulders. As she reached for the latch to the front door, it opened. Her husband, Thomas, stood in the opening, a smile fading as he took in the women's cloaks. He held their daughter, Minna, cradled in one arm, her black hair tousled, one pudgy hand gripping his collar. Ecke peered around him. Their faces were flushed from chasing Minna around the yard in the chill air.

"Mama," Minna burbled, extending both arms and hanging precariously from her father's arms.

Ragan took her daughter and propped her on a hip.

"Going somewhere?" Thomas asked.

"I'm taking Gallia to visit Beadu," Ragan said.

Thomas' head tipped back. "Ah." He stepped aside to make way. "Want me to start dinner?"

"We won't be long," Ragan said. After pulling Minna's hand from her nose, she rested her hand on Thomas' chest. "Sit by the fire and enjoy a quiet house." Reaching up on her toes, she gave him a quick kiss on a scratchy cheek. "Ecke, you should come, as well," she said, then swept out the door.

They crossed the wide yard that separated the house from the Imperial Highway, crossed the road and slipped into the forest.

"Where are we going?" Ecke asked.

"To meet a powerful witch, apparently," Gallia said with a smile in her voice.

"It's not far," Ragan said. She shifted Minna to the other hip, pulled a kerchief from a pocket inside her cloak and wiped her daughter's nose.

Minna pushed her hand away. "No!"

"She *really* likes that word," Ecke mumbled from the back.

Ragan grinned and Gallia said, "She knows what she likes, is all."

"Knows what she doesn't like, at least," Ecke said.

"Is that right? You know what you don't like, Minna?" Ragan asked.

"No!" Minna said and took a handful of her mother's hair.

"Ow!" Ragan buried her face in Minna's neck folds and blew, eliciting giggles and freeing her hair.

The path rose, the footing made tricky by debris from long-gone glaciers hidden beneath autumn's litter.

"Um," Gallia said.

"It's just up here," Ragan said. "Honestly, you would think you were the one six-months pregnant." She put her hand to her mouth and called, "Beadu! I'm bringing visitors." Moments later, they emerged in a clearing on top of a hill. A small hut nestled up against the trees on the far side.

"Oh my," Ecke and Gallia chorused.

Ragan knew they weren't talking about the old woman who stood in the door, wearing a smile that touched all the wrinkles on her face. It was the cloud of spirits that swarmed the clearing. The *lan'and,* land spirits, appeared as small, luminous orbs swirling through the air. Ragan paused, took a deep breath and allowed herself to enjoy the moment. The joyful *lan'and* were as unlike the *sjel'and* as could be imagined. The spirits, curious about the new arrivals, streamed across the space, swirled around the three women, washing them in lambent spirit light, before spiraling up into the darkening sky.

"So many," Ecke said.

"Yes, the spirits are fond of Beadu," Ragan said, and started across the clearing.

While they were watching the spirits, the old woman settled herself on a log in front of her hut. When the three women arrived, she was stirring the contents of a small pot suspended over a fire.

"Beadu," Ragan said. She handed Minna to the older woman and eased herself down to sit next to her with Gallia's help. Minna settled back into the old woman's lap, sucking furiously on a thumb and gazing at the fire.

"This is—"

"They could be no other than Ecke and *Sister* Gallia," Beadu said.

"I'm no longer a sister of the Seidi," Gallia said.

"Of course, my apologies."

Ragan threw an apologetic smile at Gallia. "Beadu likes to tease," she said.

"Just so," Beadu said. "Though, in my defense, my people have suffered much at the hands of the sisters. I rather expect I might be allowed a bit of gentle teasing."

Gallia stared at Beadu, her face showing she wasn't quite sure what emotion to settle on. Then Beadu's face split into a wide smile.

Her face reddening, Gallia gave Ragan an embarrassed smile and said, "We were going to talk about prophecy."

"Yes, we were."

"You've seen something," Beadu said, making it a statement rather than a question. She put her finger in Minna's hand, allowing her to wrap her fist around it.

"When I arrived in Fennig, Beadu helped me explore what gifts the spirits might grant me," Ragan said, not surprised at the doubt in Gallia's expression. Ragan's deficiencies were no secret while they were novices at the Seidi. Though she could sense Daga's essence, she displayed only meager gifts. When she showed not the slightest talent, the sisters concluded Daga found her wanting.

It was Beadu who explained their gifts came from the spirits, not Daga. Ragan could see the *lan'and.* Beadu called it *and'ssyn,* spirit sight. But knowing the truth didn't provide the answers she hoped to find. It was the spirits who decided to whom they would grant their gifts rather than Daga, but the result was the same. Like the sisters at the Seidi, Beadu almost concluded Ragan had no affinity for any spirit. But there was one remaining possibility. Beadu was reluctant to explore it, but Ragan pestered her until the old *saa'myn* relented.

"Turns out there is one spirit who has a gift for me," Ragan said. "The *sjel'and.*"

"Prophecy," Gallia said flatly. Though it was not what the Seidi taught them, she couldn't help make the connection.

Ragan nodded. "It is the worst sort of irony to call it a gift."

"You mean that thing in Kartok?" Ecke asked, horrified.

Ragan nodded. "Time is measured differently in *annen'heim.* Freed from the constraints of the physical realm," Ragan lifted her hands and gestured around them, "the *sjel'and* see the full *shehdi'enun,* the cause and effect, of creation. The spirits of the dead choose to reveal some of what they see, glimpses into the future, or I should say, possible futures." She looked at Ecke and said, "And yes, they are as horrible as the one you saw in Kartok."

"The *sjel'and* revel in misery and death," Beadu said, rocking gently. "They delight in showing you what is most difficult for you to see."

"What have you seen?" Gallia asked in a hushed tone.

Ragan reached out and cupped her daughter's foot. "The Inquisition will come for my daughters. I've seen it, over and over again. The details change. The inquisitors are different, but it always ends the same way. Our children are taken and Thomas is dead."

The crackle of the fire and the call of a nightingale were the only sounds in the clearing.

"But they're just visions. You said there are many possibilities. You don't *know* what you've seen will come to pass," Gallia said.

"No, I don't," Ragan said. "There are so many possible futures, it was difficult to tell which ones are most likely. I dismissed it at first. After all, the future turns on such small events. But it drew me back, time and again, a horrible fascination. I went back to the spirits, looking for reassurance." Ragan looked sadly at Beadu, repeating an argument she used many times to convince her friend. "I've learned so much. At first, I couldn't tell which futures are more likely. But now I know the river of time finds its path, and some courses are more likely than others, some currents irresistible."

"But Beadu said the spirits show you what they know will hurt you," Ecke said. "Maybe they're lying."

"The spirits can't lie," Beadu said.

"But maybe they aren't showing you the good futures."

"That was my wish as well," Ragan said. "But, as I said, I have come to understand how likely it is a vision will come to pass."

"Leave the empire," Gallia said. "Come with me."

"I've considered it," Ragan said. "Across the Southern Sea to the Union or Kai. East to Tsada. All are perilous, all with dangers I understand less than those here."

"Is there no hope?" Gallia asked.

"None, but one," Beadu said.

The women grew silent. Ecke and Gallia leaned forward. "I saw an inquisitor, standing in the forest watching Minna and Thomas sitting on the porch of our home." Ragan lifted a hand, reaching out as if she could touch the vision. "Minna looked to have ten summers." Her brow furrowed, her eyes lost focus as she gazed into her memories of a vision she had seen a dozen times. "The inquisitor … he was like so many of the others, except he had gray eyes."

"Gray?" Gallia whispered. "Are you sure he was an inquisitor?"

Ragan nodded.

"What happened?" Ecke asked, breathless.

"He watched for a time, then he turned away." She emerged from her memories and looked at Gallia. "He left Thomas and Minna alive."

Gallia stared at her through a shroud of smoke. "I don't know any inquisitors with gray eyes. The Inquisition would never allow a half-breed to become an inquisitor. Would they?" She glanced at Ecke, then remembering who she was, she shook her head and looked at Ragan. "Would they?"

"But wouldn't some other inquisitor come later?" Ecke asked.

"Maybe," Ragan looked away from Gallia. "But if I can find out who the inquisitor with the gray eyes is, find out why he left them, maybe ... I don't know. Maybe I could talk to him. Maybe he would help protect them. Having an ally in the Inquisition could only help."

The four women fell silent. "Mama," Minna said and nearly fell sideways out of Beadu's lap, reaching for her mother.

Ragan lifted her and settled her onto her lap. She bent forward, burying her nose in her daughter's bushy hair, breathing her dusty scent.

"But you have seen something else," Beadu said. "Something new."

"Yes," Ragan said. She looked up at Gallia. "I saw the inquisitor, the man with the gray eyes, again. He will die only weeks from now." She turned to Beadu. "Something I haven't seen before has happened, something that changed his future."

"We have to save him," Ecke blurted.

"Can we?" Gallia asked, her voice revealing her doubt. "Will it help?"

"You can, of course, try," Beadu said. "But, as I have already told you, Ragan, this is folly. It is one thing to try to bend events for a day or a week, or to foresee the weather months from now. It is quite another to do what you are trying to do. The *shehdi'enun* of humans is too volatile, the alternatives too many, and they turn on the smallest events. The *saa'myn* learned this, long ago."

"Eight years. That is not so long. Is it?" Ragan asked. It was well-traveled ground. When Beadu first chided her about trying to steer the future, Ragan acquiesced meekly. But her horrible fascination wouldn't let go. As Beadu's admonishments became firmer, so did Ragan's belief she could defy centuries of the *saa'myns'* accumulated wisdom. She lifted her chin and looked away from Beadu to Gallia. "Minna and her sister will be powerful. Perhaps more powerful than any *saa'myn* or sister who ever lived. I've seen it. All I need to do is give them time to grow into their strength." She turned back to Beadu.

They stared at one another, until Beadu said, "As I have said, you can try, but you, and everyone you love, will pay a terrible price."

"And what if I don't try? Will the price they pay be any less?"

Beadu's head tilted forward and her lips pursed. "Perhaps not." She held up a finger to forestall Ragan's response. "But you will have to make choices about the futures of many others, the innocent as well as the guilty. Are you so sure you know the minds of the gods that you can make such choices? How are their lives measured in your accounting?"

The women fell silent, until Minna said, "Mama, home."

Ragan hugged her daughter tighter and said, "I have to try. I'll … I'll have to make those choices when I come to them."

Before Beadu could respond, Ecke burst out with, "What do we do?"

Ragan's eyes lingered for a moment longer on Beadu, then she turned to Ecke and said. "The inquisitor dies in Richeleau."

"Richeleau?" Gallia asked.

"Oh!" Ecke said. "We have to go find Alar and Tove. They'll help."

"You're going to ask *Alle'oss* rebels to help you save an inquisitor?" Gallia asked. "I want to be there for that conversation."

***

Ragan closed her worn pack and was setting it on the floor when Thomas appeared in the door to their bedroom, Minna on his hip. "I think she wants some mama time before bed," he said, glancing at the pack. His tone was light, but Ragan heard his worry and fatigue.

They entered the common room and Ragan settled into the rocking chair beside the hearth. "Ecke and Gallia?" she asked.

"In their room," Thomas said. He hesitated for a moment, emphasizing the word when he said, "Packing."

Minna molded herself to Ragan's stomach, her green eyes on the fire in the hearth. Her mouth worked at one thumb, while the other hand worked the edge of her quilt, caressing her cheek. Ragan smiled. It was how she settled herself. "She's feisty, this one."

Thomas eased himself into the chair opposite her, extending his legs with a groan and giving her a weary smile. "You can't look away for a minute or she's into something."

They sat quietly for a time. "It's been good to have you home," he said.

"It's been so good to be home. To see you." Ragan looked down at her daughter. "To see her."

Thomas watched tears moistening Ragan's cheeks, then looked into her eyes, his face falling in resignation. "You're leaving again." It wasn't a question. When Ragan dropped her head to bury her nose in their daughter's hair, he asked, "Do you think you should be traveling so close to the birth?"

Ragan looked up at the note of anger in his voice. "Erik Lothan is taking a caravan to Richeleau. He will make a place for me in one of the wagons. I'll be fine."

He let his head fall back and stared at the ceiling. Thomas fell in love with her when most of the villagers regarded her as an oddity. They weren't openly hostile. Fennig was too remote, too far from Imperial violence, for them to hate her. She was simply the outsider with the strange tattoo on her face. She could only imagine how difficult their marriage made his life. And her frequent absences only made it worse. She wanted to tell him she would stay, be the wife and mother her family deserved. At least, until ... But she could not let doubt turn her aside from her task, so she lied.

"Besides, I have three months. I'll be back in plenty of time."

His gaze dropped so he was looking at her, his brow furrowing as he did the calculations.

"Vada will help with Minna. She always does," Ragan blurted, feeling ashamed for using the feelings she knew were growing within him for Vada to distract him. She didn't blame him—Vada was here, Ragan was not—but she hoped the guilt he felt would derail the argument. To no avail.

He nodded to Minna who had fallen asleep, her mouth still working her thumb. "Your daughter will grow up thinking Vada is her mother. She won't even remember you."

Ragan flushed. It was her biggest fear, a fear she confessed to him when she first began to understand what she would need to do. For him to use it against her was unfair. He knew the consequences if she did nothing. Glancing down at her sleeping daughter, she gave herself enough time to gain control of her voice before she spoke. "At least she will be alive. If she believes Vada is her mother, that's a price I'm willing to pay."

"You may come to regret that one day," he sat flatly.

"Yes. I'm quite sure I will," she snapped. They glared at one another for several thudding heartbeats. Then she bent down and kissed Minna's head. When she spoke, the anger had given way to despair. "What else can I do, Thomas?" She looked up expectantly, hoping he had an answer. Instead, he shook his head. Ragan sighed. "If I stayed, could we be happy, knowing what is to come?" His anger melted away, leaving behind the hopelessness they both kept hidden from one another.

His gaze returned to the fire. "When you come back, will you stay? Will this … thing you are going to do make that much difference?"

"You know I can't promise that."

"When will you know it's done?" He turned away from the fire and looked into her eyes. "Will you ever know it's done?"

Ragan let her head drop back and smiled sadly. "One day, our daughters will be women. Powerful women able to take care of themselves. Then my job will be done."

Chapter 23

A Tangled Web

Chagan's voice droned on, but Adelbart, distracted by the man's wobbling jowls, wasn't listening. The governor sighed, let his gaze drift to the window of his office and tuned the man out. The only thing he wanted to know was when Chagan and his mercenaries were leaving. Of course, he may have already said, who could tell with that accent? Noticing Chagan had fallen silent, Adelbart's head swiveled toward him and found him watching the governor expectantly. "Excuse me?"

Chagan's brows drew together, and he pushed his lips out. It was an expression Adelbart came to recognize as deep disapproval. "I was explaining that I am raising our price," he said in perfectly accented Vollen.

Adelbart stared at him. "We have a contract," he spluttered, before he remembered he insisted nothing about their agreement be set down in writing. "An implied contract. We agreed on a price, and we shook on it."

Chagan's fleshy lips stretched into a wide grin. "Oh, yes. I remember clearly. However, you will have to admit, you were not entirely forthcoming on the … particulars of the task."

Adelbart's mouth dropped open, but no argument came to mind because Chagan was entirely right.

"Indeed, if you had been more forthcoming, I would have demurred." The mercenary popped his lips and waved a hand. "Still, we were successful, of course." Pointing a fat finger at Adelbart, he said, "But your deception cost me five good men. Replacing them will be very expensive."

"But surely, you knew it would be risky," Adelbart said. "That is your job. You *are* mercenaries, are you not?"

Chagan's face stilled. "Let me make sure you understand the situation. You did not inform us who we were retrieving for you, nor did you tell us from whom we were retrieving her. I think we both know why." He let the silence underline his statement, then the froglike grin returned. He removed a folded sheet of paper from a pocket and slid it across Adelbart's desk. "This is not a negotiation. We will have to retain control of her until payment is received, of course. However, I'll allow you some time to gather the funds. I'm not an unrea—"

Gerold's distinctive tap on the door interrupted him. Staring at the folded paper as if it were a snake, Adelbart called, "Come."

Gerold entered and closed the door. He came around behind Adelbart's desk, glanced at the Union man, leaned forward and whispered, "Governor, you have a visitor. It's an inquisitor from Brennan."

Adelbart's heart lurched. "An inquisitor?" He looked into Gerold's eyes, inches away. "Hoerst?" he whispered.

"No, sir. He said his name is Harold Wolfe."

"Wolfe?"

"Yes, sir." Gerold waited, but when Adelbart didn't respond, he glanced again at Chagan and asked, "Should I show him in?"

The mercenary heaved himself upright and said, "I suppose you must." He made his way to the door to Adelbart's private rooms and winked. "Must keep up appearances, right, your excellency?"

Gerold and Adelbart watched him disappear. He hadn't even asked permission to enter the governor's rooms. "Show him in," Adelbart said.

Gerold dragged his eyes away from the door through which Chagan disappeared. His gaze rested on Adelbart, his face as carefully blank as ever, but somehow conveying reproach. Sweat trickled through the governor's thinning hair. "You can show him in," he whispered.

Gerold gave him a curt nod and left the office. When he returned, two men in the white uniforms of the Inquisition followed him. The shorter of the two stood in front of Adelbart's desk, hands clasped behind his back. Adelbart squinted at him, trying to decide what was odd about him, then realized he had gray eyes.

"Governor," the man said. "My name is Harold Wolfe, and this is Brother Henrik Matison."

"You're a novice," Adelbart blurted.

Wolfe paused, a smile slowly curving his lips. "Yes, your excellency. Very observant."

In the silence that followed, Adelbart's relief soured. "The inquisitor who accompanied you couldn't find the time to pay his regards?"

"I'm afraid I'm on my own, your excellency."

"Alone? And you're here on Inquisition business?"

"Yes."

"That is most unusual," Adelbart said. "Isn't it?" He glanced at Gerold for confirmation.

"Nevertheless, here I am," Wolfe said, and handed Adelbart an envelope.

Adelbart nodded to Gerold, who took the envelope. "And what is that business?" the governor asked.

"Novice Harold Wolfe has been tasked with investigating rumors of a rebel group called *oss'stera*." Gerold, reading the letter, answered before the novice spoke.

"*Oss'stera?*" And then Adelbart remembered. The prisoner he shipped to the Inquisition in Kartok. It had been a whim, but somehow she escaped, sending shock waves far beyond the borders of Argren. He had privately congratulated himself on handing the problem to the Inquisition before she escaped. Unfortunately, that whim had apparently brought the Inquisition to his doorstep. Once again.

Still, they only sent a novice. How seriously could they be taking the threat? Wolfe was watching him, still smiling like he knew something he wasn't letting on. Adelbart didn't like him. "Oh, yes," he said, and cleared his throat. "The girl I sent to Kartok. The one the Inquisition allowed to escape." He meant it as an insult, one he would never have made to an inquisitor, but he was disappointed when the novice's smile didn't waver. He waved a hand dismissively. "You may investigate, but I'm confident you will find there is nothing to it."

The novice frowned and cocked his head slightly. "And yet, you thought it serious enough to transfer the girl to the Inquisition for interrogation." He glanced at Gerold, his brows drawing together. "You do have your own intelligence branch, do you not?"

"Yes, of course. It was a simple misunderstanding. A clerical error. One that we have since corrected."

"A clerical error?"

Adelbart froze for a second, then said, "Isn't that correct, Gerold?"

Gerold started. "Oh, yes ... uh ... sir. That's correct. A clerical error." He laughed nervously. "My mistake, actually, but, as the governor said, that error has been cor ... rected."

The novice, who turned to face Gerold while he spoke, glanced at the other brother, who shrugged, then he turned back to Adelbart and asked, "And you don't think the *Alle'oss* who were involved in this prisoner's escape in Kartok had anything to do with this rebel group, *oss'stera?*"

Adelbart opened his mouth before he had an answer and cursed himself for hesitating. "Novice Wolfe, I can assure you, our intelligence apparatus has investigated and found no evidence of an *organized* rebel group called *oss'stera*. There might be a small band of vagrants with delusions of glory using that name, but they are no threat to the Empire."

"That is good news," the novice said, his smile stretching. "But as I've been tasked by Inquisitor Hoerst to investigate, I'm sure you understand. I must investigate and draw my own conclusions."

Hoerst. Of course. "Yes, yes, you must do as you're instructed, but while you are in Richeleau, I expect you to keep me informed on your progress."

"We will provide regular reports," Wolfe said briskly. "And you will inform your organization that we should have their full cooperation."

"Yes, yes."

"Thank you, governor," Wolfe said, bowing slightly, before turning and leaving. The other brother's eyes narrowed as he looked at the painting on the wall behind Adelbart's desk. Then he turned and followed.

Adelbart sagged back in his chair, so relieved the man was gone, he didn't even mind he left without being dismissed. He looked up at Gerold. "Make sure that man is watched. Choose your own people. I want to know everything he does." Gerold nodded and left.

Adelbart massaged his chest absently. Now, on top of everything else, he would have to keep an eye on these two. Did Hoerst know what he was looking for, or was he just harassing him? It had to be the latter. He only sent a novice, after all. He jumped as the door to his private rooms opened and Chagan appeared.

The Union man crossed to the window and peered out, careful to stay out of sight. "Is this going to be a complication?"

"No, he's just a novice. Besides, he'll be occupied chasing these nonexistent rebels for weeks."

Chagan turned away from the window. "Weeks? Is that our timeline now?"

Adelbart glanced at the folded paper lurking on his desk. "I will need to … juggle some finances, reschedule some payments." Chagan pushed his lips out again, but before he could reach full disapproval,

Adelbart said, "You and your men are well taken care of. Living in luxury, truth be told. For Daga's sake, you're already being paid by the emperor to man the garrison. You have no right to complain. After all, *you* are changing the terms of the agreement, not me. Now that you know who you … retrieved, you know how anxious I am to bring this to a close. I *will* find a way to meet your usurious demands as soon as is practicable."

Chagan's face smoothed. "I can't complain about the accommodations. That is true. We certainly have had worse." He nodded and turned back to the window. "However, we are deep in the Empire and my men are growing increasingly nervous. If this novice were to become curious about our arrangement and came snooping around …" He turned away from the window and shrugged. "Also, you have a company of cavalry and rangers at your disposal. One can't help feeling insecure under such circumstances." He stepped in front of the governor's desk and leaned forward. "I will do what I think necessary. Take steps I think necessary to ensure we leave the Empire safely and well paid."

Despite the man's oily smile, Adelbart couldn't help hearing the threat. "I'll have my people keep an eye on him. Just make sure your men stay out of trouble. We've had too many incidents between the locals and your mercenaries."

"Don't worry about us. We know our business." Chagan straightened and dabbed at a tear that had escaped a watery eye. "My men are becoming impatient. I know you will need some time, but don't take too much." He nodded at the paper on the governor's desk, then turned and left the office.

Adelbart eyed the folded paper. He reached out and pushed it with his finger. Taking a deep breath, he picked it up by the corner with trembling fingers and held it up so it fell open. When he saw the number Chagan wrote in his precise hand, he gasped and dropped the sheet as if it were on fire.

***

Adelbart sat at his desk, staring into space. He spent the afternoon after Chagan left, scouring his brain for some way out of his predicament. The payment he would soon receive from Lirantok, generous as it was, wouldn't be enough. And he needed that money to pay another debt. A debt to very dangerous people.

He rose and left his office, hurried past Gerold with barely a nod, slipped into the anteroom and peeked into the hallway. Muffled voices, but no one was visible. Hurrying to the end of the hall, he found the decorative molding embedded in the chair rail and pushed. There was a click and a section of the wall pivoted slightly inward. He pushed it open, stepped through the door and closed it behind him, leaving himself in pitch blackness. With practiced hands, he found the flint on a small table and lit an oil lamp. He lifted it and peered down a narrow flight of stairs. It was silent. Taking a deep breath, he descended as quietly as he could.

On the ground floor, he opened another heavy, locked door, and continued down a narrow winding staircase. Stepping onto the stone floor at the bottom of the stairs, he set the lamp down on a shelf mounted beside a heavy oak door, unlocked the door, and eased it open. His sudden appearance startled the lone guard, one of Chagan's men. The man rose quickly and started to speak, but Adelbart put his finger to his lips and motioned up the stairs. Though the mercenaries showed Adelbart no respect, they obeyed Chagan, unerringly. The hulking man hesitated, then slipped out of the guardroom without a word. Though Chagan insisted his men guard the prisoner, he granted Adelbart one concession. The governor could visit her in private.

After the guard disappeared, the governor crossed to the door that led to the cells, unlocked it and heaved on the massive door. The hinges creaked. Adelbart froze, holding his breath and listening. Dammit, he told Gerold to have the hinges oiled.

"Father."

Adelbart sagged. He came to expect the note of derision in her voice, but it still hurt. One night, he was lucky enough to catch her singing softly to herself and listened, tears pooling in his eyes. But it was the last time he caught her in an unguarded moment. Taking a deep breath, he let it out slowly, hitched a pained smile onto his face, and stepped out of the shadows to stand before the bars of his daughter's cell. "Elois."

Though it was a cell in the dungeon, the governor did his best to make it comfortable. He had the furniture, rugs, and tapestries from her room arranged just so. He provided enough lamps to chase the gloom away, though she only ever lit one. It was on the table beside her chair. If he hadn't been here when the Union mercenaries dragged her into the cell, he wouldn't believe this demon was the same person as the child who used to squeal in delight at his appearance. She lounged in the chair, her head tipped so that the lamp, illuminating her face from below, made her eyes shadowy pits. One leg was thrown over an arm of the chair. Adelbart winced at the vulgar display. She still wore the filthy pants and blouse she arrived in. He noted the pile of fabric in the cell's corner that was likely the fashionable garments he had brought down. At least her hair was growing out, though it was obvious she wasn't taking advantage of the baths he insisted the guards provide.

"Elois," he said. "Would it kill you to take better care of yourself?"

"What's wrong father? Does my appearance offend you?"

"Well, yes, it does, and I'm not sure what you're trying to prove."

"Prove?" She sat up so suddenly, Adelbart flinched despite the bars separating them. "I don't need to prove anything! To you or anyone else. I proved everything I needed to when I left."

"What did you prove?" Even to his own ears, the question sounded disingenuous. He knew why she left, and when he visited her, seeing echoes of his little girl, he couldn't find any blame for her in his heart.

Before she could respond, he tried a different tack. "Remember that Winter Festival in Lachton? What was it, three years ago? That was a happy time, wasn't it? And not so long ago." The pleading note in his voice spoiled his attempt to distract her with happy memories.

"That was before you tried to sell me to be that inquisitor's whore."

"Concubine." The word, a confession of guilt, was out before he could stop it. Adelbart sighed. It was the same opening gambits of all their conversations. He would appeal to her childhood memories, happy memories. She would bring up his betrayal. Then they would argue. When he spoke again, it was with the same flat, hopeless tone he always ended with. "Hoerst will be the Malleus one day, the head of the Inquisition. You would have been at the heart of the true power in the Empire."

"In the perfect position to help your political career."

"That is not the reason!" he snapped, then slammed his mouth shut. In truth, the question of a suitable match for his daughter, an advantageous match, had been on his mind since the day she was born. His plans had fallen apart when Inquisitor Hoerst came sniffing around. Hoerst had his eyes on Elois since the ball in Brennan when she was formally presented to society. She was thirteen then. Adelbart would have offered her hand that night, but unfortunately, Inquisition brothers were not allowed to marry. Apparently, though, the Inquisition turned a blind eye to concubines.

Adelbart was sure Hoerst worked to sabotage Adelbart's efforts to find a match for his daughter. None of the elite Imperials who expressed an interest before the ball would even talk to him. When Elois reached the age of consent, the inquisitor made his desires plain. Adelbart demurred at first, but Hoerst persisted. When Adelbart refused outright, the inquisitor began to dig into Adelbart's affairs. Given the governor's predilections, it wasn't hard for Hoerst to find what he needed.

Adelbart offered Elois to him to buy him off. He regretted it, but it was that or disgrace and a short trip to the Inquisition's dungeon. Hoerst's acceptance meant the governor would have been free and clear. That was, until his daughter objected and fled in the middle of the night. The complicated series of events that followed plunged him into his current predicament.

Hoerst was furious, of course, and not even Adelbart's mother could save him from the Inquisition. It was the worst sort of irony that what saved Adelbart was he owed money to people who were far more dangerous than the emperor. The Desulti. That enigmatic organization had its fingers in every part of the Empire. Their wealth was unimaginable. And they were ruthless. They forced Hoerst to back off, though Adelbart suspected Novice Wolfe's appearance meant the inquisitor hadn't forgotten. He sagged as the true breadth of the tangled web he ensnared himself in came into focus. If he *didn't* pay the Desulti, they would kill him, and if he *did* pay them, they would abandon him to Hoerst's whims.

He forced his fists to unclench and willed his anger and dismay into the background. Regardless of his daughter's betrayal, he still held out hope they could repair their relationship. After her mother died, she was his only family. Not counting his parents, and who would? He missed her.

"They'll come for me, daddy."

"They already came," he said with a heavy sigh. He glanced at his hand, which had come up unbidden, then rested it awkwardly on the bars that separated them. "But it wasn't for you. The assassin came only for the ransom I paid to buy your freedom." Though he rehearsed it in front of the mirror until it tripped off his tongue, even he could hear the lie.

"Liar!"

"No, Elois, your Desulti sisters have abandoned you." A smart woman, she ran to the only people who could protect her from Hoerst. The mercenaries left no witnesses when they raided the safe house. It was the only reason they hadn't come for her already. Chagan kept her here, in the dungeon, because there was nowhere else her presence wouldn't be noticed. Adelbart couldn't imagine her whereabouts would remain a secret from the Desulti forever.

Still, the lie he practiced delivered, he forged ahead recklessly. "Perhaps we can share dinner and discuss your future," he said, wincing at the hopeful note in his voice.

"Oh, daddy."

Adelbart let his hand drop from the bars. "I'll … I'll visit again tomorrow," he mumbled, turned and shuffled away.

He climbed the stairs back to his office in a trance. Gerold looked up as he entered. Adelbart could only guess what his stoic assistant was thinking. The governor broke his gaze first, passed into his office, then slipped into his darkened private rooms. What was he going to do?

He felt her presence before he saw her. One moment he was sure he was alone, then the shadows in the corner shifted. It occurred to him she might be there to kill him, and was surprised to find relief rising to the top of the swirling emotions that thought aroused. He chuckled.

"Something funny?" she asked, gliding out of the shadows.

"No, not at all. I'm afraid I find very little to laugh about lately," Adelbart said.

The Desulti came closer, turning so the light leaking around the heavy curtains illuminated the interior of her hood. Linen strips wrapped her face, leaving only narrow slits for her eyes and below her nose. In the shadows, her eyes were black holes.

"Your time is up," she said. "Do you have what you owe us?"

So, it was the money. They hadn't found Elois. Yet. Adelbart's gaze lifted from her face to the painting on the wall behind her. It was nearly invisible in the dim light, but he saw it in his mind as he let his eyes slide shut. Called *The Dance*, it depicted one of the traditional folk dances the *Alle'oss* reserved for festivals. The artist, a man named Valdemar, managed to capture the color, the movement, the energy of the festival, in a way that no artist outside Argren could. It was one of Adelbart's favorites, reserved for a place of honor above his bed. His eyes flew open as the Desulti took a silent step toward him.

"Wait!" he said. "I have a proposal."

Chapter 24

Alar Takes Charge

Alar looked up at a cerulean sky through the burnt orange leaves of a stand of maple trees. A chill wind plucked leaves from the branches and sent them swirling. The bite in the wind reminded him he still had to find winter clothing for *oss'stera's* new arrivals. One of many problems requiring his attention.

He looked down the hill and found his quarry approaching: a small, stoop-shouldered man, bent against the wind. While Alar watched, the wind caught the man's hat and sent it tumbling down the street. Alar was watching the man chase after the hat when he became aware Scilla was speaking.

"Hmmm?" he prompted her. Scilla leaned her shoulder against the same trunk he was leaning against, so close he caught a whiff of her scent, before the wind whisked it away. She had tied her hair back, leaving a few stray locks to play about her face in the wind.

One corner of Scilla's mouth curled up. "I was talking about Tove and Ukrit," she said. "You're worried about them."

"Oh, right," Alar said and cleared his throat. "Yeah, I'm worried. It's been over three months. How long could it take to make a bow?"

"Bows," Scilla said. "Ukrit said they were going to make bows." When Alar looked unconvinced, she added, "Three weeks' travel in each direction, assuming they don't walk themselves ragged like you did." She paused to grin at him. "And they aren't just *making* bows, Ukrit is teaching Tove how to do it. He can be very … exacting." Scilla blew a breath through pursed lips. "I have no idea what they're telling our older brother. Then there are arrows, strings—"

"Will that be a problem? Your brother?"

"I would think so. He came home to find his parents dead, then his only other family ran off, leaving him to run the business by himself. I'm glad I wasn't there when Ukrit told him he and I are joining *oss'stera*. Assuming he told him anything." Her gaze rested on Alar for a moment. "Wouldn't you be angry?"

"Yes, I suppose I would." Alar's voice trailed away as he looked down the street at the small cobbler shop.

"Anyway, I'd be surprised if they're back soon." She followed his gaze. "Are you going to tell me what we're waiting for?"

Alar grinned at her, then stepped into *annen'heim*.

*****

When he returned, he paused, still in *annen'heim*, relishing the opportunity to gaze openly at Scilla. He expected her to look frightened or worried. Instead, she leaned casually against the same tree, arm's crossed, a cat's grin on her face. He stepped in front of her, drinking in what he only had the courage to glimpse when she knew he was looking. Round eyes, the color of the lake near her home. They crinkled slightly at the corners when she smiled. She had a small dimple in her cheek that deepened when she smirked. Full, red lips, so quick to curl into a smile. Fascinating, distracting, mysterious.

The rumbling huff of a spirit, feeling for his presence, caught his attention. Taking one last look at Scilla, he stepped back and returned to the physical realm.

Scilla let out a startled gasp, one hand going to her throat. He lifted the boots he carried and smiled.

"Wish you wouldn't do that," she said, then noticed what Alar held. "Boots?" she asked. "That's what we're here for?"

"Nice boots," Alar said, tipping them so she could see the interior lined with rabbit pelts.

"Ooh," she said, dipping her hand inside to feel the soft fur. "He'll like those."

"Yeah," Alar said and crouched to shove the boots into his pack.

"Still, I thought you said no more stealing from our people?"

"I said we'll *try* not to steal from our people," Alar said. He nodded down the street to the cobbler's shop. "Besides hera cobbler happens to be the only Imperial cobbler in Richeleau." He stood and settled the pack on his shoulders. "Think of it as a tax for his countrymen's depredations."

"You've done this before," Scilla said. When Alar grinned and nodded, she looked down at the boots he gave her soon after they arrived.

"Can't dip into the well too often, but for special people ..." Alar shrugged. "What's next?"

"Wilton," Scilla said and led them away.

"Do I know him?"

"No, he owns the Nervous Goose on Sky View Lane, the one I told you about. Gives us old vegetables."

"Oh, yeah."

Scilla led them through the winding streets, climbing steadily as they made their way east. They diverted into side streets twice when they encountered groups of Imperials. Though the Imps had no reason to suspect Alar and Scilla of anything, the less they saw of them, the better. Familiar faces tended to stick out in a crowd. Finally, they made it to the top of the ridge that wrapped around the eastern edge of the city.

Alar knew the street but didn't know the Nervous Goose tavern. The businesses ran along the eastern side of the narrow, cobbled street. To the left, the city's rooftops emerged from autumn-tinted foliage. Spotting a signboard depicting the goose of the tavern's name, he asked, "How did you stumble onto this?"

"Lief found it," Scilla answered, stopping to allow a larger party to pass. "I don't know how he does it, but he knows almost every tavern and inn owner in the city. The *Alle'oss*, anyway."

Alar wasn't surprised. He watched Lief working a room before. He had a quiet way of inserting himself into almost any conversation. Maybe it was because he looked so young or his unassuming nature, but people took to him. The boy may never be able to swing a sword, but he had made himself more valuable to their fortunes than almost anyone else in *oss'stera*, Alar included.

Scilla paused when they reached the tavern and scanned the crowded street. The tavern, a two-story half-timber framed and stone building, appeared to be one of the more prosperous on the street. Snatches of boisterous lunchtime conversations leaked from inside when the door opened.

"Want me to stay here?" Alar asked.

"No, Wilton wants to meet you." Scilla slipped into the alley between the tavern and the neighboring building. The businesses on the street backed up against the granite spine of the ridge, leaving a narrow shadowy space, still wet from recent rains. Scilla walked along the tavern to a back door, lifted an iron bar suspended from a chain and rapped on it.

Minutes later, the door was thrown open, forcing Alar to jump back. The man who stepped out wasn't much taller than Alar, but he sported the most impressive set of blond whiskers Alar had ever seen. His eyes lit up when he saw Scilla. "Scilla," he said in a piping voice. "Been expecting you." He glanced at Alar and asked, "Lief not with you, today?"

"No, Lief's got other duties today," Scilla replied. She glanced at Alar and lifted a hand toward him. "This is Alar. Alar, Hera Wilton. He's the proprietor of the tavern."

"*Lehasa*, Hera Wilton," Alar said with a smile.

Wilton turned to face Alar, hands on his hips. He looked him up and down, one bushy brow rising up his forehead. "This is Alar?" he asked doubtfully. "Naught but a boy." Before Alar could respond, the man leaned forward, his eyes narrowing. "To hear these two talk, I was expecting Sigard himself to appear at my door," he said in his reedy voice.

Alar threw on his widest grin, lifted his arms out to his sides. "Sigard was a boy once too, wasn't he?"

The man straightened, both brows rising. "'Spect he was, at that." He let out an improbably deep laugh and clapped Alar on the shoulder. "Hold on," he said and disappeared into the tavern.

Scilla gave Alar an amused smirk. "Young Sigard?"

Alar grimaced. "You've got to stop telling tales. I'm not sure it's a good idea to spread the word I can go into *annen'heim*."

"Oh, we don't tell anyone about that," Scilla said. "It's just, after listening to Lief's stories, people draw their own conclusions. Sigard was known for a lot more than the realm of the dead thing." Before Alar could protest, she rushed on. "You wouldn't believe how attitudes change when Lief spins tales of the great hero, Alar." When Alar frowned, Scilla asked, "You want to eat, don't you?"

"Yes, of course—"

The door swung open, and Wilton appeared, carrying a crate which he set on the ground. "Had a little extra this week." He winked at Scilla and said, "In honor of meeting the hero."

Alar looked down at the crate. Cabbages, carrots, yellow squash, potatoes.

"*Tok*, Hera Wilton," Scilla said, bent down and started stuffing the produce into her pack. She stopped, peering at a cabbage, then looked up with narrow eyes. "These are fresh."

"Yes, well, we didn't have any leftovers yesterday, so I bought extra today." He glared down at her. "You don't want them?"

Scilla stuffed the cabbage in her pack, stood and gave Wilton a hug. "Thank you."

"S'nothing," he said, a red flush appearing above his whiskers. "Just don't want to see you in the state you was when you first came around." He regained his composure and winked at Alar. "Got to make sure the great hero has enough to eat." He laughed again. "Now, I got to get back to the kitchen. Just leave the crate when you're done."

"Funny man," Alar said, staring at the closed door, then stooped to help Scilla stow the vegetables.

***

Alar looked up as they neared their base. Lief waved from the top of the ridge then disappeared. When he and Scilla reached the top, they found the boy sitting on a granite shelf, Alar's copy of *The History of the Empire*, open on his knees.

"You reading that?" Alar asked.

"Trying to," he answered.

"It's a tough read," Alar said. "In more ways than one." Though Lief learned the basics of reading before joining *oss'stera*, Alar completed his education using a primer he stole from a school in a nearby village. "You finished the reading primer, maybe you should try *Tales of the Seidi Sisters* before tackling this." *Tales* was a children's storybook, but it was the only other book Alar owned.

"Read it, already," Lief said, closing the thick tome and setting it aside.

"You read it already?" Alar asked. "When did you do that?"

"When you weren't watching, apparently."

Alar glanced at Scilla. "Apparently."

He dropped his pack to the ground, fished out the boots, and held them out.

"What's this?" Lief asked.

"Boots. For you," Scilla said. "Yours are in such a state, we got you a new pair."

Lief took the boots, peered into the interior, then set them on the ground. He removed his old boots, put on the new pair, and stood, looking down and wiggling his toes. He looked up at Alar and said, "These are nice. *Tok.*"

Laughing, Alar clapped him on the shoulder, retrieved his pack and followed Scilla.

"I think he liked them," she said.

"Positively gushing," Alar answered with a grin.

They paused at the edge, looking down into the crowded space around the fire. Along with everything else, fuel for their fires was becoming problematic now that they had food to cook. At least the chore of gathering and bringing firewood to the base of the cliff was one made easier by their growing membership.

"Getting crowded," Scilla said, breaking into his thoughts.

"That is one problem I may have a solution for," Alar said. Before he could elaborate, someone called his name.

Alar looked toward the voice and found Stolten waving. Tall and rangy, the man arrived a week before with his wife, Inga. The two of them were exactly the kind of people Scilla and Alar were looking for; full of cheer, enthusiastic, quick to volunteer when something needed to get done. His call alerted others to Alar and Scilla's presence, and soon, more people were waving and calling their names. Alar smiled, scanning the upturned faces, until he noticed Sten and Erik. The two sat alone, as far from everyone else as they could get in the small space. Unlike the others, they weren't smiling. Erik put his hand on Sten's shoulder, leaned in, and spoke urgently. "Uh oh," Alar murmured.

Alar, Scilla and Lief returned from Kartok full of plans, determined to capitalize on their victory over the Inquisition. Alar was sure their exploits would energize Sten, and with his old fire rekindled, the man who inspired Alar would breathe life into *oss'stera*. It would be like the old days, except this time, Alar would be an equal partner. He was determined to make the older man's vision real.

What they found when they arrived home was far from that fantasy. In their absence, *oss'stera* dwindled to six disconsolate members. There were never so few, not even in the early days. Instead of the triumphant return Alar imagined, Sten greeted him with the same flat resignation he had shown for months. Erik could barely bring himself to hide his disappointment that Alar survived.

Feeling they arrived in the nick of time, Alar launched into their tale, confident he would win Sten's approval. Instead, the man who had been as a father to him, rebuked him for provoking the Inquisition. A heated argument ensued. It was a crushing disappointment, and in the morning, they discovered two more left during the night. Alar began to wonder if it was worth the effort. It was Scilla, still fired by the *oss'stera* of her imagination, who lifted him up. With the imperturbable Lief in tow, she dragged him into the nearby villages and started making friends. They began to build a network of sympathetic *Alle'oss*, people in a position to help, even if it was in small ways. People trickled in, most of them familiar faces. Some of them brought others they met while away. The old hands were surprised to find food, organization, and a renewed sense of purpose. The new members, having never experienced the bad times, were full of optimism.

Initially, Sten watched this with a hint of his old fire, but as Alar, Scilla and Lief's status rose, he soured. The new arrivals didn't regard him with the same reverence as the old members and weren't afraid to scoff at some of his more unlikely ideas. Alar suspected Erik, whispering in his old friend's ear, didn't help matters. A confrontation with the two men was inevitable.

When Alar and Scilla climbed down, Sten and Erik were waiting for them.

"We need to talk," Sten said.

Alar handed his pack to Scilla, and asked, "Can you take care of this?" He looked Sten in the eye and asked, "What's this about?"

"It's getting a bit crowded, is what it's about," Erik answered before Sten could respond.

Surprised, Alar hesitated. He expected a discussion about leadership, the deference the two men felt they were owed, strategic priorities, or the shift in leadership of the group. "Crowded?" he blurted. He glanced at Erik, then stepped closer to Sten. "'The *Alle'oss* will flock to our cause.' That's what you used to say." The lines on Sten's face smoothed. "Did you mean that, or was that just wind?"

"Of course, I meant it. It's just ... we're not ready," Sten said, his eyes cutting to Erik.

Alar looked from Sten to Erik. "It's been years. When, exactly, will we be ready?"

Sten started to speak, closed his mouth, and glanced at Erik.

"We don't have enough space," Erik said, waving his arm around the camp.

Alar laughed. "When the great revolution comes, when the flocks arrive, did you think we would squeeze them all in here?" Before Erik could respond, Alar leaned toward Sten and said, "We'll find more space. I have a plan for that."

Sten hesitated. "It's not just the space. How are we going to feed and clothe all these people?"

"I'm sure he has a plan for that, too," Erik said with a snort.

Alar pointed across the clearing to where Scilla and Stolten were sorting through the vegetables. "I'm sure you've noticed we haven't eaten this well in years."

"Vegetables," Erik scoffed. "What are you going to do in winter?"

"Most of these people showed up with only the clothes on their back," Sten said more gently. "They'll not make it through the winter."

The two men had been at this game far longer than Alar. They were right, and they knew it. Noticing Alar's uncertainty, Erik grinned in triumph. "We're not ready. Yet." He waved a hand that took in the entire camp. "You'll need to tell these people they need to go home."

Alar stared at him. "Home? You think they left their comfortable homes to sleep on the cold ground, eat whatever we can scrounge, because they had a choice?" He tried to catch Sten's eye, but the older man looked away. "You're right, more people means more problems. But if we ever want to make the changes you used to talk about, we'll need this many and a lot more. *Oss'stera. Our* struggle. It doesn't take a holiday in the colder months. We'll figure it out. We'll have to." He appealed to both of them. "You can help." He slammed his mouth shut before adding, "instead of sitting around the fire all day, complaining and eating the food we find."

"Maybe, if we wait until Spring. After the thaw. It'll give us a chance to plan—" Sten said.

"Plan?" Alar asked. "The same plans you've been talking about for years?" Alar noticed the pain on the older man's face and forced himself to take a breath. "Sten, we're putting a network together. *Alle'oss* who want to help. Like you always talked about." Erik snorted, but Alar ignored him. "Sure, they're not ready to show their support openly, but that takes time. If we show them they can trust us, that they can believe in us, others will flock to our cause and be willing to help. Isn't that what you said?"

"Yes, yes," Sten said. "It's good, what you, Lief and the girl are doing. But it's like Erik said … let's wait until Spring."

"Why? Why should we wait?" Alar waved to the gathering, who grew quiet as the confrontation intensified. "They're here now, and they want to believe in something. Let's give them something to believe in."

"How are you going to feed them?" Erik asked stubbornly. "No one's going to give us vegetables in the winter."

Alar hesitated. Erik was nodding, but there was a hopeful expression on Sten's face as he waited for Alar's response. "I … I have a plan," Alar said.

"A plan?" Sten asked doubtfully.

"What plan?" Erik asked.

"I'm not ready to talk about it. Yet," Alar said. "We'll be able to feed and clothe everyone. Get everyone through the winter."

"Right," Erik said. "Well, when you're ready to reveal your plan, I'm sure we'll be impressed." He turned and walked away.

Sten hesitated. Alar wanted to speak to him without Erik present, but before he could think of what to say, Sten spoke. "Erik is right about the winter. Whatever your plan is, it needs to come to fruition before the snows come. Otherwise, you should tell most of these people to find a safe place to winter." He turned and followed Erik before Alar could respond.

Alar, his breath coming shallow and fast, watched Sten picking his way through the crowd. They were right. Unreasonable, unfair and unhelpful, they might be, but they were right. A hollowness yawned inside him and swallowed his anger. He had been worrying at the problem for weeks, but was no closer to a solution. In the past, there were so few of them, they could scrounge, trap and hunt for what little they needed. Even so, it was a near thing most winters. Many left during the cold months and some died. A bad winter would be disastrous and squander the momentum they worked so hard to gain.

"You have a plan?"

Alar turned and found Scilla, one eyebrow raised, staring past him at the two men.

When Alar didn't answer, she asked, "You mind sharing what that plan entails?"

"I'm open to suggestions," Alar said.

Chapter 25

Rumors and Less

It took Harold only minutes to conclude Governor Adelbart would be considered corrupt even by the loose standards of Imperial provincial officials. Though he came across as a bit of a blowhard, there was cunning behind his shifty eyes. Still, though he could barely hide his glee at the Inquisition prison break, his confusion when Harold mentioned *oss'stera* appeared genuine. The governor knew nothing of the *Alle'oss* rebels. A perfunctory visit to the local Inquisition commander produced the same results.

Resigned to starting from scratch, he and Henrik shed their uniforms and immersed themselves in the city. In this, Harold had an advantage over most brothers. Having grown up in the streets in Brennan, he had an intimate knowledge of the dark underworld pathways all cities shared. A subversive organization like *oss'stera* couldn't help leaving traces if one knew where to look. Even so, after two weeks, the only hint they uncovered was the wisp of a rumor centered on a small alehouse called the Black Husky. Harold suspected the girl Adelbart conveyed to Kartok was a garden variety criminal. Or, more likely, the governor used the story of rebels as an excuse to escape an embarrassing situation. Harold would have already left had it not been Hoerst who sent him. The inquisitor didn't need an excuse to make Harold's life miserable. He decided long before he reached Richeleau, his only way out was to investigate thoroughly and document everything.

Still, it wasn't all bad. Even though he had only been in Argren for a short time, he thought he understood why the *Alle'oss* loved their mountainous home. For a man who had known little but the dirty streets of the Imperial capital, Argren was a revelation. Clean air, scented only as nature intended, snow-capped mountains soaring above teeming forests and silence, free of the clamorous drone of the capital. All of it was a balm for his clenched soul.

And Henrik had been a pleasant surprise as well. Used to his fellow brothers' oppressive hostility, Harold found Henrik's amiable company liberating. He actually found himself looking forward to their conversations by the fire each night. Dancing the careful steps necessary in the authoritarian Inquisition, they slowly discovered they were of a like mind on many delicate issues. Though Henrik remained guarded about his own story, he slowly loosened up and Harold discovered a thoughtful, educated man behind the stoic exterior. Between the countryside and Henrik's company, Harold felt the accumulated defenses he erected against a hostile world trembling as they climbed into the foothills.

But it was wandering the winding streets of Richeleau that was the true revelation. The city had a relaxed vibrancy that was as different from Brennan as it could be. Unlike Kartok, Richeleau still had the feel of an *Alle'oss* city and the citizens of Argren made up the majority of the populace. Like Brennan, there were also Imperials, Unionists from across the Southern Sea, a handful of Tsadans from the east, and even dark-skinned Tituun from the far north, but free from the Empire's oppressive caste system, the people of Richeleau lived in easy harmony.

He returned from his thoughts and focused on the door to the Black Husky across the street. For the past three days, he and Henrik loitered in nearby establishments, allowing people to become accustomed to the Imperial newcomers. Though they weren't wearing their uniforms, they couldn't hide their black hair. Fortunately, the district attracted a mix of revelers, so it wasn't long before people got over their curiosity.

Harold turned his gaze on Henrik. Though they spent six weeks together, Harold knew no more about the brother's background than when they left Brennan. If the man bobbed and weaved as deftly in combat training as he did when Harold asked about his past, he would be a formidable opponent indeed.

"Henrik, you realize we're trying to blend in," he said.

Henrik lifted his ale stiffly and took a sip. "Yes, sir."

"You look as if you're standing at attention, even when you're sitting," Harold said. "And stop saying sir."

Henrik glanced down at himself. He appeared to give it some thought, then he slumped in his seat and threw one arm over the back of the chair. The effect was even more awkward than before.

"That's ... better."

"Thank you s ... inquis ..." Henrik's mouth snapped shut. He stared at Harold for a moment, then pivoted in his seat toward the window. Noticing his arm draped over the back of the chair, he winced and rearranged himself so that he merely appeared painfully introverted.

Harold shook his head and looked out the window. They woke that morning to a cold, gray day, and while they sat in the alehouse, the first snowflakes of the season began drifting in the still air. Even so, as evening approached, the scene gathered energy. A variety of scents wafted through the open window; the rustic, uniquely spiced fare of the *Alle'oss*, the elegant, rich cuisine of the Empire, and even a whiff of the bold spices of the Union.

He watched a group of Union mercenaries in their elaborately decorated leather armor making their way down the opposite side of the street. They towered over the natives, who parted before them like a bow wave. "What do you suppose Union mercenaries are doing in Richeleau?" he mused.

"The emperor is draining the local garrisons to fill the ranks of the legions in the south," Henrik said. "Rumor has it the skirmishes with the Kaileuk are only a precursor to something bigger."

"Hmm. I hope Ludweig isn't that stupid." Harold cut his eyes to Henrik, gauging his reaction to what could be considered treason, but the brother, watching the Black Husky, didn't react. Harold followed his gaze. "Hold on," he said, sitting up.

"Sir?"

Harold lifted a brow.

"Sorry."

"That boy, the one with the blond hair." He looked to be in his teens. His clothes were typical of the *Alle'oss* who lived outside the larger cities, but his worn garments had seen better days.

"What about him?" Henrik asked.

"A little young for this crowd, don't you think?"

"Could be."

When the boy reached the cafe next to the Black Husky, he stepped into the doorway, affected a casual slouch and looked back the way he came. "That looks like someone checking for a tail," Harold said.

They watched as the boy stepped onto the walkway and entered the Black Husky. Harold and Henrik looked at one another. "You go around back. I'll give you five minutes before I go in," Harold said.

Henrik started to speak, checked himself, then nodded and stood to leave. They scouted the neighborhood and knew the only other entrance to the tavern let out into a small alley in the back. Once he gave Henrik enough time to get into position, Harold crossed the street, keeping an eye out for anyone paying attention. He stepped into the tavern door and paused to give his eyes time to adjust to the dim interior.

***

Jora nodded to Alar when he entered the tavern. Alar hesitated, scanning the room for the mercenaries he tangled with the last time he was here. Finding the room nearly empty, he ambled to the back of the tavern and leaned on the bar. Jora plopped a mug down in front of him.

"What news, Jora?"

"Your last visit caused quite the stir," Jora said.

"No problems, I hope."

"Nah. Fact, business perked up a bit for a while." Jora wiped the bar down while he spoke. "Everyone wantin to hear the tale of the *Alle'oss* boy who took down some Union mercs." He nodded to two old men at a table in the corner. They were leaning close, talking excitedly and glancing at Alar. "Evert and Olaf were here. Never been so popular."

Alar scowled. For a member of an underground resistance, being recognized was a liability. He would have to explore disguises. "Anything else? Something useful?"

"Rumors and less," the proprietor said. "Seems someone attacked the Inquisition prison in Kartok." Misinterpreting Alar's expression, he said, "I know. Bit farfetched." He rested both hands on the bar, thick fingers drumming, and let his gaze go to the ceiling. "Let's see. The only story going around with the ring of truth was that a couple of inquisitors arrived a couple of weeks ago. Heard that from multiple people."

Alar was about to take a sip, but stopped, the mug suspended above the bar. "They still in Richeleau?"

"No idea. No one's seen them lately."

"And no one saw them leave?"

"No."

A customer called Jora away. Alar, noticing the mug in his hand, took a sip. Inquisitors in Richeleau was bad enough, but if they were keeping a low profile, it meant they were looking for something. Of course, they may have left unnoticed, but given the level of fear the Inquisition inspired, it didn't seem likely.

"If you want a good brandy, you can't do worse than *Alā llok*."

Jora's words knifed through Alar's musings. *Alā llok* meant run. He turned and made for the back of the room. As he entered the back hallway, he glanced at the man standing at the front of the tavern. He was backlit, so his face was in shadow, but his hair was unmistakably Imperial black.

As soon as the door closed, Alar sprinted to the exit, then stopped, hand hovering over the latch. If they were coming in the front door for him, they would have the back covered.

Alar looked back toward the door into the tavern in time to see the latch lifting. As the door swung open, he stepped into *annen'heim*.

He crouched, listening. Seeing the spirit leave the body of the Imp in Kartok left an indelible impression on him. Hearing only distant wails, he turned his attention to the man frozen in the act of pushing the door open. The door was only open halfway, but there was enough room for Alar to squeeze through. He studied the man. He wore no uniform, but the cut of his hair suggested military. Or Inquisition. The only anomaly was his eyes. They were lighter than they should be for an Imperial. Alar rested his hand on the knife at his hip. He didn't know this man, or what crimes he may have committed. Was the accident of birth enough to condemn him? Did he deserve death just because he was Imperial? No, but Alar knew, somehow, this man was one of the inquisitors Jora mentioned. He let his gaze drift across Jora and the patrons in the tavern who were focused on what was happening at the back of the room. If this was an inquisitor, killing him might condemn these people to the Inquisition's dungeons, even if they weren't involved.

Alar took one last, lingering look at the man, committing his face to memory, then made his way out the front door. Once he found a private spot far from the busy street, he returned to the physical realm. What was an inquisitor doing in Richeleau? But even before the thought was fully formed, the answer came to him. The rescue. Scilla was sent to Kartok from Richeleau, so it wasn't a stretch to believe the Inquisition sent someone to investigate. He thought about Jora. Surely, they wouldn't connect him to *oss'stera*.

***

Harold's eyes adjusted in time to see the boy disappearing through the door at the back of the tavern. He hurriedly wove through the tables, ignoring the shout from the man behind the bar. As he was pulling the door open, he thought he saw something move, but by the time he was standing in the doorway, the hall was empty. He rushed to the back door and pulled it open. Henrik was waiting in the small yard.

"You didn't see anyone come this way?" Harold asked.

"No, sir."

Harold stepped back, holding the door open so Henrik would follow. They positioned themselves on either side of one of the privy doors and Harold knocked. "Come out in the name of the Inquisition." There was no response. He pushed the door open and found it empty. The other privy was empty as well. Harold stood in the hallway, hands on his hips, studying the floor and the ceiling.

"Sir?" Henrik asked.

Harold stomped on the floor. "I saw the boy enter that door. You didn't see him come out. Where is he?"

They examined the walls, floor, and ceiling, but found nothing that might indicate a way out.

Eventually, they exited the back door and studied the back of the tavern.

"Sir?" Henrik asked again.

"Go out front and locate some gendarmes. Get them to seal the tavern. No one in or out. Then go to the garrison. Adelbart has a company of Imperial cavalry. Get a squad and take this place apart."

"Yes, sir," Henrik said, and turned away.

"Bring manacles and a wagon. I think it's time for some more direct questions."

Chapter 26

Propitious Return

Alar blinked in surprise when he found himself at the bottom of the ridge on which their base perched. He had been so occupied by his encounter with the inquisitor, he had no memory of getting home. Reaching mechanically for the first familiar handhold, he glanced up and forgot all about the inquisitor. Scilla was watching him. When she saw him look, the soft smile on her face widened. She waved and disappeared. With the possibility they might be alone when he reached the top in mind, Alar climbed with purpose.

Pulling himself over the lip at the top, he stood, wiping his hands on his shirt. They were alone. Alar held her gaze, recognizing his own feelings in her expression. It was more than physical attraction. That was there from the start. What was new, what he never expected, was how comfortable they had become with one another. They fit. That was the only way to describe it. They studied one another silently until the breeze lifted a lock of hair across her face. Tucking it behind her ear, Scilla grinned and dipped her eyes, breaking the spell.

"Any news?" she asked.

Caught off guard, Alar managed, "News?" One of Scilla's brows lifted, her grin sliding into a smirk. "Oh, right, news," Alar said. He indicated a rock shelf they used as a bench, and they sat, shoulders touching. "So, news," Alar said, waiting to see if Scilla leaned away. "Someone attacked the Inquisition prison in Kartok, apparently." They grinned at one another.

"Do tell."

"Yeah. Quite the ...," Alar said, looking from Scilla's hand next to his leg to her blue eyes, which were very close. Scilla's smirk softened. A small lift of her brows added meaning Alar couldn't identify. He looked away, gazing out over the treetops. "And ... uh ... let's see, a couple of inquisitors came to Richeleau." When he looked back, he was disappointed to find the tantalizing smile replaced by a worried frown.

"Inquisitors?" she asked. When Alar nodded, she asked, "What do you suppose they're doing in Richeleau?"

Alar sighed inwardly. The moment apparently passed, he leaned away, opening a gap between their shoulders. "I was wondering about that myself."

Scilla stared at him for a moment, then looked toward Richeleau. "They could be looking for *oss'stera*."

Alar felt a chill go through him. It was the same thought he had. They always kept an eye on the local inquisition brothers, but never considered them a threat. But, out of all the establishments in Richeleau, the inquisitor entered the Black Husky and followed him when he ducked out the back. It didn't feel like a coincidence. "The prison break," he said.

Scilla nodded. "The man who told me they were handing me over to the Inquisition said it was because I was asking about *oss'stera*."

"And then we broke you out of their prison," Alar said. If *oss'stera* had come to the attention of the Inquisition, they would come to regard their deadly cat and mouse games with the local Imps as the happy times. "Even if that was true, what can they find? We've been careful. At least before you and ... Sorry."

Scilla bit her lower lip and sat up straighter, widening the gap between them. "No, you're right. We put everyone in danger."

Alar shifted around to face her. "You didn't know." She lifted her hands from her knees and started to speak. Alar took her hand and said, "We've been living this life a long time. You couldn't have known."

Scilla didn't answer. She gazed down at their hands, then entwined her fingers with his and peeked up at him.

Alar stared at their hands. How did that happen? He looked up. Finding the smile returned, his mind went blank. Free from worries about inquisitors, the corners of his lips rose into a smile that mirrored hers. Suddenly, somehow, they were close. Their lips touched. Tentative, only a brush. Then they were apart, and he was gazing into her eyes, unsure what came next.

Alar had eight summers when the inquisition killed his parents. For years, that horrible event eclipsed his memories of what they were like with one another. Eventually, he was able to recover happier memories. His father sweeping his mother into his arms. His parents gently teasing one another while his sister rolled her eyes. He liked to think they were affectionate with one another. But those were faded memories, more emotion than detail. As he entered his teenage years, he hung onto the stories told by the changing cast of rebels; boasts about love conquests or reminiscences of lost lovers. There were even a few couples who made their small camp home briefly, though cramped space and desperate circumstances kept them chaste. It wasn't that he didn't know about sex. He grew up on a farm, after all, and had worked out how it must work for people. But the ways of men and women, the gulf between that simple kiss and intimacy, was deeply mysterious. Scilla's kiss, as simple and brief as it was, left him breathless, prickly hot and overwhelmed. He stared as Scilla leaned forward, her eyes sliding shut.

Alar pulled away. When Scilla opened her eyes and frowned, he put his finger to his lips. He was sure he heard Tove laughing. He heard it so rarely, her distinctive laughter, free and unrestrained, was imprinted on his brain. He stood and waded through a confusing mix of relief and regret to the edge of the cliff. When he caught sight of the two people approaching, his mouth fell open. Tove climbed the low slope toward the base of the ridge, laughing and glancing over her shoulder at Ukrit, who was gesturing expansively and speaking animatedly. He felt Scilla come up beside him, felt her heat where she pressed against him. He glanced at her, hesitated when he saw her eyes so close, then asked, "What's going on there?"

"Looks like they made friends," she said and stepped away, breaking contact.

"Friends?" Alar asked doubtfully, glancing down at his abandoned shoulder. "Tove and Ukrit?"

"You'd be surprised," Scilla said with a chuckle. "Ukrit can be very charming."

"Ukrit? You sure we're talking about your brother?"

"Every girl in the valley has eyes for my brother," she said. "Quite irritating at festivals, to be honest."

Her lips twisted in a distracting way. When she noticed him watching, her mouth curved into a grin. His gaze lifted to her eyes. The blue of her irises darkened toward the center, becoming almost a rich Argren blue near her pupil. How had he never noticed that?

"Hello! Anyone up there?" It was Tove's voice.

Alar dragged his gaze away from Scilla's tantalizing smile and looked down. When she saw him, Tove smiled broadly, waved and begin to climb.

She arrived at the top of the ridge, breathless, sweaty and excited. Alar reached down, took her hand, and pulled her up into a hug.

"Wait!" She fought free of his arms and unslung a wool pack from her back, from which she extracted a bow. It would have been two paces long had the last eight inches of the tips not curved. Holding a hand up to forestall any questions, she dug into the pack and retrieved a length of sinew she used to string the bow. Nearly vibrating with excitement, she grinned up at Alar, plucked the string producing a sharp twang, then held it out to him. Alar took the bow and drew the string back experimentally.

"That's yours. I made it," Tove said and blushed when Alar returned her smile. She ran her finger along the belly of the bow. "It's mountain yew. That's the best wood to use."

Alar grinned down at her, but she was so intent on her explanation, she didn't notice.

She ran her finger along the back. "It's backed with sinew. It makes it less likely to crack. Did you know you can make glue out of deer hide?" she asked, a serious frown on her face. She glanced up, the furrows on her brow smoothing. Alar lifted a brow, and Tove nodded vigorously. "Yeah, it's called hide glue. Who knew, right?" She plucked the string. "That's elk sinew." Her smile grew wider. "I shot the elk with the first bow I made."

"It's beautiful, Tove," Alar said.

"Yeah," she said, reaching out to touch the bow with one finger.

Alar handed the bow to Ukrit, who had arrived red-faced and puffing, and pulled Tove into a hug.

"Wait, wait," she said. She struggled free, bent down, picked up the pack she discarded and held it in front of her with an expectant smile.

"Bows," Alar said in wonder. "A lot of bows."

"Ten and Ukrit has another fifteen, plus arrows."

"How did you make so many?" Scilla asked and thumped her brother's chest.

"Ouch!"

"Ukrit spread the word," Tove said and gave him a grin.

"There are a lot of people in the valley unhappy with the deal the governor forced on them," Ukrit said. "Once we let them know what we were doing, people volunteered. We could have brought more if we could carry them."

"I can't believe it," Scilla said.

Alar rested his hand on the bows. "Tove," he glanced at Ukrit. "And Ukrit. You may have just saved us."

"What do you mean?" Scilla asked.

"I think I have a plan to get us through the winter," Alar said.

***

Harold settled himself in the chair across from the proprietor of the Black Husky. The man watched him warily. The inquisitor glanced down at a document Henrik handed him. He waited, allowing the prisoner to become nervous. When Harold looked up, Jora was putting on a brave face, but he couldn't hide the fear haunting his eyes.

"Jora Wotan," Harold said.

"Aye."

"You've owned the Black Husky for ten years. Nothing on your record. No arrests, nothing to suggest treason."

Jora's face went slack for a moment. Harold watched, knowing whatever expression emerged would reveal a lot. The guilty were careful about showing fear. Outrage was what they thought was the less guilty response.

"Treason! No, course not."

Harold studied the man's face. Fear, but something else as well. "Why, then, do I hear rumors you've been associating with known rebels?"

"You're talking about those kids who come around asking about rebels," Jora said quickly, as if he was expecting the question. "That what the emperor's got you doing? Chasing rumors of kids playing rebel?"

"What does *alāllok* mean?"

Jora sat back, suddenly nonchalant. "It's, uh, brandy, a local specialty."

"It must be very local because no one else I've asked has heard of it. In fact, they tell me it's an *Alle'oss* word that means 'run'."

The blood drained from the man's face. His eyes flicked to Henrik, then he leaned forward, resting his manacled hands on the table. "Listen, the boy, the one you chased. He lost his entire family to the Inquisition. Inquisitor came for his sister. His parents fought back. Left the boy alone. Thought it was funny, apparently. None of his neighbors would take the boy in, count of the inquisitor told them they would be punished if they did." Jora's eyes rested on the symbol of Harold's rank on his collar. When he looked up at Harold's face, there was defiance in his eyes. "The boy was seven or eight. Been livin on his own since. I told him to run because he's had enough of the Inquisition's attention already."

Harold studied Jora's face. It was probably true. At least he didn't see any deception there. It was a sad story. Still, if the boy turned his anger on the Empire, he was a threat that had to be dealt with. "How did he get away?"

Jora looked confused. "He must have slipped out the back."

Harold shook his head and glanced at Henrik. "We had the back door covered."

"Well, how would I know?" Jora said, his suppressed anger surfacing for a moment. "You near took my place apart. You tell me how he got away."

That had the ring of truth as well, unfortunately. Harold sighed. "Okay, I need his name and the names of any associates."

"He, uh, calls himself Joran. Might be his real name, maybe."

"Hera Wotan, I'm guessing you aren't a member of this *oss'stera.*" Harold noted the small flinch when he said the word. "They come to your tavern for a bit of normalcy, have a drink, share some stories. Maybe you tell them the latest news and rumors. Unlike my colleagues, I'm not a violent man. If I'm right about you, I would be willing to release you with the caveat you refrain from associating with rebels in the future. However, if I were to decide you were withholding information from the Inquisition, that would be treason." He let Jora consider his words before saying, "Punishable by death."

"His name's Joran, as far as I know. Don't know of any associates."

Harold stood abruptly drawing a flinch from the prisoner. "I'm leaving you in the capable hands of Brother Henrik. Perhaps he will be able to jog your memory." The look Henrik gave him as he swept from the room was enigmatic. Not one who relishes the bloody work. Interesting.

Chapter 27

Honutok

Alar gazed at the others expectantly.

"Caves," Lief said.

"They just look like caves." Alar pointed toward the top of the rock formation. "The top is mostly open. They're more like ravines or slot canyons."

"Ravines," Lief said.

"Whoa there, Lief," Ukrit said. "Calm down."

Alar gestured expansively as he explained. "That outcrop in the center makes it look like there are two caves. But if you look closely, it doesn't join the sides at the top." He pointed to one of the dark openings. "It goes back about thirty paces and then it opens out into a large space. A space more than big enough for everyone. At least for now." He pointed to one of the stone cliffs. "The cliffs protect the space from the wind." He looked around at the others as they considered.

"We could get trapped in there," Tove said.

"There's an exit on the far side," Alar said. "The small entrances will be easy to defend and keep us hidden from prying eyes."

"We'll have to build shelters," Scilla said.

"Yep," Alar said. He rested his hands on his hips and beamed down at their new home. "We'll call it *Hanutok.*"

Tove squinted at him. "Shelter town?"

Alar waved a hand. "More or less, but you don't have to translate it literally."

Lief looked up at the snowflakes drifting in the still air. "We better hurry," he said, and headed down the hill toward one of the openings.

Alar grinned at Tove, clapped her on the shoulder and followed.

***

That one hurt. Alar lay on his back, eyes closed, working his ankle, evaluating the extent of the damage. He pulled, letting the rush emanating from the spot in his mind dampen the pain. Deciding it wasn't significantly injured, he opened his eyes to find Tove looking down at him, her pale face framed by dark, snow-laden clouds. When she saw his eyes open, one brow climbed her forehead.

"That one looked like it hurt," she said.

"You *could* try jumping off something a little lower," Ukrit said, offering a hand to help Alar up.

Alar stood and looked up at the boulder from which he jumped, brushing twigs and leaves from his hair. "No, it's got to be high enough to give me time to, you know ..."

"No, we don't know," Lief said.

Ignoring him, Alar clambered back to the top of the boulder. Tove, Ukrit, Scilla and Lief were arrayed around the bottom, looking up at him with skeptical expressions.

"Tell us again what you're trying to do," Tove said.

Alar rested his hands on his hips and looked beyond his four hecklers to a gathering crowd. The members of *oss'stera* were supposed to be toting materials to build shelters into their new home. Apparently, the sight of Alar throwing himself to the ground was too alluring to resist. They sat in small groups amid the piles of thatch, clay, and sticks, chattering and laughing at his expense.

Looking down at Tove, he said, "In Kartok, when I fell—"

"Jumped," Lief said. "Right?" He looked at Tove. "It looked like he jumped."

"That's what I saw."

Alar's lips twisted. "You said you didn't see because you were keeping watch."

"We lied."

"My trusted lieutenants," Alar said to Scilla. "Anyway, as I was saying …" He paused and glared. "When I *fell* off *Zhot ti* and crossed into *annen'heim,* I stopped falling. I sort of hung there." He mimed his efforts to turn over, twisting at the waist and waving his arms. "I couldn't move."

His effort to explain himself only drew grins.

"So, you're trying to figure out how to fall in the underworld?" Ukrit asked.

"No, not fall. Sort of …" He bent his knees, extended his arms to his sides and made small flapping motions. "Glide." He let his arms fall. Ignoring the snickers, he said, "Something Ragan said made me think I could move around *annen'heim* like a spirit."

"What, exactly, did she say?" Scilla asked.

Alar screwed his face up and gazed up into falling snowflakes. "It was something like, while I'm in *annen'heim* I'm not fully physical, but I'm also not fully a spirit. The part I remember clearly was when she said, 'At first you can't move through *annen'heim* as a spirit would.' I'm sure she said, 'at first'."

"So, you're thinking that means you can *learn* to move like a spirit, float around like a *sjel'and?*" Tove asked.

"Right."

Thoughtful expressions settled onto their faces.

"How is it you can walk?" Lief asked. "I mean while you're in there?"

"That's a good question," Ukrit said. "I mean, if you just sort of float instead of fall, how is it you can push off with your feet to walk?"

"And you said you sink into things," Scilla said. "Why don't you sink into the ground?"

Alar's mouth opened, then snapped shut when he realized it was a good point.

"Maybe because you know how to walk already," Tove said.

"What does that mean?" Lief asked.

"I mean, he and his spirit ..." She wiggled her fingers in front of her forehead. "They walk around in this world." She gestured around with her arms extended. "So, you know, you and your spirit already know how to work together to walk. You move your legs and the spirit knows what you want to do."

"But he already knows how to fall," Lief said. "He just proved that. Repeatedly."

"But he doesn't have to *do* anything to fall," Tove said. "He doesn't have to tell the spirit ... or the other way around, whatever ... how to fall. He just falls. He has to *decide* to walk. He doesn't have a choice when he falls."

"Right," Scilla said. "I get it."

"You understood that?" Ukrit asked. "What did she say?"

Waving off Scilla's response, Alar asked, "So, you're saying I have to tell my spirit how to fall?"

"Don't give me that look," Tove said. "You're the one with the ..." She lifted her hand and wiggled her fingers beside her temple this time. "But yes, that's what I'm saying. More or less."

"Right," Alar said. He focused on the spot in his head. It had to be his spirit. *How do I talk to it? Maybe it understands me, even if it can't answer?* He looked down, but before he jumped, Lief spoke.

"Maybe you should wait until you're closer to the ground before you, you know?" He gazed up at Alar for a moment, then added, "So you don't fall so far."

"Right," Alar said. Focusing on his spirit, he stepped off the boulder, waited a split second longer than before, then crossed the boundary. When he opened his eyes, he was hanging upright, his toes a pace above the forest floor. Scilla and Ukrit were wincing. Lief watched with his usual impassivity. Tove grinned in anticipation.

Alar stretched his toes toward the ground, bent his knees, and thrust his feet downward. Nothing. He hung helplessly. Fortunately, the cries of the *sjel'and* were far away. He closed his eyes, relaxed, and focused on his spirit, picturing himself standing on the ground. Nothing happened. *This is ridiculous.* He exploded into motion, flapping his arms and kicking his feet, willing himself toward the ground. Falling limp, he hung like the creepy scarecrow in his father's cornfield, gazing at Tove's grinning face. *Glad she didn't see that.* He was preparing to return to the physical realm when it came to him.

Stairs! Walking, but downward. Focusing on his spirit, he closed his eyes and pictured himself descending stairs, his feet moving in sympathy. The hum that suffused his mind warbled, then rose in pitch for a moment. *Did my spirit answer me?* Distracted by that thought, he didn't notice himself descending. There was no sensation of movement, but when he opened his eyes, he was *standing* on the ground.

He threw his hands above his head and whooped, but before he recrossed the boundary, his eyes fell on Tove. It would be childish to return the favor of her prank in Kartok. Unbecoming of the leader of *oss'stera.* Still … He walked around behind her and recrossed the boundary. Unfortunately, the gasps of the gathered members of *oss'stera* alerted his quarry. She whirled around and caught him with his hand extended.

"You did it!" Scilla and Ukrit said together.

"You flew?" Tove asked.

"Like a bird," Alar said with a grin. "Or, more like a falling feather, but you get the idea."

"Can you fly up?" Lief asked and nodded to the top of the boulder.

Alar looked up and noticed the dusting of snow on top of the boulder. He looked up at the sky, then turned toward the watching crowd. "Maybe later," he said. "Alright everyone, back to work! We all want warm places to sleep."

***

"Anything?" Harold asked as Henrik entered the small office the local gendarmes allowed them. They could have taken an office at the local Inquisition house, but when Harold reported to the commandant, the man made no effort to hide his contempt. The less time he had to spend in that man's presence, the better. The gendarmes were *Alle'oss*, and though Harold could tell they weren't quite sure what to make of brothers sharing their space, they kept their opinions to themselves. Besides, if you wanted to get some information in an unfamiliar city, it was a good idea to cozy up to those charged with keeping the peace.

"Nothing so far," Henrik said, sitting and leafing through the daily reports.

It was what Harold expected. They distributed descriptions of the *oss'stera* members the tavern owner gave them, but the descriptions were generic enough to apply to most of the *Alle'oss* in Richeleau. Besides, he was beginning to wonder if it was worth all the trouble. Based on Jora's description, *oss'stera* sounded like a group of kids who suffered from the Empire's rough handling and were living out revenge fantasies in the forest. So far, they had been no more dangerous than garden variety thieves. If it weren't Hoerst who sent them, he would turn it all over to the locals and go home.

"He going to be okay?" Harold asked Henrik.

The brother looked up. "Who, Jora?" When Harold nodded, Henrik returned his attention to the report he was reading. "Eventually. Nothing permanent. You want me to spring him?"

Though he tried to hide it, Harold could hear Henrik's concern for the tavern owner. It was little things, like the fact he referred to the man by his first name. Harold hadn't seen Jora since handing him over to Henrik, but he guessed Henrik hadn't resorted to the harshest of their arsenal of interrogation tools. "Not yet. Let's see if we get lucky before word gets out."

Harold watched Henrik poring over one of the pages. The question of why this man was a brother of the Inquisition was on the tip of his tongue before he pulled it back. It would only be met with the same evasiveness as all of Harold's attempts to get to know him. There was also the danger such a pointed question might push him further into his shell, and Harold would regret that. He liked the taciturn brother. Henrik hadn't once insinuated anything about Harold's caste, and his indifference seemed genuine, not in deference to Harold's position. His humanity was a nice change from the typical thuggery Harold was used to.

His eyes unfocused as his thoughts turned once again to how the boy escaped in the tavern. Jora was right, they nearly took his tavern apart looking for an explanation. Harold even made the cavalry troopers explore the privy, an act he was sure confirmed their dark opinions of the Inquisition. He resisted the possibility for as long as he could, but with no other explanation available, he was forced to consider magic. He didn't know a lot about the sisters of the Seidi. He had long suspected their reputation was more myth than reality. But the boy seemingly vanished into thin air. It certainly seemed like magic. And there *were* sisters involved in the prison break in Kartok.

Feeling slightly embarrassed, he asked, "Have you ever heard of anything like this before? Maybe something in the lore of the Seidi?"

"Hmmm … sir?"

"The boy disappearing."

Henrik paused, gazing at Harold as if he were considering.

"Yes?" Harold asked.

Looking uncomfortable, Henrik said, "My father used to tell a story about sisters called realm walkers."

Harold's brows rose. "Realm walkers?"

"Supposedly, they could enter the Otherworld. While they were in the Otherworld, time sort of stopped in the real world." When Harold frowned and started to ask a question, Henrik rushed on. "I don't remember exactly how it worked, but it would look like they disappeared, then reappeared somewhere else in an instant." He hesitated, then shrugged. "It was just a story my father told."

"Realm walkers."

"Yes, sir."

"But they were women?"

"Yes, sir. I assume so. They *were* sisters."

That was another problem. As far as he knew, only women could wield magic. "Could they take others into the Otherworld with them?"

"I've no idea. Like I said, I don't remember how it worked."

Harold sat back and gazed up at the ceiling. "So, we have runaway sisters who have an ability not seen for hundreds of years. *And* they are in league with a rag-tag rebel group in Argren." He lowered his gaze, and they stared at one another. "I'm having a hard time putting those two together."

***

Alar watched the arrow sink to the fletchings into the practice target.

"That's pretty good."

He glanced at Tove who hovered at his shoulder offering tips. "Pretty good?" he asked with arched brows.

Rather than answer, she plucked an arrow from the dozen or so thrust into the ground at his feet, held it out and met his gaze. "Do it again."

When her hair grew out, Alar expected her to retreat behind her veil. To his surprise, she sheared off the black tips, leaving her hair shorter than it was in Kartok. The scar that descended from below her eye and crossed her lips near the corner was as livid as ever, but Alar had always suspected the scar on her face was only an excuse. The wounds Tove hid from the world cut much deeper. She still instinctively dropped her head. But since she returned, Alar watched her fighting her reflexive need to hide, forcing her chin up, bunched jaw muscles, revealing the effort it took. Though he hadn't said anything to her, it filled him with so much pride he could barely contain it.

Taking the arrow, he nocked it, drew and released, putting the arrow within inches of the first. When he turned a grin on Tove and found Scilla approaching, his smug boast died on his lips.

"Course it's only twenty paces away," Scilla said.

"That's all we'll need," he said, returning her grin. Conscious of Tove watching them, he forced his gaze away from Scilla and looked down the line of people practicing with their new bows. Ukrit was on the far end, demonstrating the proper form to Stolten and Inga. "How are the others doing?" he asked.

Tove set off behind the line of archers, with Alar and Scilla following. "Scilla and Ukrit have been using bows since they were wee," Tove said. "They're naturals. A handful of the new people are pretty good. Most of the others … well, like you said, it's only twenty paces."

"I don't see Sten or Erik," Alar said.

"No, and I'm not surprised after that row you had with them," Scilla said.

"They weren't fond of the plan," Alar said. "Said I'm going to get us all killed."

"Yeah, I heard that," Tove said. "We all heard it. You ever think it may be time for the two of them to move—"

Alar came to a stop, putting out a hand to stop Tove. "Who's this?" he asked, pointing to a wisp of a girl as she released an arrow. The girl glanced back, revealing crystalline blue eyes. When she saw him pointing at her, she turned around, set her feet and glared.

"That's Zaina," Tove said. "Zaina, this is Alar. Our leader."

Alar turned toward Tove and Scilla. Ignoring their smirks, he asked, "She's had, what, ten summers?"

"Twelve," Zaina said. The set of her mouth dared him to contradict her.

"Twelve," Alar said to Tove. "Why does she have a bow?"

Tove nodded to Zaina. Alar turned to watch as the girl retrieved an arrow, nocked it, and drew in one smooth motion. With the string at full draw, she looked back at him over her shoulder and loosed. The narrow nestled among a cluster of arrows sprouting from the center of the target that was twenty paces past the others. The girl's eyes narrowed. She waited a moment, then turned away and retrieved another arrow.

Alar had the distinct impression he had been dismissed. He took in the women's grins. "She's twelve."

"You had ten summers when Sten found you," Tove said.

"That was—"

"Not different," Tove said.

Noting Zaina's furtive glances as she listened to their conversation, Alar took Tove's arm to pull her away when his attention was drawn to someone approaching at a run from across the meadow. "That doesn't look good."

Tove turned around and followed his gaze. "No, it doesn't."

It was Keth, a recent arrival from the small hamlet of Illiantok.

"Lief," Alar said. Keth accompanied Lief to Richeleau to check on Jora.

Keth's strides lengthened as he drew close, until he stumbled and fell, ending up on his hands and knees at Alar's feet. Alar knelt beside him, resting his hand on the boy's sweaty back. "Take your time, Keth. Get your breath."

Keth sat back on his heels, raising a hand and wincing. "Lief said I needed to tell you—" Grimacing, he fell forward, gasping.

Alar looked up as others gathered around and was surprised and disappointed to find Sten and Erik among them. He caught Scilla's eye and stood.

"He must have done something stupid," Erik said, drawing a nod from Sten. "Got caught stealing or something."

Alar caught Tove's frown and put a hand on her shoulder before she could gain momentum. "Let's give Keth a moment, hear the story, before we jump to conclusions." He glanced at Scilla and saw she was thinking the same thing he was. In the excitement after Tove and Ukrit's arrival, he forgot to mention to anyone about the inquisitors in Richeleau. He threw a guilty look at Tove. When she caught his look, her face clouded over. Alar mouthed the word 'later.' Her eyes narrowed, but she looked away without saying anything.

Finally catching his breath, Keth reached up, took hold of Alar's shirt, and pulled himself to his feet. Alar helped him stand and held him until he was steady.

The boy wiped his mouth with the back of his hand, and said, "Lief … that gendarme he knows. The supply train to Ka'tan. It's leaving early."

It took Alar a moment to put the pieces together, but when he did, he took the boy by the arm and asked, "How early?"

"Lindenlatha."

Alar stared at him. "This Lindenlatha? That's … what day is it?"

"Two days from now," Ukrit said.

"You sure?" Tove asked Keth.

"Yeah. Lief said to get here soon as possible, cause you got a long way to go," Keth said.

"Where's Lief?" Scilla asked.

"He stayed," Keth said, sounding relieved now that his message was delivered. When he noticed everyone staring at him, he said, "We went to the Black Husky, and it was all torn up."

"Jora. Is Jora okay?" Alar asked.

"Don't know. That's why Lief stayed behind. He was going to try to find out."

"Jora wasn't at the Husky?" Tove asked.

"No. The neighbors said the Imps took him away in a wagon."

Sten started to speak, but Alar cut him off. "You did good, Keth." Ignoring Sten's glower, he said, "Sten, take him down to the stream, get him some water." Sten glanced at Erik before turning a mutinous frown on Alar. Alar leaned toward him and spoke in low tones. "See if you can get a little more detail out of him."

Sten stared at him. For a moment, Alar thought he would argue, but when Alar gave Keth a gentle push to get him moving, Sten glanced around at the others. His expression hardened, and he nudged Erik as he turned away. Erik gave Alar a look that was difficult to read, then turned and followed Sten.

"Hmmm," Scilla said, watching the two older men walking in the opposite direction as Keth.

"Yeah, hmmm," Alar said. He turned to face Tove who was watching him expectantly.

"Alright, everyone. Back to your practice," Ukrit said.

Once Alar was alone with Tove, Scilla and Ukrit, he said, "In all the excitement, you and Ukrit getting back, the bows, the plan. I forgot to mention something." When her eyes narrowed, he looked down at his feet and said, "Something that might be important."

"Might be?"

"Probably is," Scilla said.

"She knows?" Tove asked.

"When I got back to camp, I told her. She was here. Then, after you got back, I started thinking I might have overreacted."

"Just spit it out, already," Ukrit said.

"I was in Richeleau, visiting the Husky for news."

Tove, hands on her hips, nodded.

"I might have been chased by an inquisitor. I mean, I don't *know* he was an inquisitor. I just had a feeling."

"Forgot to mention?" Tove's voice rose. "Forgot to mention an inquisitor chased you?"

"Shhhh," Alar and Ukrit said.

Tove looked at Scilla. "You too. The two of you knew, and you didn't think it was important enough to mention?"

Scilla threw an apologetic frown at Alar and said, "I only knew an inquisitor came to Richeleau. He didn't tell me about being chased."

Tove turned her glare on Alar. He lifted his hands in a placating gesture, but Tove wouldn't be deterred. "You, who always lectures the rest of us on security?" She slammed her mouth shut and looked at the ground. When she looked up, she had regained control of her voice. "Tell me what happened. Everything."

Alar told her.

"He said *alā llok?*"

"Yes."

She let her gaze linger on him for a moment, then let her head drop. When she looked up, she said, "I know you had your reasons for not telling me. Both times. But they aren't good enough." She looked at the ground. He heard her sigh. "I thought I was important enough to you that you would have found a way to tell me about this realm walking thing. Then not remembering to tell me about an inquisitor chasing you, even if you weren't sure—" Her voice cracked.

Alar reached out to her. "Tove—"

She shook his hand off. "If we're going to keep to your plan, we need to get everyone moving," she said, turned and walked away.

Chapter 28

Oss'stera Rising

The towering spruce fell across the road with a deafening crack, as if expressing its outrage at being felled after such a long life. Alar acknowledged the two men who emerged from the forest. "That will do," he said.

The men tossed axes into the ditch beside the road, retrieved their bows, and followed Alar to join a small group waiting quietly in the middle of the road. Alar checked on Keth in the distance, keeping watch where the road began a long, gradual descent. The boy's posture, slouched against a granite outcrop at the side of the road, suggested they still had time. The supply caravan leaving Richeleau two weeks early forced them to leave immediately and race to this spot. Though the pace left them little time to sleep and no time to prepare meals, it was worth it. They arrived with just enough time to prepare and rest for a few moments.

Alar took in the faces watching him expectantly. Tove, Scilla, and Ukrit stood in the middle, their hands resting on the tops of their bows. Scilla grinned. They were surrounded by the old hands. The newer members gathered around Stolten, who had taken them under his steady wing. Stolten gave him a nod. Sten and Erik stood alone, their expressions guarded. Twenty-four of the fifty members of *oss'stera*. Ragged, gaunt, exhausted. Most of them still handled their bows awkwardly. Few had killed before. But they were all *Alle'oss* who suffered at the hands of the Empire, and they were eager to strike back. Beneath the fatigue, Alar saw excitement, anticipation. Confidence.

"Everyone ready?" he asked.

They didn't cheer. Though the snow relented, the forest lay hushed beneath a thin white blanket, and the caravan was likely close. Instead, they lifted their bows, held them aloft, and said as one, "*Otsuna.*"

"*Otsuna,*" Alar answered. "Okay, everyone. Remember, stay out of sight until Scilla's arrow." Nods. "No one gets away." More nods, though with some hesitation. "Alright, *andsutra.* Get into position."

Ukrit stepped up beside Alar and watched the group disperse. "Just hope they don't all fall asleep while they're waiting. Be a shame to wake up and find the wagons already gone."

"That crossed my mind, as well," Alar said.

After a few moments, Ukrit asked, perhaps for the twentieth time, "You sure about the escort?"

"As sure as snow," Alar said. "A platoon of Imp calvary, twenty or so."

The caravan left Richeleau every three months, laden with supplies for the garrison guarding the coal mines in the mountains around the city of Ka'tan. If they could capture it, there would be enough food, clothing and other supplies to see *oss'stera* comfortably through the winter.

Alar watched Sten climbing the embankment on the far side of the road. In Alar's younger days, he looked on the older man as a father figure, but Sten rarely cared enough to track Alar's whereabouts. Alar would leave on various adventures, sometimes for weeks, and return to find his absence barely noticed. He didn't hold it against Sten. After all, they were rebels, not family. He had thirteen summers the first time he followed the supply wagons as they climbed laboriously into the mountains along winding roads. Even at thirteen, he recognized the significance of this particular spot as soon as he saw it. In the years since, he came often. He would perch in the densely packed

247

evergreens crowding the slopes, spinning wildly speculative plans while he watched the wagons trundle slowly past. When he related his unlikely stratagems to Sten, the older man would smile indulgently and say, "A simple plan is the best plan."

Alar's plan was simple. A sharp bend in the road hid the old spruce blocking the road. The Imps wouldn't see it until it was too late. The wagons wouldn't be able to turn around on the narrow road. Scilla and Ukrit, their best archers, were stationed at the bend so they could shoot down the length of the caravan. The attackers could pop up at various spots from the dense foliage and loose, but the cover and elevation would make it difficult for the Imps to respond. If they were extraordinarily lucky, they would eliminate the escort with the first volley. Then they would finish off the drivers, clear the road and make their way back to Richeleau on a seldom used road that intersected the main thoroughfare five leagues farther on. Simple.

Wiping damp palms on his shirt, he studied the trees, checking to be sure none of the rebels were visible. Icy rivulets of sweat snaked their way down his ribs. "I'm more nervous than before I rescued your sister," he said to Ukrit.

"That nervous, huh?"

Alar whirled and found Scilla standing beside her brother.

Oblivious to the sparks flying right next to him, Ukrit asked, "You sure about them?"

Alar followed his gaze and found Sten and Erik talking and peering down at them. "No, I'm not." He turned back and said, "But how much damage can they do?"

Ukrit grunted, unconvinced. "*Andsutra*," he said, glanced at Scilla, then set off at a slow jog to take his place.

"*Andsutra*," Scilla said. She hesitated for a heartbeat, then leaned in and gave him a quick kiss on his lips. With an impish grin, she turned and followed her brother.

"Huh," Tove said. Alar dragged his eyes away from Scilla's retreating form. In the week it took them to get into position, Tove's demeanor had not softened. They had little time to talk, so Alar wasn't sure where they stood. When she saw Alar's discomfort, she snorted. "Don't worry about it. You two been hovering around each other since I got back."

Not sure whether she was ready for the easy familiarity they used to share, he gave her a small grin and asked, "You ready?"

"More than ready. Been waiting for this, or something like it, for a long time," she said and turned away.

Alar nodded at her back, took one more look to make sure everyone was hidden, then followed.

***

Men's laughter. The creak of the wagon wheels and the horses complaints on the hill. Alar jerked awake from a light doze. They were coming. He caught Tove's eye and grinned. The corners of her mouth twitched up before she pressed her lips together and looked away. Alar let his gaze linger on her, but she didn't look back. He looked across the road and saw Sten whispering to Erik. While he watched, they disappeared from view. He caught movement in the corner of his eye; Tove nocking an arrow and tugging on the string. The flat, white light filtering through a thin layer of clouds painted the scene in somber hues. The air hung heavy, the forest holding its breath. Alar closed his eyes and breathed deeply, letting clean evergreen scents calm his nerves. He pulled and shivered at the energizing rush.

"*Sheoda*," Tove said softly.

Alar's eyes flew open. Tove, eyes wide, was nodding urgently toward the road. Alar pulled the brush aside so he could see the Imps leading the caravan appearing at the top of the hill. He swore under his breath. They wore the green uniforms of Imperial Rangers, rather than the blue of Imperial Cavalry. These were the elite. Men trained to operate in the mountains. Alar hoped to panic the escort with a sudden onslaught from unseen attackers. These men would not panic. The caravan's normal complement of guards was twenty, but it was clear before the wagons finished coming into view, there were at least double that number this time.

"What are they guarding?" Tove whispered.

Alar could tell from her expression, she was wondering the same thing he was. Could they afford to slink home, empty-handed? Sten and Erik were right, they could not hold *oss'stera* together in the winter without these supplies. But, more importantly, the effect on their morale would be devastating. It could undo all the good work they did since coming back from Kartok. "Let's find out," he said. He nocked an arrow, counted the Imps on this side of the road and picked out his assigned target. The man, a sergeant, slouched in his saddle, rocking gently with the horse's gait. When the ranger neared, Alar drew back on the string and waited on Scilla.

A hint of motion in the corner of his eye was the only evidence Scilla launched the arrow. The lead rider grunted, shivered, then slid from his horse. There was a moment of silence, a shout from the Imp beside him, then *oss'stera* loosed. Though they were not born to the bow, their targets were nearly stationary and close. A dozen Imps fell from the first volley. This was going to be easy. But in the time it took Alar to pluck another arrow from the ground at his feet, the Imps reacted.

As he fit the arrow to his string, a fluttery hum, like a large winged insect, passed by his ear. He ducked and looked up. The Imps were firing into the surrounding trees, loosing arrows faster than Alar thought possible. The wagons accelerated, bouncing as they rolled over the bodies of the fallen soldiers. Alar fired again, missing, then ducked to retrieve another arrow. He looked up, hearing a thock and found an arrow, still vibrating, protruding from a tree inches above Tove's head. The staccato flicking of another arrow passed through the underbrush nearby. He tried to rise to fire again but had to duck down to avoid the rain of arrows flying their way.

"*Vo Kustak*," Tove shouted.

The caravan slowed suddenly as the lead wagon rounded the corner and encountered the barrier. When the remaining Imps saw what was happening, they wheeled their horses around and headed back.

"Uh, oh," Tove said and snapped off a wild shot.

Ukrit and Scilla downed another two, but the rangers were getting organized. They began to coordinate their fire, sending a steady barrage of arrows into the trees. Two rangers concentrated their fire on Scilla and Ukrit, while two more dismounted, drew swords and headed into the trees below their position. Eight more dismounted rangers approached the embankments along both sides of the road. The few arrows the rebels managed to loose, went wildly wide of the mark.

Alar looked across the road and saw Sten disappearing up the slope. There was no sign of Erik. "We will not run away this time," he growled. He crawled over to Tove. "Be ready. I'll distract them, give you time." She nodded, tight-lipped. Alar stepped into *annen'heim.*

He made his cautious way to where the embankment dropped to the road and looked out over the scene. Death was drawing the spirits. The mist roiled, as the *sjel'and* swarmed the glittering spirits of the recently dead. He could only hope they were too preoccupied to notice his presence. He practiced descending in *annen'heim* until he was sure of himself, so when he stepped off the rim, he glided to the ground two paces in front of the dismounted rangers. Nocking an arrow, he drew, aimed and returned to the physical realm.

Shock froze the ranger's face as the arrow entered his heart. Alar recrossed the boundary into the underworld. He repeated the performance on a ranger approaching the far side of the road. When he returned to the underworld, a spirit's deafening roar greeted him, so near it felt like a physical blow. He flinched, ducking on instinct. The mist roiled, as a shadow swept over head. He dove, crossed the boundary, rolled, came to his feet, and sprinted toward the cover of the wagons.

Panic engulfed the rangers' discipline. Casting frantically around for the phantom, they loosed poorly aimed shots at him as he ran. The pressure on *oss'stera* released, they rose as one and rained arrows down on the rangers. Alar looked up and saw Scilla, only her upper body visible, her face twisted by fright, backing up the slope. As he watched, a ranger rose up in front of her.

"Scilla!" he shouted. But before he could step into *annen'heim*, Ukrit appeared behind the ranger and thrust a knife into the man's back. He yanked the knife out and threw the ranger's body sideways. Alar came to a stop and watched Scilla throwing her arms around her brother.

Suddenly it was over. Alar turned in the middle of the road, not quite believing it. Slowly, his comrades rose from their hiding places, staring around at each other with incredulous expressions. A whoop rang out, another, then they were all stumbling out of the brush, sliding down the embankment, grinning stupidly, cheering, laughing, embracing.

Alar's gaze swept across the bodies. Red blood, green uniforms dotting a snow white blanket. Noticing a wounded ranger's feeble movements, his smile faded, the celebration suddenly seeming obscene. But these were Imperial Rangers. They weren't drafted. They volunteered. Volunteered to take on the Empire's dirtiest jobs.

Tove slid down the embankment and thrust her arms into the air, a wide smile stretching her face. She rushed him and threw her arms around him. Alar returned her embrace, rocking her side to side, unable to suppress his smile. He wouldn't let the deaths of Imps darken their victory.

***

Alar let *oss'stera* celebrate for a few minutes, sharing their experiences, laughing the giddy laughter of those who narrowly escaped death. But there was work to do. Grabbing Stolten, he set him to accounting for everyone and tending the wounded. The tree blocking the road had to be cleared. They removed the saddles, tackle and saddlebags from the few horses that hadn't fled, then set the horses free.

Eventually, everyone busy with their assigned tasks, he was forced to confront the issue of what to do with the wounded rangers. It was something they never faced before. When they killed, it was always in the heat of battle, a matter of life or death. At least for most of them. The issue came to a head when Tove and Stolten dispatched a pair of wounded rangers who tried to slink away. Now, while archers kept an eye on the rangers, a small group gathered behind the last wagon, debating the issue.

"They're Imps," Tove said as if she were speaking to a child.

"I know they're Imps," Scilla said, exasperated. "But you just can't kill helpless men, even if they are Imps."

Ukrit and Alar remained silent, listening to the argument. The murder of Scilla's parents was a single incident. Tragic, but merely coloring a moral core forged by a life free of trauma. The blotchy flush on Tove's face set the evidence of what the Empire made of her life in stark relief. Neither would give in, and though they didn't say so, they were waiting for Alar to decide. He knew what he would decide. It was the only choice possible.

"We can't take care of them," Ukrit said, entering the debate for the first time and momentarily quieting Tove and Scilla.

"No, we can't," Sten said. The man appeared after the battle with a pronounced limp. Erik was still missing. "How long before someone notices the caravan is late and comes looking for it? If these men tell anyone what happened, they'll never stop hunting us."

"And if we leave them …" Ukrit said. "What are their chances?"

"How long before anyone finds out?" Scilla asked.

"Three weeks from here to the mines near Ka'tan," Alar said. "Say, a week before they start to wonder if there's a problem, week and a half for a patrol to get here." He shrugged. "Make it five weeks." He gave Scilla a look that invited a counterargument.

"We *could* take care of them," Scilla said, though with less conviction than before.

"Where? And, say they get better, what do we do with them?" Alar asked.

"Be better if the Imps weren't sure what happened here," Ukrit said. "Especially since they saw Alar's little trick."

"Right. Meaning, we can't let them go," Tove said. "And we can't keep them. Who's going to guard them?"

The group was silent, waiting for Alar's decision. Finally, he looked at Tove and gave her a nod. Tove spun around, drawing an arrow as she walked toward the nearest body. Scilla watched her go, then met Alar's eyes and said, "You can't *make* anyone take part in this." When he nodded, she turned and walked in the opposite direction.

Ukrit grimaced at Alar before turning to follow his sister.

Alar sighed and retrieved one of the rangers' fallen swords from the ditch at the side of the road. "Let's get it over with," he said to Stolten.

He approached a young private laying against the embankment, an arrow protruding from his side below his armpit. He wasn't much older than Alar. His eyes widened as he watched Alar approaching. *It's the only way.*

"No!" the ranger said weakly and coughed, splattering his chin with red flecks.

Alar lifted the blade and brought it down on the man's head, cutting off his next words. He yanked the blade free, let his gaze linger on the dead ranger for a moment, then turned away.

***

Miraculously, of the *Alle'oss* only Tiall, a young man from Kartok, was killed outright, though it didn't look good for one of the three who were wounded. Alar put their fortune down to the dense foliage and the embankment.

The wagons were packed with the supplies they expected, and the ones who were able took the opportunity to fill empty bellies.

Alar returned from supervising the removal of the barricade to find Tove and Scilla standing at the back of one of the wagons. He was relieved that there didn't seem to be any lingering animosity between them after the argument over the wounded.

"What is it?" he asked and peered inside the dark interior. Ukrit stood over an ornate chest, out of place among the utilitarian barrels and crates.

"I have no idea," Ukrit said.

"Did you try to open it?" Scilla asked.

"It's locked and none of the Imps have the keys," Tove said.

Alar hopped into the back of the wagon and nudged the heavy chest with his foot. "We better move," he said. "We can figure it out later." He took the winter apple Ukrit handed him, started to take a bite then changed his mind. When the wagon lurched forward, he sat heavily on the chest and gazed into the falling snow. It was a great victory for *oss'stera*. Perhaps in time, it would feel like it.

Chapter 29

The Noose Tightens

The Desulti pulled on her reins, slowing her horse to a stop. She sat motionless in the saddle, her head swiveling as she took in the scene. Fat, fluffy snowflakes drifted slowly in the still air. Only her horse's misty breaths disturbed the quiet. In most ways, the lonely stretch of road was like every other in the mountains. But something was off. Leaning over, she peered at the ground beside the road. *Was that ... ?* Dismounting, she knelt to get a closer look. It was blood. A lot of blood. She stood and gazed around. Now that she knew what she was looking for, she spotted other congealing pools. Minutes later, falling snow would have obscured the evidence.

"Adelbart, you fool," she said aloud. She intended to trail the caravan to keep an eye on it. But since it wasn't scheduled to leave for a few weeks, she took the opportunity to take care of other business. When she returned to Richeleau and discovered the governor sent the caravan early, she left immediately and rode hard to catch up. The first sign of trouble was the Imperial horses she encountered on the road, alone and some of them still saddled. Now, signs of a battle. She had a bad feeling she was too late.

Leading her mount down the road, she studied the ground, trying to gauge the scale of what happened. From the amount of blood, it looked big. Glancing up into the falling snow, she wiped moisture from the stubbly fuzz on her scalp and pulled her hood up. At least she could dispense with the linen wraps on the isolated road.

"No bodies," she said. "What do you suppose happened?" Her horse, no doubt grateful for the rest, merely snorted in response. Noticing a spot of black beside her boot, she bent down and plucked the back half of an arrow shaft from the snow. "Not Imperial," she said, examining the fletchings. "*Alle'oss.*" She let her hand fall to her side and gazed around. "Very confusing." She remounted and walked her horse forward until she rounded the bend in the road and encountered the spruce. The tree was dismembered recently with axes, the remains piled haphazardly beside the road.

She stared at wood chips disappearing beneath the falling snow in the middle of the road. After glancing behind her, she looked at the blue-green needles of the spruce, lifted a bent arm and let it rotate until her forearm was horizontal. "Drop a tree across the road." Turning her horse so she was looking back the way she came, she extended her arms and brought her palms together. "The road is narrow, so the wagons can't maneuver." Lifting her hands outward toward the forest on the slopes, she said, "Ambush the escort from the high ground." She dropped her arms and retrieved her reins. "Hide the bodies so no one knows what happened until spring." The mystery solved, she grinned in satisfaction. "But who would attack an Imperial caravan?" She lifted the broken arrow shaft and flicked a feather. "The *Alle'oss?*" It seemed unlikely, but who else could it be in these mountains?

Whoever it was, if they stole the wagons, they stole from the Desulti. Though she suspected that was incidental, they were in trouble.

She looked down the road, past the remains of the tree. They would have to continue on to Ka'tan, until they found a place to turn around or a take side road. Based on the state of the blood, she was hours behind. The snow already obscured whatever tracks would be visible on the hard surface of the road. Still, there were few places the wagons could leave the road. If she hurried, she should catch them.

She urged her tired mount into a reluctant trot.

**

Harold descended the steps of the gendarmerie, pulling on his gloves. "Is it always this cold this time of year?" he asked Henrik. It occurred to him it would still be warm in Brennan. Breathing deeply of air free of the Imperial capital's stench, he let it out in a misty cloud and thought of his cramped room in the Academy dormitory. Perhaps he should look into one of the thick cloaks the *Alle'oss* wore.

"I imagine so," Henrik said. When Harold gave him an amused look, Henrik added, "We're pretty far north. I expect it's going to get a lot colder, before …" He pursed his lips, looking as if he were gathering himself. "I've been meaning to ask—"

"When do we know we're done?"

Looking relieved, Henrik said, "It's just, I'm beginning to think Jora was right." When Harold lifted his brows, Henrik grimaced and added, "This *oss'stera* seems to be a local problem. The whole thing is beneath the Inquisition."

Harold suspected Hoerst knew that before he sent them, which begged the question: Why *did* he send them? Harold couldn't help thinking he was being set up. Somehow. "Do you think we've done enough to satisfy Inquisitor Hoerst?"

Henrik sighed and looked away. "No." Before he could continue, his face grew attentive.

Harold followed his gaze. Traffic was light, and though it was late in the afternoon, there was enough light to see two men standing on the corner two blocks away. "That gendarme, there … what was his name?"

"Torva," Henrik said. "Look at the one he's talking to."

Harold looked closer. "Looks like a boy."

"Yeah, notice anything about him?"

Harold watched him. Whatever they were talking about, the boy looked upset. Then he understood what caught Henrik's notice. "He's got the same scruffy look and fidgety wariness as our magic man."

"One of the rebels Jora mentioned was a boy. Lief or Leath or something like that."

"We'll never get close on this street."

"You keep an eye on them. I'll go over a block and try to get close."

Harold grunted an affirmation, and Henrik set off at a jog. Harold stepped behind a corner and peered at the pair. Suddenly, the two turned and looked down the side street. A moment later, the boy fled in the opposite direction. Harold set off as Henrik appeared at a run. Torva stuck a shoulder out, but merely brushed Henrik as he passed. The gendarme turned toward Harold, stuttered to a stop when he saw him approaching, then turned and strode away.

"Torva," Harold called.

Torva took two more steps before stopping, shoulders sagging. He turned halfway around and pressed his back against the brick front of a millinery.

When Harold caught up, he said between pants, "Gendarme Torva." He paused to take a breath and give the young man a chance to speak. Torva only glared at him.

Henrik returned, holding the boy by the neck of his tunic. The boy's face was curiously expressionless, and he didn't struggle as Henrik led him to the gendarmerie.

"He's just a boy I know, lives on the street."

Harold dragged his gaze away from Henrik. The gendarme's sullen expression hadn't changed. "What's his name?" Harold asked.

Torva's eyes flicked to the side as he searched for a believable lie. Licking his lips, he started to speak, but Harold interrupted him.

"Think before you speak, Torva," Harold said. "Your future as a gendarme is likely over. That may seem disappointing, but if you lie to me, I can assure you, you'll have larger problems."

Torva searched Harold's face, then seemed to sag within himself. "Lief."

Bingo.

"He's one of them you put out the notice on, but believe me, he's just a boy. He's no rebel."

"Well then, it won't hurt to question him. Or you. Come along."

***

Adelbart leaned back in his office chair and gazed at the empty spot on the wall where *A Summer Day* used to hang. A tap at the door interrupted dark thoughts. The governor sat up, cold sweat breaking out on his scalp. From the cadence of the taps, he could tell Gerold had something urgent to share, and lately Gerold only seemed to bring him bad news.

"Come," he called.

His assistant entered and came to stand before Adelbart's desk. He handed Adelbart a sheet of paper and said, "Odd news from Captain Brennerman. It seems some of our horses wandered into Richeleau on their own."

The governor hadn't read half the report before he sat forward and flattened the document on his desk. He looked up at Gerold's taut face, gave his head a small shake, then read it again. When he finished, he gazed past his assistant. "What does this mean?"

Gerold hesitated. "I checked the identification numbers from their hooves against our inventory." He retrieved another document and handed it to Adelbart. When the governor made no move to take it, he set it on the desk. "All of the horses were issued to the rangers."

Adelbart felt the office shift around him. He focused on Gerold, asking numbly, "Are you sure?"

"Quite sure."

"The wagons? Was there any sign of the wagons?"

"No."

A trickle of sweat dripped down the governor's cheek. "Have we heard from Ka'tan? Did the caravan arrive there?"

"No, nothing so far. But there hasn't been enough time, even if they were aware something was amiss."

Adelbart wiped sweat from his upper lip. "Yes, maybe on the way back ... something ... Send a rider to Ka'tan. Tonight." He loosened his collar and stood. "Tell ... uh ... Captain Brennerman to send a squad ... No, send the entire company. Search the road to Ka'tan."

"Yes, sir."

"I ... uh ... have another appointment, so if there's nothing else." Adelbart barely heard his assistant's response and was only vaguely aware of the man leaving his office. When the door closed, he hurried to the door to his private suite. In the darkened room, he glanced at the far corner where he knew the door to the tunnel was. There was no one there. He wanted to have the door sealed after her first visit, but he was afraid of what they would do to him if he did.

A nervous giggle escaped his lips before he could clamp them shut. He was overreacting. He sent a full complement of Imperial Rangers and had heard nothing from them. Even if something happened to the caravan, surely some of them would have survived to bring news. But the horses. If something happened to the shipment, *she* would come. He crossed to the window, checked the latches and peered into the darkening street below. As if she would simply walk up the street. "Being foolish," he mumbled.

Adelbart counted the days since the caravan left, trying to decide how much time he had. Even if the Desulti knew already, it would take them weeks to arrive. But, for all he knew, the damn Desulti could fly. They always seemed to be where you least expected them. He reached up for the heavy curtain and froze. As before, she made no sound, but the room felt different, as if it were holding its breath. Calling his guards would do no good. He would be dead before he got the words out. For one brief, terrified moment, he considered throwing the windows open and leaping the three stories to the cobbles below.

Instead, he said, "I sent it." When the voice whispered into his ear, he nearly lurched through the glass.

"It didn't arrive," she said. "You sent the caravan early."

"Yes, yes," Adelbart managed. "The interest on the debt—"

"Someone stole the wagons."

"I sent forty rangers to guard it. It's Argren, for Daga's sake. Who in Argren would attack a company of rangers?"

"Turn around."

Adelbart swallowed, licked his lips, turned and pressed the small of his back against the windowsill. Even in the low light filtering through the windows, he could make out the linen strips obscuring the Desulti's face. This time he could see her eyes, but it made her no more human. He didn't see her move, but something cold pricked the soft flesh beneath his chin, pressing until his head tipped back. Something hot, sweat or blood, trickled down his neck, tickling the soft hairs on his chest.

She didn't speak. Didn't ask questions. Didn't need to.

"It was …" Adelbart cast about for a likely culprit, someone to blame, and from the jangling clamor in his mind, he came up with, "Rebels." He saw the Desulti's eyes narrow slightly until the increasing pressure on his throat forced his head back so he could no longer see her. "Rebels. The *Alle'oss*," Adelbart forced through clenched teeth.

"*Alle'oss* rebels?"

What was the name Wolfe mentioned? "Oss … o*ss'stera*," he said triumphantly.

The pressure eased. In the stillness that followed, Adelbart forced a swallow past the blade still pressed to his throat. He breathed deeply through his nose and caught the Desulti's scent. Lavender. An irrational need to giggle almost overwhelmed him.

"Our struggle?" The woman's voice sounded doubtful, but the tip of the knife pulled back infinitesimally.

"What? No. It was oss—" The pressure returned, forcing a whimper from the governor. He waited. Would he feel the blade entering his mouth, plunging through his sinuses before it entered his brain? How quick would it be? Suddenly, the knife was gone. Adelbart sagged.

When she spoke again, it was from the darkness on the far side of the room. "There is nowhere you can run that we won't find you."

There was the whisper of a door, and the room sighed its relief. Adelbart was alone. He slid to the floor, swiping at his neck, and gazing at the blood on his fingers. "Always, the threat before she leaves," he mumbled. "As if I didn't know, already." He took a deep breath that threatened to become a sob, then pressed his mouth shut. After long moments, he sighed. He wasn't sure how, but once again, he managed to kick a problem down the road.

He took hold of the windowsill and pulled himself upright. Maybe he would be lucky, and it really was this group who took the shipment. *Oss'stera.* The Desulti would eliminate that band of rebels and recover her blood money. One problem solved. Another hysterical giggle bubbled up out of him and he let it have its way. "I should have told her it was Chagan."

Chapter 30

One Community

It took the rebels nearly two weeks to return to *Hanutok*. Riding in the wagons over bumpy, winding roads was no treat, but by the time they made it back, they were well fed and rested. They brought the wagons as close as they could to their new home, then set about lugging the contents through the forest.

Stolten's wife, Inga, was waiting at the mouth of the openings in the granite edifice when Alar and Stolten appeared, dragging a travois laden with a barrel of barley. When he saw his wife running toward them, Stolten dropped his load and ran to meet her. Alar leapt out of the way of the falling travois, then settled on to the barrel and smiled at the sight of the two greeting one another.

Inga extracted herself before her husband was ready to relinquish his hug. "Lief isn't back," she said to Alar.

Alar's good feeling drained away in an instant. "He hasn't sent word?" he asked, coming to his feet. When she shook her head, he turned, intending to head to Richeleau. Tove, a coil of rope draped across her body like a sash and a canvas bag containing blacksmith's tools in one hand, stepped in front of him.

"You can't go," she said. Before Alar could protest, she continued, "That inquisitor saw you, knows what you look like. If they got him, you'll try to rescue him and kick up a hornet's nest. You'll get yourself caught and give away our biggest secret."

"Isn't he worth it?" he asked testily.

Her eyes narrowed, but instead of the angry retort he expected, she said softly, "We don't know he's in trouble. Let someone else go check."

"I'll go."

He turned around. Keth was setting a crate of potatoes on the ground. "I know his friend, Torva. I'll go ask him if he's seen Lief."

"You need someone to go with you," Alar said.

"I'll go with him."

Zaina stood next to Inga, a familiar, challenging tilt to her mouth. She was furious when he wouldn't allow her to go with them to ambush the caravan. He caught her twice, trying to hide among the group.

Alar glanced at Tove, who shrugged. He sighed. "Be careful."

"We'll be back tomorrow," Keth said.

He watched the two climbing the hill side by side, trying to make sense of his swirling emotions. Worry for Lief was there, certainly, but in the mix were a sense of helplessness, guilt and something else he wasn't used to. He felt useless. Lief's life may be in danger. The fault was his, but he would have to rely on others to fix the problem. If possible.

"Not like the old days," Tove said, stepping up beside him. "Got responsibilities now. Gotta look at the bigger picture. Can't dive in and hope for the best."

Alar looked down at her and was relieved to find his friend looking back at him. For the first time since she found out about the inquisitor, there was no anger in her expression. Instead, there was sympathy and a hint of the playful grin she reserved for him.

"Your spirit's luck has to do for all of us now," she said. "Not just you."

***

Alar sat on a granite shelf, gazing out over the community they were building. Small roundhouses dotted the space. Shelter from the elements, and for Alar, the first thing that felt like home since he wandered away from his family's farm one rainy day a lifetime ago. *Oss'stera* would not want for sustenance, either, at least for the winter, courtesy of the Imperial governor.

On most nights, there were four fires, one for each of the groups that were coalescing. Sten and Erik still had a small following among the old hands. Ukrit, Scilla and Lief were the center of a mix of old timers and newcomers. The newest, the families, some with children, gathered around Stolten and Inga. The fourth was the misfits, the castaways from society who didn't fit anywhere else. But to everyone, and especially to Alar, they were one community, bound together by shared purpose, not just the circumstance of birth.

Tonight, there was one fire. A massive bonfire in the communal space in the center of their camp. Someone found a bodhran, and the drum was soon joined by a flute. Dancing followed, encouraged by casks of Imperial ale they found among the plunder. All agreed, the dark brew paled in comparison to *Alle'oss* ale, but it flowed nevertheless. They celebrated their good fortune, *oss'stera's* first real victory over the Empire and the lives of their fallen. Alar didn't know what came next for *oss'stera*, but for at least this night, he would try to stop worrying.

"You worried?" Ukrit, sitting beside him, asked.

"Worried?" Alar responded with a soft chuckle. "Always, seems like, but if you're asking if I'm worried about Lief, yes, I am."

Ukrit didn't comment. He sipped his ale and gazed toward the revelers. "Tove looks happier than she's been."

Alar followed Ukrit's gaze and found Tove sitting on a boulder near the fire, outside the ring of dancers. Some of the newcomers gathered on the ground around her, looking up as she spoke. She lifted her hands and mimed aiming a bow, the hand of her extended arm holding a mug. "Mmmm. She's resilient," Alar said. He swiveled to look Ukrit in the face. "I thought you two were— Why are you sitting here with me?"

"Oh, well," Ukrit said. He looked down and cleared his throat. "I *was* thinking along those lines. Never met anyone like her. She's tough but kind of vulnerable at the same time. Like, you want her by your side in a fight, but, at the same time, you want to take care of her."

Alar chuckled. "That sounds right."

"It was a long walk to Lirantok, you know. At first, it was mostly me doing the talking, to fill the silence. But one night, she sort of relaxed and started talking."

"About what?"

"Oh, everything. You, *oss'stera.* I suspect she was just tired of listening to me. Anyway, we were getting to know one another." He cleared his throat. "I let her know what I was thinking one night. About her and me." In response to the sharp look Alar gave him, he lifted his hands in a placating gesture. "Respectful, just letting her know what I felt." Alar turned back to watch Tove, and Ukrit continued. "Tove has had some tough ... experiences ... with men."

Alar turned back to Ukrit to make sure he understood what he was saying. Ukrit nodded. Alar knew Tove suffered as a girl living on the streets of Kartok. Soon after he found her and brought her into *oss'stera,* he probed gently, but she threw up an impenetrable wall. Not wanting to scare her off, he let her know he was available, then left it alone. "I didn't know, not that. Though, I suppose it wasn't hard to guess."

When Alar didn't continue, Ukrit said, "She wouldn't talk too much about it. Just let me know where we stood. She talked about you. A lot." Before Alar could ask, he said, "Not that way. She's just glad to have you as a friend. Sort of restored her faith in men. Up to a point."

Alar looked in his empty mug, then set it aside.

"Turned out really well," Ukrit said in a more cheerful tone. "Once that was out of the way, she sort of opened up, like she was worried I would think there was something wrong with her." Ukrit must have read the hurt on Alar's face, because he added, "Couldn't be you. I think she knows you wouldn't think less of her if you knew. She just didn't want that to be part of your friendship. She doesn't like people feeling sorry for her."

Alar was mulling that over when Scilla emerged from the shadows.

"Hey, Scill," Ukrit said and hopped down.

"Hey," she said.

"Want more ale?" Ukrit asked Alar. When Alar declined, he gave Alar a funny grin. "You two be good," he said and made his way to the party.

Scilla smiled up at Alar. "You want to go for a walk?"

"Love to," he said and dropped to the ground. They stood, looking at one another for a moment, then Scilla hitched up the hem of her oversized, Imperial issue cloak and beckoned him with a nod.

They walked in silence for a time until Scilla stopped. "This is your place, isn't it?" she asked.

Surprised, Alar glanced at the small dwelling he shared with Ukrit, Lief and Keth. "Uh, yes." Suddenly aware of Scilla's closeness, he turned and looked toward the celebration.

"Are you wor—"

Alar reached around her waist and pulled her close. When he saw her impish grin, he said, "I'm tired of worrying. Just for a bit, let's not talk about any of those things."

She gave him a small nod. "Okay." Her eyes cut to Alar's house. "You want to show me around?"

Alar pulled the door open and ducked to enter, then had to step back when he collided with Scilla. He caught her arm to steady her, feeling his face warm. "Sorry. You first."

The interior was lit only by the soft glow of embers in the fire pit in the center of the single room. He set to stoking the fire while Scilla watched, her hands clasping the edges of her cloak at her throat. After coaxing the fire to life, Alar stood and brushed his hands together, eyes wandering the room.

"Which bed is yours?" Scilla asked.

He pointed behind her. "That one." He started to point to the others, reciting who occupied them, then clamped his mouth shut. Taking a slow breath, he sighed it out in a cloud of mist. Though it was warm for the time of year, it was still cold, and the fire would take time to warm the space. He wiped his sweaty palms on his tunic, feeling awkward and foolish. Where was that recklessness he was famous for? He raised his eyes to Scilla, who stood quietly, returning his gaze through a veil of smoke. Gathering himself, he strode around the fire and stopped in front of her. She startled, but didn't back away.

She tipped her head to the side, watching him quietly as he studied her face. When his eyes found hers, he took the edge of her cloak and tugged gently. Scilla let her hands drop, allowing him to reach inside and pull her close. He bent toward her upturned face, his lips hovering over hers. A light brush, an exhaled breath, then he kissed her. He knew, theoretically, that in a real kiss, tongues were involved, but when the tip of Scilla's tongue caressed his teeth, he sucked in a breath in surprise. Tentatively, he reached out and tasted her.

Scilla moaned, lifted her arms around his neck and pressed herself against him. Embarrassed by his body's response, Alar pulled back. Scilla wrapped her arms around his waist and pulled him close. Her frustrated growl, an expression of their shared need, swept away youthful bashfulness, exposing the raw urgency that had been building in both of them since they met in Lirantok.

Alar relinquished the kiss and worked at the clasp of her cloak. Scilla released the belt that cinched his shirt, then tugged the tail up, giggling when Alar mumbled, "How does this work?" Finally, the clasp came free. Letting her cloak fall, Alar tugged his shirt and undershirt over his head and tossed them aside. He bent to kiss her again, but Scilla put a hand to his chest.

"Whoa," Alar exclaimed and pulled back. To Scilla's alarmed expression, he said, "Cold hands."

"Sorry," she said, chuckling. She cupped her hands over her mouth and breathed, then chaffed her palms together. She peeked up, her hands hovering over his chest, then pressed them to his skin. When Alar didn't flinch, she shuffled closer, pressing her lips to his chest and let her fingers trail down his ribs, until they reached his waist. She hesitated, then slid her fingertips inside his waistband and pushed down

Alar released the tie that held his leathers closed and let her push them off his hips. Her fingers danced up his thighs, then reached around and cupped him. While he worked the buttons that secured the blouse of her dress, she let her hands wander. Alar groaned, his fingers losing purchase on the buttons as she wrapped him in a warm hand, squeezing and tugging gently.

Moaning, Alar let his arms fall limply to his sides as they both gazed at her hand. She looked up from their connection, a mischievous twist to her lips.

With an embarrassed giggle, she let go, dropped her eyes and began working at the last few buttons of her blouse. When she glanced up at him, Alar slid his arms around her waist and pulled her tight. She hung limp, her arms imprisoned in her half discarded blouse, surrendering to his kiss. He let her lips go and watched as she freed her arms, dropped the dress to the floor, then shimmied out of her undergarments. She stood naked, except for her boots, her arms crossed over her breasts, gazing up at him.

Alar pulled her arms away. She reached out to him, but he held her away. Sinking to sit on the edge of his bed, he lifted her foot, resting her boot on his knee while he undid the laces. After removing their boots, he turned her slightly so he could see her in the flickering light of the fire. Letting his fingertips rest lightly on her chest, he traced a line between her breasts, then reaching around her, he pulled her close, bringing a nipple to his lips. Her inhaled breath was shivery. Alar pulled back, relinquishing her nipple, and noticed the goosebumps rising on her skin. "Oh, sorry," he said and pushed her gently back so he could stand. She stood, arms crossed over her chest, watching while he lifted the corner of his blankets and invited her into his bed.

She ducked under the covers, lay on her back, spread her arms and invited him to follow. Alar hesitated, until Scilla grinned, took hold of him again and pulled him gently on top of her. Afraid to put his weight on her, he supported himself awkwardly on his elbows and knees, until she reached around, took his hips and pulled him down. He kissed her, thrilled by the pressure of her heels on the backs of his thighs.

"I've never done this," she whispered.

"Neither have I," Alar murmured. He ran the tip of his tongue along her collarbone, eliciting a low moan. "We'll figure it out."

***

Harold suppressed a yawn. The gendarmerie was silent late at night. The small interrogation room, lit only by a single lamp on the small table, was stuffy. He shook his hands, flicked his fingers, then brought his palms to his face, rubbed vigorously before running his fingers through his hair. The Inquisition had many techniques to extract information from prisoners. In Harold's opinion, most of them were more likely to satisfy the sadistic urges of the interrogator than produce useful intelligence. There were more effective methods. One of his favorites was to drag prisoners from a deep sleep and interrogate them while they were disoriented.

The problem was the blade cut both ways. An hour of sleep only left him feeling groggy, his mind sluggish. Not the best state to be in for an interrogation. "He's only a kid. Probably scared out of his wits," he said, speaking aloud to keep himself alert. When he heard footsteps approaching, he took a breath, blew it out, and arranged himself into an intimidating posture.

Henrik appeared, pushing Lief ahead of him. From the boy's puffy face and tousled hair, it appeared the brother roused him from a deep sleep. Henrik guided him roughly into the seat across from Harold, then stepped back, just far enough so that he loomed over the prisoner.

The boy glanced up at Henrik, then leveled his gaze on Harold. Fear, caution, anger. All were emotions a prisoner might display or attempt to hide under the circumstances. Lief yawned widely. Harold waited in vain, hoping to see something that revealed the boy's state of mind. The moment stretched, Harold and Lief gazing at one another. Henrik coughed.

Finally, Lief asked, "What did Jora do?"

Caught off guard, Harold glanced up at Henrik, before saying, "I suggest you worry about your own predicament."

The boy's head cocked slightly. "What predicament is that?"

"You've been arrested for suspicion of treason against the Empire."

His eyes narrowed slightly. "Treason?"

Disappointed by the mild reaction to the loaded word, it took Harold a moment to realize Lief was asking what the word meant. "Treason is the offense of acting to overthrow the empire or to harm or kill the emperor, or a violation of allegiance to the emperor or to the empire," he recited, then fell silent. He watched Lief's face as he worked through that information but was disappointed once again at the lack of reaction.

Lief glanced at Henrik. "How did I ... all those things, the emperor, state and all that?" he asked. "What did I do?"

"You are suspected of participating in a prison break at the Inquisition headquarters in Kartok."

The boy's eyes narrowed again, then he gave a small nod. "You mean when someone rescued that girl, the one everyone is talking about? The one accused of ... what was she in prison for?"

"Suspicion of treason."

He nodded, glanced at Harold's uniform and asked, "That what you inquisitors do? Arrest kids for suspicion of treason?"

"I'm not an inquisitor. I'm a novice," Harold answered automatically, then swore inwardly.

"So ... you're *learning* to be an inquisitor?"

Harold bit back his irritation. How did this boy get him so unsettled? He looked down at his hands cupped on the table, took a deep breath and sighed it out. When he looked up, Lief was watching him expectantly. Henrik's face displayed mild alarm. "Have you ever been to Kartok?"

"Yes."

"Are you familiar with the Inquisition Headquarters in Kartok?"

"*Zhot ti lios.*"

Harold glanced at Henrik, who shook his head.

"House of death," the boy said.

Harold stared at him. The *Alle'oss* language had been outlawed for generations. In fact, he had never heard it spoken and assumed it was nearly a dead language. Yet, it was prevalent enough that they would have an *Alle'oss* name for a building that obviously referenced its use for housing prisoners for interrogation. That was a relatively recent development. "I could put you in prison for speaking *Alle'oss.*"

"You can put me in prison for speaking my language?"

"I can put you in prison for anything I want," Harold snapped, then cursed himself for showing his irritation.

"So, is there a law against speaking *Alle'oss,* or is it just something you don't like?"

"No, there is a law. The Imperial decree of—" He knew the decree, had studied it along with many others that applied to Argren and the *Alle'oss* before he came, but he couldn't bring it forth from the murk in his mind. He looked up at Henrik, whose gaze wandered the room, the ghost of a smile playing at the corners of his mouth. Feeling suddenly exhausted, Harold put his hand to his forehead, trying to decide if it would be prudent to retreat, when the boy spoke again.

"Is rescuing a person who was unjustly arrested to save them from torture by *inquisitors.*" He looked pointedly at the insignia of rank on Harold's collar. "Is that as bad as speaking my own language?"

"I suggest you consider your own situa—"

"Is breaking an innocent person out of prison disrespecting the emperor, or whatever you said? Is that treason?"

Harold pushed his lips out in frustration. "No, that is not treason."

"I thought you said I was suspected of treason?"

"You are accused of treason for being a member of the rebel group called *oss'stera*."

"That's *Alle'oss*."

"What?"

"Our struggle."

"So, it *is* a rebel group?"

"No, that's what it means."

Harold stared.

"I think he's saying *oss'stera* means 'our struggle'," Henrik said. "It's *Alle'oss*, sir."

Harold sighed. "Are you a member of *oss'stera*, Lief?"

"Assuming *oss'stera* exists, what if I was a member? Do you have any proof we did anything? Break into *Zhot ti* or whatever?" He pointed toward the wall and asked, "Is living up in the woods, starving and cold, because the Imps took our homes and families treason?"

Emotion. Finally. A moment of truth. But what? Harold groped for it, while Lief and Henrik watched him expectantly. Something ... but his tired mind wouldn't cooperate.

And then he had it. He sat back, letting a grin grow slowly on his face. "No, living in the forest is not treason, Lief. Thank you." He nodded to Henrik and stood. "Brother Henrik, if you would escort the prisoner to his cell and meet me in our office."

Henrik looked as surprised as Lief, but the brother took the boy by the back of his tunic, lifted him to his feet, and led him through the door. Harold followed and found a gendarme waiting outside the room. "Helga, isn't it?" When the young woman nodded, he said, "I need a topological map of the area."

Chapter 31

Something's Different

Harold looked up as Henrik entered their office. The brother paused, filling the doorway, fighting to keep the grin from his face.

"You have my permission to mock me, Henrik," Harold said. "The boy ran circles around me."

"So, it wasn't some clever plan to get him to confess something?" Harold chuckled. "You've seen through me."

Henrik looked uncertain until he noticed Harold's grin.

"But he did say something important," Henrik said, and took a seat at his desk.

"Yes, I believe he did." Harold rested his index finger on his chin, looking down at the map spread out on his desk. "When he became angry, he asked if we have 'proof *we* did anything.'" Harold let his finger fall to point at the forest east of Richeleau. "His exact words were 'is living *up* in the woods, starving and cold, because the Imps took our homes and families treason'." He looked up. "That was awfully specific, and not at all germane to the line of questioning. I believe Lief gave us two vital pieces of information. First, that *oss'stera* exists, and second, that they are living in the forest."

"So, they're living in the forest. That wasn't hard to deduce."

"He said '*up* in the forest,'" Harold said. He rotated the map, inviting Henrik to join him. When the brother was standing next to him, he said, "The only sighting of members of *oss'stera*, except, perhaps, the prison break in Kartok, is in Richeleau. As you say, we can assume they are living in the forest somewhere nearby. So, we need to find somewhere forested, close to the city *and* which could be described as up from the point-of-view of Richeleau." Harold pointed to the map. "Richeleau sits at the eastern edge of the foothills of the Eastern Mountains. To the north, west and south are foothills. They are forested, but thinly and one wouldn't describe them as up. That leaves the east. It's heavily forested. The bones of the mountains emerge, providing many defensible hiding places, especially to the northeast."

They gazed at the map in silence until Henrik said, "Still a lot of ground to cover, and as you say, it's pretty rugged."

"Yes." Harold looked up from the map and noticed for the first time the sheaf of papers Henrik carried. "The morning reports?"

Henrik looked down at the papers. "Yes," he said, returned to his desk and began shuffling through the reports.

"Anything?" Harold asked when Henrik stopped and held a page up to read.

"Could be," Henrik said. "Unusual, anyway." He held out the sheet of paper.

Harold took it, sat and scanned it, then looked up. "A Desulti? Is that possible?"

"I know. It seems farfetched," Henrik said. "But there have been multiple sightings, complete with descriptions of the face wraps."

"So, now we can throw a Desulti assassin in with the ancient realm walkers and rebels. What is going on in this city?" He read through the brief report again. "All of them in a neighborhood called the art district."

"Desulti and art. What's the connection?"

"Who would know? Bit mysterious, aren't they? May be a coincidence," Harold said. They sat quietly, staring at one another. "You know, one thing I noticed when we met Adelbart?"

The corners of Henrik's mouth twitched. "A lot of art. Unsanctioned art. Art frowned on by the Inquisition," Henrik said.

"It's probably nothing," Harold said, returning his smile. "Still, I have a mind to pay the governor a visit. We need manpower to search the forest. I'm sure the governor wouldn't mind if we commandeered his cavalry once again." When he noticed Henrik's frown, he asked, "What is it?"

"Well, it's just that I ... we've had very little sleep."

"Right, and apparently, the governor is a late riser. Okay, let's catch a few winks first."

***

Fueled by ale, plentiful food, and a new sense of optimism, *oss'stera's* celebration lasted until the wee hours. Even so, the sun was only just making its arrival known when Alar opened his eyes. He rolled onto his side. Something was different. Something both profound and ephemeral. He was the same person, had the same worries and hopes. But when he gazed around the dark roundhouse, lit only by coals in the fire pit, it looked different.

After walking Scilla home the night before, he made an appearance at the party before retiring. Despite his fatigue, he lay awake for a time, unwilling to let go of the images of Scilla in the firelight, her body painted in gold and shadow. At some point, after he surrendered to sleep, Ukrit came home. The big man lay on his back, arms flung out, snoring like a grizzly. Alar grinned until he noted the empty beds. Keth and Lief were still absent.

He rolled out of bed and danced around the cold room, searching for his discarded clothing. Once he was dressed, he ripped the blanket from Ukrit. "Get up, you big bear. We have work to do."

With a great snort, Ukrit sat up, staring around the room. When he saw they weren't under attack, he dropped onto his back and reached for the blanket. Alar held it just out of reach, coaxing Ukrit to lunge for it, until he hung halfway out of the bed.

"Don't you ever take a day off?" Ukrit grumbled. He rolled over on his side, huddled against the cold. After a moment, he growled in frustration and sat up. "Okay, *okay.*" He stared blearily around the room. "What's for breakfast?"

"Let's go see," Alar said and ducked out the door into the gray morning. Full of energy, despite the late night, he roamed the community, rousting people from their beds. When he got to the roundhouse Scilla shared with Tove and two other women, he knocked, feeling an unfamiliar fluttering in his stomach.

Tove pushed the door open, her short hair tousled, her face paler than normal. "Oh, it's you," she said, not bothering to hide her smirk.

"A good morning to you too, Tove," Alar said brightly. "Always a pleasure."

Tove looked back over her shoulder. "Scilla, you have a visitor."

Scilla appeared behind Tove, clutching a blanket around herself. "Morning," she said, her cheeks darkening.

Alar felt a silly grin growing on his face. "Morning."

Tove rolled her eyes and disappeared.

"Breakfast?" Alar asked.

"Oh, yes," Scilla said. They stared at one another.

"You ... want to get dressed?" Alar asked.

"Yeah, right. Be right back." She gave him a grin and disappeared.

***

Ignoring their grumbles, Alar set people to work. One party dismantled most of the wagons for the lumber. After much discussion, Ukrit convinced him to keep a wagon and the team to pull it. A corral and shed for the animals to shelter in the winter had to be built in a nearby field. Alar tasked another group with releasing the other animals far away. While the rest of the community got on with daily chores, Alar, Scilla, Ukrit and Tove inventoried their newly acquired supplies.

Now, with the inventory complete, Alar stood at the mouth of the ravine, staring toward Richeleau.

"You worried?"

He glanced at Tove. "I wish people would stop asking me that."

"Sorry."

"Sorry," he said with an apologetic grimace. "I'm not worried about Keth and Zaina. Not yet. They have to find Torva and they can't just walk into the gendarmerie. It might take them a while to get him alone."

"Lief."

"Yes. I can't think of any reason for him to be gone so long."

"We'll find him," Tove said. After a moment, she added. "It's time to open the chest. Come on. Keep your mind off your worries."

They waited to investigate the ornately decorated chest until they accounted for everything else. Alar turned to find a small group that included Ukrit, Scilla, Sten and Erik gathered around it. Ukrit was working at the lock with a hammer and chisel. Alar had a moment to wonder where Sten and Erik came from when Ukrit interrupted his thoughts.

"There you go," he said. He set the tools aside and lifted the top of the chest.

There was a rustle as they shuffled forward to get a better view, then only the sounds of the forest. Alar wasn't sure what he was expecting, but the pile of leather tubes nestled in the chest was decidedly underwhelming. The tubes were a pace long and four inches in diameter. Leather caps enclosed the ends.

"What are they?" Tove asked.

"I know what these are," Ukrit said excitedly. He plucked one from the chest, slid the cap off one end, and holding it up to the sunlight, he peered into the tube. "Bless the Mother," he said softly. "Could it be?" He tipped the tube up and let a roll of canvas slide into his hand.

Handing the tube to Tove, he laid the canvas on the top of a crate and unrolled it with shaky hands.

"It's a picture," Tove said.

Ukrit looked at Scilla, his face slack for a moment, then the two of them threw their heads back and laughed.

"What's so funny?" Tove asked, leaning over to get a better look. She glanced back at Alar. "It's a picture, right?" She reached for the canvas.

Scilla clamped her hand around Tove's wrist, her good humor gone in an instant. "Don't. Touch."

"What is it, Scilla?" Alar asked.

Scilla let Tove's wrist go, and watched the hand retreat, then she let her hands hover over the canvas, trembling fingers betraying her excitement. "This, this is a Valdemar."

Alar saw the same confused expressions on the others' faces. All except for Ukrit, who appeared lost in some other world.

"What's a Valdemar?" Tove asked.

"Valdemar is, or was, the greatest of the new school *Alle'oss* artists," Ukrit said. He glanced at Alar, his expression animated. "This painting was the one that got him arrested by the Inquisition. Most people say they executed him. I saw this hanging on the wall in Adelbart's office." Anger swept his features. "They murder a great man like Valdemar, then they slap his greatest work on the wall of a *numana* like Adelbart."

Scilla rested her hand on Ukrit's shoulder.

Not sure that Scilla wouldn't tackle him if he got too close, Alar leaned forward to get a better view. The painting depicted an *Alle'oss* woman standing on a rocky promontory, feet set firmly apart, her hair and dress caught by the wind. There was a slight arch to her back, and her arms extended gracefully above her head, elbows bent. Alar was reminded of a troupe of Tituun dancers he saw on the streets in Richeleau. He had twelve summers at the time, and the women's sinuous movements teased at thoughts he was only just becoming aware of. But, while the impression conveyed by the woman in the painting was of an overwhelming ecstasy, it was not sexual.

"What are those … lights around her?" Sten asked.

Ukrit chuckled. "This is Wattana." He pointed to the woman, then pointed to the orbs that floated around her. "Those are the—"

"The fairy lights!" Tove said.

"But every *Alle'oss* child knows that story," Alar said, sounding unsure. "Wattana and the fairy lights. Papa used to tell it all the time. It's beautiful, but why would they arrest the main who painted it?"

"I can't say. You would have to ask an inquisitor," Ukrit said. He pointed to the woman's face. "But what does the story say about Wattana at the end?"

"She was insane, sick," Sten said. "She threw herself from the cliff when she realized what chasing the fairies did to her family."

"Madness is not what I see," Alar said softly, and everyone leaned in for a closer look.

"Me neither," Tove said. She looked at Ukrit. "Still, why would the Inquisition care about that?"

He shrugged.

"More pressing for us," Alar said, "is what was it doing in an Imperial supply caravan from Richeleau to Ka'tan?"

They all stood, staring down at the painting, until Alar asked, "Is it valuable?"

"Oh, yes," Scilla said with a chuckle.

"How valuable?" Alar asked.

Ukrit started to speak, stopped, then looked down at the canvas, his lips pursed. "I wouldn't have any idea," he said. "But I know a man in Richeleau who would."

Chapter 32

A Generous Offer

Alar couldn't remember a time he felt so wary walking the streets of Richeleau, and he could tell Tove felt the same. His experience in the Black Husky set them on edge. Fortunately, their destination was on the outskirts, north of the city. Excited for some reason Alar couldn't fathom, Ukrit and Scilla's pace sped up as they neared their destination. Alar reached out and took Ukrit's arm to pull him to a stop.

"You trust this guy?" Tove asked before Alar could.

"Completely," Ukrit said.

"Do you trust him enough to show up with an unimaginably valuable, stolen painting by a late, great artist?" Alar asked.

Ukrit hesitated. "Yes," he said finally, but with less certainty.

Alar glanced at Scilla, who nodded firmly.

Tove met Alar's eye behind Ukrit's back and shook her head.

They stood on a nearly empty street in a neighborhood Alar never visited. Noticing Alar examining the signs above the shop doors, Ukrit said, "This is the art district."

"They have a district for art?" Tove asked.

Ukrit ignored her. "Richeleau is at the center of the new school. *Ākana si.*" He gestured around. "Many of the best artists of the new school have their studios near here. Artists from all over the world come here when the Empire lets them." He pointed to a narrow two-story townhouse across the street. "That's where Olaf had his studio, before he fled." He and Scilla gazed reverently at the nondescript building.

"Uh-huh," Tove said. She and Alar grinned at one another, careful to keep their amusement to themselves.

"So what's the deal with the new school?" Alar asked.

"*Ākana si,*" Ukrit said. "Sune can explain it better than me."

"How do you know all this stuff?" Tove asked.

"The Ishian River valley is a haven for artists," Alar said.

Ukrit and Scilla stopped and stared at him.

"What?" Alar asked.

"How did—" Ukrit started before Alar interrupted him.

"This is the place, right?" he asked, pointing to the sign above the door of the shop behind Ukrit. "Sune's Gallery." It was an unseasonably warm day, but even so it was too cold to have the large window that fronted the gallery open. Yet, it was. A man stood in the center of the room in front of an easel. Alar thought, at first, he was painting. His brush hovered above a canvas, the tip twitching as if he were applying paint, but the brush wasn't touching the surface of what looked like a completed painting.

"Right," Ukrit said. "Come on, but let me do the talking."

"You afraid we'll embarrass you?" Tove asked.

"Yes," Ukrit said and stepped into the street.

Their entrance was announced by the tinkling of a small bell. It didn't look like any shop Alar had ever seen. The walls were bare, but canvases, some blank and others splashed with color, were stacked against the walls or piled on the floor. The middle of the room was empty, save for the man and his easel. The painter looked up, his surprised expression enhanced by short red hair that stood straight out, as if it were trying to leap from his head. His blue eyes roved over Tove and Alar, but when he saw Ukrit, a wide smile stretched his lips.

"Ukrit! You brought friends." He stepped away from the easel, the hand holding the brush still aloft. "And Scilla, of course. What a treat."

"Sune," Ukrit said. "These are my friends Alar and Tove."

Sune's eyes slid past Alar, but when he saw Tove, he froze and sucked in a breath. "Toe vahhh," he breathed. His head tipped back, eyes half-lidded. The brush came slowly around until it dabbed at the air a foot in front of Tove's face, as if brushing paint on an imaginary canvas.

Alar glanced at Tove. In the past, this type of direct attention would send her into hiding. She stood stock-still. Curious, he watched the inner struggle playing out on her face. When a dangerous scowl began to coalesce, he cleared his throat and said, "Ukrit." Ukrit startled and tore his eyes from Tove and Sune. Alar nodded toward the leather tube.

"Um, yes. Sune," he said, raising his voice to get the artist's attention and held the tube out.

The man's eyes focused, his head cocked to the side. "What have you got for me this time, Ukrit?"

The attention gone, Tove's face relaxed, though she shuffled closer to Alar. Alar caught her eye and shrugged.

"I'll show you, but you have to promise, no questions, and you have to keep it a secret," Ukrit said.

Sune hesitated, once again studying Alar and Tove. "What have you gotten into, Ukrit?"

"No questions," Ukrit said. He held the tube up again and said, "Believe me, it will be worth it."

Sune stared at the tube, holding the fingers of the hand without the brush to his lips. Suddenly, he hurried to lock the door, then lifted the support for the shutter and eased it down to close the window. The room was now lit only by a small lamp. When he returned, he stood rigid, hands down by his sides. After seeming to gather himself, he said, "Okay, Ukrit, show me."

"Here, clear a space," Ukrit said, indicating a table along the back wall. Once the space was clear, Ukrit slid the cap off the tube and carefully unrolled the canvas, then stepped back to allow Sune room.

The artist didn't move from his position. He stared at the canvas, then his eyes pivoted toward Ukrit, a small furrow appearing between his brows.

Ukrit nodded. "It's real."

"Oh, Ukrit, what have you done?"

"No questions," Scilla said.

Sune hurried back to the window and raised the shutter, flooding the room in light. He leaned out and looked in both directions, then rushed back and stood before the canvas. Hands beside his head, fingers splayed, he bent at the waist so that his nose was only inches above the image. His head swept back and forth as he studied the brush strokes. After several long minutes, he straightened, one arm across his stomach, the hand cupping the elbow of his other arm. The tip of the brush hovered next to his head. He looked at Ukrit. "It's *Spirit Light*," he whispered.

"Yes."

"Spirit light?" Alar asked.

Sune glanced at him, but didn't answer. He leaned over the canvas again, exclaiming softly to himself.

They let him pour over the painting for a time until Tove lost patience. "Maybe you can explain why it's such a big deal now."

"Yeah," Alar said. "Why is this new school a big deal?"

Sune jerked upright, one hand going to his mouth. He stood for a moment, then rushed to one of the stacks of canvases and shuffled through them. "Ah-ha!" he said, extracted a small painting, scurried back and propped the frame next to the Valdemar. He stood back, gestured expansively with both hands toward the two canvases, a triumphant smile on his face.

Alar looked uncertainly at Scilla and found a matching smile.

"I don't get it," Tove said.

Ukrit, Scilla and Sune shared an irritatingly smug chuckle, then with a sweep of the brush, Sune spoke as if he were lecturing to a class. "The *Alle'oss* have always had a unique love of color, of course."

"Of course," Tove said.

Sune ignored her sarcasm and twirled a finger before the smaller painting. "This work is by a Styrian artist by the name of Manon. Styrian culture has been so entirely subsumed by the Empire that it may as well be the same. Look at the color palette. What do you see?" He stood back, cupping his cheek in the palm of his hand.

Alar and Tove shuffled over to stand next to the artist and studied the two canvases.

"This one is a lot duller," Tove said, indicating the Styrian work.

"Yes!" Sune exclaimed, causing Tove to jump.

"Argren blue," Alar said. Wattana's dress was the same vibrant blue his sister used when she depicted his eyes. His fingers touched his chest, above her painting, and for a moment, he was sitting on the stump in his family's yard, trying his best to sit still for his sister. When he came back to the present, Scilla was watching him, her furrowed brow showing she noticed his mood. He smiled and mouthed the word 'later' to her unspoken question.

Unaware, Sune smiled and nodded knowingly. "Yesss. You see, blue is a very rare pigment in nature. There is only one place in the known world where blue this brilliant is found."

Alar, still gazing into Scilla's blue eyes, said, "Lirantok."

"That's right," Sune said, sounding mildly surprised. "And of course, though blue is the rarest—and most valuable—there are many other hues that are only found in Argren."

"So, it's the colors," Tove said.

"The colors are of utmost importance, it's true." Sune's finger tips rested briefly on Tove's shoulder. "Perhaps because the *Alle'oss* have always had access to a variety of pigments, they have learned to be bold in their use." He made an extravagant gesture with the hand that held the brush, then paused and grinned. "But that is not what elevates the new school to such heights." Gesturing toward the two works, he said, "Look at them. Imagine them as depictions of something real, rather than pictures on a canvas. What do you see?"

Alar and Tove looked from one to the other. Finally, Tove pointed to the smaller painting and said, "That one's flat."

"Yes!" Sune said, and tapped Tove on the shoulder with his brush. Tove flinched, but Alar could see she was pleased.

Sune waggled his fingers in front of the smaller painting. "Outside of Argren, artists use various tricks, ineffective tricks, to imply *perspective* in their works." He smiled, taking in Alar and Tove's confused expressions. "Perspective makes a picture on a flat canvas look as if it has *depth*."

Alar looked at the Valdemar, surprised he hadn't noticed it before. "The things in the background, the trees," he said, pointing at a copse of trees that clustered at the base of the promontory. "They look smaller, like they're farther away."

Sune stepped forward and raised his hands over the sides of the canvas. Bringing them toward the center, he explained, "The new school artists have discovered how to add perspective by drawing the focus to a single point." His hands came together, and he pointed the brush tip at a spot above Wattana's left shoulder. "It is called the *vanishing point*, and all lines converge there."

"And no one else can do the same thing?" Tove asked doubtfully.

"In the Empire, art is a means for reminding people of the proper order of things, not for depicting the world as it is," Scilla said.

"Yes, and if that is your goal, to remind the viewer of the Empire's preeminence, the artist need only *evoke* the idea in the viewer's mind," Sune said. "The faithfulness of the depiction to reality is immaterial, and, *in fact*, it is a detriment to the intended message." He swirled his hands above the Valdemar. "The *Alle'oss* artists strive to capture the world—its color, its movement, its *wonder*—in all its glory."

The room fell silent as everyone gazed down at Wattana's beatific expression, until Tove poked Ukrit in the ribs and said, "How is it you and Scilla know all this?"

"Scilla!" Sune's exclamation startled them all. The man was staring at Scilla and Ukrit, horrified.

"I—" Scilla started, before Sune dashed to the far side of the room and shuffled through another stack of canvases. He withdrew one, stood back, held it up and said, "Ukrit." He nodded at the easel.

Ukrit removed the painting from the easel and found a place for it. Sune settled the canvas he held onto the easel and stood back, using both hands to wave Alar and Tove forward.

Tove gave Alar an uncertain look then they stepped up beside Sune. It was a view of a valley from the heights of the mountains. Alar leaned forward and studied it. Something was familiar about the scene. Straightening, he said, "The Ishian River valley." He turned to find Scilla blushing. Lifting a finger to point at the easel, he said, "You did this?"

"Oh, yes," Sune said. His brush sprung into action again, the soft bristles caressing the air above the depiction of the Woodsmith's home. "There is some clumsiness, of course. Especially in the finer details, but there is also great *promisssse.*"

Too flustered to notice the intensity of Alar's gaze, Scilla said, "You showed mine. You have to show Ukrit's."

"Ah, yes, of course," Sune vanished through a door in the back of the room and returned moments later, carrying something heavy covered by burlap. "Ukrit, if you will," he said and nodded at the Valdemar.

Ukrit carefully rolled it up and returned it to the tube.

Sune hoisted his burden onto the table, stood back, then, with a flourish, swept the covering off.

It was a small statue, or more accurately, an unfinished statue. The bottom half was untouched by the chisel, but the top half depicted a woman, her head thrown back, her arms upraised as if she were struggling to emerge from her stone prison.

"It's Wattana," Tove said.

Alar took a step closer. It *was* Wattana. "Ukrit," he said. "It's beautiful."

"It's not done," Ukrit said. "And I never saw the painting. All I had to go on were third-hand descriptions."

"Oh posh," Sune said. "Yes, it is not done, *but* already, you can see the potential. It will be great."

Tove punched Ukrit's shoulder. "Who knew we had a couple of artists among us? Not like you ain't had time to mention something like that."

Ukrit rubbed his shoulder. "I—"

"How much is it worth?" Tove asked. When everyone looked at her, she added, "The Valdemar." She took in their blank faces. "That is why we came, right?"

"Worth? How can you put a price on a work such as *Spirit Light?*" Sune asked, gesturing toward the leather tube Ukrit held.

"Okay, let me ask it a different way," Alar said. "How much would someone be willing to pay?"

Sune stopped, then threw his hands up. "One could only imagine. Tens of thousands. At least. Imperial Eagles. Gold Eagles." He gave them a sly grin. "But who would risk the wrath of the Inquisition for even such as this?"

"Why does the Inquisition care?" Alar asked. "About this particular painting, I mean?"

"Ah, if we only knew," Sune said wistfully.

***

The four young people gathered on the nearly deserted, sun-washed street outside Sune's gallery.

"We're in trouble," Tove said.

"What?" Ukrit asked. "Why?"

"Because whoever put this in that wagon, and the people who were expecting it to arrive in Ka'tan, will want it back," Alar said. "You steal gold from someone, they'll be unhappy, but they can go out and earn more gold. You steal something like this, something irreplaceable—"

"They'll come looking for it, and they won't give up until they find it," Tove finished.

"It belonged to the governor," Ukrit said. "I saw it in his office."

"Then why was it in a wagon to Ka'tan?" Scilla asked.

"He was shipping it to someone. That's why the rangers were there. Maybe he sold it. All of them, the paintings," Alar said. "Come on. Let's go home and figure out how to give them back to whoever they belong to before they come looking for them."

"Give them back?" Ukrit and Scilla chorused.

"Come on," Tove said. "We can argue while we walk."

***

The Desulti spotted the four ragged-looking *Alle'oss* when they arrived in the art district. While the neighborhood attracted its share of bohemians, those wannabe artists' dishevelment was carefully arranged. These four looked as if they lived hard. They were as out of place in the tony district as a sewer rat in a parlor. She recognized the leather tube the big man carried and followed them.

It was warm, the sun beat down on the roof of Sune's Gallery where she crouched, waiting. Sweat dripped down her body and soaked the linen strips, making her scalp itch.

She hadn't expected to find any truth to the governor's excuse for losing the shipment. She only investigated because the term *oss'stera* used an archaic construction she was sure Adelbart couldn't come up with on his own. To her surprise, it turned out there may be something to it. Not only did she uncover rumors of the group herself, she discovered there was an Inquisition novice in Richeleau investigating *oss'stera* as well. A recent raid and arrests suggested he found something. Fortunately, whatever he found, it was not related to the attack on the supply caravan. If that was the Inquisition's concern, she would have seen their agents in the art district. She needed to recover the art before the Inquisition found its way to it.

When the four *Alle'oss* emerged from the gallery, she was surprised by how young they were. They stopped, stood close together, and spoke in urgent tones. When the blond boy turned away, he raised his voice loud enough for her to hear. It was as she suspected. They attacked the caravan for the supplies meant for the garrison in Ka'tan. The art was unexpected. She was a bit surprised they were smart enough to recognize the jeopardy they were in. This would be easy. She would follow them to where they kept the art, approach them and make a generous offer; the paintings for their lives.

When the four rebels left, the Desulti followed.

Chapter 33

Desulti

Alar put out an arm to bring the others to a stop. "It's awfully quiet." He peered up at the top of the cliff and was relieved to find someone on watch. The man waved when he saw Alar looking his way. As they neared the entrance to the ravine, Stolten emerged, appearing flustered.

"Where is everyone?" Alar asked, instantly wary.

"Some are off practicing archery, Inga's got the kids in school and the others are off gathering firewood," Stolten said hurriedly, then he leaned forward and said in a hushed voice, "Three women arrived not long after you left. They're asking for you."

"Three women?" Alar asked, trying to think of who, outside *oss'stera*, he knew.

"Two of them got marks on their face," Stolten said. "Like those—" He stared over Alar's shoulder, eyes narrowing.

Alar whipped around.

A figure was entering the flat space in front of the entrance to the community. At first, Alar couldn't understand what he was seeing. The tight, black leathers and blouse revealed the athletic body of a woman, but her head was entirely covered by cloth wrappings, leaving only thin slits that allowed her to see and breathe. The way she moved across the clearing, like one of the great lions that lived high in the mountains stalking its prey, sent a thrill of fear through him. She set her feet, leaned out, and looked past Alar.

He caught movement from the corner of his eye and looked in time to see Tove raising her bow. "No," he shouted too late.

Tove loosed her arrow. Alar was sure the strange woman would die before he had a chance to find out who she was. Incredibly, she shifted to the side, turning her shoulders so the arrow flew harmlessly by. In a blur of motion, her arm whipped toward them. Alar stepped into *annen'heim*.

He tensed, listening, but the moans of the spirits were far away. Relaxing, he approached the woman and studied her. Her arm was frozen in her follow-through. A small, star-shaped projectile hung in the air halfway between her and Tove. The cloth wrapping appeared to be fine linen. Her eyes, intense, focused on her target, were the black of an Imperial. "Who are you?" he muttered to himself. The quavering cry of a *sjel'and* seemed to answer him. Still far away.

Returning his attention to the woman, he walked around her, noting the variety of clever weapons secured in a harness that bound her torso. Would the Inquisition use an assassin? It didn't seem their style. Not regular Imps, either. They would arrive with a full company. When he cast about for someone else who might want them dead, he came up with Adelbart. The art belonged to the governor. Either Adelbart sent her, or, more likely, the intended recipient of the paintings did.

It was a question for later. The first order of business was to subdue the assassin. He examined the projectile, hanging, nearly motionless. The razor-sharp edges on the points of the star glinted in a frozen sunbeam. Drawing his knife, he positioned it so the blade would deflect the projectile to the side, then crossed the boundary. He was used to encountering a wall of sound when he returned to the physical realm, but the clearing was eerily silent, save for the bright ping of the star ricocheting from his blade.

The assassin hesitated, her eyes meeting Alar's before he recrossed the boundary.

Strolling toward the woman, he considered the problem. He had questions for her. The trick was to subdue her without harming her. First, he needed to disarm her. At some point, she produced a knife and held it in her right hand. He walked around to her side, lifted his knife above her hand, counted to three, then swung down as he crossed the boundary.

The brass butt of his knife impacted her wrist, sending the knife clattering to the ground. Before his mind could register his satisfaction, he was flying backward. Crossing the boundary arrested his fall, leaving him floating a foot above the ground. One hand, thrown out to catch himself, sank into a stone and went instantly numb. When he got his feet under himself, he stared at the woman, his good hand rubbing the spot where her fist struck his sternum. Two inches higher and he would have sustained real damage. *Who had reactions like that?* She couldn't be human.

He retrieved his knife and walked around behind her, flicking tingles from his hand as it reawakened. Hefting his knife, he brought the butt end close to the back of her head. No. It would be hard to judge the force of the impact, since he couldn't be sure how her head would be moving when he returned to the physical realm. He cozied up behind her, reaching around and holding his knife close to her throat. She was shorter than he was, so he had to crouch to reach his other arm around her waist. It was awkward, but surely, no matter how fast she was, she would have to respect a blade at her throat. Steeling himself, he crossed the boundary.

"Now—" was all he got out before the woman twisted in his arms. His mind went white, pain like he'd never felt before erupting from his groin. He fell back, glimpsing a metallic flash through slitted eyes, before escaping into *annen'heim.*

Bent at the waist, Alar rested his hands on his thighs, fighting nausea. After several minutes listening to the *sjel'and* drifting closer, he was able to stand. "*Vo kustok,*" he muttered. She had to be a demon.

The wrappings, which made a blank slate of her face only heightened the illusion. She was, once again, frozen, but somehow, as she twisted around, she retrieved another blade. Short and wicked, it protruded between the fingers of her fist. He was lucky she used her knee rather than the blade. The stuttering grunt of a spirit nearby raised the hairs on the back of his neck. A spirit feeling for his presence. He was running out of time. He would have to kill her.

He positioned himself so he could get the tip of his knife against her throat, then noticed Tove behind the woman, stilled in the act of approaching the assassin, her face set in the cool concentration Alar recognized as her fighting face. She held a log, thick as her arm, in front of her. He needed to give her time. He stepped back, crouched and crossed the boundary.

The woman's eyes flashed, the hand holding the blade swiped sideways. Alar crossed the boundary, stepped to the side, away from the blade's path, and returned. Impossibly, she reversed her stroke almost as soon as he reappeared. The tip sliced through his shirt sleeve, nicking his forearm. She drew the blade back in a blur and punched toward his abdomen. Alar lunged backwards and retreated into *annen'heim*. He stepped to her side, chopped the hilt of his knife down toward her wrist, and returned. She swiped sideways, avoiding his blow and slicing through his shirt, grazing the flesh beneath. Alar threw a jab toward her face. His still numb fist exploded in fiery tingles when it contacted her cheek. Without waiting to see what effect the punch had, he crossed the boundary again to the deafening roar of a *sjel'and*, so near it vibrated in his chest. The mist swirled around the dark bulk of the spirit.

Alar leapt back and returned to the physical realm. This time he appeared far enough from the assassin that she hesitated, crouched, the fist clenching the knife held at the ready. They watched one another, the assassin still barely breathing, Alar puffing, sweat pouring down his back. Somehow, despite the fact he could retreat into *annen'heim* and freeze her in place, she was kicking his ass.

Tove was almost there, picking her way to avoid making a sound. Alar dropped into a crouch, hoping to keep the woman's attention on him. He pointed his knife toward her, waved the tip, and offered her his widest smile. "Brrrrrrrr apa!" he trilled theatrically.

She didn't react, but just as Tove was bringing the log up before drawing it back over her shoulder, the woman whirled, blindingly fast, and struck out with the knife.

"Ahh!" The surprised shout escaped from Alar and Tove at once. Tove dropped the log just as the assassin's fist struck it, sending it flying. Alar lunged, stepping across the boundary. Ignoring the spirit's frustrated shriek, he flew across the narrow gap, chopping down with his knife as he returned to the physical realm. The butt thudded into the woman's cloth-covered head, dropping her like a stone.

Only Alar's heaving breaths disturbed the silence until Tove shouted, "What the *sheoda* was that?!"

"Quick, tie it up," Alar said, peering over Tove's shoulder at the others. "Everyone okay?" he asked. When they nodded, Alar said. "Make sure you tie her up good."

Stolten appeared with a coil of rope. Tove and Ukrit set to binding the woman while Scilla examined Alar's wounds.

"Superficial. Mostly," Scilla concluded. "Should probably have a stitch or two on your arm."

"She's awake," Tove said over her shoulder. She stepped back, drew and nocked an arrow.

Alar joined her and looked down at the assassin. She was sitting with her legs extended in front of her. Her ankles were tied and rope wrapped her torso, from her waist to her shoulders, locking her arms in place.

"You sure you tied her up well enough?" Alar asked.

"I'd'a tied her up more if I had more rope," Tove said, not returning his smile.

"She say anything?"

"Not a word," Ukrit said.

Alar and the assassin studied one another.

"We taking the wraps off?" Tove asked.

"Seems a bit rude," Alar said. Their eyes met, both of them aware of what the other was thinking. What was she hiding? To Tove, who until recently might have wanted to hide her face from the world, the fact that this deadly woman did so must have been fascinating.

"She attacks us, without provocation, mind you, she loses her privacy rights," Tove said.

Technically, Tove attacked first, but sensing the contradiction wasn't helpful, Alar shrugged and nodded. Tove set her bow aside, drew her knife, stooped behind the woman, slit one of the wrappings and began unwinding the linen. To his surprise, the woman didn't react. The face that emerged was startling.

Tove dropped the linen, came around to stand next to Alar and said, "Well, that's a letdown."

She was beautiful. She watched them with large eyes above high cheekbones. Her head was shaved recently, but the black stubble emerging from her scalp confirmed she was Imperial. The only sign of her recent exertion was a light blush on her pale cheeks. She gazed past them, her heart-shaped face carefully blank, no hint of the anger Alar expected. He knelt and put himself in her line of sight, sifting through the many questions he wanted to ask when she spoke.

"What are you?"

"Uh uh," Tove said. "Seeing as how we kicked your ass, we get to ask the questions."

The assassin's only reaction was a slight pursing of red lips.

"Why don't we start with that?" Alar asked. He lifted one end of the linen wrap. "What are *you?*"

No response.

"Do you have a name?"

No response.

"This is going to get old," Tove said. "You want me to rough her up?"

Alar chuckled. He didn't think Tove was serious, but he couldn't be entirely sure. He studied the woman, who watched him expectantly. "Your head okay?" No response. Her eyes flicked toward

Ukrit and Scilla. Before her gaze came back to rest on Alar, it lingered for the briefest of moments on the tube containing *Spirit Light,* which Ukrit held.

"If you're looking for the paintings, we burned them," Alar said. If he hadn't been looking for it, he might not have noticed the tiny movement of the muscles around her eyes. Not a flinch, but a reaction nearly as intense on her placid face. "So, it *is* the art." He studied her face. "Let's see. Adelbart?" An ever so slight flaring of the nostrils that might have been disgust. "No. But if not him, who was Adelbart sending them to?"

"What's in Ka'tan?" Ukrit asked.

The destination of the caravan had been a topic of speculation since they first opened the chest, but the conversation spiraled without landing on any satisfying conclusions.

"There's an Imp garrison and the mines," Tove answered mechanically, then stated what they already concluded. "They don't seem likely."

"No," Alar said.

"Maybe they were going somewhere else," Scilla said. "The supply wagons were going to Ka'tan, but the art wagon was going another place."

"But where?" Alar said.

"The Desulti."

Alar stood abruptly and whirled toward the voice. Tove drew back the string of her bow and pointed the arrow at the three women emerging from the mouth of the ravine.

"Ragan," Alar said. He put his hand on Tove's bow, urging her to lower it. "I'd say I was surprised, but this makes a sort of sense. You are fond of the dramatic entrance." He noticed Gallia had a hand on Ragan's back and the other on her elbow, helping Ragan negotiate the uneven ground. When they came to a stop, Alar nodded to the other women. "Gallia, Ecke."

"Alar," Ragan said. "Nice to see you survived." She looked around at the others and added, "All of you. It's a bit of a miracle when you think about it."

"Wouldn't have, if it weren't for you two," Ukrit said.

"You're pregnant," Tove said. She glanced up at Alar. "*Really* pregnant."

"Very observant, Tove," Ragan said with a chuckle. Gallia helped her lower herself to sit on a boulder.

"Didn't know you were married," Tove said.

"Didn't mention it," Ragan said. "Not sure it's any of your business."

"Not trying to pry. Just, Seidi sister and all," Tove said. She glanced up at Alar. "Didn't know that lot *could* get married."

"We're no longer Seidi sisters," Gallia said.

"Right," Tove said. "I knew that."

Ukrit cleared his throat. "We never got a chance to thank you for helping rescue Scilla."

Ragan's eyes grew distant, a sad smile appearing on her face. "I only hope others will return the favor someday."

Ukrit hesitated. "Not sure what that means," he said under his breath. He looked at Alar and shrugged.

Alar returned his gaze to Ragan and stepped aside to give her a view of their prisoner. The assassin was staring at Ragan and Gallia with an intensity that was startling on her placid face.

"You were saying," Alar said to Ragan.

"She's a Desulti."

When everyone gave her blank looks, she explained. "The Desulti are women, Imperial women, who have rejected the roles forced on them by the Empire's patriarchy."

Alar looked at Tove, whose face showed no more understanding than he had. Noticing him looking, she shrugged.

Ragan tried again. "In Imperial society, women who aren't Seidi sisters have few options. They can be wives and mothers, concubines, or spinsters. In some ways, for a woman who is smart or ambitious, being Imperial is worse than being a member of a lower caste."

"My heart bleeds," Scilla said.

"Yes, I know," Ragan said, chuckling. "Hard to be sympathetic with women, forced to idle their lives away on their grand estates, servants tending to their every need."

"How horrible," Scilla said sarcastically.

"That would suck," Tove said at the same time.

The two women exchanged frowns.

"*I* wouldn't want to live like that," Scilla said. "But being bored hardly compares to Imps burning your home and murdering your family."

"So these women, Imperial women, they run away from home and join the Desulti ... to do what, become trained killers?" Alar asked. He looked down at the Desulti who was watching the exchange with interest.

"Not all of them," Ragan said, resting her hands on her stomach. "Our friend here is a Murtair. They carry out the more ... delicate tasks for the order. Most of the women are involved in politics or commerce, both black market and legitimate. Some are artists, farmers, whatever the order requires of them. But most importantly, they have some say in the course of their lives. The Desulti have their own expectations and rules, but there are far more options available to them than elsewhere in the Empire. At least for Imperial women. Outside the Inquisition, they may be the most powerful institution in the Empire, and they are as wealthy as the emperor, maybe more so."

Alar glanced at Tove, who was staring at the Desulti, fascinated.

"So these women just leave and say, 'to the Otherworld with all of you, I'm doing my own thing'?" she asked.

Curious about her reaction, Alar looked at the assassin in time to catch a small twitch at the corner of her mouth. It might as well have been a guffaw. Her eyes met his briefly before returning to Ragan.

"So Adelbart, I'm guessing," Alar said, "is sending priceless art, banned *Alle'oss* art, to the Desulti, a mysterious order with dubious business dealings. We always assumed our governor was no more corrupt than your typical Imp official, but apparently we've underestimated him."

"What are they going to do with the paintings?" Ukrit asked. "They can't sell them."

"There are those in the Empire who would pay, secretly, for *Alle'oss* art, but I don't think that is what they intend to do with it," Ragan said.

"Outside the Empire," Scilla said.

"The paintings might be priceless to the *Alle'oss*," Ragan said, "valuable to a certain segment of Imperials, but in other parts of the world, the works of Valdemar and the other new school artists are valued beyond imagining."

"They burned them."

Alar looked down at the assassin. She glared up at him, the carefully controlled expression gone. Alar grinned and her scowl fell away, replaced by an accusing glare. "You lied," she said.

"Yes, he lied," Ragan said.

Alar was no longer surprised when Ragan made pronouncements about things she couldn't know, but he also knew she had her own agenda. He looked closer and noticed dark circles under her eyes. Her skin, normally the darker hue of an Imperial, was almost pallid. She looked unwell. "Why are you here, Ragan?" he asked.

Chapter 34

A Lot of Apples in the Air

The governor's assistant stood in front of his boss's door clutching a sheaf of papers in front of him like a shield. "The governor is not in his office."

"It's Gerold, isn't it?" Harold asked.

Gerold nodded stiffly.

"I've been more patient than the governor has a right to expect, but my patience is wearing thin," Harold said, putting some steel in his voice. "When will the governor return?" Before Gerold could answer, voices raised in anger drifted through the closed door.

Gerold stared at Harold, his cheeks darkening. "He … should be back by three this afternoon."

"Three," Harold said.

Gerold nodded.

"We shall return then," Harold said. "Make sure the governor is available." He nodded to Henrik, turned, and left.

Henrik caught up to him in the hall. "He was lying."

"Yes, he was." Harold stopped beside ornately carved double doors and glanced back the way they came. "But what man in his position has not?" Not seeing the assistant, he pushed open one of the doors and slipped through into a large room. It was similar to the grand ballrooms in the Imperial capital, but in the smaller space, the elaborate decorations designed to impress appeared cheap and garish. Harold examined the room while Henrik entered and closed the door behind him.

"Sir?"

Harold pulled Henrik out of the way and opened one of the doors a crack so he could see down the hall in the direction away from the governor's office. Satisfied, he ambled over to a painting mounted beside the door.

"What are we doing?" Henrik asked.

"Waiting," Harold said, studying the painting.

Henrik joined him. "Who would keep an inquisitor waiting?"

Harold chuckled. "Technically, I am not an inquisitor yet."

"Still, he has to be aware you won't forget this slight."

"Yes, that is rather curious, isn't it? That's why I suspect the governor has more pressing concerns than playing petty games. We are waiting to find out what those might be," Harold said. Before Henrik could reply, Harold gestured to the painting and said, "I have to say, I appreciate having the time to examine this art more closely."

Henrik grunted.

The canvas depicted a woman working at a spinning wheel, smiling down at a small child on the floor at her feet. The boy looked up at her, a pudgy hand lifted, finger extended toward the spinning wheel. The artist captured the boy's expression so faithfully—the furrowed brow, the slightly parted lips—Harold could almost hear the conversation between the mother and her curious son. "They're really quite remarkable. The colors." He swept this hand across the canvas. "The depth. It almost looks real."

"Hmm," Henrik said. "But what's the purpose of it?"

Harold gave Henrik a curious grin. "What do you mean?"

Henrik pointed to a neighboring canvas, a depiction of a woman standing at the edge of a cliff, staring out over plains far below. It was Abria, the first Seidi sister, whose power enabled the Vollen people to wring the Empire from much larger countries. It was typical of Imperial art, flat and pale. "That one shows Abria before the Vollen tribes descended from their mountains." He looked at Harold. "It was a pivotal moment in the history of the Empire. It reminds us who we are."

"Is that all we are?" Harold asked. When Henrik lifted a brow, Harold turned back to the *Alle'oss* painting. "Isn't this also who we are?"

"We?"

Harold waved his hands. "We, the collective we, people. Aren't these the moments that make us, as individuals, who we are? The simple moments that make up life?"

Henrik gazed at the painting, then shrugged. "Perhaps." He turned his back on the image. "Don't you believe in the Empire?"

Harold sighed. He wondered when this would come up. Though it was hard to see into the brother's heart, he hoped Henrik's views were near to his own. Knowing he may be about to poison their friendship, he answered in measured tones. "Of course, I do. The Empire brings order." Henrik gave him a look that was difficult to interpret. Harold clasped his hands behind his back. "I'll be the first to admit, in private, the Empire is not perfect. But the Empire is here, and it is stable." He forgot his audience, speaking more to himself as he continued. "This foolish provocation of the Kaileuk will stir up a hornet's nest that only the emperor's armies can contain. There are others, like the Union, waiting to take their share if the Empire fails. Imperial governance is necessary to maintain order in the conquered districts. Without the Empire, economies would fail, starvation and war would follow. There would be decades of bloodshed and chaos." He paused, nodding to himself. "No, the Empire has its faults, but it is far better than the alternative. It is much better to work within the system to tame its worst excesses." He stared, unseeing, at the wall. "What is the alternative?"

"But it's illegal."

"Hmm? What?" Harold said.

Henrik turned around and pointed to the depiction of the mother and son. "The art. It's illegal."

"Oh. Yes," Harold said. "This so-called new school attracted unwanted attention for depicting ordinary subjects so faithfully, but were it as simple as that, the Inquisition would be content with quietly confiscating their works and intimidating the artists."

"But why did they execute that one, what was his name?"

"Valdemar."

"Yes," Henrik said, "That wasn't very quietly done. In fact, it was quite the spectacle."

"Yes, but as you said, no one knows why they executed him. Have you wondered why?"

Henrik started to speak, then stopped, his brow furrowing. "Now that you mention it, I don't remember the reading of the charges."

"That's right. There were none. They wanted to send the message to a small, very specific audience, without drawing widespread attention to his crimes."

Henrik lifted his brows. "What crimes, specifically?"

"Some of the new school artists have chosen dangerous subjects," Harold said. "I don't know what Valdemar painted, but it raised alarms at the highest levels of the Church. The High Priest himself signed the edict condemning the new school artists."

Henrik let his eyes linger on Harold's face for a moment, then turned and studied the mother and child. Harold knew what he was thinking. It wasn't uncommon for the Inquisition to confiscate art deemed heretical and even arrest the artists in the most egregious cases. But it was hard to imagine what could attract the personal attention of the High Priest. Certainly, it wasn't subjects such as this mother and son.

While they were contemplating, voices drifted through the open door. Harold hurried over, pressed himself to the closed door, and peered through the opening. A group of men appeared, their backs to Harold. He pulled the door open wider to allow Henrik to watch the men receding down the hall. There was a short, round man in the front, accompanied by two enormous men in Union uniforms. Following the others were two scruffy-looking *Alle'oss*. One of them was limping and carrying a leather tube.

"Were those Union men?" Henrik whispered.

"Yes, they were." When the five turned and disappeared down the staircase to the lower floors, Harold said, "Follow them, but be careful." Henrik hurried after them. Harold watched him go, then headed in the opposite direction. He entered Gerold's office, and ignoring the assistant's protests, he pushed through the door to the governor's office.

Adelbart, sitting behind his desk, startled and spluttered, "What is the meaning of this? Gerold, what is this?"

Gerold followed Harold into the office and took up position beside and slightly behind the governor. He opened his mouth to speak.

Harold pointed at him. "You. Don't speak unless I ask you a question."

Gerold's mouth snapped shut.

Harold let his arm drop and clasped his hands behind his back, noting the painting behind the governor's desk was missing. Adelbart watched him as if he were a snake.

"Governor, who were those men who just left your office?"

"I don't have—"

"Yes, governor, you do."

"You're just a novice."

"With the full authority of the Inquisition behind me. Inquisitor Hoerst, himself, sent me." The governor went still. Interesting. There was something there, some history between Hoerst and Adelbart. "Now, who were those men?"

"Novice, if I may?" Gerold asked.

Harold nodded.

"The party included Chagan Koutman. He is the commander of the Union company the emperor contracted to replace the infantry that was recalled. He had two of his captains with him."

"And the two *Alle'oss?*"

Gerold hesitated, concocting a plausible lie. "Chagan hired them as guides."

Harold gazed at Gerold until the man dropped his eyes, but decided to wait to find out what Henrik discovered before confronting them about the lie.

Adelbart was watching him expectantly. "Is there something else?"

"Yes, I require the use of your ranger company to search the forest for *oss'stera*."

The governor's face drained of all color. His eyes flicked to Gerold, but when no help was forthcoming, he cleared his throat and said, "The rangers are on assignment."

"On assignment?"

"Yes, we've … had reports of unrest at the mines in Ka'tan." He spoke slowly, but he finished in a rush. "The garrison commander requested assistance."

Harold glanced at Gerold and caught the smallest shake of his head.

"Don't the mines have their own garrison?"

"Yes, but you see, the rangers are there to hunt down troublemakers in the mountains *around* the mines," Adelbart said. He watched Harold, the slightest arch in his brows, gauging the effectiveness of the lie.

"Your cavalry then?" Harold asked.

Adelbart chuckled and gestured vaguely with his hand. "Funny story and quite the coincidence, but the cavalry is," he seemed to lock in place, his mouth hanging open. Then he straightened in his chair. "You have no idea what we have to deal with in the districts. Besides, I'm an Imperial governor, the emperor's representative in Argren. I don't have to reveal all my affairs to you. Even if you do represent the Inquisition and Inquisitor … Hoerst. How I deploy the forces under my command is not within your purview."

Technically, the governor was correct, but Harold was not used to being lied to. Especially in such a brazenly clumsy manner. He stepped forward so that he loomed over the governor. Adelbart shrunk back in his chair. Before Harold spoke, he caught motion out of the corner of his eye. He glanced at Gerold. The governor's assistant nodded toward the door.

Harold looked down at the governor, who was coiled to spring from the chair at Harold's slightest movement. Harold took a moment to suppress his anger. When he was sure he could speak calmly, he said, "Governor, we will continue this conversation at a later date." He turned and exited the office, followed by Gerold.

The governor's assistant slipped past him in the outer office and exited to the hall. He paused to ensure Harold followed, then led them to the ballroom. Before Gerold could speak, Harold said, "Whatever you say to me better be the truth. All of it."

"Yes, of course, novice." He took a breath and let it out. "You are aware of the governor's lineage?"

"He's the nephew of the emperor."

"Yes. The emperor appointed him at the behest of the emperor's sister, the governor's mother. She is quite a formidable woman." Gerold was looking at Harold's chest, but when he said the last, he glanced up at Harold's face. "Her son ... well, he is not an *unintelligent* man, but he has never lived up to his mother's rather high expectations. I think she was hoping he would rise to the occasion."

"I take it he hasn't."

"The governor," Gerold's mouth moved as he searched for the right words. "Has struggled to adapt. I'm afraid he has become rather rudderless without his mother's influence."

"She put you here to keep an eye on him."

"Yes." A word laden with regret and relief, as if he was confessing a shameful secret. "She asked me to keep him out of trouble." He gave a nervous laugh, his fingers coming up to rub his forehead. "I thought, well, how hard could it be?" His eyes found Harold's again, for a moment, "I am finding it a challenge."

Harold gazed up at the ceiling, his lips pursed. Where to start? "The men who were meeting with the governor, Chagan ..."

"Chagan Koutman." Gerold sagged slightly, looking relieved that Harold took the lead in the conversation.

"They were arguing when you told me the governor was absent."

"Yes."

"Why?"

"The governor owes Chagan a great deal of money."

Harold considered the likely possibilities. "Has the governor embezzled the funds the emperor designated to pay the mercenaries?"

"No, the … uh … the governor contracted Chagan to carry out a task. A separate task."

Harold waited, but when no further explanation was forthcoming, he said, "Gerold, if you make me drag this out of you, I will become angrier than I already am."

Gerold startled and lifted his hands in resignation. "It's just, it's a very complicated situation. The governor has a lot of apples in the air." A weak smile flitted across his face, but fled when his eyes flicked up and saw Harold's expression. "The governor's daughter ran away and ended up with the Desulti."

The Desulti again. Coincidence? "Can't say I'm surprised," Harold said.

"Yes, well, the governor hired the Union mercenaries to retrieve her from the local Desulti safe house."

Harold stared at him, his anger forgotten. The Desulti responded aggressively when anyone attempted such a thing. Women had to know if they came to them, the Desulti would protect them. Many of them would face retaliation if the men they left were allowed to retrieve them. How was Adelbart still alive? He glanced at the door. "The Desulti don't know who attacked their safe house," he answered his own question.

Gerold shook his head. "I assume not."

Harold gazed over the man's head. "But they will find out. The Murtair spotted in the art district is here to investigate."

Gerold shook his head again, peeking up at Harold. "No."

Harold sighed. "Just tell me."

"The governor has run up a rather sizable debt with the Desulti. He was attempting to settle that debt using the *Alle'oss* art." He gestured to an empty spot on the wall. "He sent it on the regular supply caravan to Ka'tan."

"The rangers were sent to guard it."

"Yes, it was my idea to send the rangers as an escort. It was an extraordinarily valuable shipment, after all."

"But?"

"The caravan never arrived and the rangers have disappeared."

"A company of rangers? Disappeared?"

"Yes, one can only imagine." Gerold shook his head. "We sent a squad of cavalry to search for them, but so far we've heard nothing."

"Only a squad? Adelbart implied the company was on assignment."

"The governor wanted to send the entire company. However, Captain Brennerman and I felt it unwise to leave the garrison entirely in the hands of the mercenaries. The tension between the mercenaries and the cavalry has escalated alarmingly."

Remembering the missing art in the governor's office, Harold turned, noting the irregular arrangement of the remaining canvases. Others had been removed. "The Desulti lurking in the art district ..."

"Yes, I believe she is attempting to find the stolen art."

"Then who else could have stolen it?" Harold said, more to himself than Gerold.

"Well, funny you should ask. Chagan was here to demand payment, which the governor doesn't have. And, quite the coincidence, the two *Alle'oss* men showed up and said they know who stole the paintings." He looked up at Harold. "They even brought one as proof."

"So Chagan has agreed to take the paintings in payment."

"Much to the governor's displeasure, as you can imagine."

"Because he has no way to pay the Desulti."

Gerold nodded.

"Not that it will make much difference if he did. The Desulti will find out who attacked their safe house," Harold mused. "What became of his daughter?"

"Elois is being held prisoner by the Union, pending payment."

"At the fort?"

Gerold shook his head and pointed at the floor. "In the dungeon. It was the only secure place away from prying eyes. The governor didn't tell Chagan they were raiding a Desulti safe house, and he is rather anxious to keep it secret until he leaves."

Harold was rarely, if ever, at a loss for what course to take, but the governor's tangled affairs had him flummoxed. He wasn't even sure which malfeasances were within his purview, and which he should refer to more secular authorities. The only thing he was sure of was the man couldn't be left in his position. The trick was how to remove him over the objections of the emperor and his sister. It might be easier to allow the Desulti to take care of the situation. In any case, this mess was quite clearly above his pay grade.

"Have you reported any of this to the governor's mother?" he asked.

"Daga, no!" Gerold said. "At first, I thought I could get things under control. I mean, after all, it was just small debts, extravagant parties, women—" Gerold looked up at Harold and said, "Then one day I woke up and ..." He threw his arms out. "This!" He let his arms flop to his sides and said morosely, "My only hope is the old woman dies of shock before she can have me killed."

The easiest thing to do was to drop the entire affair into Hoerst's lap. Remembering the governor's reaction when he mentioned the inquisitor, Harold asked, "What history does the governor have with Hoerst?"

"The inquisitor wished to have Elois as a concubine. The governor refused." Harold was amused to hear a note of pride in Gerold's voice. "Inquisitor Hoerst found something he could use for leverage against the governor. I mean, how hard is it, really?" Gerold laughed weakly.

"Anyway, the governor was forced to relent. Unfortunately, his daughter objected and ran to the Desulti."

"And Hoerst?" Harold asked, his heart sinking.

"When the inquisitor threatened to have Adelbart arrested, the Desulti objected, and who could blame them? The governor owes them quite a large sum of money." Gerold fell silent. When Harold didn't speak, he looked up. "Novice?"

Harold's eyes focused on the governor's assistant.

"What should I do?" Gerold asked. He looked up at Harold, relief in his expression. He was undoubtedly hoping Harold would extract him from his predicament. Unfortunately, Harold's brain was frozen. He needed to get away, find a quiet place to think, and wait for Henrik.

"Nothing for the moment," Harold said to Gerold's obvious disappointment. "I need to consider this ... tangle ... to find the best course of action. For the time being, do nothing. And for Daga's sake, try to keep the governor from making it worse." Gerold nodded meekly. Harold turned and fled from the room.

Chapter 35

Or Some *Sheoda*

Ragan gathered herself and smiled. "I came to ask a favor of you, Alar."

"Oh, no, no, no," Tove said. "Don't you talk to her, Alar. Whatever it is, it won't be good. She's going to tell you someone's in trouble and needs your help, you're the only one can help, or some s*heoda*. You'll run off like you always do 'cause you're reckless and you got a soft heart." She waved a hand at Ragan. "You can't talk to him. We already done you all the favors we owe you."

Alar studied Tove. She was right. He looked at Ragan, prepared to say no, but something in her face stopped him. She was always so sure of herself, giving off an air of someone who knew more than everyone else. Though she was trying to project the same confidence, it was obviously a veneer. Whatever she was trying to hide found its way to the surface as tightness around her eyes and lips. Her hands cradled her belly as if she held something precious and fragile. Alar looked at Gallia and Ecke standing behind her and saw something there as well, some suppressed emotion. Ecke nodded encouragingly, and Alar dropped his head.

"*Sheoda*," Tove said.

"I can, at least, hear her out," Alar said.

"You know that won't be all you do," Tove said.

Ragan looked for a moment as if she would burst into tears, but she mastered her face and scooted forward to get her feet under herself. Gallia and Ecke hurried to take her arms to help her up.

"What do we do with her?" Scilla asked, pointing at the Desulti.

"You can let me go!" the assassin snapped. "It's all very dramatic, what you have going on here, but that art belongs to my order. I heard you saying you *wanted* to return it to the owners. Well, we own it. Just let me go. I'll go get some help, come back and take it off your hands. When I leave, I'll gladly forget I ever heard of any of you."

"No, Alar. No," Ukrit said. "Those paintings belong to the *Alle'oss*. They don't mean anything to the Desul — whatever. They're just going to sell them and we'll never see them again."

"Alar," Ragan said quietly. "I'm afraid time is of the essence. Perhaps, you can make a decision on the art when time allows more careful consideration."

Alar looked from Ukrit to the assassin. He pointed at Ragan and said, "She's right."

"*Sheoda*," the Desulti spat.

"Whoa! Some mouth on you," Tove said.

The Desulti ignored her. "You will regret this decision, Alar."

"I haven't made a decision," Alar said. He nodded to Tove. "We can at least get her out of the cold. Take her to your roundhouse, and have Stolten keep an eye on her."

"Actually, I'd like to … I mean, it should be me, keeps an eye on her," Tove said, glancing up at him then looking away.

"You sure?" he asked her. When she nodded, he said, "Okay. I'll let you know what Ragan wants before I make a decision." Tove gave him a single, quick nod. Alar gestured to the woman trussed up on the ground. "You want to cut her legs free?"

"No!" Ukrit, Scilla and Tove chorused.

"Right, good idea," Alar said with a grin. "Guess you'll have to carry her."

The Desulti struggled against the ropes binding her. "You will not carry me like some child."

"Hush," Tove said. "Stolten, you want to get the head, I'll get the feet."

Alar turned away and followed Ragan with Scilla and Ukrit. "Ukrit, you should put the painting back with the others." When Ukrit started to protest, Alar called back to Stolten, "Stolten, put a couple of guards on the chest."

"Right," he grunted, struggling to control the squirming assassin.

***

Alar led them to his roundhouse. He pulled the door open and stepped out of the way to allow the others to enter. Ragan, supported by Gallia, stopped, bent over slightly, wincing and panting.

"You okay?" Alar asked.

She nodded and, after a few moments, she straightened and entered the house.

After the three women were inside, Scilla whispered to Alar. "She's in labor."

Alar's eyes widened. "You sure?"

"Pretty sure. I used to assist the midwife at home."

"How long?" Alar asked.

Scilla shrugged. "Impossible to tell without doing an exam. The contractions are still pretty far apart. Probably hours, but if she's had other babies, could be much sooner." She ducked inside.

Ukrit watched her go, hitched a brow at Alar and said, "Weird day, huh?"

Inside, Ukrit set to stoking the fire. Scilla pulled Alar onto one of the beds, tugged his shirt over his head and examined his cuts. Ragan perched uneasily on the edge of the opposite bed. Gallia sat beside her and Ecke stood on the other side.

"Okay," Alar said. "You got me here. What's the favor?"

Ragan's eyes flicked to the side and her mouth moved as if she were whispering to herself. Alar readied himself for a long, complex justification for whatever she wanted. Instead, she looked him in the eye and said, "I need you to save the life of Harold Wolfe, a ... novice of the Inquisition."

Alar stared at her, sure she would crack a smile, but instead, she held her face rigid. Thinking it must be a Seidi sister's idea of humor, he looked at Gallia. She was watching him, curiously. Ecke appeared to be holding her breath, eyes wide. Alar glanced at Ukrit and Scilla, finding as much shock in their expressions as he felt. He sighed, looked down at Scilla's hand pressed against his stomach and shook his head. "What are you trying to accomplish, Ragan?"

"Alar, surely you aren't—" Scilla began before she was interrupted.

"She sees the future," Ecke said in a rush. When all eyes turned to her, she hurried on. "From the *sjel'and.*" She gave a small shrug before continuing, her hands helping to tell the story. "Or many futures, and in all the futures, inquisitors come and kill her family. Because they will be witches. Her daughters." She waved her hand at Ragan, presumably pointing out the unborn baby. "*Powerful* witches. She's trying to change the future to save her daughters." She glanced to the side and shrugged. "But every time she changes it, a *different* inquisitor comes." She looked directly at Alar and raised a finger. "BUT, there is one inquisitor, a man with gray eyes, who lets them live." She paused for a breath and Ragan tried to speak, but Ecke started again. "The man with the gray eyes is going to die tonight, in Richeleau and Ragan needs you to save him so he'll be around to save her daughters." She slammed her mouth shut, stood stock still and stared with wide eyes at Alar.

All eyes shifted from Ecke to Ragan. "Well, that was a little blunt," Ragan said with a weak a smile, "with less nuance than I would have used, but it did save a lot of time. A bit loose on the details, but essentially correct."

"You communicate with the spirits of *annen'hein?*"

"Yes, and it is as unpleasant as you would imagine."

"They show you the future?" Alar asked, feeling heat rise on the back of his neck. When she nodded, he asked, "So while we're all muddling through, afraid of what the future will bring, you already know. No wonder you always seem so smug. Might be helpful if you let others in on your secrets."

"It's not that simple," Ragan said, an uncharacteristic note of pleading in her voice. "The future is always shifting. There are many possibilities, and it's difficult to determine which are most likely. Telling someone what *might* happen can do far more harm than good. Acting on the wrong vision could be far worse than making your own choices. Believe me, I know from personal experience."

"But this vision of your daughters, you're *sure* of that one?" The words came out harsher than Alar intended them.

"Yes, as sure as it is possible to be." She glanced down. When she looked at Alar again, she bent forward slightly and raised a hand in supplication. "There are many futures in which they die, but there is only one where they live. If this man, this novice, dies, even that slim hope will be gone." Her voice cracked as the veneer flaked away, allowing the depth of her desperation to show.

Alar nodded to her swollen stomach. "So, if I refuse, I condemn your daughters to their deaths?"

Ragan's face fell. She dropped her eyes to her hands caressing her stomach. When she spoke, Alar could barely hear her. "I know I'm asking too much. You don't owe me or my family anything. But you are my only hope." She looked up at him. "I have no choice but to ask." She paused. "Yes, if you refuse, the Inquisition will kill my daughters."

Alar studied her face, searching for signs of deception. He looked at Ecke, who nodded rapidly. "You've seen evidence she can see the future?" he asked, and looked from Ecke to Gallia.

They looked at one another and shook their heads, reluctantly.

"If you can see the future, then why do you need to ask?" he asked Ragan. "Don't you already know what I will say?"

"It doesn't work like that. I'm not omniscient." When she saw the doubt in Alar's expression, she said. "How else could I have known Scilla was in *Zhot tl?*"

Alar had worried at that question for a long time without coming up with a plausible explanation.

"She's got a point," Ukrit said. "And she knew you were a realm walker even before you did."

He looked at Scilla, who was threading sinew through a needle. When she noticed him looking, she shrugged and the corner of her mouth twitched up. "I've seen stranger things lately."

Alar sighed, then he looked at Ragan and asked, "What would we have to do?"

***

The big man and the woman with the scarred face finally managed to wrestle her into a small one-room house. The Desulti made sure it wasn't too difficult for them, only wanting to distract them while she worked at the bindings on her wrists. Unfortunately, the red-headed woman knew her business. When they tossed her roughly onto a small, hard bed and stood back to watch her roll into a sitting position, she was no closer to freeing her hands.

Breathing hard, the man said, "I were you, I'd get as far from her as you can in here and keep an arrow nocked."

The woman nodded, but didn't look away from her captive. There was something there, something going on behind those blue eyes.

"I'll send someone to help you keep an eye on her," the big man said.

The woman barely acknowledged him as he turned and left. She moved to the far side of the room and worked the fire. The Desulti watched her, waiting for her to come close. Unfortunately, when she was done, she sat on the bed across from the Desulti and stared at her.

"Your name is Tove," the Desulti said.

The red-headed woman nodded. "And your name?"

The Desulti didn't answer.

Tove's lips twisted. She glanced to the side, then looked as if she were gathering herself before asking, "So, you and all those other women, you live together up near Ka'tan?"

There it was. The Desulti smiled inwardly. It wasn't her place to reveal anything about the Desulti, but what could it hurt? The Imperial witch already told her as much. She nodded.

"No men?"

The Desulti shook her head, keeping her amusement off her face. This woman hid deep wounds. Weaknesses she could exploit.

"They teach you how to fight like that?" Tove asked, nodding toward the door.

"Not everyone. Only the Murtair. The elite."

The woman's lips twitched. Her hand came up and rubbed at the scarred corner of her mouth. "But ... it's just Imperials, the women?"

There was something in her expression. Something the Desulti recognized, and for a moment, she felt sympathy for this young woman. But she was Murtair. She couldn't afford to let her guard down. "Yes," she said. The truth. But then she lied. "But there are those who say we should welcome others. The *Alle'oss*." It was easy. The young woman tried to hide it, but there was a hunger there. Something the Desulti could work with. She hitched a sympathetic mask onto her face to encourage that hunger.

The door swung open and the big man came in, followed by a boy.

The Desulti wiped the expression from her face.

"Tove, Alar wants a word," the man said. "Willen and I will keep an eye on our guest."

Tove pressed her lips tight. She stood, peeking at the Desulti as she hurried toward the door, her head bowed, as if someone caught her in a shameful act. The big man and Willen took a seat, staring at her nervously. The Desulti let a wide smile stretch her lips.

***

Alar, Ukrit and Scilla waited outside for Tove to appear. As soon as she saw their expressions, her face clouded over. "You let her talk you into something stupid and reckless," she said before Alar could speak.

"Yes," Ukrit said and shrugged when Alar glared at him. "Well, you can't say stupid and reckless don't describe it."

Alar turned back to Tove and sighed. "I'll go along with reckless. Let's hold off on stupid until we see how badly it goes wrong." He lifted a placating hand toward her. "Frankly, I wasn't going to tell you, because I knew how you would react, but I've made that mistake before."

"Tell me," Tove said.

"She asked us to go to Richeleau and ... you remember the inquisitor I—"

"Oh, no, no, no," Tove cut him off. "She asked you to kill an inquisitor?"

Alar stood still, hand aloft, mouth hanging open. "Not exactly, no."

"For the Father's sake," Ukrit said. "Get to the point."

"She asked us to *save* the inquisitor, or novice, whatever he is, to keep him alive," Alar said quickly, then took a step back and watched Tove warily.

Tove burst into laughter, but when she saw the expressions on all their faces, her laughter trailed away. "She asked you to do what?"

"Listen, Tove," Alar said. "This is why I wasn't going to tell you. There is some sort of prophecy about what this man is going to do sometime in the future—"

"What are you talking about?"

"It's complicated. I don't have time to explain it," Alar said. "Do you want to come with us or not?"

Tove hesitated, then glanced over her shoulder at the roundhouse. "No," she said. "Someone needs to watch the prisoner, and I don't trust anyone else."

Alar wasn't fooled by her smile. There was something going on here, but Alar wasn't sure what it was. He returned her grin and said, "You're right." He took her arm and led her away from the others. He meant to ask her what had her troubled, but when he saw the apprehension in her eyes, he only asked, "You'll be careful, right?"

"Always am," Tove said. "Besides, I'm not the one off to rescue an inquisitor from a death they deserve."

"Alar!" It was Ecke, running down the path from his house. "Ragan's water broke."

"The baby's coming," Scilla said.

"Do you have a midwife?" Ecke asked. "Me and Gallia, we don't know anything about babies."

"Scilla?" Alar asked. "Can you handle this?"

"Yes, I suppose," she said hesitantly. "I've never delivered a baby by myself, but I've seen it plenty of times." She gave Alar a pleading look. "But—"

"We'll be careful," Ukrit said. "I'll keep him out of trouble."

"Hurry," Ecke said and took a few steps towards Alar's roundhouse.

Alar put his arm around Scilla's waist and pulled her close. He kissed her, feeling the same thrill he did the night before. He broke the kiss and said, "We'll be careful."

"Hurry." Ecke took off at a run.

Scilla followed, letting her fingers linger in Alar's hand until she was forced to let go.

Alar watched her go, then turned to Ukrit, who was watching him with one brow raised. "I assume you're intentions are honorable, despite you being a disreputable scoundrel."

Alar gave Tove a hug, then winked and said, "Be careful." He slapped Ukrit's shoulder and started walking. "I am always and ever an honorable man." Weeks of worry and anxiety fell away, leaving him suddenly light and energized. Off on a reckless adventure, no one to worry about but himself. Well, and Ukrit, but he would keep Ukrit safe.

***

Tove watched them walk away, then turned back toward the roundhouse where the Desulti was probably toying with poor Willen the same way she toyed with Tove. Tove knew predators when she saw them. Stepping away from the situation for a moment was exactly what she needed to regain her composure. Before she could pull the door open, Stolten emerged. "Ah, good," he said when he saw Tove approaching. "I've got to get back. Didn't want to leave Willen alone with her. Been eying him like a hawk watching a mouse."

Tove nodded as he passed, then pushed through the door to find Willen on a knee at the Desulti's feet, knife in hand.

"What are you doing!?"

Willen jumped up, stepped in the fire, then leapt aside, stomping his boot. When he was sure his foot was safe, he gestured toward the Desulti with his knife hand, forcing her to lean away. "She's got to pee. I was just going to cut the ropes around her ankles so she could walk to the privy."

Tove shook her head and pointed to one of the four beds. "No, no, no. You just sit down over there and keep quiet."

"But she's got to go," Willen said.

"She can go right where she is. It's not my bed." Willen started to argue but when he saw Tove's expression, his mouth snapped shut. She watched him sheath his blade. Once he was seated, glowering up at her from lowered eyes, she settled onto the bed across the fire from the assassin. When she noticed a smile appearing on the Desulti's face, she said, "You know your smiles might be more convincing if it didn't look like you were selecting something out of your wardrobe to try on."

The prisoner's smile fell away, replaced by a speculative gaze. "You attacked me first," she said.

"You snuck up behind us," Tove said without hesitation. "Might want to announce yourself, you want to sneak around wearing a mask." The Desulti's lips pursed. "Besides, you tried to kill me with that star thing."

"I was trying to cut your bowstring."

Tove barked a laugh. "You got some stones on you." She glanced at Willen, who was staring at her, his cheeks darkening. Her laughter died away. She and the Desulti watched each other through a curtain of smoke. "You that good?"

Instead of answering, the Desulti asked, "What's the deal with your friend, Alar? What is he?"

"Sorry," Tove said with a chuckle. "That's privileged information."

Chapter 36

An Unexpected Offer

Harold returned to the office he shared with Henrik in the gendarmerie, barely aware of his surroundings. It was finally clear why Hoerst sent him, alone, to Richeleau. The inquisitor knew it would be impossible for Harold to ignore Adelbart's peccadilloes. Hoerst was probably even aware of the arrangement between Adelbart and the Union. Harold couldn't believe the Inquisition didn't have informants in the governor's organization, especially given the man's obvious unreliability. Hoerst knew Harold wouldn't simply walk away, wouldn't be content to simply pass on the knowledge to his superiors. He was counting on Harold's deep-seated need to prove himself. It wouldn't matter to Hoerst which of them, the Desulti or the Union, Harold ran afoul of, he would be just as dead.

He paced the small office, considering his options. He could defy Hoerst's expectations, return to Brennan and report everything Gerold told him. The fly in that ointment was Hoerst blackmailing the governor. Even if he left Hoerst out of his report, the inquisitor would suspect Harold knew. Would he allow Harold to keep that secret, knowing he could reveal it at any time? That didn't seem like Hoerst. He came to a stop, inches from the wall, and stared at the minute flecks of mica embedded in the granite. Hoerst obviously hoped to rid the Inquisition of the half-breed novice. If he suspected Harold knew about the blackmail, he would make Harold's life a living hell, if he allowed him to live.

Harold came around his desk and dropped into the chair. Maybe he could have Hoerst killed. The thought sprung fully formed into his mind, leaving him momentarily stunned. Breaths coming short and shallow, his eyes flicked to the open door. He never heard of the Desulti hiring out the Murtair, but perhaps in this case. They did have reason to want Hoerst dead. He shook his head. The Desulti wouldn't hire themselves out, and he didn't have the coin to pay for such a thing, anyway. Maybe he could goad Hoerst into a duel. No, the inquisitor was too smart for that. Some thugs in a dark alley? Messy and unreliable. He took a deep breath and blew it out. It was a ridiculous idea.

His gaze fell on the map of Richeleau and its surroundings still spread out on his desk.

"*Oss'stera*," he said aloud, a whisper of an idea hovering just out of reach. He grew still, allowing his mind to follow the breadcrumbs. The *Alle'oss* he saw in the governor's office, the one's who offered to sell the art, they knew where the paintings were. Could the *Alle'oss* attack an Imperial caravan, steal the art, improbably wiping out a ranger company in the process? Who else could it be? The Desulti were apparently still looking for it, so it wasn't them. No one else operated in these mountains. He chuckled humorlessly. Perhaps *oss'stera* were not so feckless as everyone believed. His grin fell away. "Realm walkers and renegade sisters," he whispered.

So, it was feasible the *Alle'oss* stole the art, but would they sell it to the Union? It didn't feel right. His time in Richeleau, his first extensive exposure to the *Alle'oss*, had been a revelation. He let his eyes unfocus, remembering a recent evening. He and Henrik were returning home from a meal in one of their favorite taverns when they stumbled on a troupe of street performers. Knowing a likely mark for their japes when they saw one, they descended on Henrik like hawks. The recalcitrant brother stood, red-faced, enduring the good-natured hoots of the crowd, doing his best to play along. Harold laughed so hard, his eyes streamed. A simple moment, unremarkable in many ways. But it left him disoriented, breathless ... exhilarated. At first, he attributed the feeling to an extra brandy over supper, but that was too simple. He felt different in Richeleau. Lighter, less guarded. For the first time in his life, there were moments when he felt safe enough to let down the emotional armor that kept the world at bay.

Alone in his silent office, he finally understood what he so clumsily tried to explain to Henrik in the governor's mansion. Why take the care to paint a simple moment, to render the mother and child in such exquisite detail the observer couldn't help feeling echoes of their happiness? It was, Harold thought, because the *Alle'oss* took joy in all that life offered, even, maybe especially, the small, everyday moments. It was so unlike the relentless pragmatism of the Empire, where life was often to be endured until you died and submitted to Daga's judgment.

Would the *Alle'oss* sell the paintings? Would rebels who thought they were fighting for their homeland discard the art for which their greatest artists were persecuted by their oppressors? Would they allow it to fall into the hands of Union mercenaries, where it would likely be lost to them forever? He didn't think so, or he didn't want to think so. That meant the two *Alle'oss* who were selling the art to Chagan were traitors. He couldn't know it for sure, but he was certain enough to gamble.

And then the idea he pursued through his thoughts coalesced. He chuckled. The chuckle became a laugh, then grew into deep belly laughs that brought tears to his eyes.

The gendarme, Helga, the woman who found the map for him, the one he concluded was assigned to keep tabs on him and Henrik, appeared at the door. Harold's laughter died away. "Yes," he asked hopefully, wiping away a tear that escaped his eye. "Have you had word from Brother Henrik?"

"Um, no, sir. Sorry," she said. "I just heard you laughing and … was wondering …"

Harold assured her he was okay, then sent her back to lurk in the hallway. Alone again, he shook his head and grinned. How ironic if the pretense Hoerst used to trap him in this quagmire, *oss'stera*, turned out to be a real threat to the Empire. He stared at the empty doorway, index finger tapping the map. *Oss'stera*. Threat to the Empire. He chuckled again. It was a crazy idea. Still, after all, Argren was part of the Empire, so the *Alle'oss* were technically its citizens. He needed Henrik's opinion. Harold was sure the stuffy brother would disapprove, was rather hoping he would talk Harold out of it. But he was too restless to sit still and wait. He stood and retrieved his cloak. He would check a few of the more likely spots where he might find Henrik and come right back.

He paused in the doorway. Helga watched him warily. He was about to turn right, toward the exit, but instead, he turned left and headed to the prison block.

***

Lief was stretched out on the narrow cot, staring at the ceiling, one foot propped on the bars. When Harold stepped in front of the cell, the boy craned his neck up to see who his visitors were. His placid expression didn't change when he saw Harold, but when he saw the proprietor of the Black Husky standing behind Harold, he rolled to his feet, a guarded expression on his face. Harold nodded to the gendarme who accompanied him and gestured toward the door. The man unlocked it, pulled it open and stepped back.

Lief didn't move.

"He wants to talk to you," Jora said.

The boy looked from Jora to Harold and Harold nodded.

Harold led the two *Alle'oss* out onto the street in front of the gendarmerie. Lief watched him with narrowed eyes while Harold composed his thoughts. It was such an outlandish idea, he wasn't sure how much to tell this boy. He needed to talk to someone with more authority.

"I would like to meet with the leaders of *oss'stera*," he said.

Lief stared at him. He looked at Jora, who shrugged. "I've never heard of *oss'stera*," he said, but there was the slightest twitch at the corner of his mouth.

"Of course not," Harold said. "After an extensive investigation, my conclusion, the conclusion I expect to report to my superiors is that rumors of a rebel group called *oss'stera* are just that, rumors." He paused, then added. "Still, I would like for you to arrange a meeting with the leaders of this rumored group. Soon."

Lief visibly relaxed. "I could tell you I would, then walk away and you would never see me again."

"I'll take that risk," Harold said.

"Why would we want to meet with you?"

"I have a proposition, or a warning, depending on circumstances," Harold said. "In either case, it will be of enormous benefit to *oss'stera* and the *Alle'oss*"

"When do you want this meeting?"

"Tonight, if possible."

"It would be on our terms. You would have to put yourself at our mercy."

"Of course," Harold said.

"Where do I find you?"

"I'll return to the gendarmerie in two hours. Ask at the front desk. I'll leave word."

"Okay, Hera *Novice*. You wait here. I'll go *arrange* a meeting," Lief said. He gave Harold a level look, then turned and walked away with Jora by his side.

Harold watched them go, wondering if he would see them again. He turned and walked toward the small flat he shared with Henrik. After that, he would check the taverns they frequented. It was likely a waste of time, but he needed to walk while he thought.

***

Alar sent word ahead while Scilla stitched his arm, so the wagon was waiting, horses hitched and ready to go when he and Ukrit arrived at the newly finished corral. It was dark, a full moon peeking over the mountains in the east. He stopped and stared at the wagon. Hana and Estrid, relative newcomers to *oss'stera* who adopted the horses, were watching him, a hint of pride in their expressions. He pointed and asked, "Is this the same wagon?"

Hana answered, "Ayuh. We removed the canvas, of course." She slapped the side of the wagon. "Took down a couple of planks, lowered the sides to make it look different. Couple of coats of Argren green to cover the Imperial marks." She ran her hand along the side. "Spruced right up."

"Sure did," Alar returned Estrid's grin, then he noticed the big Imperial draft horses waiting patiently in their harnesses. "Can't really slap a coat of paint on the horses, though."

"Nah," Hana said with a frown. "Can't do much about them. We filed the numbers off their hooves. Course, that just makes it obvious we stole them." She shrugged. "I were you, I'd stay clear of busy roads."

"Good idea," Ukrit said, one brow arched.

"It'll be late by the time we get to Richeleau," Alar said.

"Richeleau?" Estrid asked. She exchanged a worried look with Hana.

"Don't worry, we'll take good care of the horses," Alar said.

"Sigard and Ulfson," Hana said.

"Excuse me?" Alar asked.

"The horses," Estrid said. "That's their names."

"Oh. Well. Of course," Alar said. "We'll take good care of Sigard and Ulfson." He thanked them and was preparing to climb onto the driver's seat when someone shouted his name. He turned to find Keth and Zaina arriving at a run.

"Stolten told us you were here," Keth said between breaths.

"Take your time," Alar said.

When he could talk, Keth said, "We couldn't find Torva. We were afraid to ask at the gendarmerie, so we asked around and found out where he lives."

"Who'd you ask?" Alar asked.

"Lief said Torva hangs out at that tavern, the Bull. We asked a woman serving tables there."

Alar nodded. "And?"

"His wife says the Inquisition arrested him."

"*Sheoda*," Ukrit said.

"What about Lief?" Alar asked.

"Torva's wife visited her husband in the gendarmerie," Zaina said. "She said she thinks she saw Lief in another cell."

Alar and Ukrit looked at one another. "The gendarmerie? I thought you said the Inquisition arrested him?" Ukrit asked.

Keth shrugged. "That's what she said."

"Could be a good sign he's there, I suppose," Alar said.

Ukrit shrugged. "Maybe we can ask this novice."

"I have a feeling he won't be in the mood to volunteer any information," Alar said. "Not sure he'll believe Ragan's story. I'm not sure I believe it."

"Then what are we doing here?" Ukrit asked.

"Because, like Tove said, I have a soft heart," Alar answered, noticing Keth and Zaina's heads swiveling back and forth, following the conversation. "You two get back and get some rest. Good job," he said and climbed onto the wagon's bench.

Ukrit climbed up beside him and looked at Alar expectantly.

"What?" Alar asked.

"You going to drive?"

Alar looked at the horses doubtfully. "I don't know how to drive a wagon. Didn't your father teach you?"

"My pa taught me to make bows and furniture. I've never driven a wagon. My brother did that. I've *seen* it done." Ukrit looked uncertainly at the horses, whose ears were twitching back, as if they were following the conversation.

Alar looked past Ukrit to Hana and Estrid's horrified expressions. "Good enough," he said to Ukrit and waved at the reins. "Come on, we don't have time to argue."

"You want me to drive?"

Alar and Ukrit looked down at Keth. "You've driven a wagon?" Ukrit asked. Keth nodded. "You got the job," Ukrit said, and before Alar could protest, he climbed into the wagon's bed.

Keth took his place, glanced up at Alar, and took the reins. Zaina made to climb into the wagon until Alar pointed at her. "You. Go back and get some rest."

She dropped to the ground, her expression closing. Alar recognized the defiant twist to her lips, but before he could reinforce his command, the wagon lurched forward, throwing him backward. When he glanced back, Zaina was walking to the middle of the road, watching them ride away, bow hanging from her hand.

Chapter 37

The Union Attacks

Sten peered through the branches of a spruce at the wagon trundling past in the moonlight.

"Who is that?" Chagan asked.

"That's Alar and Keth in the front. In the back is Ukrit," Sten said. Though he hoped to retrieve the art without raising an alarm, there were no guarantees. But their chances of success were considerably higher with Alar gone.

Perhaps noticing the relief Sten couldn't hide, Chagan studied his face. "Is it usual, them going somewhere this late?"

"No," Sten said. "But what difference does it make? Believe me, it's a good thing Alar won't be there."

Chagan watched the wagon disappearing around a curve.

"Remember, we agreed," Sten said. "You get the art, and you leave. No one gets hurt." He glanced up at Chagan's lieutenant standing quietly behind the Union commander. The huge man returned his gaze with the same flat expression Sten found so disturbing when he first saw him in the governor's office.

"Yes, of course," Chagan said, turning to face him. "We have no interest in bloodshed. In and out, quick and efficient. At your request,

I've only brought Captain Topol." He gestured to his silent companion. "How much damage could the two of us do?" He nodded in the direction from which the wagon appeared a moment ago. "The community is, as you said, over the rise, then east?"

Sten glanced at Erik, who said, "We want to see the money first?"

"Ah, yes," Chagan said, gesturing to his captain. "The money."

The man came around Chagan, lifting the strap of a satchel over his head. When he came close to Erik, he opened the satchel's flap, withdrew a heavy truncheon, and clubbed Erik in the head with a wet crunch. Erik dropped without making a sound. Then, moving surprisingly fast for such a large man, Topol sprung at Sten, drawing the club back.

Reacting on instinct, Sten lifted the leather tube. The blow caved in the tube's side and knocked it from his hand. He backed away, scrabbling at the hilt of his sword. The mercenary, his expression the same blank mask, stalked toward him. As he pounced, Sten tripped, fell backwards, and took a glancing blow to his forehead. Stunned, he lay on his back, fighting to stay conscious. Topol loomed over him, lifting the club. Sten's hand closed on a stone. Desperately, he flung it at the mercenary, too stunned to feel surprise when it hit the man's forehead with a hollow thock.

Topol stumbled backward, hand to his forehead. Sten tried to stand, but collapsed to one knee when his injured ankle gave way. For a moment, he gathered himself for one final effort to stay alive, but then he sagged to sit on the cold ground. Even if it was possible for him to escape this monster, where would he go? He had no place to call home, no one to call a friend. Not anymore. Alar would find out who led the Union to *oss'stera's* home. It was Erik, whispering his poison in Sten's ear, who suggested the betrayal. Sten knew Erik only wanted to escape the grinding poverty that had been their life for years. But Erik was always weak and venal. Sten's betrayal was far worse. He told himself he would use the money to make a real difference, something *oss'stera* could only dream of. He would return triumphant, regaining the respect that was now Alar's. He bowed his head. He was once a true believer. The fiery speeches were not just a show. "I'm just so tired," he whispered.

***

Chagan watched Topol finish the traitor. The big man tossed the club into the underbrush, then stood silently, wiping blood from his forehead. "Signal the others," Chagan said. "Let's get on with it." Topol bent to retrieve a hooded lantern. He walked to the middle of the road, raised the hood, and waved it back and forth. Noticing the damaged tube the traitor dropped, Chagan retrieved it and waited for his men to arrive.

***

"You said you had another month," Gallia said.

Ragan, leaning against one of the posts anchoring the wall of the roundhouse, said, "I lied." She paused to pant through a contraction. When the crisis passed, she pushed herself upright. "I had to lie, for Thomas's sake."

"You should keep walking," Scilla said.

"You sure?" Ecke asked. The young girl hovered nearby, hands clutched at her waist. "It looks awfully uncomfortable."

"Walking will speed up the delivery," Scilla said.

"You didn't just lie to Thomas," Gallia said. She pushed through the door and left the roundhouse.

"She's really mad," Ecke said.

"Yes," Ragan said, exhaustion softening her voice. "She has a right to be."

***

The traitors, Sten and Erik, wanted to persuade the outlying sentries to allow the mercenaries to pass, but that was a foolish plan. It would only take one to refuse and raise the alarm. Chagan's experienced men quickly dispatched the inattentive sentries. The *Alle'oss* were still amateurs. Silent as ghosts, the mercenaries approached the entrance to the community, using the terrain to hide their approach. There was another sentry on the top of the cliff, but Chagan wasn't concerned about that. If the traitors were correct about where the art was stored, his men could recover it before the rebels had time to respond to the alarm. He hadn't lied about wanting to avoid bloodshed, though it wasn't because he cared about the lives of this rabble. Violent confrontations were unpredictable. He wanted to retrieve the art and leave the Empire with as few complications as possible.

The entrance to the community was as Sten described, two ravines cut into a granite cliff. The art should be a few paces inside the ravine on the right.

"Two guard," Topol said.

"Guardsss," Chagan said, emphasizing the s. Months in the Empire hadn't improved his men's grasp of Vollen. But Topol was correct. He could see a man and woman inside the ravine, illuminated by a lantern propped on a crate. They looked as if they were playing cards. Laughing. Not paying attention. Chagan nodded to Topol, and the mercenaries moved forward.

They were nearly at the entrance to the ravine when the horn sounded. The two *Alle'oss* guards only had time to look up before Union arrows cut them down. Topol lifted the hood of the lantern halfway, and he and Chagan followed his men. Chagan had his eyes down, picking his way over the rough ground when the small circle of light fell on the linen wraps. Stopping abruptly, he stared at the pile of fabric, then bent over and took the strip of linen between a finger and thumb, as if it might come alive and strike at him. "Desulti," he whispered. What did it mean? She must be here searching for the art. But why were the wraps here, on the ground? Did the *Alle'oss* kill a Desulti? For a moment, he entertained that hopeful thought, but it was too unlikely to take the risk.

He turned to Topol and held up the fabric strip. "Find the Desulti. Avoid becoming engaged more than you have to, but find her. Or her body. Be quick." As Topol turned away, Chagan added, "Alive if possible."

Topol nodded and hurried forward, shouting orders in their language. Mercenaries headed deeper into the ravine as Chagan arrived. Topol pointed to a chest. The lid was open, revealing the leather tubes. "Art," his captain said.

Chagan returned the damaged tube to the chest and closed the lid. "I'll return to Richeleau with the chest. Bring the Desulti to the dungeon and inform me at the fort."

Topol nodded and turned to follow his men into the ravine.

Chagan watched two men lift the chest, then, with a worried glance at Topol, he turned away and followed the chest, his personal guard arrayed around him. It was likely the Desulti was operating alone. The Murtair usually did. But that didn't mean she didn't report the location of the paintings to her superiors. If the Desulti discovered who took the paintings, he wouldn't be safe, no matter where he ran. He considered, for a fleeting moment, ordering Topol to eliminate every last rebel, but dismissed it as unrealistic. No, he would have to hope the Desulti was alive. Then he could have Muustak work on her. If anyone else knew of the art's location, his torturer would get it out of her.

***

The Desulti lay on the bed, pretending to be asleep. Willen lay on his back, snoring loudly, arms and legs splayed. Tove sat back against the wall, watching the assassin through half-lidded eyes. She desperately wanted to learn more about the woman and her order, but the way the Desulti toyed with her when she let her guard down, shamed her. She pressed her lips into a thin line. Though the woman was pretending to sleep, Tove knew she was listening. "Embarrassing," she muttered, watching the Desulti for a reaction, disappointed when there was none.

Suddenly, the horn sounded.

***

Gallia threw the door open and entered the roundhouse. "What does that mean?"

"We're under attack," Scilla said.

"Do you have a plan for this?" Gallia asked.

Scilla nodded, helping Ragan to kneel beside the same bed on which she spent an exhilarating hour with Alar the night before. "They will try to slow the attackers while most of the community escapes out the back."

"Ragan can't leave," Ecke said. "We can't leave now." She looked at Gallia. "Can you do something? That singing thing?"

Ragan, emerging from a contraction, said between pants, "It's the Union. They're here for the art."

"That would have been nice to know before you sent Alar way," Scilla snapped, standing and taking a step back.

"I wasn't sure," Ragan said. "It was one of dozens of possibilities for tonight. It seemed … unlikely." She looked up at Gallia. "A spirit song isn't likely to affect the mercenaries as much as the *Alle'oss.*"

"Maybe they'll just take the art and go," Ecke said.

Scilla knelt beside Ragan and gripped her arm. "Tell me. All of it."

"They came for the art, but they'll search for the Desulti." She winced as another contraction built. They all looked up at the sound of a scream cut short. "That's all I know. I promise," Ragan said, and started to pant.

"Fog," Gallia said. She looked at Scilla. "Your people should be able to find their way more easily in the fog. They know the ground." Scilla nodded and Gallia ducked through the door.

***

The Desulti sat up, instantly alert. Her eyes met Tove's. "You're under attack."

Tove kicked the still sleeping Willen, then came around the fire, pulling her knife. The Desulti tensed until Tove knelt at her feet and worked at the rope binding the assassin's legs.

"Imperials?" the Desulti asked.

Tove shook her head. "Imperials would be a single blast. This signal means the sentry doesn't recognize them." Finished with the bindings on the woman's feet, she moved up to work on the rope wrapped around her torso, regretting how thoroughly she bound her.

Willen was staring wide-eyed at the door. "Willen, make sure people are moving to the exit." The boy nodded and bolted through the door.

"Can you hold them back?"

"Probably not," Tove said. Working on the last bit of rope. "We have maybe twenty bows here. With Alar gone ... Depends on how many there are."

Finally free, the Desulti stood and shed the last of the bindings. "Where did Alar go?"

A scream joined the alarm and then was cut short.

"Not relevant," Tove said. She caught the woman's arm as she moved toward the door. "You have to help," she said. When the Desulti's face hardened, Tove said, "They might be here for the art." She had no reason to believe that was true, but she could see from the woman's expression she hit the mark. The assassin gave her a nod. Tove snatched up her bow and followed the Desulti out the door.

Outside, they assessed the situation. People were visible between the houses, streaming toward the narrow cleft that climbed up through cliff face at the back of the community. Already, there was a small crowd there waiting for their turn. Tove spotted Stolten as he loosed an arrow toward the front of the community. But who was he shooting at?

The Desulti headed toward the ravine where the art was stored. Tove followed, but before they took ten steps, they heard deep, guttural voices. The assassin stopped. "Union." The men were hidden by the roundhouses. She listened, then said, "They're looking for me." As she said it, the moonlight dimmed. She turned slowly and lifted her hand to wave in front of her face. "What's happening?"

"Fog," Tove said. "One of the sisters must be making it." She slipped into the lead and kept going. The fog thickened rapidly. Soon, she could only make out vague shapes around her. Choosing her steps carefully, she made their way slowly, the assassin pressed up close behind her.

She had no time to react. Dark shapes emerged from the fog so quickly she couldn't avoid them. In the moment before they collided with her, she recognized the shape of a giant man, sprinting heedlessly through the murk. She turned her head in time to avoid smashing her face on his chest, but she was caught between the man's bulk and the Desulti. The side of her head impacted the assassin's forehead and the two women were thrown backward. The Desulti grunted, then screamed when Tove landed on top of her. Before Tove's vision faded entirely, she glimpsed the ghostly shape of the man casting about as if he wasn't sure what he collided with.

When she opened her eyes, the fog was thinning. Through slitted eyes, she watched two men standing over her arguing in the same guttural language she heard before. One of them gestured to Tove and shook his head. She recognized the word Desulti. Her eyes swiveled to the side. The assassin lay on her stomach, hands bound behind her, lips pulled back from her teeth as if she were in intense pain. Tove's fingers closed on a familiar shape, one of her arrows, scattered by the collision.

Their argument settled, one of the men bent forward, reaching toward the assassin. Tove launched herself off the ground, thrusting the arrow toward his neck. Reacting faster than she thought possible, he flinched back, lifting his arm so the arrow only pierced his shoulder. He jerked back, snapping the arrow shaft. No scream. Not even a grunt. She stood unsteadily over the Desulti, tossed the broken arrow shaft away and pulled her knife. The men watched her impassively. The one she stabbed examined the broken shaft protruding from his shoulder, then gestured to Tove and spoke. The other man shrugged, then quick as a snake, he lunged at her, one hand wrapping around her throat and the other trapping her wrist. She clung to his wrist with her free hand as he lifted her slowly off the ground. Her attempts to kick him only brought a smile to his face. He jerked her up and slammed her down on her back. Light exploded in her head. She squeezed her eyes shut, gasping for air, fighting to remain conscious, not wanting to die unaware of her fate.

Stunned, she couldn't resist when he rolled her onto her stomach, pulled her hands roughly behind her and bound them. When the mercenary rolled her onto her back again, the sharp edge of an arrowhead cut into her palm. As he grasped her arms and jerked her up, she closed her hand around the arrowhead, bending her wrists to snap the shaft against the ground. Cupping the arrowhead in a hand slick with blood, she grunted as he threw her over his shoulder like a sack of potatoes.

***

The baby was coming. Ragan rested on her knees beside the bed, her forehead pressed to her forearms. The panicked shouts outside the small house, Ecke's frantic voice, Scilla's soothing reassurances were muffled echos. Even the rippling contractions forcing her daughter from her body were only a distant sensation. She sought refuge in the meditative state where she sensed her spirit and she communed with the *sjel'and*. But she would not call forth the soul spirits. When Minna was born, she sensed her daughter's spirit entering her body. For one fleeting moment, their spirits, mother and daughter's, greeted one another before they separated. She knew this baby would be her last. A child who, if her visions were correct, she would barely know. She was determined to know her spirit.

She waited, barely aware of Scilla behind her, preparing to catch her daughter. Tears forced their way between her eyelids. She groaned. Her body told her to push, but she needed the moment to last. And then she sensed it. The *lan'and* which would give her daughter life. The spirit emerged into her awareness, swooping joyfully in the manner of its kind. She was used to approaching the *sjel'and*, knew how to protect herself from their manipulation, knew not to provide them with weaknesses they could exploit. But she didn't want to shield herself now. She wanted to open herself to the spirit who would animate her daughter, to allow her to know her mother in this moment, as she wouldn't in life. Ragan's spirit song swelled as she reached out to the *lan'and.*

And then there was another spirit. "No, no, no," Ragan moaned. The *sjel'and* could not take Ragan's spirit, bound as it was to her body. But what could it do to her daughter's spirit before it entered the baby's body? She tried to send the *sjel'and* away, but distracted by pain and exhaustion, it was a weak effort that only earned the spirit's amusement. She waited, panting and moaning, expecting the *sjel'and* to lunge for her daughter's spirit. Instead, it hesitated. She sensed curiosity, then it surged fully into her awareness, joining her daughter's spirit for a moment before the *lan'and* disappeared. *What happened?*

"Here it comes," Scilla shouted. "One more push."

Scilla's voice brought Ragan's awareness back to her surroundings. There was a scream outside. A moment later, the door crashed open. Ecke screamed, and the world exploded.

Suddenly, Ragan was far away, dragged into the vision by the *sjel'and.* She was standing on a darkened city street. The gray-eyed novice, sword in hand, faced two Union mercenaries. Others were fighting in the background. "Alar, help him," she whispered. But Alar didn't come. As she watched, one of the mercenaries trapped the novice's sword, and the other cut him down.

"No!" she screamed.

The vision faded, replaced by darkness, screams, flames, and chaos. She was on her knees, buried beneath the wreckage of the roundhouse, an intense heat on her back. "Alyn," she said, though she was too weak to say it loud. Almost as if in answer, a baby cried out, a strong, lusty screech. Ragan tried to stand, but her legs wouldn't support her. Suddenly, the debris holding her down was lifted away. Someone beat at her back. There were confusing shouts. Strong hands wrapped around her arms and pulled her roughly to her feet.

She opened her eyes, as an *Alle'oss* man lifted her and carried her like a baby away from the remains of the roundhouse. The thatch from the roof fell into the fire when the house collapsed, sending flames leaping up into the night sky. A woman's body lay on the ground near the conflagration. She tried to get the man's attention, but he ignored her. He carried her into another house and lay her on a bed. She reached up, but he was gone before she could catch him. Scilla appeared, holding a bundle in her arms.

"She's perfect," Scilla said and lay the baby on Ragan's chest.

Looking down at her daughter's pinched face, Ragan asked, "Where's Ecke?"

Scilla nodded to the man returning with Ecke's limp body.

"She's alive," Scilla said. "I don't know what she did, but one of those mercenaries tried to enter the house and Ecke sort of … exploded."

"Gallia?"

Scilla pressed her lips together and shook her head.

Ragan let her head drop back, tears leaking into her hair. The *sjel'and* hid that from her. In none of the futures they showed her, did her friend die. "Folly," she whispered.

Chapter 38

Otsuna!

Alar stood and glanced around. "This is good," he said.

Keth tugged on the reins, bringing Sigard and Ulfson to a halt. He looked around the deserted street, a twist to his lips signaling his uncertainty. The moon wasn't yet visible in the narrow strip of sky above them, but it painted the intersection with the east–west alley in its pale blue light. "What's here?"

Ukrit hopped to the cobbled street. "Nothing yet," he said and caught Alar's eye when he joined him. "And I'll lay long odds there won't be anything or anyone, anytime soon."

Alar brushed past him, approached the intersection and peered both ways. "Not sure if I'll be disappointed or relieved either way. What time you think it is?"

Ukrit pulled his cloak tighter and looked up at the narrow slice of sky visible between the buildings. "I'd say seven, seven–thirty."

"Sounds right," Alar said and followed Ukrit down the alley. He glanced back at Keth standing on the driver's deck and said, "Might as well get comfortable. This might be a while."

Lief slowed from a jog to stand in the middle of the road, listening to voices on the road ahead. He had been running since he left the novice and was nearing his limit. Stilling his heavy breaths, he listened. They were speaking another language. He ducked into the brush at the side of the road, crawled under a spruce and watched figures approaching. He knew from their size who they were before they were close enough to see their uniforms. Union mercenaries. There were ten of them. It looked as if two of the giants carried something over their shoulders. When they passed close to his hiding place, he saw by the light of the full moon, they carried people. Though he couldn't see who they were, the moon was bright enough he could tell one of them had short red hair. *Alle'oss.* They were coming from the direction of his home.

As the men passed, he crawled backward until he could stand. Backing away to free himself from the prickly needles, his heel struck something soft, and he sat on the cold ground. It took him a moment to realize what his leg was draped across. When he did, he scooted backward, stood and stared at the body. It slumped over, as if the person was sitting on the ground when they were struck in the back of the head. He knelt and pulled the hair back from the face. Sten's cloudy eye gazed sightlessly back at him. Lief rose and turned slowly, wiping his hands on his shirt. Erik's body lay nearby, the side of his head a bloody ruin. Lief had no love for either of the men, having joined *oss'stera* after Sten lost his way, but he was aware how important Sten was to Alar. Deep, rumbling laughter rose up in the distance for a moment, then faded away. The mercenaries sharing a joke.

Lief pushed through the sticky needles of the spruce, hit the road at a run and raced toward home.

***

In the chaos of the attack and the aftermath, no one was exactly sure when the mercenaries left. The fire, which they managed to confine to one roundhouse, was nearly extinguished. Ragan was asleep, or pretending to be, wrapped around her new baby on Scilla's bed. Scilla and Stolten tamped down the worst of the panic and were organizing a search for injured and dead when Lief appeared.

When he noticed them, he veered in their direction.

"Lief!" Scilla said before he could speak. "Where have you been?"

"Prison," Lief said. "Where's Alar?"

"Prison?" Stolten asked.

"Alar's not here," Scilla said at the same time.

Lief started to speak, then noticed the ashes of his home. He spun around, taking in the signs of the community recovering from the attack. When he came back around to face Scilla, he said, "Sten and Erik are dead."

Scilla glanced at Stolten. "Where?"

"A couple of leagues up the road. Union mercenaries attacked," he said matter-of-factly. Before Scilla could ask, he added, "I saw Union mercenaries heading toward Richeleau carrying two people. One of them was *Alle'oss.*"

"They came to take the art," Stolten said to Lief, then he asked Scilla. "But why take prisoners?"

"The Desulti," Scilla said. "Ragan said they were searching for the Desulti. Who do you think the other person was?"

"Have you seen Tove since the attack?" Stolten asked. "She was watching the assassin."

"Did you see what they looked like?" she asked Lief.

"Couldn't see much. Short red hair. It could have been Tove." He shrugged. "Where's Alar?"

"He's in Richeleau," Scilla said absently. "Why would they take Tove?"

"I need to see Alar," Lief said. "Tonight."

Scilla focused on him, her attention caught by a rare note of urgency in his voice. "Why?"

"I was arrested by a novice of the Inquisition. That's why I was in prison. He was asking about *oss'stera.* Then today, he let me go, and said he wants to meet the leaders of *oss'stera.* Says he has a proposition for us."

Scilla and Stolten exchanged a look. "Could be a trap," Stolten said.

"That's all he said?" Scilla asked.

Lief nodded. "Said he needs to meet tonight." When Scilla didn't respond, he said, "Do you know where Alar is? I could go tell him."

Scilla glanced up at the moon, doing a rough calculation. "My guess is the novice will get his wish soon."

***

Henrik still hadn't appeared by the time Harold returned. For the past hour, he alternated between pacing the small office and sitting at his desk, fidgeting and studying the map. He didn't know if he was more anxious to hear from Lief or Henrik.

"Helga," Harold shouted.

The young gendarme appeared at his door almost instantly. "Yes, sir."

"What is the time?"

"I'm not sure. It was six when you returned."

"Thank you," Harold said. Helga nodded and disappeared from view.

He couldn't wait any longer. Regardless whether his request to meet *oss'stera* bore fruit, he needed to put a lot of pieces in motion, quickly. It was time to talk to Captain Brennerman.

He searched his desk for a sheet of paper to write a note for Henrik. When he couldn't find anything suitable, he rummaged through the drawers of Henrik's desk. He was reaching for a stack of paper when Inquisitor Hoerst's name leapt out at him. His hand hovered over the page. It was a field report, written in the Inquisition's formal style, addressed to Hoerst. Taking the top sheet of paper off the stack, he held it to the lamp and read it. The brief paragraph described the incident at the Black Husky, ending with a damning statement.

... the novice doesn't seem to have any idea how to proceed under these unusual circumstances.

Harold dropped into Henrik's chair, pulled the stack of papers from the drawer, and spread them out on the desk. They all contained similar descriptions of their activities. Though they were accurate in the main, they shaded events in a negative light, often calling Harold's decisions into question.

He sat back and stared at the wall. Henrik was reporting on him to Hoerst. A dozen and more moments played out in his mind. Their careful dance as they made their way to Richeleau, neither of them sure of the other. After all, Hoerst threw them together. It was not Harold's choice. Between the big sergeant's natural reticence and Harold's customary distrust, the first few weeks were difficult. But over time, they both carefully shed their defenses. Or so he thought. Harold sighed and rested a hand on the scattered papers. He had been a fool. Henrik was just like everyone else in the Inquisition Academy.

Giving his head a firm shake, he stood abruptly and gathered the papers into a pile. He didn't have time to feel sorry for himself. Returning the stack to the drawer, he slammed the drawer closed, retrieved his cloak and swept from the office.

According to the pendulum clock in the lobby, it was nearly half-past seven. He left a message for Lief with the desk sergeant, then stepped onto the street and took a moment to pull on his gloves while he searched for his tail. They were good. It was a week before he realized they were being followed, but they had a nearly impossible task. While they switched out frequently, there were too few of them and they had been at it for weeks. Familiar faces were easy to spot, even in crowds. The only question was who they worked for. Considering what he just found in Henrik's desk, he would guess they were Inquisition.

Resisting the urge to give the familiar man loitering at the corner a nod, he turned and headed toward the fort. It was just beyond the city limits to the northwest. As he moved north, the crowd thinned. Two blocks from the fort, he was walking alone on a dark street, idly wondering how the men following him were managing the difficult task. He just turned off the main thoroughfare into a narrow lane when he felt a prick on the back of his neck. Whirling around, he crouched, his hand on the hilt of his sword. The street was empty. He felt a warm trickle at his collar and put his hand to his neck. In the dim starlight, the blood on his fingers looked black. Putting his back to the brick front of a warehouse, he searched for his assailant. The windows in the buildings were small and shuttered, and there were no obvious hiding places. His gaze rose past the eaves of the building across the street. As he searched the roofline, the stars slid across the sky, twisting and leaving purple trails. He sucked in a breath, squeezed his eyes shut, and gave his head a shake. When he dared look again, the stars were racing toward him, as if he was rising up into the sky. Dropping to the street, he dug his fingers into the cracks between the cobbles, but the world would not stay still. He sank, pressing his cheek against the cold stone. His vision shrank to a small circle, but before the world went black, a pair of boots stepped into his field of view.

***

Ukrit stepped up beside Alar. "That the guy?"

Alar knelt and rolled the man onto his back. "Yeah."

"Have to give Ragan credit," Ukrit said. "I had my doubts, but she got it right. This time, anyway."

Alar stood. "Yeah, I suppose." He lifted the small knife. The razor-sharp blade, coated with witchbane, glinted in the moon's light, which was peeking above the rooftops. "We should see about getting some of this." Carefully, he returned the blade to its sheath and shoved it into his pocket.

They gazed down at the man lying at their feet. His white uniform seemed to glow in the moonlight.

Ukrit knelt and pressed his fingers to the novice's throat. After a moment, he stood and said, "He's alive."

Alar grinned at the note of disappointment in his voice. "That *was* the idea."

"Right." Ukrit shrugged. "We could leave him." He glanced around the empty street. "Seems pretty safe here."

"You want to get that end?" Alar asked, pointing to the novice's head.

"I suppose." Ukrit came around the prone man and nodded to Alar. They bent over, hoisted the body up, and shuffled down the narrow alley. When they emerged from the alley, Keth was standing on the driver's bench.

"On three," Alar said. They swung the novice between them, counting out loud, then heaved the man into the back of the wagon, where he landed with a thud.

"Heavier than he looks," Ukrit said with a grin.

"You killed an inquisitor?"

Alar and Ukrit looked up at Keth who was grinning down at the novice.

"Technically, he's a novice," Alar said. "And he's not dead. In fact, we're trying to keep him *alive*, if you can believe it." He climbed into the back of the wagon and threw the canvas that used to cover the wagon bed over the body.

Ukrit climbed onto the driver's bench.

Keth, still standing and watching Alar, asked, "Where are we taking him?"

"We need to get to the Black Husky with as few people as possible seeing us," Alar said. "If you go down *Shonuma* Street, you can pull the wagon into the alley in the back."

Keth tilted his head, lips pursed. Then, with a nod, he sat, gave the reins a flick, and set them in motion.

***

Alar tried to catch the novice as Ukrit rolled him over the side of the wagon, but he lost his grip and the man hit the hard ground in the alley behind the Husky. He looked up at Ukrit, who shrugged.

"Oops," Ukrit said.

"You know you can let the back of the wagon down," Keth said.

"Good to know." Ukrit exchanged a grin with Keth and dropped to the ground next to the novice's head. "He'll live."

Alar was about to tell Keth to return home with the wagon, but when he saw his defiant expression, he said, "What about the horses?"

Keth glanced at Sigard and Ulfson.

"Could be here a while," Alar said. "They need water and feed. Don't they?"

Keth sighed, hopped to the ground, walked to the front of the team and started coaxing them to back down the alley.

"Nicely done," Ukrit said to Alar. "You're learning." When Alar, watching Keth retreat, turned back, Ukirt asked, "How we getting in?"

Alar walked over to stand in front of the alehouse's back door. Starting at a brick next to the latch, he counted five to the right, then wedged his fingers into the cracks above and below the brick and worked it free. Grinning at Ukrit, he fished inside the cavity and extracted a key.

"Jora told me about it, in case I needed a place to hide," Alar said. He unlocked the door and pulled it open.

"You want to get the head this time?" Ukrit asked.

Alar bent and worked his arms under the tall man's armpits. They heaved him up and lugged him through the door. Once they had the novice lashed to a chair, Ukrit asked, "How long will he be out, you reckon?"

"Ragan said an hour or two. Should we blindfold him?"

They searched the room for something they could use but came up empty. "I guess we stay behind him," Alar said. Remembering when Gallia woke up after being dosed with witchbane, Alar said, "I'll go out back and get some water from the well."

"Right," Ukrit said, righting a chair someone tossed into the corner when the gendarmes searched the tavern. "I'll keep watch." He sank down, crossed his arms, and tipped the chair back until his head rested against the wall.

***

It took them two hours after Lief arrived to gather the remaining members of *oss'stera* in the community space. Of the hundred who were present when the Union attacked, nine were found dead, including the sentries and Sten and Erik. Twenty were missing, hopefully having escaped, but not yet returned. They confirmed that Tove and the Desulti were among the missing. Ragan was no help. She told Scilla the *sjel'and* had nothing useful to offer. Something about the near future moving too fast to predict. Scilla thought it more likely she was grieving for her friend.

"Ready?" she asked Stolten and Lief. The three of them discussed what she would say to the gathered community, but coming from her instead of Alar, there was no telling what the response would be. Stolten and Lief nodded. She stepped onto a boulder and gazed out over the faces turned her way, seeing expectation, worry, and anger.

She cleared her throat and took a moment to imagine how Alar would approach this. Then she said, "As all of you likely know already, we were attacked by Union mercenaries."

"Why?" someone called. "Why attack and leave most of us alive? What did they want?"

Scilla glanced at Stolten. "You all know about the paintings we found on the supply caravan." There were nods. "They came to steal them, and they were successful." She was disappointed to see relief rather than anger on many of their faces. That would make what she was going to ask more difficult. Taking a deep breath, she let it out and lifted her chin. "We have to go get it back. The art."

Silence.

"How are we going to do that?" The speaker was Ogden, one of the community's few trouble makers. He wiped his hand across his bald scalp. "It's one thing to ambush a supply caravan. By the time we catch up with the mercs, they'll be behind the walls of the fort, along with the Imp cavalry. What are we going to do against stone walls with these?" He lifted his bow. There were mutters of agreement.

Unable to respond to that, Scilla instead made the appeal she discussed with Stolten and Lief. "That art is part of our heritage, a part the Empire was trying to steal."

"But it's only art. Why is that worth getting killed for?"

Scilla took a breath. To avoid the skeptical faces turned her way, she gazed over their heads. "Art, this art, is far more than canvas and paint." She raised a hand in supplication. "Ask yourselves, why would the Empire confiscate it? Why would they persecute the artists?" She closed her hand into a fist and allowed her anger to show. "Why did they execute Valdemar?" Letting her gaze lower, she was encouraged to see her anger reflected back at her. Not everyone knew about Valdemar. Alar and Tove were evidence of that. But his execution struck a spark that fell on dry tinder in parts of Argren. Scilla had seen it among her neighbors in the Ishian River valley. It was, yet, a small flame. But if it were tended, given air, it might grow into the conflagration they would need to win their freedom. "They executed Valdemar, because he dared to tell the truth. A truth they don't want the *Alle'oss* to know."

"What truth?" someone asked.

Scilla spread her arms and let passion color her voice. "Art is a reflection of who we are as a people. Of why we fight to be free from the Empire's oppression. At its greatest, it represents truths we can't express in words, truths that speak directly to our heart." She paused to let her words sink in. "The kind of truth that inspires people to rise up against impossible odds." She let her arms fall to her side. "Listen, we'll never defeat the Empire on our own. Not with bows and swords. We need all of Argren with us. And to do that, we need to stoke a belief … a passionate belief … that we can win, that truth will win out, that there are ideals worth dying for."

There was more silence, but it was a thoughtful silence this time.

"They have Tove," Lief said.

"Why?"

"We don't know," Scilla said.

"Flowery words are all great. But, again, what do you expect us to *do?*" Ogden looked around. "We have, maybe, twenty bows left."

"We can do it with Alar," Scilla said.

"Where is Alar?" someone else asked.

"He's in Richeleau, taking care of something very important," she answered.

"He should have been here," Ogden said. Others nodded and Scilla felt the moment slipping away.

"We can't always expect Alar to save us," she said. "He's only one man. We can't expect to defeat the Empire with one man."

In the uncertain silence that followed, one voice rang out. "I'll go."

Zaina had elbowed her way into the front row. A head shorter than the people on either side, she stood with one hand propped on her hip, her bow dangling from the other. Noticing everyone looking at her, she thrust her chin out. "Alar's in Richeleau. We go find him, we go get Tove, then we get the art back." There were a few mutters and shuffling feet. "No one comes into our home and attacks us, and we don't abandon any of our own." She looked around and raised her voice. "*Ērtsa jīla oss'stera, da* (Are we *oss'stera*)?"

Sensing the crowd teetering, Scilla pushed them over the edge. "*Ērtsa jīla Alle'oss, da?*" she shouted.

"*Da!*"

"*Otsuna!*" Zaina shouted, and *oss'stera* answered her.

Chapter 39

Always Unexpected

Adelbart leaned on the heavy door to the dungeon, expecting it to creak as it always did. Instead, it swung easily on well-oiled hinges. He would have to remember to thank Gerold. He entered the short hallway and pushed the door closed. As he turned away, a glimmer of white in the usually empty cell across from his daughter's caught his eye. Taking a hesitant step, he peered into the dark cell. A man lay on the damp floor against the back wall. The governor straightened, fingers covering his lips. Even in the low light, he could discern the white Inquisition uniform. Edging forward, he squinted into the shadows, but couldn't tell who it was.

"They brought him in a few hours ago."

Adelbart turned to face his daughter, who leaned on the door of her cell, hands dangling through the bars. "Someone local?" he asked her

Elois shook her head. "Never seen him before. They beat him up pretty bad. Not even sure he's still alive."

Adelbart's eyes lost their focus. *What does this mean?*

"You're wondering how deep the shit is now, aren't you?"

He focused on his daughter's face, barely registering the vulgarity.

"If you weren't sure, it means I'll be dead before dawn," she said.

It was so unexpected, Adelbart took a moment to find meaning in the words. When he did, all he could say was, "What? Why?"

Elois snorted. "You don't think Chagan ever intended to let me live, do you?"

"Of course," Adelbart said, taking a small step forward. "He said he would. I paid him to rescue you."

"Father, Chagan is terrified of the Murtair. He doesn't intend to leave any loose ends. He can't." She straightened and worked her fingers through her filthy hair. "He can't risk me telling them who attacked their safe house."

"We wouldn't tell." But wasn't that exactly what he considered doing after the last time the Desulti visited him? Unable to bear his daughter's withering look, he dropped his eyes.

"It won't take long for the Inquisition to notice they're missing someone," Elois said.

Adelbart glanced back at the dark cell.

"The emperor won't ignore an attack on a brother of the Inquisition." She gave up on her hair and propped her hands on her hips. "My guess is the mercenaries will leave at first light. They have a long way to go to get to the port in Lubern. Chagan will want a head start."

Adelbart shook his head.

"That means ..." Elois drew a thumb across her throat.

"No," Adelbart whispered. "I'll call the caval—" He gave his head a vigorous shake. The cavalry was somewhere in Argren, looking for the rangers. He gave the order himself. "Why keep you here all these weeks if they just plan to kill you?"

"To keep you in line. You and your men." Her lips pursed and her head tilted to one side. "The only question is whether they let *you* live."

Before Adelbart could respond to that shocking revelation, a commotion outside the dungeon interrupted his thoughts. A woman's angry complaints punctuated the clank of sheathed weapons and the scuffs of feet on the stone stairs.

"Put me down, you ugly *wota*!" the voice shouted. "I told you, I can walk."

The outer door to the guardroom crashed open, raising the volume of the voice. It was joined by the guttural rumble of the new arrivals greeting the mercenaries left to guard the dungeon. Adelbart and his daughter's eyes met. She pressed her face to the bars, trying to see the door to the guardroom at the end of the hall. Adelbart pressed his back against the stone wall. There was movement in the small window, then the door banged open. Two giants came through, carrying people over their shoulders. It was the woman the second man carried who was the source of the complaints. The first man paused when he noticed Adelbart, then he dumped his burden onto the floor, stepped over her and approached the only remaining empty cell at the far end of the hall.

Adelbart watched the woman lying at his feet, struggling into a seated position. Shaved head, familiar black leggings and blouse. A Desulti. It must be. Recognition lit her expression when their eyes locked.

"Brie!"

Adelbart looked up, startled, at the sound of his daughter's voice. She dropped to her knees and extended a hand through the bars.

"Elois?" Though the Desulti's hands were bound behind her back, she rolled onto her knees and shuffled close to his daughter's cell. "What are you doing here?"

"Oh, Brie," his daughter said, tracing her fingertips along the other woman's cheek. Her eyes met her father's. Adelbart watched her, knowing she was weighing her anger at him against what remained of their frayed relationship. Then she said, "The Union. They attacked the safe house. They're using me to blackmail my fath—"

The Desulti pressed her lips to his daughter's mouth, cutting off her words. Adelbart stood absolutely still, unable to put the pieces together. His daughter was kissing a Desulti assassin. His head swiveled toward the other woman brought in by the mercenaries and was surprised that it was an *Alle'oss* woman. She stared at the couple, her face reflecting the shock he felt. When she felt his gaze on her, she scowled and turned her scarred face away.

One of the mercenaries hoisted the assassin up by her upper arms, forcing a scream from her. He dragged her to the cell at the end of the hallway and threw her through the door. Then he wrapped a hand around the arm of the other woman and shoved her into the same cell. He locked the door and returned to the guardroom, leering down at Adelbart as he passed.

Once they were alone again, Adelbart looked at his daughter. Tears streaked the filth on her face. "I didn't know," he said.

Elois climbed into the chair he had conveyed to her cell. He gazed at the pile of her fashionable garments thrown into the corner, the unmade fourposter bed, the dolls that brought her such delight as a child, strewn across the floor. Did he really think such trivial things would rekindle his daughter's unconditional love for her father? As he watched her, her face buried in her hands, the enormity of what he did to his daughter finally sank in. Knowing how colossally inadequate anything he had to say would be, he turned away and shuffled to the exit.

***

Adelbart passed through Gerold's office, only vaguely aware of his assistant trying to get his attention. Inside his empty office, he dropped onto his chair and stared at the spot once occupied by the painting of the young couple walking along a country road. When Gerold stepped in front of him, blocking his view, Adelbart's eyes wandered up to his assistant's face.

"Governor, we've had news from the men following Novice Wolfe."

Adelbart stared at him without comprehension.

Gerold came around the desk, took Adelbart's arm, spun him around and rested his hands on the arms of the chair so his face was inches from the governor's.

It was so unlike his meek assistant, shock finally penetrated Adelbart's haze. "Gerold, what is the meaning of—"

"Governor, the *Alle'oss* have captured the novice."

Adelbart blinked. So many incomprehensible events in such a short time. "*Alle'oss?*" Adelbart whispered. Gerold nodded. "So, the brother in the dungeon … Are the *Alle'oss* and Chagan working together?"

"Governor, what are you talking about?"

Adelbart gave a weak chuckle. "The *Alle'oss* captured the novice, and the Union have his companion in the dungeon."

"The Union put a brother in the dungeon?" Gerold straightened and took a step back.

Adelbart nodded absently. "A Murtair and an *Alle'oss* woman, as well." Adelbart frowned. That didn't fit. The Union couldn't be working with the *Alle'oss*. He looked up at Gerold. "What does it mean?"

Gerold turned away, his fingers going to his forehead. "Chagan is terrified of the Desulti," he mumbled. He glanced at Adelbart who nodded. It was the same thing Elois told him. Gerold continued his line of reasoning. "He will want to erase anything that can lead them to him. We have not enough cavalry to defeat them." Adelbart was about to mention they had no cavalry, but Gerold pressed on. "We need …" He turned so quickly toward Adelbart, the governor flinched.

"The *Alle'oss* that left with Chagan. The men who brought the painting," Gerold said and waited until Adelbart nodded. "They impressed upon Chagan their desire that none of their people would be hurt when they took the art. They implied the others didn't know what they were up to."

"Yes," Adelbart said. "That was my impression."

Gerold covered his mouth with his hand. After a moment, he let his hand drop. He straightened his jacket and said, "Governor, we must go speak with Novice Wolfe."

***

Tove winced. She didn't want to think of what the razor-sharp edges of the arrowhead were doing to her hands. The leather thong binding her wrists was slick with her blood, and she could no longer feel individual nicks on her hands and wrists. But she was nearly there. While she worked, she stared at the Desulti. Brie, she reminded herself.

A shadow cut Brie's face in half, one eye glinting in the golden light from the torch on the wall outside their cell. She sat cross-legged, gazing past Tove. She hadn't said a word since they were locked in the cell. Tove hoped for some hint of the emotion she displayed with the other woman. Some window into her heart. But she was, once again, behind her implacable shield. Still, Tove saw her face when Elois recognized her. Surprise, delight, a tenderness that transformed her. Watching the two women unleashed a confusing swirl of emotions in Tove. But she forced herself to clamp down on them, to shove them in the same place she kept the fear and despair that defined her childhood. If she dwelt on them now, allowed herself to be distracted, there would be no time to try to understand later.

The thong gave way. Wincing, she stretched her arms carefully, easing the ache in her shoulders.

"Finally," Brie said.

Tove scooted over and pressed her palm to Brie's chest. Brie looked down at the bloody print, then looked up at Tove. "Maybe if you weren't such an asshole, you'd have more friends," Tove said. She came around behind the other woman and set to work on her bindings. When the Desulti grunted, Tove pulled her hands away, afraid she cut her.

"My arm," Brie said. "It's broken. It happened when that oaf ran over us."

Tove returned to her task. Once the thong was severed, Brie cradled her arm against her stomach. Tove knelt in front of her and reached for the arm. The Murtair flinched away. "Let's see how bad it is," Tove said. Brie hesitated before relenting and letting Tove examine her arm.

She pushed the sleeve up and felt for the break. The Desulti hissed a breath through clenched teeth.

"Hasn't broken the skin. Feels like a clean break," Tove murmured. She let the arm go and cast about for anything she might use for a splint. Finding none, she dropped into a sitting position and studied the other woman's face.

Despite the obvious pain she was in, Brie tried to pull the same blank mask over her features. Only a tightening at the corners of her mouth betrayed her. She cradled her arm in her lap, her eyes cutting to Tove. "Thank you," she said.

"Now, was that so hard?" Tove asked. "You're welcome." She nodded to the broken arm. "We could set it, but without a splint, I'm not sure how much good it would do."

"It won't matter," Brie said. "The Union torturer will be here soon. Once he starts working on me, a broken arm will be the least of my agonies."

"Torture?"

Brie nodded. "They're worried I told my order where the art was. They'll torture me to find out if I did, then they'll kill us all before they leave Richeleau."

Just like that. Tove searched Brie's face, looking for some outward sign of the fear and horror Tove felt. There was nothing. "If I hadn't just seen you and that other woman, I'd guess you were an empty vessel. No emotion, no feeling," she said.

Brie's head swiveled toward Tove. Tove expected her to speak, wanted her to reveal something of the woman behind the mask, but she was disappointed. Brie only gazed silently at her.

"Why'd they bring me?" Tove asked.

"When you tried to defend me, they thought you might be in the order," Brie said. "Wasn't your best move. Sorry."

Tove felt her face flush. She turned away, dropped her head, then stopped herself. Instead, she lifted her chin, met Brie's gaze, and said, "You and ... that other woman." When she saw Brie's smirk, she dropped her eyes, feeling her face warm. *Sheoda.* For the Mother's sake, they were locked in a cell, likely dead before the night was over. She looked into Brie's eyes. "You're lovers, aren't you?"

Brie's grin fell away, and the mask slipped. Tove held her breath, but instead of answering the question, Brie said, "She's the governor's daughter."

"What? What's she doing in the governor's dungeon? Wasn't that Adelbart we saw earlier?"

Brie ignored the question again and gazed at something Tove couldn't see. "We met when I came to pay the governor a visit." Her eyes flicked to Tove. "We have an informant in the governor's house. She told me Elois would be a good source of information, someone we could use for leverage." A small smile curled her lips, and she shook her head. "Love is a mysterious thing. Impossible to explain. Always unexpected." For a moment, Tove thought she could see the girl Brie once must have been. She watched, transfixed, but then a scowl chased the smile from Brie's face and broke the spell. "Her father tried to sell her to an inquisitor to be his whore."

"Her father sold her?"

Brie's eyes narrowed. "I told her to run away. She refused." She shook her head and let her chin drop. "But then she disappeared. I didn't know whether her father succeeded or she changed her mind and ran away. All I knew was she was gone." Her voice trailed away. She sat quietly for a moment, then shook herself. "Anyway, at least we found each other before we die."

The finality of her words brought Tove out of her trance. "But why is she here?"

"Does it matter?"

Tove started to say, of course it mattered, but did it? "Don't you want to live?"

Brie gave a quiet chuckle. "More than anything."

The cold-hearted assassin was gone, hidden behind a smile so sad Tove felt her heart breaking. "Alar will come for us," she said.

"Brie." Elois's voice.

"Alar doesn't know we're here," Brie said before she stood and crossed to the door.

***

Alar paced. Each time he neared the window, he peeked through the space between the closed shutters into the street in front of the tavern. The nightlife was picking up, people finishing meals and moving onto less healthy pursuits. If he had to guess, he would say between nine and ten o'clock.

"You're making me nervous."

Alar turned around. Ukrit sprawled in a chair, legs stretched out in front of him. Alar glanced at the novice, who was still unconscious, bound to a chair, facing away from the two of them. "What's to be nervous about?" he asked and resumed pacing.

"I don't know. You're the one pacing like a caged wolf," Ukrit said. "How long you think he'll be out?"

"Ragan said an hour or so, but she wasn't sure. Been longer than that already," Alar answered, pivoting around to make another circuit. "Best case scenario, he's out till morning. We leave. He never sees us. Thank the Mother, we only have to keep him alive until morning."

"You're not lying. Kidnapping an inquisitor *sounded* like quite the adventure."

"Novice."

"Whatever."

"Anyway, you're right," Alar said, coming to a stop. "I can't help feeling we could be doing something more useful."

Ukrit grunted. "Could just leave him here." He sat up. "He looks safe to me."

"Been considering it."

The novice groaned.

They exchanged a disappointed frown. "Oh, well," Ukrit said and settled back.

The novice's head came up and swiveled from side to side.

"Don't look behind you," Alar said.

The novice's head stopped.

"I imagine you're thirsty," Alar said. "I'll give you some water, as long as you keep your eyes closed."

The novice nodded. "Don't think I can open them, anyway. I'm afraid I'll throw up."

Alar retrieved a ladle from the bucket of water, then came around to the novice's side and lifted the ladle to his lips. When he drank his fill, Alar asked, "How do you feel?"

"Fuzzy. Nothing wants to stay still and everything is purple."

"It wears off," Alar said. "Eventually." He shared a grin with Ukrit. "You're Novice Harold Wolfe?"

"Yes."

Alar was sifting through the many questions he thought of while he paced when Harold spoke again.

"When Lief said we would have to meet on your terms, I have to admit, I was thinking along the lines of a blindfold and bindings."

Alar turned a startled expression on Ukrit who shrugged. As the silence lengthened, Harold's head turned slightly. "You did get my message, right? You are the leaders of *oss'stera?*"

"Right," Alar said. "Well, we have to be careful. Especially with your kind."

After a pause, Harold said slowly, "Yes, I suppose I understand that."

Alar looked again at Ukrit who shrugged unhelpfully, again. After a moment, he gestured to the novice and mouthed, "Ask him what he wants."

Alar frowned and asked, "You wanted to meet with us?" Ukrit nodded encouragingly.

"Yes," Harold said. "I have a proposal that might be of benefit to both of us."

"That's hard to believe," Ukrit said under his breath.

Harold's head jerked to the right at the sound of the new voice, but he stopped short of looking. "I would like to … hire … or more properly, join forces with *oss'stera* to attack the Union mercenaries."

When Alar reassured himself he understood, he laughed.

"Who says inquisitors have no sense of humor," Ukrit said, joining him.

Noticing Harold's silence, Alar's laughter died away. He lifted a hand to quiet Ukrit. "And why would we do that?"

"The art you stole from the caravan? I assume you didn't intend to sell it to the Union?" Harold asked.

Alar and Ukrit exchanged a look. Ukirt started to shrug, until he noticed Alar's expression, then shook his head instead. "Assuming we know anything about art and a … caravan," Alar said, "we would have no intention of selling it to anyone."

The novice, who was sitting absolutely still, sagged slightly. Alar heard a soft whoosh of released breath. "I know for a fact some *Alle'oss* are selling the art to the mercenaries."

"You're a liar," Alar said.

"Two men. One with red hair. The other with blond hair."

"That's not very helpful," Ukrit said.

"I didn't see them very well, but the blond man had a limp and looked as if he had a scar on the side of his face, near his eye."

Alar and Ukrit exchanged worried looks.

The novice continued. "They brought one of the canvases to the governor's office, said they knew where the rest were and offered to sell them. When I saw them, they were on their way to retrieve the rest of the paintings."

"How long ago did you see these men?" Alar asked.

"Was maybe half-past four today. What time is it?"

All three men started at the sound of a key being inserted into the lock of the front door. Alar tensed, prepared to step into *annen'heim*. The door swung open, and a man stepped through.

"Jora!" Alar said.

Jora looked up, a wide smile on his face. "Alar." He took in the novice tied to the chair. "I see you've had an interesting day."

Before Alar could reply, two more men entered. They wore the formal suits popular among the Imperial elite. "Novice Wolfe," the older man said. "I see you've made progress in your investigation." He let a small giggle escape his lips. "You appear to have *oss'stera* right where you want them."

Chapter 40

Unusual Alliances

Alar was too shocked to come up with a response. A quick glance at Ukrit showed no help was coming from that quarter.

"Governor," Harold said. "I have to admit, I'm more than surprised to see you here."

Alar dragged his eyes away from the newcomers to stare at Harold. The novice, tied to a chair in a ruined alehouse, spoke as casually as if he just happened upon the governor on the street one fine sunny day. Ukrit caught Alar's eye and mouthed the word 'governor.'

"Yes, well, as you have no doubt realized, we were having you followed," Gerold said. He gestured to Alar and Ukrit. "Our men were able to report where you were being held."

"And, as you previously arrested the owner of this establishment, the gendarmes could provide his name," Adelbart added, gesturing to Jora, who was inspecting the damage to his business.

"Some plan," Ukrit mumbled.

Alar let his gaze drift to the ceiling. Of course, the novice had a tail. No one in the Empire trusted one another. How stupid could they be?

"Gerold," Harold said. "Is this you keeping the governor out of further trouble?"

The governor looked down at Gerold, who gave him a sheepish look. Adelbart started to speak, but gave his head a shake and addressed Alar and Ukrit. "*Oss'stera*, I presume?"

"I don't know what you're talking about," Ukrit said.

When Ukrit looked to Alar for confirmation, Alar pointed at the window.

Ukrit hurried over and peered through the gap in the shutters. "Imps." He stepped back, his hand going to his sword.

The governor smiled and waved his hands. "No, no, no. Nothing to worry about. My personal guard. I can assure you they are only here for my protection. However, I hope that when you hear my proposal, they will not be needed." He paused. "Or I should say, Gerold's proposal."

"Our lucky day," Ukrit said to Alar. "Everyone has something to sell us."

Adelbart and Gerold exchanged confused looks.

"We were just discussing something similar," Harold said.

"Ah," Adelbart said. "Well, let us put all proposals on the table. Then we shall see what we have to choose from." He waved his assistant forward. "Gerold."

Gerold stepped forward. "Novice, in answer to your earlier question, I believe I've found a way out of our predicaments, yours and ours." He glanced at Alar and Ukrit. "It … uh … however, requires some unusual alliances."

"You are going to suggest that *oss'stera* join the cavalry in attacking the Union," Harold said flatly.

Gerold's mouth snapped shut and his head rocked back. After a moment, he asked, "How did you know?"

"It was the exact proposal I made," Harold said.

Alar looked from Harold to the governor. The older man gave him a grin and nodded. "Now, before you reject the proposal out of hand, let me fill you in on some facts of which you are likely unaware."

"Before you do that," Harold said. "Since we are all on good terms here, can someone UNTIE ME?" When Alar and Ukrit made no move to comply, Harold added in a calmer voice, "I already know what one of you looks like. I saw you in this same tavern."

"It's a bad idea," Ukrit said.

"Let's hear the governor out before we make a decision on that," Alar said.

Harold sighed. "Very well. Governor."

"Yes. As Gerold has informed you, novice, Chagan …" He said to Alar and Ukrit. "The leader of the company of Union mercenaries who are garrisoned at the fort." His eyes rolled up for a minute, then he continued. "As I was saying, Chagan has been holding my daughter in the dungeon of the governor's mansion." When he noticed Ukrit's frown, he waved his hands and hurried on. "The reason is not relevant. However, I was visiting her today and became aware of two facts that *are* relevant."

"Will you get to the point?" Harold asked.

"The Union has imprisoned your companion, Brother Henrik, after beating him rather badly, I'm sorry to say." He looked at Alar. "And while I was there, the mercenaries arrived carrying two prisoners, a Desulti and a red-headed woman with a rather unfortunate scar on her face."

Only the muted music of a fiddle and bodhran from a nearby tavern joined by revelers on the street disturbed the silence. Alar suddenly found it difficult to catch his breath. He glanced at Ukrit, who was staring intently at the governor.

"Someone you know?" Adelbart asked.

"Henrik? You're sure," Harold asked.

"How could this be?" Alar asked at the same time.

"We believe the Union attacked the *Alle'oss* camp in order to recover the paintings. In the process, they captured the Desulti. We presume Chagan intends to kill the Desulti to prevent her from informing her order what became of the paintings," Gerold said. "As for the *Alle'oss* woman, one can only guess why she is there." He gave

Alar and Ukrit a sympathetic smile. "But I'm afraid she will share the same fate as the others."

"Are they alive now?" Ukrit asked.

"They were when I left," Adelbart said. "How long that remains true is a question I can't answer. As we speak, Chagan is preparing to leave Richeleau. So time is of the essence."

Alar drew his knife. Adelbart flinched back, but Alar only sliced the ropes binding the novice. Harold rose unsteadily. Alar took his hand and pressed a small vial into his palm.

"What's this?" Harold asked.

"Antidote," Alar said. He turned away from Harold's scowl and asked Gerold, "What's the plan?"

"As the governor mentioned, we must move quickly if this is to work. First, someone will need to enter the dungeon, overpower the guards, and rescue the prisoners."

"Let's go," Alar said, heading toward the door.

"Wait," Adelbart said. "There's more."

Alar stopped.

"The second part of the plan is for *oss'stera* to join forces with the cavalry remaining in Richeleau to attack the Union mercenaries."

"Why, in the Father's name, would we do that?" Ukrit asked.

"Why, to recover the *Alle'oss* art," Adelbart said. "I assume the presence of your companion in the dungeon is evidence Chagan was successful in recovering the paintings."

"If I may," Gerold asked Harold. "Were you proposing the same strategy?"

"It's the only way I can see our way clear." He gestured to Alar. "*Oss'stera* assists undermanned Imperial forces in ridding the Empire of an enemy force that wiped out a company of Imperial Rangers and threatened the Imperial governor. I will be able to report to Hoerst I rooted out the threat. The *Alle'oss* recover the art, a worthy incentive from what I can tell." He drank the antidote, winced, and said to Alar, "In return, *oss'stera* agree to hide the art from those who would find it offensive." He paused until Alar and Ukrit nodded. "Destroying Chagan's forces releases the governor's debt to them and frees his daughter. The only loose end is the governor's debt to the Desulti, but the Murtair's capture might turn out to be fortuitous in that regard."

"And the governor will have done a great service to the Empire and the *Alle'oss*," Gerold said.

"Ukrit," Alar said. "Go get *oss'stera* organized."

"Right."

"Bring as many bows as you can find to the governor's mansion." Ukrit turned to go and Alar called after him. "Find out how Scilla is."

Alar looked at Adelbart. "You can get me in the dungeon?"

Adelbart nodded.

Alar headed to the door, taking a protesting governor by the arm as he passed. Harold followed until Gerold stopped him. "Novice, I will need your authority." Before Harold could protest, Gerold said, "The captain of our cavalry, Captain Brennerman, will need official incentive to join forces with the *Alle'oss*. He is a rather narrow-minded man when it comes to the locals."

Harold waved at Adelbart. "Have the governor order him to cooperate."

"I'm afraid the captain has a low opinion of the governor," Gerold said. "My apologies, governor, but I believe only a threat from the Inquisition can move him to cooperate."

"I'll get your companion out," Alar said to Harold.

The novice looked him up and down. "Have you seen the Union mercs?" he asked.

"What are you saying?"

"They're huge. Inhumanely quick. Well trained. They're monsters, and we don't know how many there are." He raised a hand and gestured vaguely toward Alar. "And you're ... well, there's only one of you."

"Don't worry," Ukrit said with a lopsided grin. "They'll need an *army* of monsters."

Alar winked and followed Ukrit out the door.

***

Hanutok was a brisk two-hour walk from Richeleau, mostly uphill. Ukrit set out at a jog, but it wasn't long before he slowed to a ragged walk. He was steeling himself for another effort, when he heard the jangle of a wagon's traces. Edging over to the side of the road, he peered ahead, ready to slip into the brush. The moon, nearing its zenith, illuminated a wagon pulled by two familiar horses rounding a bend in the road.

Ukrit stepped onto the road and waved his arms.

"Whoa!" Keth said, pulling the team to a stop.

"Ukrit?" Scilla said and jumped down from her spot beside Keth. "Ukrit, where are you going? Where is Alar?"

"To get you," Ukrit said. He looked past her to the back of the wagon. It was so full, people were hanging onto the sides.

"The Union attacked *Hanutok*," Scilla said. "They came for the paintings and they took Tove."

"I know," Ukrit said.

"Wait," Scilla said. "How do you know?" Before Ukrit could answer, she asked, again, "Where's Alar?"

"It's complicated, and we have to hurry. Let's talk while we ride."

Scilla climbed back onto the bench. Ukrit took one look at the crowded bed of the wagon, then scooched in beside her. Once they were rolling, he said, "Alar is rescuing Tove and the Desulti from the governor's dungeon. The novice is going to threaten the captain of the cavalry to get him to cooperate with us so we can attack the Union mercenaries and recover the paintings."

"We're going to fight on the same side as the Imp cavalry?"

Ukrit turned to find Lief pressed up against the backrest of the driver's bench. "I know. It's all very confusing and last minute," Ukrit said. "But what do we do that's not?" His grin faded when he saw Scilla's face. "Alar will be okay. You know him."

"Yeah, I do. That's why I'm worried."

"Yeah. Me too. Let's pick up the pace."

Chapter 41

Alar Will Come

The governor's mansion was nearly deserted once they got past the guards posted at the door. The two Imps scowled at Alar's cocky smile as he followed the governor into the building. Adelbart dismissed his personal guard, then they climbed to the third floor. Adelbart had not spoken to him on the way, but after leading Alar down a darkened hall to a dead end, he paused and said, "The stairs behind this wall take us to the ground floor. From there we pass through another door and then it's another two stories down to the lower dungeon."

"There isn't a way to get into the dungeon on the lower floor?" Alar asked. Adelbart blinked and stared at him. When no further explanation was forthcoming, Alar shrugged and asked, "How many guards are there?"

The governor pursed his lips. "Normally, there are only two. Under the present circumstances, who can tell? There were four when I left." He looked Alar up and down and asked, "Should we wait for your companions to arrive?"

"Time is of the essence, remember?" Alar asked, hitching a brow. "Let's get it over with."

A few minutes later, they were standing on a landing on the ground floor before a heavy oak door. The governor set a lamp on a small table and retrieved a key ring. It was silent except for the scuff of their feet on the stone floor and the governor's labored breath. As Adelbart fit a key into the lock, voices speaking another language drifted up from below. The governor froze. He turned wide eyes on Alar, shook his head, and started to pull the key from the lock. Alar put his hand on the governor's, turned the key, and slipped the key ring into his pocket. Putting a finger to his lips, he whispered, "Stay here," then he slipped through the door.

The stairs were steep, narrow and wound down to the left. The dim light leaking through the window in the door only enhanced the shadows. Alar waited for his eyes to adjust, listening to the approaching voices. They were getting louder, but echoes in the stone passage made it difficult to judge how close they were. He took a breath, let it out slowly, pulled and shivered. He was about to step into *annen'heim*, when he glanced back at the governor's wide eyes watching him through the window. Deciding it would be best if the governor didn't know his secret, Alar descended toward the voices.

He just stepped outside the governor's line of sight when the darkness ahead of him retreated, chased by a shifting light. A moment later, a man came into view. The mercenary, looking down as he carefully navigated the narrow steps with oversized feet, didn't see Alar step into *annen'heim*. Alar paused, listening. There were spirits nearby, but they were not close, so he turned his attention to the man in front of him. He was enormous. Even though Alar was several steps above him, their heads were on a level. The mercenary's wide shoulders nearly brushed the walls. Alar leaned over, peered past him, and was relieved to see only one other man. The trick was how to get to the second man after killing the first. He would only have moments before the *sjel'and* arrived once the first man died. He needed to incapacitate him without killing him outright. After considering the situation, he drew his sword and his knife, descended so he was two steps above the first man, then stepped across the boundary.

The mercenary was still looking down when Alar's boots appeared in his line of sight. He looked up, startled, and hesitated a fatal moment before Alar reached up and drove his knife into the side of his neck. Blood gushed sideways, soaking Alar's hand and splashing the stone wall. The man dropped the lantern and clamped both hands to his neck. Alar put his foot on the man's stomach and shoved. The idea was to get the second man entangled with the body of his companion, then strike before he could free himself. But as Alar shoved, his heel slipped off the edge of the step and he only managed to thrust himself backward. Throwing out a hand to catch himself, he dropped his knife.

Surprised to be sitting on the cold stone steps, he only barely scrambled out of the way as the wounded man, pushed by his comrade from behind, fell toward him, his face a mask of hatred painted in dark and light by the flickering lantern. For a second, he and the second mercenary stared at one another. The Union men all looked the same to Alar, but there was something familiar about this one. When the mercenary cocked his head, light from the fallen lantern fell on a milky eye and Alar recognized him. It was the mercenary he tangled with at the Black Husky.

"You!" the man bellowed and lunged.

Fortunately for Alar, the body sprawled on the steps between them hindered the mercenary's attempts to reach him. Recovering from his surprise, Alar raised his sword and thrust at the man's chest. To his astonishment, the man caught his blade in gloved hands.

The mercenary guffawed, gave the sword a shake, and rumbled something Alar couldn't interpret.

Bracing his legs, Alar grasped the hilt with both hands and jerked. It was like yanking a rope tied to a stone wall. Leering, the merc clambered awkwardly over the shifting body beneath his feet. Alar backed slowly away, sawing the blade back and forth, to no avail. *I might need to spend more time sharpening my blade.* Distracted by the stray thought, he was nearly jerked off his feet when the mercenary yanked the blade. Only a firm grip on the sword saved Alar from flying down the stairs. *What a ridiculous situation.*

His opponent laughed again. "Not this time, little *l'oss.*"

The merc gathered himself, but Alar was ready this time. In the instant before his opponent jerked the blade, Alar stepped into *annen'heim.* His swelling spirit's song was nearly drowned by the howls of approaching *sjel'and.* He knew he should flee, but he hesitated when the glittering orb of the dead mercenary's spirit rose and hovered just before him, a beacon of light in the shadowy realm. There was no malevolence emanating from this spirit as it did from the *sjel'and.* He reached up as if he could touch the spirit, but pulled his hand back. Dark specters, emerging from the stone walls, woke him from his trance and chased him across the boundary.

Back in the world, he was gratified to see he timed it perfectly. When the sword disappeared, the mercenary only threw his bulk backward. Hands scrabbling at the smooth stone walls, feet tangled with the body, he couldn't stop his momentum. On the steep stairs, he was nearly vertical when he landed on the back of his neck with a wet crunch. Alar watched as the body tumbled limply out of sight around the bend.

"Bless the Mother," he whispered, listening for anyone who might have heard the altercation. Hearing nothing, he retrieved the lantern and climbed over the body, trying not to think about what was happening to the man's spirit in the underworld. He found the second body wedged against the walls in the tight space.

He knew he was approaching the dungeon when a dim light lifted details from the pitch dark outside the small pool cast by his partially hooded lantern. A few steps later, he heard voices. He paused and listened, but the voices were muffled and were not coming nearer. He set the lantern on a step and continued down until he emerged onto a flat space in front of a heavy oak door, centered on the opposite wall. The light came from a small window in the door. The guard room to the dungeon. He withdrew the key ring from his pocket and was considering how best to approach the situation when a shout rang out. Others followed it, then the sound of a slammed door, running feet, and an anguished roar.

"Tove!"

***

Tove sat on the cold stone floor, staring at the wall. Though she knew it was rude to listen to Brie's conversation with Elois, she couldn't help it. She was fascinated, both by Elois's story and by the feelings the two women's relationship stirred in her.

The governor's daughter learned of the Desulti house from the informant in the governor's mansion. The woman, who was aware of Brie and Elois's feelings for one another, revealed herself when Adelbart made his deal to sell his daughter. Elois slipped out of the mansion in the middle of the night with the help of the informant and made it safely to the Desulti house. They accepted her. She had been so happy, she wept tears of joy while they shaved her head in a ritual that represented leaving her old life behind. The Union attack on the safe house came that night, before her presence was reported to the order.

As the women's conversation became more intimate, Tove pressed her eyes closed, ashamed to be eavesdropping but desperate to hear what they said to one another.

When the volume of the voices in the guard room rose, abruptly, Brie hurried back to her spot on the floor across from Tove. "The torturer comes," she said. The door to the guardroom opened.

Tove gathered the remains of the leather thongs and shoved them under herself, then put their hands behind her back just before two men appeared at the door to their cell. She recognized the giant who carried her to the dungeon, but the other was new. He was much shorter, thin, with sallow, pockmarked skin and thinning hair tied in a tail at the back of his neck. He peered through tiny spectacles into the cell, a leather case held in front of him with both hands. When he saw Tove, his nose wrinkled, and he said something in their language.

The other man shrugged. The torturer considered Tove, then pointed at her and spoke. The giant produced a key ring, unlocked the cell, entered and bent over, reaching for Tove.

Before Tove could decide whether to reveal her hands were free and fight back, she caught a flicker of movement in the corner of her eye. One moment, Brie was sitting quietly, the next she drove the fingers of her uninjured arm into the mercenary's throat. The man dropped to his knees, gasping to pull air past his ruined esophagus.

Tove was up before the torturer reacted, leaping over Brie, who was administering another blow. The torturer squeaked, dropped his case and fled. Tove slammed the cell door closed, reached through the bars, and extracted the key from the lock. Before she could back away from the door, another guard, approaching at a run, slammed against the bars, shoved his arm into the cell, and wrapped an enormous hand around her upper arm. Pulling futilely at his grip, Tove stared at the strangely blank face pressed against the bars. Then the giant yanked her off her feet. She twisted, letting her momentum do the work when she drove the heavy key into his eye.

The roar he emitted echoed in the stone hallway. His hands went to his ruined eye. Tove backed away from the door and watched another guard help his wounded comrade to the guardroom. She lifted the bloody key and glanced at Brie, who appeared beside her.

"Quick thinking," the Murtair said. "Though I'm sure they have a spare."

"Probably," Tove answered. "But it will give Alar a little more time to find us."

Brie snorted.

Her smirk fell away, and both women looked toward the other end of the hall as chaos erupted in the guardroom.

***

Alar took a quick look through the small window into the guardroom. Across from him, another door opened into a darkened hallway. A man, his back to Alar, looking down the hall, stepped aside to let two others enter the room. The newcomer supported a bellowing companion who held a blood-drenched hand to his face. At least three mercenaries. Alar ducked away when one of the men turned in his direction. He just got out of the way and pressed himself to the wall as the door flew open. A man emerged at a run and disappeared up the stairs. He would encounter the bodies soon, but if Alar was quick, he could take care of the others before the one who went for help returned.

Sword in hand, he stepped into the doorway. The injured mercenary sat in a chair, bent over, his blood spattering the floor between his feet. The other man looked up as Alar stepped into *annen'heim*. He crossed the room, raising his sword. He swung horizontally as he returned to the world and cleaved the man's head. Before the injured mercenary realized he was there, Alar reset his sword and swung at an angle, striking the injured man at the base of his neck. Footsteps and shouts from the returning mercenary echoed in the small stone space. Alar's sword was stuck fast in the man's ribcage. Letting go of the sword, he whirled around just as the mercenary entered the guardroom at a run. He spotted Alar and drew a sword.

Alar glanced down and stooped to pull a knife from the sheath of the headless mercenary. He stepped into *annen'heim* just before the mercenary's sword embedded itself in his head. The howls of approaching *sjel'and* were deafening. He was hemmed in against the wall and the bodies of his victims and had no time to extract himself. Ducking just low enough to avoid the sword, he recrossed the boundary. The blade brushed his hair as it passed, and Alar drove himself upward, thrusting the blade under his opponent's ribcage.

The body fell backward and lay spread eagle on the stone floor. Alar stood alone in the silent room, breath coming in ragged gasps, surrounded by bodies and pooling blood. Pressing his eyes closed, he fought to stand on wobbly legs. Opening his eyes and staring down at his victims, Ragan's words in Kartok emerged from his muddled thoughts; '… being in *oss'stera*, I'm sure you have much to atone for.' Yes, he had much to atone for. But not yet. Pulling, he let the rush calm his heart and shore up his legs. When he was sure he could walk without stumbling, he picked his way past the pools of blood, crossed to the door that led to the cells and peeked into the darkened hall. A short, thin man holding a leather case looked nervously back at him from halfway to the other end.

"Tove," he shouted.

"Here," a familiar voice answered.

Alar heard a key turning in a lock. Weak with relief, he checked the cell on the left and found a brother of the Inquisition standing behind the bars. His face was battered, his right eye swollen shut.

"Henrik?" Alar asked.

The brother's undamaged eye widened. He nodded.

"Harold sends his regards. We are, at least temporarily, on the same side," Alar said. A woman was looking at him through the bars of the cell on the opposite side of the hall. "The governor's daughter."

"Who are you?" she asked.

Alar ignored the question. He dropped the knife and braced himself just before Tove crashed into him. She wrapped her arms around his chest, then stepped back and shoved him. "You stupid *wota*," she said. "What do you think you're doing coming down here by yourself?"

Alar grinned. "You're welcome." He pulled her into a hug.

"*Sheoda*," she said, fighting to get free. "Let go of me. You're a mess."

Alar let her go and bent down to retrieve the knife. It was longer than any knife he had seen. More like a short sword, but the steel was pristine, the balance perfect, and though the hilt was bigger than he was used to, it was comfortable in his hand. He looked up at the sound of a key turning in a lock. The Desulti was opening the door to the brother's cell. The small man with the leather case was peering at him from between the bars of the cell Tove previously occupied.

"It's a seax."

Alar looked up to find the brother looking at him, leaning against the bars of his cell. "Say axe?" Alar asked, looking down at the knife.

"It's a style used in the Union. They are renowned for their metalwork. That blade will never chip or rust. You should hang on to that."

One corner of Alar's mouth lifted. What, he wondered, were the odds of that? Still, it was a nice knife.

"Brie!"

The governor's daughter was glaring at the Desulti, who apologized and opened her cell door. *Brie?* The governor's daughter wrapped her arms around the other woman. She glanced at Alar and said, "Thank you." Then she kissed the Desulti.

Alar found himself staring and snapped his mouth shut with a click. Feeling as if he was intruding, he averted his eyes and sought Tove. When he saw the intensity with which she was watching the two women, he grew still. She bit her lip and her eyes flicked to him. He expected the scowl that usually appeared when someone caught her revealing something of her real self. Instead, she gave him a sad smile and leaned against him.

The two women parted, and Tove's expression cleared.

"Hold on," he said. When she looked at him, he asked, "How did you have the key?"

Someone snickered. He looked up and nearly dropped the knife again when he found the Desulti grinning at him.

"She kept her *eye* open," the Desulti said.

Alar glanced at the brother who was standing in the open door of his cell. He shrugged.

"You might say," Tove said, elbowing him in the ribs. "I found an *eye-popping* opportunity."

Alar watched, fascinated, as the two women broke into giggles. To his surprise, Tove stepped forward and punched the Desulti's shoulder. "Told ya," she said.

To Alar's even greater surprise, the Desulti's only response was to shrug her shoulder and give Tove a crooked smile.

"This is Brie, by the way," Tove said. When she noticed Alar gaping at her, she scowled. "What?"

"Nothing." Alar cleared his throat and dragged his gaze away from her. "Right. We need to get—"

"Elois."

Alar whirled and found the governor standing in the door to the guardroom, looking past Alar to this daughter.

He gestured to Alar. "I found someone to rescue you."

Alar had no context to understand their relationship, but even so, he could feel the awkwardness in the silence that followed. "Yes, well … As I was saying," Alar said. "We need to get going."

"Where?" Brie asked.

"We're joining the Imperial Cavalry to attack the Union mercenaries."

"Let's go," Tove said.

Alar retrieved a torch from a sconce. "The stairs are dark," he said and stepped up to stand in front of Adelbart, who blocked the door. "Governor," he said and flicked his fingers.

The governor retreated, pressed his back against the wall and watched Alar with wide eyes as he passed.

He heard a low whistle behind him and looked back. Tove and Brie were examining the bodies. The Desulti hitched a brow at him.

"There are two more on the stairs," Adelbart said. When Brie and Tove looked at him, he lifted a finger and pointed.

Chapter 42

The Battle of the Fort

Alar led them up to the top floor of the mansion. They found Harold, Gerold and a man in the blue uniform of the Imperial Cavalry in a large ornate room arrayed around a table. The Imp was tall, as tall as the novice, thin, even cadaverous, with graying stubble for hair. Alar returned his pinched expression with his biggest smile. To be fair, the man's disgust might have been because Alar was covered in the mercenaries' blood, but he guessed that wasn't the only reason. Alar veered over to stand beside him, forcing him to retreat around to the other side of the table.

"You must be Captain Brennerman," he said. He turned when Tove elbowed him. She nodded at the captain and waggled her brows. Though Alar was no expert on Imp military kits, the captain's immaculate uniform seemed to be festooned with an inordinate amount of gold. Gold shoulder brushes, two rows of golden buttons, gold, woven ropes looped across his chest. A large gold buckle closed his belt from which an ornately gilded sword hung.

Alar forgot his amusement at the captain's discomfort when he noticed the two brothers standing apart, staring at one another. After a moment, the novice turned his attention to the table.

"Novice Wolfe," Alar said.

Harold gave him an appraising look, his eyes lingering on the blood staining his tunic. "No army, then?" he asked.

Before Alar could answer, the captain said in a surprisingly deep voice, "A Desulti?"

Alar had to admit, he was either brave or stupid to refer to the Murtair with such distaste.

"A Desulti *assassin, nāminu,*" Tove blurted.

The captain's head rocked back. He looked as if he wasn't sure how offended he should be at the unfamiliar word, but before he could say anything, Harold spoke.

"Yes, well, can we turn our attention to the problem at hand?" He gestured to the table where a map of the area surrounding the fort lay. Oil lamps held the corners down. He caught Alar's eye and said, "The captain was just briefing us on the tactical situation." He pointed to a roughly square outline in the center of the map. "This is the fortress."

"Are the mercs in there?" Brie asked.

"No," he said. He pointed to rows of rectangular buildings to the left of the fort. "The Union and the cavalry are housed in the barracks west of the fort." He waved his hand over an empty space between the fort and the barracks. "The Union have been busy loading everything they can lay their hands on into wagons on the parade ground. Most of them are there." He straightened. "There are four sentries on the allure on top of the fortress walls, another two guarding the fortress gate, and the last we knew of Chagan, he was in his office inside the fortress with four of his personal guard. The other two left to bring their intelligence man to the dungeon." He paused and hitched a brow at Alar.

Alar set the big knife on the table with a clunk. "There are five in the dungeon we won't have to worry about," he said.

"Six," Brie said.

Harold looked at Adelbart who shook his head and wrinkled his nose. "Quite messy."

"Yes," Harold said. "Good. As you say, that's six fewer we have to worry about."

"Governor."

Everyone turned toward the voice. An Imp Alar recognized as one guarding the front of the mansion was standing in the door.

"Yes," Adelbart said.

The man glanced at Alar and Tove, then said, "There is a wagon load of *l'oss* out front who say you are expecting them."

"Yes," Adelbart said, turning back to the table. "Show them up."

The guard looked as if he would ask a question, but then shook his head and said, "Yes, sir," and disappeared.

"I suppose we should wait until everyone is here," Gerold said.

In the awkward silence, Alar studied the two brothers, standing at opposite sides of the table, glancing furtively at one another. The captain looked as if he couldn't decide which offended him most, the two *Alle'oss* or Brie and Elois, who were leaning against one another. Elois kept trying to catch Brie's eye with small smiles, which Brie was trying, and failing, to ignore. When he noticed Alar watching him, the captain harrumphed, crossed his arms and turned away from the table.

"Did he harrumph?" Tove whispered. When Alar chuckled, she asked, "Was everyone else okay? At home?"

"I don't know."

They heard voices approaching, Ukrit's voice louder than the others. "I'm sure he's okay."

A crowd of boisterous *oss'stera* appeared in the door, led by Ukrit and Scilla. Ukrit spread his arms, a big smile on his face. "Look what I found on the way to *Hanutok.*"

When she saw Alar, Scilla stopped, a smile transforming her face. She crossed the distance between them in a few quick steps and threw her arms around his neck. Before she could kiss him, she stepped back, nose wrinkling.

"Yeah, he's a mess," Tove said.

Scilla stepped up to the table on the other side of Tove and said, "You'll have to wait to see how happy I am you're alive."

The *Alle'oss*, carrying their bows, spread out, surrounding the table and jostling one another to get a better view of the map.

"Captain," Harold said, a coldness in his voice that drew every *Alle'oss* eye in the room.

The captain shuddered, hands curled into fists at his side. He turned to face them. When he noticed the *Alle'oss*, blocking his access to the table, he stepped up behind Lief and peered down at him. "Excuse me," he said.

Lief looked up. "Sure," he said and shuffled over to make room.

"Yes, now that we're all here," Harold said. "The captain can continue with the tactical briefing."

The captain pursed his lips, hands clasped behind his back, jaw muscles working. When he spoke, he sounded as if he were reading from an excruciatingly boring book. "When the mercenaries returned earlier tonight, they confined my men in their barracks. There is a contingent, maybe twenty, assigned to keep them bottled up there."

"How many men do you have?" Ukrit asked.

The captain glanced at Ukrit, but looked at Harold when he answered. "The governor has left me with only fifty troopers."

"Can you communicate a plan to them?" Alar asked.

"That would be difficult," he said to Harold. "However, the situation is a tinderbox. My men need only a small excuse."

"A signal, perhaps?" Gerold asked. When everyone looked at him, he said, "To attack, that is."

The captain sniffed. "Perhaps if my bugler was not up in the mountains."

"What about a flugelhorn?" Gerold suggested.

The captain blinked. "A … flugelhorn?"

When the captain let his eyes drift to the ceiling, Alar bent over and studied the map. He looked at Harold and asked, "You say most of the mercs are on the parade ground?"

Harold nodded. "As of a few minutes ago. It looks as if they're almost finished loading the wagons. I don't know what will happen after that. And I assume it won't be long before they find out what happened in the dungeon." He raised an eyebrow, but when no one answered his implied question, he finished, "If that happens, the situation becomes much more fluid and difficult to control."

Alar pointed to the western fortress wall that bordered the parade ground. "If we can get on top of that wall undetected, we'll be able to shoot down on them from cover." The captain started to speak, but Alar talked over him. "Once we get their attention, and hopefully thin out their numbers a bit, Gerold," he gave him a quick grin, "sends the signal and the Imps attack the mercs from behind."

Alar looked across the table at Ukrit in the silence that followed. Ukrit rolled his eyes and nodded toward the captain, who was frowning down at the map.

After a moment, the captain said, "You will have to get past the gate guards and eliminate the sentries on the allure without alerting anyone."

Alar pointed to the corner of a building a hundred paces from the fortress gate. "We take out the guards from here. Scilla and," he looked up and spotted Zaina peeking between Ogden and Harold, "and Zaina take the shot."

The captain dismissed Scilla quickly, but when he saw Zaina, his face froze. With a shake of his head, he said, "Assuming that is possible, there are still the sentries on the walls."

"If the guards at the gate are eliminated, can I get onto the wall without being detected?" Alar asked. When the captain nodded, Alar said, "Leave the sentries to me."

The captain's gaze fell to the knife on the table and looked as if he would speak before Brie interrupted.

"I'll help."

"With that arm?" Tove asked.

Brie nodded. "Splint it."

After studying the Desulti for a moment, the captain bent over the map, popped his lips, then said, "Assuming all goes to plan, and you get your men—people up on the wall. As soon as you open fire, the mercs in the parade ground will return fire to keep you pinned down. Then they will send a contingent to enter the fortress and sweep the top of the wall clear." He pointed to a building in the fortress yard, nestled up against the opposite wall of the fortress. "Chagan's personal guard will join that attack." He straightened and looked around at the *Alle'oss* staring at him. "The Union mercenaries are *not* a ragtag band of hooligans. They are nearly the equal of the Empire's finest."

Tove leaned toward Alar and whispered loud enough for everyone to hear in the silence, "I think we've just been insulted."

"Rangers," Lief coughed, covering his mouth.

Laughter broke out among the *Alle'oss.* Alar returned Ukrit's smile. He glanced at Harold and found a grin playing at the corners of his mouth.

When the novice noticed Alar looking at him, he grew serious and cleared his throat. He tapped the gate of the fortress and said, "Once *oss'stera* opens fire, we drop the inner portcullis." He let his finger trace the barbican which jutted out from the fortress wall, forming a tunnel attackers would have to fight through to enter the fortress. "When the Union enter the barbican, we drop the outer portcullis and trap them."

"So then, we only need to take care of Chagan's guards."

"I'll guard the bottom of the stairs with …," he looked at Brie, who nodded. "That's two."

Alar looked across the table at Ukrit, who was tipping his head toward the novice, mouthing what looked like, "Alive. Morning."

"Three," Alar said.

Harold met his eyes and nodded. "Three against four. Certainly no army."

"We catch the others in the parade ground between our bows and the Imps," Alar said, bringing the palms of his hands together. "Simple."

All eyes turned to the captain. He stared down at the map, then looked around at the *Alle'oss* who were watching him expectantly. He looked at Gerold and asked, "A flugelhorn?"

"We better move," Harold said. "Once they find out what happened in the dungeon, we lose the element of surprise."

The members of *oss'stera* looked to Alar. "Let's go," he said, and they moved off toward the door, high-spirited chatter breaking out. Harold nodded to Alar and turned to follow. Alar watched him go, noting Henrik limping along behind him at a distance.

Ukrit appeared at Alar's side. "Did Ragan tell you what time, exactly, we can stop trying to keep him alive?"

Alar pursed his lips, replaying Ragan's instructions. "No, but I'm guessing there is no time limit. He won't be much help to her daughters if he dies tonight or next week."

"It's not like we can ask him to hang back. Can we?"

"No," Alar answered. "He doesn't seem like that kind of person." When he noticed Brie listening to their conversation, he said, "It's a long story."

"Once you clear the wall, you can keep an eye on him," Scilla said.

"Right," Alar said. "We get him through this alive. That's all we agreed to. After that, he's Ragan's problem. Okay, let's go."

In the hall, Gerold was listening to the captain whistling a tune. Alar heard Tove behind him, offering to splint Brie's arm. Scilla, who was walking beside him, took his arm and pulled him to a stop. She watched Tove examining Brie's arm, with Elois standing nearby, then whispered, "What is going on there?"

"You noticed."

"How could you not?" she asked. "I haven't heard that tone in Tove's voice since ... well, ever."

Alar pulled her into motion and said, "I think Tove figured something out."

"What are you two talking about?" Ukrit asked.

"Nothing," they chorused.

Alar peered at the dark gate of the fortress, trying to ignore his trembling legs. As the adrenaline that buoyed him through the struggle in the dungeon and the planning session ebbed, a heavy lethargy settled on him. He pulled carefully, for the third time in the past half hour, clenching his teeth against the euphoric effects that set his head swimming. Still, it barely touched his fatigue.

Scilla nudged him and held his bow out.

Alar shook his head and pointed to a sentry on top of the wall, standing near a large brazier. The light from the fire glinted on the man's helm and cuirass. "Not sure an arrow will penetrate that armor."

Zaina stuck her head between Alar and Scilla and peered up at the wall. She looked up at Alar, withdrew an arrow from her quiver, and pointed a finger on her other hand at one of her sapphire eyes.

Alar stared at her for a moment, then looked up at Scilla. "I worry about this one's childhood." He took the bow Scilla offered him and muttered, "More so than most." He handed Scilla his knife and turned his attention to the men guarding the gate.

"It sounded like a good plan upstairs," Scilla said. "We forgot about it being dark."

The moon, well past its zenith, left the gate on the eastern wall of the fort in darkness.

"Right," Alar said. "Time for plan B." Their eyes met, and they both glanced back at Harold, Gerold, and the captain standing behind them. Was there a way to distract them so they didn't see Alar disappear into *annen'heim*?

Just then, a man exited the gate carrying a lantern. The other guards gathered around him.

"Quick, Zaina, Scilla," Alar said. "Ukrit, you take the third man."

Zaina stepped out of the shadow of the building they were standing beside, an arrow already nocked. She glanced up at Scilla and said, "On three." Scilla and Ukrit nodded, drew and took aim. On the count of three, all three bows twanged and a moment later, all three guards staggered and fell.

Alar glanced up at the sentries on the wall. Finding them looking elsewhere, he left the shadows and sprinted toward the gate, with Brie close behind. He stopped at the entrance to the barbican and peered into the dark tunnel, while Brie ensured the guards wouldn't raise an alarm. Finding the coast clear, he gave Brie a nod and stepped into *annen'heim.* The spirits had noticed the men's death, but they were not yet close. He jogged the length of the tunnel and entered the courtyard of the fortress. The steps to the top of the wall were to his left. He paused at the bottom, eying the stairs, and looked along the allure. The first sentry was frozen ten paces from the top of the stairs. Alar headed up.

The allure was wide enough for two people to walk side-by-side, but the mercenary was wider than a normal man, and he was walking in the center of the walkway. Alar drew an arrow and nocked it as he strolled toward him. He stopped a pace in front of the man and studied his piggish eyes. Alar's head only came up to the man's neck, so as he drew, he was forced to aim up to place the arrow tip six inches from the man's eye. He settled himself, crossed the boundary, and loosed.

It was as if the strings animating the big mercenary were cut all at once. He dropped into a heap, producing only a dull thud. He was probably dead before his brain registered Alar's appearance. "I have to give the little terror credit. That was a good idea."

He recrossed the boundary and moved on, racing the spirits and discovery. The other three sentries died as easily as the first. Not more than a minute passed in the physical realm from the moment he first entered *annen'heim.* After killing the fourth, he jogged to the wall where they saw the guard illuminated by the brazier, then leapt onto one of the crenels between two merlons and waved his arms. When he saw the others leave the shadow of the building across the plaza, he hopped down onto the walkway and found Brie waiting for him.

Her head swiveled, scanning the top of the wall. "You got them all," she said. Alar nodded and started walking. As she turned to follow him, he heard her mutter, "There's something not fair about that."

By the time he and Brie made it to the bottom of the stairs, *oss'stera* were pouring through the inner gate. Nervous energy animated their greetings as they streamed past, their moccasins whispering on the stone steps. Scilla handed him his knife, gave him a quick kiss, and followed the others.

Harold, followed by Henrik, Gerold and the captain, brought up the rear. "Captain, if you would show Brother Henrik to the winch room," Harold said. As Henrik was turning away, the novice caught his arm. "Remember, wait until the shooting starts to lower the inner portcullis, and don't close the outer portcullis until you see the mercenaries in the tunnel through the murder holes."

"Right," Henrik said. Harold was turning away when Henrik said, "Sir." When Harold looked back, Henrik said, "Good luck."

Harold hesitated, then said, "Good luck to you, brother." He watched Henrik walking away, then turned to Alar. "Once they're in place, we'll give the signal to shoot."

Alar ran up the stairs and got Scilla's attention. "You ready?"

She looked along the allure where the archers were crouched behind the merlons on top of the wall, arrows nocked, peeking at potential targets through the crenels. "Yes," she said.

Alar looked down at Harold in the courtyard and waited. Adrenaline was once again surging through his veins, but it left him feeling like a bowstring pulled too taut. He didn't dare pull again. The captain and Gerold appeared and ascended the stairs. The captain brushed past Alar without acknowledging him. Gerold, fingers working the valves of his flugelhorn, nodded despite his tight expression. Alar looked down at Harold. The city held its breath. Only the Union mercenaries' rough voices in the parade ground below the wall broke the silence. They hadn't noticed anything yet.

"Fire," Harold said in a normal voice.

Alar nodded to Scilla, who shouted, "Ready!" All along the walkway, archers stood at the crenels and drew. Scilla waited, giving them time to find their targets, then shouted, "Loose!"

Eighteen bows twanged in unison. Alar gave Scilla a nod, then hurried down the stairs. He was still on the stairs when the massive iron and oak portcullis rumbled down. Before it crashed to the ground, three mercenaries ducked through the opening.

***

Scilla nocked another arrow and peered into the parade ground, trying to gauge the effect of their attack. There were a handful of bodies scattered across the ground, but the mercenaries reacted faster than expected and most of them found shelter behind the wagons. It wasn't long before they began to fire back with disturbing effect. Already one *Alle'oss* was struck and fell from the wall into the fortress yard. The captain was peeking around the next merlon over, with Gerold huddled against the wall at his feet. She returned her gaze to the parade ground, looking for a target. There were none. The men who were shooting back at them appeared and disappeared so quickly, there was no time to target them.

"Captain!" she shouted. She could tell he heard her, but he didn't answer. She stepped past Gerold and tugged on the captain's arm. He jerked his arm free, but turned to face her. "You're men need to attack." The captain turned away from her. Another *Alle'oss* crumpled to the walkway. She reached for the captain, but was interrupted by a scream from the far end of the allure.

***

The first Ukrit knew they were under attack was when the man on his right screamed. He swung around and found a mercenary throwing the man's body from the top of the wall. Ukrit was fumbling for an arrow when the man turned a flat expression on him. Ukrit fit the arrow to his string, but before he could raise it, the mercenary lunged, covering the space in the flicker of an eye. Ukrit swung his bow in a desperate attempt to fend off the attack, knowing it was too late.

A hum beside his right ear, as of a bumblebee, then an arrow sprouted from the man's forehead. The man's momentum carried his body forward, crashing into Ukrit and carrying him to the walkway.

Another mercenary stepped on the body of his comrade before another arrow struck him in the chest. He took another step, his foot coming down beside Ukrit's head, then he fell to a knee and tumbled off the allure.

Ukrit lay on his back, looking up at Zaina. "Thank you."

She nodded. "Must be another way to get up."

She retreated, leaving him to stare at a starry sky. He heaved the dead weight to the side and climbed to his feet. "Must be other stairs," he murmured and bent to retrieve his bow.

***

Next to the closed portcullis, Brie sprang at the first mercenary, looking tiny next to his bulk. She feinted to her right, then glided left, avoiding his sword, and drew her knife across his thigh.

Alar turned his attention to Harold, who faced the other two mercenaries alone. The first man blocked Harold's downward stroke, leaving the novice open to the second man's attack. "No!" Alar shouted as he stepped into *annen'heim.*

The murk of the underworld writhed, roiled by a howling swarm of *sjel'and.* Alar froze for a heartbeat, stunned by a wall of sound. Before he could react, a shadow left the mass and swooped by his left arm, so close, he imagined he felt it brush him. He flinched away and whirled as the shape slowed and stopped. Though he could see no recognizable shape, Alar had the sense the spirit was turning to regard him. Before, the spirits had been just shadowy presences. Only in his nightmares had Alar imagined what they looked like. He stood rooted to the spot, fascinated, afraid to escape into the physical world lest time restart and Harold be struck down. The spirit hovered, an undulating cloud of polluted smoke. Suddenly, the smoke pulsed, breaking into ropey tendrils through which Alar glimpsed the glittering spirit within. The *sjel'and* reached out to his spirit. Despair, craving, and revulsion. Alar sensed the *sjel'and's* need, the emotions so powerful that Alar shrank back. His song, his spirit's song, wavered. Suddenly, he felt an unreasoning rage. The cloud contracted and emitted a stuttering grunt that vibrated in his chest, a sound he recognized as a spirit seeking him.

The *sjel'and* sprang at him, the stinking cloud spreading, the edges grasping, as if to envelop him. Something inside Alar screamed. Not a sound, but a thrill of fear so powerful, his mind went white. He fled across the boundary half a heartbeat before the cloud surrounded him. The scream erupted from his mouth, and he fell backward, tumbling down the stone steps, and coming to a violent stop at Harold's feet. The back of his head struck the cobbles. A flurry of motion, a clash of steel, a scream. Then nothing.

***

"Ukrit!" Scilla shouted and took off toward the other end of the wall, but she had only taken a few steps when she saw Zaina move out of the way and Ukrit roll a body aside and stand. Whatever happened, it was over. She retreated to her previous position, peeked down into the parade ground in time to see a group of mercenaries leaving the cover of the wagons. She snapped off a shot, then screamed, "Captain! Now!"

The captain reached down and dragged Gerold to his feet, bent over to stand nose to nose with the smaller man and shouted, "Now!"

Gerold nodded, gave Scilla a frightened glance, wet his lips, and put the horn to his mouth and blew. No sound emerged.

Scilla leaned in and said, "Breathe, relax. You're safe here."

He nodded, licked his lips once more, raised the horn. And played a rousing tune.

Scilla had no idea whether it was right, but the captain nodded, said, "Continue," and returned to look down into the parade ground.

***

Alar opened his eyes. Brie was crouched beside him. When she saw his eyes open, she said, "You're back."

It was quieter than before he passed out. He winced, started to sit up, then decided it was a bad idea. "Did we win?"

"Almost over," Brie said. "The cavalry is mopping up, and we have this lot."

Alar followed her pointing finger to a group of mercenaries peering balefully through the portcullis.

"Harold's plan worked like a charm," Brie said.

"Harold!" Alar sat up quickly, then had to squeeze his eyes shut against a wave of nausea.

"Harold is fine," Brie said, taking Alar's arm and helping him to his feet.

"But I saw … heard him being killed. Didn't I?"

"He should be dead. That second merc was about to cut him down. No way for me to reach him in time, but then he just stopped. My guess is he saw you do your thing and he froze."

Alar looked at her.

"You sort of flickered," she said. After a moment, she added, "It was disturbing."

Alar looked over her shoulder. Harold and the captain were walking toward them across the yard. "Did Harold see anything?"

"I don't think so. His back was toward you. I think your secret is safe." When Alar gave her a questioning look, she said, "I'm not telling anyone. No one outside my order, anyway. Secrets are the currency of my profession." She glanced back at Harold. "Shared secrets are the basis for relationships."

Alar looked at her placid face. Before Harold arrived, he gave her a small nod.

When Harold and the captain saw them, they stopped. The captain said something, then turned and walked away while Harold joined them. He hesitated, looking from Brie to Alar, eyes narrowing slightly.

"You're alive," Alar said, probing the back of his head with his fingertips.

"Yes, well, it was a near thing," he said. "Chagan and his guard are gone. Apparently, there is a postern gate on the northern wall the captain neglected to mention. The captain is going to organize his men to take possession of these." He nodded to the mercenaries trapped in the barbican.

Henrik arrived and stood quietly.

"You did a good job," Harold said.

"It was a good plan," Henrik said.

Alar shook his head and tackled the stairs with a groan. Scilla was looking down into the parade ground where a battle was winding down. Gerold nodded at him.

Scilla looked up when he arrived, then returned her gaze to the parade ground. "It didn't look good for the captain's men at first, even with the surprise." She waved down at the line of *oss'stera* who were watching the fight. "But the mercs had to leave their cover to fight back, and we just picked them off." They watched the end of the fight below. "May have hit a few Imps. Not on purpose, of course."

Alar tipped his head when she looked at him. "I'm sure it couldn't be helped."

"Harold okay?"

"Not a scratch," Alar said. "Chagan and his guard found a way out. The captain didn't bother to mention the postern gate on the northern wall."

Ukrit and Lief appeared. "Didn't mention there is another set of steps, either. I'm guessing the two that attacked us were from Chagan's guard."

Noticing the shadow that might have been a body lying against the wall farther down the wall, Alar asked, "How many?"

"Ogden, Kurt, Brinna," Scilla said. "Two others that I saw, but I didn't see who."

They watched the cavalry celebrating on the parade ground in silence, until Scilla said, "Now what?"

"We gather our dead, make sure the paintings are safe, then we clear out before any of these Imperials remember we're not allies," Alar said.

***

"That is Imperial property," the captain said.

Alar let his gaze roam over the Imps arrayed behind the man. There were at least twenty swords drawn, hard expressions on their faces.

"No," Ukrit said. "Those are *Alle'oss* property. They were stolen from us by Imperials."

Twelve of the remaining members of *oss'stera* gathered around Alar and Ukrit, arrows nocked. It would be ugly. Even if every archer found a target, they might not get off another shot before the remaining Imps closed the distance. Alar gazed across the parade ground where men were caring for the wounded and retrieving the bodies. After his encounter with the *sjel'and* on the steps, he wasn't in a rush to return to *annen'heim*. But what was the point if they lost the art? He pursed his lips and gazed at the captain's supercilious smile.

"Gentlemen. There is no need for further violence."

Alar looked over his shoulder. The governor was approaching, accompanied by Gerold and the governor's personal guard. That made the number of Imps thirty.

The governor stopped midway between Alar and Brennerman. He nodded to Alar, lifting a placating hand, then turned to the captain. "The paintings, in fact, belong to me."

"I would beg to differ, governor."

Alar hadn't seen the Desulti arrive.

The governor stared at her, fingers resting on his lips.

Gerold cleared his throat. "Governor, if I may." Adelbart nodded and Gerold said. "In fact, I believe the governor's debt belongs to you. As you had not actually received the paintings, they had not passed into your possession."

Before Brie could respond, Alar said, "Governor, we had a deal."

"Yes, and I don't want to gain a reputation for reneging on my word." Someone standing behind the captain snorted. Adelbart ignored the interruption. "However, there are, as we discussed, many considerations, competing claims." He gestured to Brie and Harold, who were watching quietly. "This is what I suggest. I will take possession of the art." Ukrit started to protest, but Adelbart talked over him. "For the moment. Keep it safe and we will meet one week from today to tie up any loose ends. When emotions aren't running so high."

Adelbart must have read the distrust in Alar's face, because he took a step toward him, raised a hand in a conciliatory gesture, and spoke quietly. "Alar, you saved my daughter. I owe you more than I can express. I would not lie to you."

Alar glanced at Ukrit who shook his head and said, "This is a bad idea."

Scilla shrugged.

Harold gave him a nod.

Brie's eyes narrowed, but she didn't object.

Alar looked down at the ground. It wasn't like he really had a choice, but he didn't want the governor to know that. After he felt he made them wait long enough, he looked up and asked, "One week?"

Adelbart nodded.

Alar turned away and began walking, *oss'stera* following in his wake.

Chapter 43

Destinies

Harold sat at his desk in the gendarmerie. He lifted a heavy hand and probed the cut the *Alle'oss* made in the back of his neck. He assumed that was how they administered the drug. He leaned forward, rested his elbows on his desk, kneading his forehead with his fingertips. He couldn't decide which need was greater, food or sleep. Henrik's chair squeaked as the brother settled into it, but Harold didn't look up. They hadn't spoken since leaving the fortress. He gazed at the map spread out on his desk, in particular, the rugged territory west of Richeleau. Somewhere out there, *oss'stera* was licking its wounds and, more than likely, plotting against the Empire. He sat back and gazed at Henrik. "Our struggle," he said.

Henrik looked up. "Hmm, what?" When he saw Harold looking at him, he nodded. "That's what the boy, Lief, said *oss'stera* means."

"Clearly a rebel group," Harold said.

Henrik chuckled softly. "And quite formidable, apparently." He looked at Harold. "What do you plan to do about it?"

Harold let his gaze drift to the ceiling. What indeed? On the one hand, they were clearly a threat to the Empire. On the other hand …

"Nothing," he said.

"Sir?"

Harold was quiet for a moment. "When your father told you about realm walkers, did he mention whether any of them were men?"

"No, he said they were all sisters of the Seidi. Are you thinking …" Henrik's voice trailed off.

"Brie told me what Alar did to those mercenaries in the dungeon," Harold said. "That's hard to credit if Alar was a normal man. Still, as you say, the realm walkers were all women."

They sat silently for a moment, then Henrik said, "One of the rogue sisters, staying hidden, letting Alar take the credit, maybe?"

"Maybe," Harold said, slowly. "In any case, I owe Alar a great debt." Harold met Henrik's eyes and held them.

"I didn't send them," Henrik said. He reached into the drawer and withdrew the stack of reports he wrote for Hoerst and set them on the desk.

"I noticed," Harold said. "Not after the first couple of weeks."

Henrik sat back and blew a breath out through pursed lips.

"It was a burden, keeping it a secret," Harold said.

Henrik, whose gaze had been wandering the small office, finally found Harold. They looked at one another for what felt like a long time, then Harold gave him a small smile.

"You've no idea." Henrik looked at his hand resting on the stack. "Not sure what I'm going to tell the inquisitor."

"Yeah, that occurred to me as well," Harold said. "Of course, it *was* your disappearance that led me to investigate Chagan." Henrik looked up. "It's almost the truth. We only need to stretch the time they held you prisoner."

"It certainly won't be the biggest lie we have to tell."

"No, it will not," Harold said. He stood and began rolling up the map. "If we take our time returning to Brennan, we will have time to craft an airtight story."

"You don't want to stay until this business with the art, the Desulti, and the governor is sorted out?"

"Daga, no," Harold said with a grin. "I trust everyone involved with that mess is motivated to resolve it amicably. Or at least they will want to avoid attracting Imperial attention." He came around the desk as Henrik rose. Resting his hand on the brother's shoulder, he said, "I suggest a nice meal at that tavern you like, then we get as much sleep as we need. Once we're recovered, we, very quietly, leave this fair city."

"Yes, sir," Henrik said with a smile. "I agree."

***

Ecke was standing outside the roundhouse, watching Alar approach. "She's waiting for you," she said when he drew near.

Alar stopped and searched her face. "Heard the birth was rough. She okay?" he asked. He hadn't seen Ragan since the battle at the fort a week ago.

"Are you?" she answered, but there was something that might be a smile trying to climb onto her face.

"You blew up my home," he said.

"Yeah," she said, the smile breaking out into the open. "Ragan called it a spirit wave. My first gift from the spirits."

"Congratulations."

"Thank you." She shrugged. "I fainted, so I don't really remember it."

"Any idea what you're going to do now?"

"I'm going with Ragan. Learn as much as I can."

"You're always welcome here."

"I know," she said. "Who knows?" She gestured toward the door.

Alar gave her a small smile, then ducked to enter the roundhouse. Ragan sat on the shaggy hide of one of the giant bears that lived high in the mountains. Her blouse was open, her newborn at her breast, a thatch of blond hair visible above a blanket wrapped around her mother's arms. In the fire's soft light, Ragan looked beatific.

"Ragan," Alar said. "How's the baby?"

She looked down at her daughter. "Alyn is strong and opinionated," she said and smiled up at him.

Alar sunk to sit cross-legged and watched them for a moment. "I'm sorry about Gallia."

Ragan's smile vanished. She looked down at Alyn. "Thank you," she said. "She was going to leave the Empire. Find a new life. But she decided to take this one last trip with me."

Alar didn't know what to say to that, so he changed the subject. "Ecke said you were waiting for me."

"Yes. Tove dropped by to let me know how things turned out," she said. "You kept Novice Wolfe alive. Thank you for that. You rescued the brother, Tove, Elois and Brie. And you saved the paintings. A great success for *oss'stera*, was it not?"

"We paid a high price for it," Alar said.

"Was it worth it?"

Alar opened his mouth, shut it, and considered. Finally, he said, "I don't know how to answer that."

"Were you ever under the impression you could fight the Empire without paying a price?"

Alar waved a hand. "No, I … I knew …" He let his hand drop and busied himself by picking at the tail of his shirt.

In the silence, the sounds of Alyn's pleasure filled the space.

"Alar, have you ever wondered why the *Alle'oss* produce such beautiful art?" Ragan asked.

Caught off guard, Alar hesitated. "Do we? I mean, compared to other parts of the world?"

"Oh, yes."

Alar tore a long splinter from a log stacked by the fire and tossed it into the flames. "I wouldn't know why."

"What would you guess?" Ragan asked.

"I suppose our artists feel free to express their creativity. Scilla says the Empire controls what art is allowed." Ragan watched him expectantly, clearly expecting more. Alar cast about for what she might be getting at. "The *Alle'oss* let people be who they want to be. We appreciate beauty."

"Yes, I think that is near enough to the truth," Ragan said. "But the *Alle'oss* are unique in many other ways as well. You take joy in the everyday moments of life more than any other people I've known. Family, community, art. Life. It even makes it into your language."

"*Ērtsi kalaola*," Alar said softly.

"It's life's colors," Ragan said, nodding. "What does it mean?"

Alar shrugged. "It's ..." He tapped the toe of his boot with an index finger. "Life ..." He pursed his lips in thought, dropped his eyes and plucked at the laces of his boot. Not long after Alar brought Tove into *oss'stera*, they found an old man who agreed to teach them *Alle'oss*. Suffering from a degenerative illness, he was difficult to understand. From time to time, he erupted into a strange gurgling sound. When he noticed Tove glancing uncomfortably at him, Alar whispered, "He's laughing."

Tove gave the old man an incredulous look and blurted, "What's *he* got to laugh about?"

The corner of the old man's mouth twitched in what Alar recognized as a smile and he said, "*Ērtsi kalaola*." What followed were tales from a life well lived. There was sorrow, but there was also love, joy, and warmth. When he finally fell silent, he said, "Those are the colors of my life."

Alar looked up and met Ragan's eyes. "It means that whatever life gives you, it's up to you to make of it what you can."

"To paint your own masterpiece."

"So, what are you trying to tell me?"

"Do you know why people fear the Desulti?"

Alar let his annoyance show, but Ragan merely watched him without reacting. He shrugged and asked, "They kill people they disagree with?"

"There is that," Ragan said with a chuckle. "But the real reason is more complicated. People fear them because they are powerful."

"Isn't that the same thing?"

"Oh, no, not always. Power comes in many forms. The women who are Desulti ran away from what they felt was a corrupt and patriarchal empire, because they wanted more control over their own lives. They sought to take on roles the Empire doesn't believe are their right. That puts them in danger. There are many who would do as Adelbart tried to do and drag their wives, mothers or sisters back. Put them back in their place. The Desulti knew they could never withstand the military might of the Empire, so they sought power in other ways. It is true, they are ruthless. They kill when they need to, but always as a last resort." She looked down at her daughter and stroked her hair away from her face. "No, their power comes from their great wealth. With it, they put people in influential positions when they can and buy influence when they must. They gather information they can use to intimidate or extort powerful people. They are dangerous, but the mythology they've encouraged is far more frightening than the reality."

Alar remembered Brie's implied offer. Secrets, but secrets the Desulti could exploit. "They're wealthy because they're Imperials."

"No, most of them sacrificed their wealth to be free. They have made themselves wealthy through their own enterprise. Those in the Empire who put their animosity aside and work with them become rich, and those who don't ... well, as you say, the Desulti kill people who disagree with them. They have become so integrated into the Empire's economy, they could bring the Empire to its knees if they were so inclined."

"Why don't they?"

"Because, though they ran away from the restrictions the Empire would impose on them, they are, at heart, Imperial. They have the same prejudices, the same adherence to the caste system. To them, the *Alle'oss* are Brochen, the broken caste. They grew wealthy by working within the system they ran from. Don't ever forget that."

Alar waited as Ragan rearranged to offer Alyn her other breast. When she was settled, he asked, "Why are you telling me this?"

"Though they are few and have no military, the Desulti exist and thrive in the shadow of the Empire."

Alar gazed into the fire. "You're telling me the *Alle'oss* should follow their example?"

"The *Alle'oss* can never expel the Empire from Argren through violence alone. No matter how many you kill, the Empire has more to take their place. You are too few, too peaceful, and the effort will leave you a changed people. The price will be paid in more than blood. You will lose what makes you a unique, joyful people, the part of you that can produce transcendent artists like Valdemar. The people for whom life is a canvas to be painted." She fell silent for a moment, then said softly, "Once that is lost, it is lost forever."

A frightened face of a young, wounded ranger, begging for his life escaped the dark place where Alar tried to bury it. Would he ever be the same after that monstrous act? How many more memories like that would he have before his people were free? "How could we be like the Desulti?" he asked. "We are scattered without a strong central authority. We trade to earn a living and to help one another, not to accumulate wealth and influence."

"I'm not saying the *Alle'oss* should mirror the Desulti, I'm suggesting *oss'stera* should."

Alar stared at her. "I don't know anything about business."

"Alar, you have something far more important. You inspire loyalty. You will find people who can help you. You can start with Scilla and Ukrit. The two of them have watched their father conduct his business affairs their entire lives."

"I wouldn't know where to start."

"Go to Lachton."

"The Imperial city?"

"It was once an *Alle'oss* city, and it still has a large *Alle'oss* population. Argren has much to offer the world and you can help sell it to them. Make *oss'stera* wealthy and use that wealth to buy power and influence. You'll help your people far more than you will by hiding in the forest."

"We still have to defend ourselves."

"Of course. Build your forces. Become strong. One day, the Empire will be vulnerable, and you must be ready. But keep your eye on the bigger picture. When the rest of the Empire burns, be ready to lift Argren from the ashes."

Alar watched Ragan cupping her daughter's small head. Deciding she was done, he asked, "Why did the Empire execute Valdemar for that painting? Spirit Light?"

Ragan glanced at him before looking down again and answering absently. "The Empire is terrified the *Alle'oss* will discover the power of the spirits." Alyn had fallen asleep. "That's why they work so hard to eliminate girls with spirit sight when they are young. If people knew the true story of Wattana, they would begin to question."

Alar nodded. It was what he worked out on his own. He rose to his feet. "What about you, Ragan? You always seem to know more than you should. You obviously have an agenda. What are you really trying to accomplish?"

"I just want to save my family."

"Is that it?"

It was Ragan's time to show her annoyance. "Isn't that enough?"

"You should listen to your own counsel, Ragan. Think of the bigger picture. If you have some influence on the future, use it to save more than your own family. Your daughters will always be in danger as long as the Empire exists."

Ragan stared at him, her brow smoothing. She let her head drop and gazed at her sleeping daughter.

"If they will be as powerful as you say, they can help their own people," he said. When she didn't reply, he said, "I have to go. I have to go see the governor."

As he was pushing his way through the door, Ragan said, "Adelbart and the Desulti owe you, Alar. Don't let them off easily."

Scilla was waiting for him outside, the bright sun lifting highlights from her hair. Ecke was gone. Alone for a change, he and Scilla gazed at one another. She stepped up to him and touched his chest. He looked down, then lifted his brows.

"You said you would tell me later," she said. "At Sune's gallery." She tapped his chest with her finger.

Alar guided her to a boulder beside the path and sat, pulling her down beside him. He scanned the small community busy coming back to life after the twin traumas of the Union attack and the battle at the fort. Most of the people missing after the attack returned, many of them bringing new friends. Between the roundhouses, he could see the community space where Zaina was instructing some newcomers on the basics of archery. The sounds and smells of an *Alle'oss* village surrounded them, but they were momentarily alone. He reached inside his tunic and withdrew the folded oilcloth, laid it in his lap, and unfolded it carefully. His own blue eyes looked up at him. His sister's gift to him.

"Oh." The sound escaped Scilla's lips. "It's you."

Alar nodded, the sting of tears behind his eyes. It was the first time he ever showed it to anyone. "My sister painted it," he said. He pressed his lips together and swallowed. Scilla held her hand out and Alar set the painting in her palm. "She had ten summers. A few months before the Inquisition took her."

Scilla leaned her shoulder against him. "It's very good."

Alar didn't answer. He didn't care, really, how good it was.

"So, this is what you looked like as a boy," she said. She held the painting in the palm of her hand and brushed her fingertips along the eyes. "Argren blue," she said.

"My parents bought the paints for her," Alar said.

"They must have recognized her talent." She handed the painting back to him and leaned her head against his shoulder. "Thank you."

Alar nodded slowly, gazing down at a more innocent version of himself. He folded the paper and returned it to the spot next to his heart. He looked up at a cerulean sky, dotted here and there by puffy, white clouds. "Argren blue," he said softly.

"Hmmm?" Scilla asked.

"Nothing," Alar said. He stood and took Scilla's hand. "Come on, we have a meeting with the governor."

***

"You can't have them." It was Ukrit's voice. "They belong to the *Alle'oss*."

Alar and Scilla entered the governor's office to find Ukrit and the Desulti standing toe to toe in front of the governor's desk. Adelbart sat at his desk, looking like a child who knew he was in trouble and was waiting to find out the nature of his punishment.

The Desulti looked up at their entrance, her face set in a stubborn mask. She said in a calm voice, "They are the property of my order, a payment for his debt." She pointed at Adelbart who eyed the finger pointed his way warily.

"I don't care—"

"Excuse me," Alar said.

Ukrit glanced over his shoulder. When he saw it was Alar, he turned and pointed at Brie. "She says the art belongs to the Desulti. They'll sell it to people outside the Empire. We'll never see it again."

"I gathered that," Alar said. He took in the others in the office. Elois was standing behind Brie. Somehow, Alar wasn't too surprised to see Tove standing with her, but she averted her eyes when he looked at her. Gerold stood beside Adelbart's desk. Alar asked, "Captain Brennerman and Novice Wolfe?"

"The captain is searching for Chagan and, in any case, this is none of his affair," Adelbart said.

"The novice is returning to Brennan," Gerold said. "He mentioned he would prefer not to know what happens here."

Alar nodded. "That is probably wise." He eased Ukrit aside and took his place, looking down at Brie, who watched him expectantly. "Surely, there is some agreement we can come to," Alar said. When she shook her head, he asked, "How much does he owe you?"

The woman eyed him speculatively. Everyone in the office other than the governor and Gerold leaned in. When she told them the figure, there was a collective gasp, and everyone turned to look at Adelbart.

"It was ... a series of unfortunate investments," he said with a grimace. "I just need to get back on my feet, and I will be able to make amends for previous ... mistakes."

"The money you extorted from Lirantok. What was that for?" Scilla asked.

Adelbart's face flushed. "Ext—" His mouth slammed shut when Gerold touched his shoulder. The governor cleared his throat. "Well, I meant to pay the Desulti with that, but then Chagan raised his price, so—" He stopped and finished with a murmur. "And in any case, this year's take was only a drop in the bucket."

Alar looked from Scilla to Ukrit. "I have a suggestion." He reached into his shirt and extracted the small bundle that held his sister's painting. Unfolding it, he gazed down at it, letting anticipation build. Finally, noticing Brie leaning forward, trying to peek at the painting, he showed it to her.

She studied the image, a small furrow appearing between her brows, then looked at him. "What is this?"

"Argren blue," he said.

She stared at him, glanced at the painting, then looked at the governor.

"And of course, that is not all. There are the other pigments, as well," Alar said. "A fortune to be made for the right investor."

"What does this have to do with what the governor owes them?" Ukrit asked.

"The Desulti and the citizens of the Ishian River valley share the profit." Alar held out the painting and Scilla took it. "The *Alle'oss* donate a portion from their share to pay down the governor's debt." He held up a finger to silence Ukrit's protest. "We won't agree to the terms Adelbart forced on Lirantok, but it will be generous. Given the size of the governor's debt, it will take some time to pay it down, but

I'm guessing your order will value the potential of a long-term partnership. Once the debt is paid, the *Alle'oss* keep their full share."

The small furrow between the Desulti's brows smoothed. "Exclusive rights?"

Alar nodded.

"Alar," Ukrit said.

Alar put his hand on Ukrit's shoulder. "Trust me." He returned his attention to Brie. "The Desulti handle sales, distribution and provide protection to the residents of the Ishian River valley." He cut his eyes to Adelbart, who was watching the exchange with dawning horror. "The *Alle'oss* keep the paintings."

"There will be interest on the debt," Brie said.

"Which Adelbart will pay," Alar said. When Adelbart started to protest, Alar gave him a look that shut him up. "Of course, you will have to get the agreement of the citizens of the Ishian River valley, but given their recent experience, I'm pretty sure they will happily agree to a fair offer."

"What about me?" Adelbart squeaked.

Alar didn't respond. He waited until Brie gave him a small nod.

"I can sell this to my order," she said.

"Alar," Ukrit said. "Why should we pay this man's debt?"

Alar turned toward Adelbart. "Governor, *oss'stera* plan to export products from Argren through Lachton. It would be beneficial for us if we could bypass complex Imperial regulations and avoid paying exorbitant Imperial taxes. Instead, we would pay a fee directly to you."

Adelbart's scowl melted away, replaced by calculation. "You're asking me to take part in a black market."

"Yes, I am," Alar said.

Adelbart studied him, then looked up at his assistant.

Gerold cleared his throat. "We would have to have some assurances."

"Of course," Alar said. "As long as you treat the *Alle'oss* with respect and justice, *oss'stera* will not cause you trouble."

"No more attacks on supply caravans."

"No more taking of slaves," Alar countered. "And you rein in Brennerman."

Gerold considered, then said, "We cannot make such guarantees for the emperor, the Inquisition or forces outside our jurisdiction."

"I understand," Alar said. "And we will defend ourselves if we find it necessary."

"We can agree that the forces under the governor's command will refrain from such activities," Gerold said. "And we will maintain open lines of communication to avoid misunderstandings."

"Agreed."

Adelbart looked from Alar to Gerold. Finally, Gerold gave him a nod.

"Excellent," Adelbart said. He stood and clapped his hands. "There are, of course, details to be arranged, but I think we can all agree that we have an auspicious beginning. Now, who would like to toast to the future?"

Alar caught Tove's eye and nodded to the exit, then said, "Brie, might I have a word with you and Tove outside?"

She nodded and headed toward the exit.

Alar raised a hand to prevent Scilla and Ukrit from following. "I just need a minute," he said. As he was turning to leave, he saw Adelbart come around his desk and say something to his daughter. She smiled and reach out to pat his shoulder.

Brie and Tove were waiting for him in the outer office. Tove was watching him with a guarded expression. He looked at her, a brow lifted, his eyes flicking to Brie. She gave him a nod.

"Brie, I've been considering what you said about secrets and relationships." He paused until she gave him a nod. "Since the Desulti will be entering into a business relationship with the *Alle'oss*, I think it reasonable that we have a representative within your order. It would help reinforce what I believe we both agree will be a mutually beneficial relationship."

Brie gazed at him, then turned to look at Tove.

"Will they allow an *Alle'oss* into your order?" Tove asked.

Brie studied her, then said, "Being Murtair has its advantages. I think I can sway the council to admit you, but I cannot protect you once you are in. You will have to find your own way. It will be difficult. Are you sure?"

Tove looked at Alar. He nodded. "Yes, I'm sure," she said and gave Brie a firm nod. Brie put her hand on Tove's shoulder and squeezed. She nodded to Alar, then entered the governor's office.

Tove and Alar looked at one another. "I'll miss you," Alar said.

"What do you mean, you stupid *wota?* You have Scilla and … Ukrit and all the others."

"Yes, I do, but none of them are you." He opened his arms, and she stepped forward, allowing him to wrap her in an embrace.

"I'm not dying," Tove mumbled into his chest. "I'm sure I'll be able to visit. Sometime."

"You always have a home. If it gets too difficult, I mean."

"I know. But you know I'm harder than that."

Alar kissed the top of her head and whispered, "I know." He let her go and said, "If they let you write, let me know how you are."

Tove stepped back, wiped her nose with the back of her hand and rested her palm on Alar's chest. "Thank you, Alar. For saving my life, giving me hope and making it all worth it."

"*Otsuna,*" Alar said quietly.

Tove grinned, laughed, put her head back and shouted, "*Otsuna!*"

***

Alar, Scilla and Ukrit descended the steps of the governor's mansion. Alar gave the suspicious guards a smile, then paused, taking a moment to enjoy the unseasonably warm weather.

"Not sure I can sell the deal to the people in Lirantok," Ukrit said.

"Remind them it isn't just the pigments. They will be able to avoid the Empire's taxes and regulations if they deal with us," Alar said.

"That … might work," Ukrit said. He looked at Scilla and said, "We should go home, talk to Old Jep."

"He'll see the wisdom in it and once we convince him, the others will go along," Scilla said.

"I trust you can convince them," Alar said. They stood on the busy street in silence for a few moments.

"That was well handled," Ukrit said.

Alar grinned at him. "I note the hint of surprise."

Ukrit waved his hands. "No, no, not sur—" He let his hands drop. "Okay, I'm shocked, is what I am."

Alar and Scilla laughed.

"Now what?" Scilla asked.

"Once you get back from Lirantok, we're taking a trip to Lachton," Alar said.

"Lachton?" Ukrit and Scilla asked at the same time.

Alar started walking. When the others caught up with him, he said, "Tell me about your father's business."

Chapter 44

Our Kind of Plan

Harold stood at attention before the desk of the Malleus. Of all the brothers of the Inquisition, Malleus Ulvan alone had shown Harold kindness since the day he admitted Harold to the academy over others' objections. Harold had just given an oral recitation of the written report he prepared for Inquisitor Hoerst. Hoerst stood beside the desk, his face carefully neutral.

"That is some story," the Malleus said. "You foiled a plot against an Imperial governor, organized the *Alle'oss* gendarmerie to avenge an attack on an Imperial Ranger company, rescuing Brother Henrik from the Union in the process."

"Yes, sir," Harold said.

"And you were in Richeleau to investigate rumors of this rebel group, this …"

"*Oss'stera*, sir," Harold said, his eyes flicked to Hoerst. "Inquisitor Hoerst sent me to investigate after the name came up in connection with the prison break in Kartok."

"You found nothing," Ulvan said.

"Not exactly, sir," Harold said. "There is a group calling themselves *oss'stera*, but they are nothing more than petty criminals. I turned over what we learned to the local gendarmes."

"Well, we were certainly lucky you happened to be in Richeleau," the Malleus said. He glanced at Hoerst, the corner of his lips twitching. He stood and extended his hand to Harold. "Good job, Novice Wolfe. You have a bright future with the Inquisition."

Harold shook his hand, thanked him, and turned to leave. His fellow novice, Stefan Schakal, was waiting in the hall. Harold gave him a smile and waited for Hoerst to appear, nervous sweat sticking his shirt to his back.

"You think the Malleus will buy that pack of lies?" Stefan asked with a sneer.

Harold remembered Stefan looking smug as Hoerst sent Harold into what he thought was a trap. He gave Stefan a big smile and said, "As a matter of fact, the Malleus commended me." Stefan gaped at him. Harold cocked his head "I have to wonder how you're privy to contents of a report labeled 'eyes only' for Inquisitor Hoerst and the Malleus."

Before Stefan could respond, Hoerst appeared and closed the Malleus's office door behind him. When he saw Harold, he drew himself up, clasped his hands behind his back, and gazed at him.

Harold stood at attention, looking into the inquisitor's ice-blue eyes, waiting him out.

"Well, well," Hoerst said, finally. "That *was* quite the story."

Harold didn't reply.

"I sent you to chase rumors, and you stumbled upon a nest of vipers."

"Yes, sir. The governor was lucky we were there. As was the Empire."

"We most certainly were," Hoerst said. He started to turn away, then paused. "Did you happen to meet the governor's daughter?"

"No, inquisitor," Harold said. "I was unaware the governor had a daughter."

Hoerst stared at him. "Elois?"

Harold shook his head, careful to keep his face neutral.

After long moments, the inquisitor let a cold smile stretch his lips. "A shame. She is quite lovely." He turned and strode away.

Stefan looked stunned.

Harold leaned toward him and whispered, "Better hurry along." He watched their receding backs until they turned a corner, then let his held breath go and sagged against the wall. He couldn't be sure Hoerst really bought their story, and it would fall to pieces if he chose to investigate, but that was a problem for another day. He grinned, imagining how Stefan must be complaining to Hoerst right now. Pushing himself upright, he strode down the hall. Henrik was waiting in a nearby tavern, anxious to hear the outcome.

**

Alar, Scilla and Ukrit stood on the crest of a hill overlooking the city of Lachton. Sunlight glinted on the Odun River which wound around the eastern edge of the city.

"So, Ragan said there were a lot of *Alle'oss* living there?" Ukrit asked.

"It used to be an *Alle'oss* city," Alar said.

"You sure Lief will be okay without us?" Scilla asked.

"He's got Stolten and Inga. Besides, you know how Lief is. Everyone loves Lief," Alar said. When Scilla didn't look convinced, he added, "We're nearby and we won't be strangers. He won't be alone."

"What do we do when we get there?" Ukrit asked.

Alar gave them his biggest smile. "Let's go find out."

"I like it. Sounds like our kind of plan," Ukrit said with a grin. They shouldered their packs and set off down the slope.

Chapter 45

A Spark on Dry Tinder

Kari sighed. "Val, do you always have to be so dramatic?" The artist stood next to an easel, the corner of the sheet draped over his latest work in his hand.

"Oh, Kari," Valdemar said. "You know you would be disappointed were it not so."

Kari returned his smile. It was true, but it wasn't always. When she moved into Valdemar's home five years ago to cook and clean, she found the eccentric artist exasperating. At first, the perpetual anarchy was exhausting. But it wasn't long before she recognized the man's genius. She supposed the chaos was the price Val paid for a mind that soared to such heights. Acceptance was followed by fondness, and, in time, love. Val was a gentle soul, full of life, full of love, but he lived only in his own mind. Kari knew he loved her, and almost as important, they both understood he would be adrift without her to tether him to the present. She looked down at her hand resting on her stomach, knowing the evidence of their love would be impossible to hide before long.

"Ready?" Val asked with a sly grin.

Kari took a breath and settled herself. She knew whatever was beneath the sheet would be special. Val worked on it twice as long as he normally did, insisting she stay out of the studio until it was done.

"Yes," she said, with a theatrical shiver.

He swept the sheet off the easel and stepped back, a shy, almost childlike smile on his face. When Kari stared at the canvas, stunned, small tremors swept across his face. "Do you like it?"

"What did you do?" Kari breathed.

Valdemar stared at her, clearly dumbfounded by her reaction. He turned and gazed at the canvas, as if to reassure himself he had the right one on the easel. Giving a quick nod, he spun around. "What? It's Wattana."

Kari shook her head and glanced involuntarily at the balcony, through the double doors, open to a glorious spring day.

Resisting the urge to throw the doors shut—who could see into the studio on the third floor, anyway — Kari tried a smile. "Yes, Val, I see it's Wattana." Her eyes flicked to the open door to the stairway that led to the lower floors.

"Then what's the problem?" Valdemar asked. Confusion and the beginnings of hurt were threatening to cloud his expression. "Isn't it good?"

"Oh, yes," Kari said. She came closer and stood in front of the canvas. The painting depicted an *Alle'oss* woman. She stood on a rocky promontory, feet set firmly apart, her hair and dress caught by the wind. There was a slight arch to her back, and her arms extended gracefully above her head, elbows bent, her head back. Small, glittering orbs swirled around her. The painting was beautiful.

Gazing at Wattana's beatific expression, Kari saw herself. She posed for Val, not knowing the subject. Had she known, she would have refused. "It's beautiful, Val. Maybe your greatest work."

Valdemar, who was watching her, a worried furrow between his brows, lit up. "I thought so." He hurried to the double doors, stopped, then stepped carefully into the sun. It was the first time he allowed himself to leave the studio for a month. Sunlight glinted on his golden locks, an imitation of the luminous spirits surrounding Wattana. Crossing the balcony with small tentative steps, he rested paint-stained hands on the rail and lifted his face to the sky.

Kari watched him, the tears pooling in her eyes spilling over. She turned back to the painting. It was so vibrant, the details so delicately rendered, she could almost feel the wind in her hair, as if she were standing on the precipice rather than Wattana. Kari knew, firsthand, Wattana's ecstasy. She was one of the few outside the Seidi who did. But those spirits were anathema to the Imperial church. It was only after she fled the Empire, that she heard about Wattana and learned the true nature of the spirits.

She gazed at the woman's face, her face, and felt Val's presence behind her.

"Val, you know you can never let anyone see this," she said gently, as if she were coaxing a frightened animal.

"What?" Val said. "Why?"

"You know why."

"But it's the truth," he said. "You know it is."

"I *know* it's the truth," Kari said, failing to keep the desperation from her voice. "But the truth doesn't matter." Val started to argue, but Kari put her hand on his arm to forestall him. "There is a reason that we didn't know any of this before we met Ragan," she said gently. "The Empire suppressed the truth, and they will do anything to keep it in the shadows." She paused, wanting to make sure he heard the next part. "That is the reason Ragan must hide. The Inquisition would kill her if they knew where she was." It wasn't the first time she cursed the day Val stumbled onto the former novice.

Val turned and gazed at the painting. "But ... it's the truth," he whispered.

"Yes," Kari said, putting her arm around his shoulders. "And someday people will know the truth. That's the way of it. It's impossible to hide the truth forever. When that time comes, we will show them this." She gestured toward the canvas.

Valdemar nodded slowly. "Perhaps you are right," he said, then he brightened. "Anyway, at least Olga got to see it."

He looked away before horror could register on Kari's face. "You let Olga see it?" she said, trying to keep her voice calm.

"Yes," Val said. "I didn't want to, but the studio was becoming unlivable. I mean," he chuckled, "I was locked up in here for a month."

Kari stepped away from Val, turned slowly, and examined the room. She didn't notice when she entered, too excited that Val was returning to the world. Never entirely clean, the room was far more orderly than she would expect. She took Val's arm and pulled him around to look at her. "Olga saw the painting?" she asked.

Val nodded. "She recognized your face."

"Did you tell her what it was? That it was Wattana?"

"Yes, of course," Val said, a small frown tugging at the corners of his mouth. "She seemed quite interested."

"You told her about the spirits?"

Val nodded.

Three stories below, someone banged on the door. Shouted words drifted in through the balcony. "Open in the name of the Inquisition."

The frightened expression on Val's face lanced through Kari's heart. She ran to the studio door, slammed it shut, and threw the bolt. Stepping back from the door, she stared at it. What to do? She jumped at the sound of splintering wood. The front door giving way.

"Kari?" Val's childlike voice.

Kari whirled, her eyes resting on the canvas. "Val, we have to get rid of the painting."

"What? No!"

The thud of footsteps on the stairs pushed her across the room. Val saw where she was headed and stepped in her way.

"No, Kari, you can't."

Kari took his arms in shaking hands. "Val, the Inquisition will kill you if they see that. We have to—" She turned away from Valdemar, searching for a way to destroy the painting. She could hide it among the canvases stacked against the walls. She only took a step to get around Val when the studio door crashed open. Before she reached the painting, strong hands closed around her arms and pulled her away, screaming in frustration.

"Kari?" Val sounded frightened.

The man who held her pulled her around. When she saw who was standing in the door, her knees buckled, only remaining upright because the man wouldn't let her fall. The inquisitor stepped into the studio, examining the room, hands clasped behind his back. His eyes slid across Kari, lingered on her black hair for a moment, then he walked over and stood in front of the canvas.

"It's the truth. You won't be able to hide it forever," Val said.

Kari had been afraid to look at him, afraid if she did, she would collapse into hysterics. But the sober note in his voice, so unlike the childlike genius, brought her eyes around. Val was watching the inquisitor, a calm that belied the danger they were in on his face.

"Truth?" the inquisitor said. He glanced over his shoulder to the man who was restraining Kari. "They always say that, as if it mattered." His eyes settled on Kari. "Who are you?"

"Kari, sir. Just a servant, a cleaning woman," she said, hating herself. Her eyes flicked to Val and was horrified to see the fond smile on his face. She dropped her eyes.

"Yes, of course, it's the *truth,*" the inquisitor said to Valdemar. "That is why we are here." He nodded to other men, who took a hold of Val and dragged him out the door. Val looked back at her, and just before he disappeared, the fear she felt rippled across his face.

"What about her?" the commander asked, nodding at Kari.

The inquisitor looked as if he had forgotten Kari was there. He glanced once more at her hair and said, "Ah yes, the cleaning woman. You might as well take her in for questioning."

As they dragged her away, she heard someone ask, "What about the art?"

She looked back over her shoulder. The inquisitor was standing in front of Valdemar's greatest work, gazing at it. "It's really quite beautiful. Ah well, cover it and bring it." He looked around at the other canvases in the studio. "Burn the rest."

Characters

Oss'stera

Alar - An orphan from Shrintok

Tove - Alar's best friend with a tragic past

Ukrit - Brother of Scilla from Lirantok

Scilla - Sister of Ukrit from Lirantok

Leif - The youngest member of oss'stera until Zaina arrives. Friend to everyone.

Sten - The founder of *oss'stera*

Eric - Sten's second in command, if they were actually organized

Stolten - A late arrival, husband of Inga

Inga - A late arrival, wife of Stolten

Ogden - One of *oss'stera's* few troublemakers

Zaina - The youngest, and best, archer in *oss'stera*

Keth - Friend of Zaina

Estrid - Horse lover and friend of Hana

Hana - Horse lover and friend of Estrid

Other *Alle'oss*

Jora - Owner of the Black Husky tavern

Jena - Jora's server at the Black Husky

Evert - Codger and teller of tales at the Black Husky

Olaf - Codger and teller of tales at the Black Husky

Helga - Gendarme

Torva - Gendarme and Lief's friend

Valdemar - A new school artist

Imperials

Adelbart – Imperial governor of the District of Argren

Elois – Adelbart's daughter

Gerold – Adelbart's assistant

Harold – Half – breed novice of the Inquisition

Henrik – Brother of the Inquisition assigned to accompany Harold to Richeleau

Hoerst – Inquisitor of the Inquisition who assigns Harold to hunt down *oss'stera*

Stefan – Novice of the Inquisition and Hoert's closest confidant

Ulvan – The Malleus of the Inquisition.

Ludweig II – The emperor

The Union

Chagan – The commander of the Union mercenaries

Topol – Chagan's captain

About the Author

Ross Hightower and DL Heim have been partners in crime for more than 36 years. While Ross built a career as a professor and Deb worked on four advanced degrees, they managed to raise two wonderful people and launch them into the world. When Ross started writing his first novel, *Spirit Sight*, they never dreamed they would work together, but after a rocky beginning, they discovered they loved writing together. It took a few beers, many intense conversations, and a few arguments to produce *Argren Blue*, the second *Spirit Song* novel. There will be many more to come.

If you would like to hear about upcoming books, short stories, and other news from the Spirit Song world, sign up for my newsletter at rosshightower.com.

Note from the Author

Word-of-mouth is crucial for any author to succeed. If you enjoyed *Argren Blue*, please leave a review online—anywhere you are able. Even if it's just a sentence or two. It would make all the difference and would be very much appreciated.

Thanks!
Ross Hightower & Deb Heim

We hope you enjoyed reading this title from:

BLACK ROSE
writing™

Subscribe to our mailing list – *The Rosevine* – and receive **FREE** books, daily deals, and stay current with news about upcoming releases and our hottest authors.
Scan the QR code below to sign up.

Already a subscriber? Please accept a sincere thank you for being a fan of Black Rose Writing authors.

View other Black Rose Writing titles at
www.blackrosewriting.com/books and use promo code
PRINT to receive a **20% discount** when purchasing.

9 781685 131982